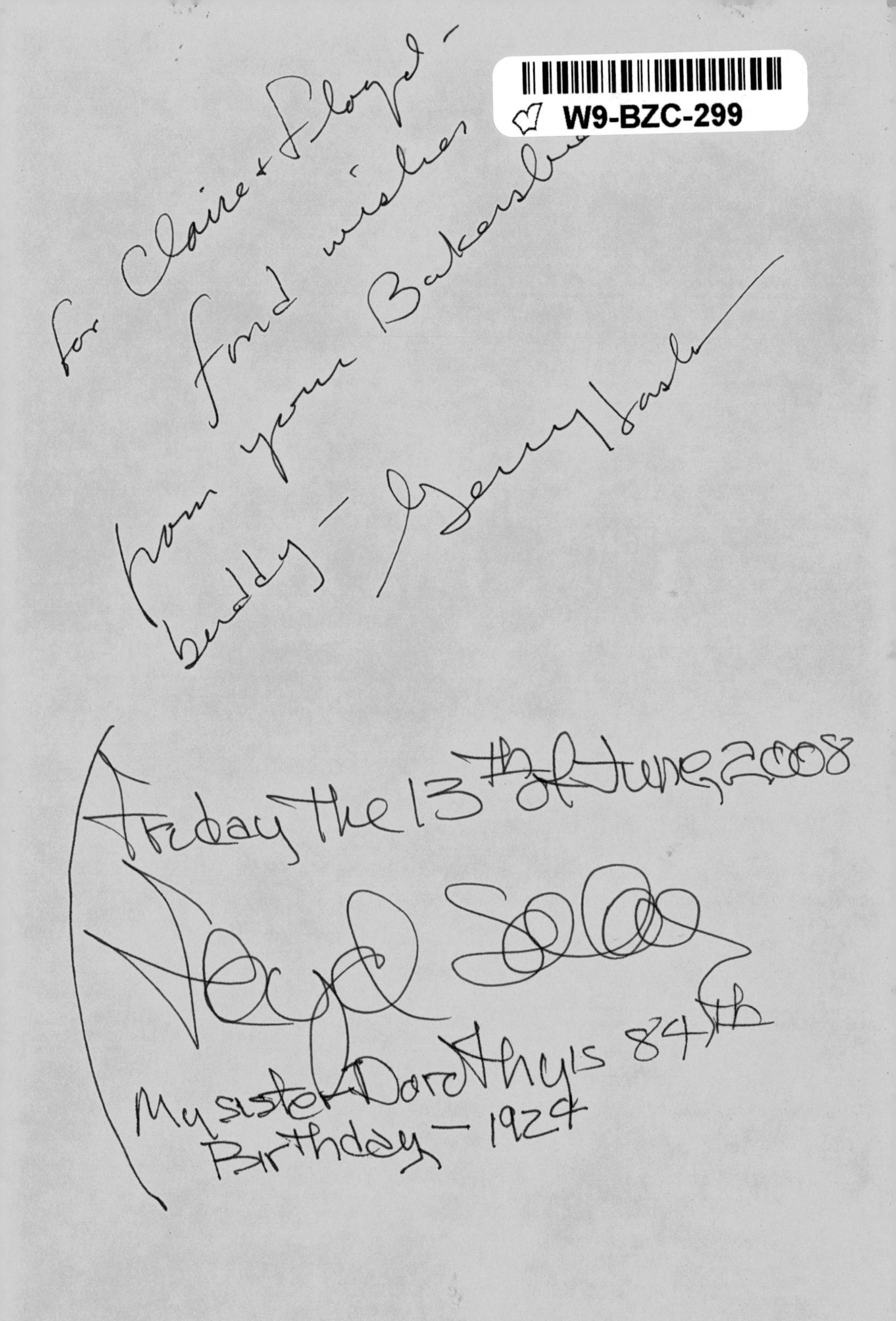
W9-BZC-299
for Claire + Floyd -
fond wishes
from your
buddy -
Friday the 13th of June, 2008
My sister Dorothy's 84th
Birthday - 1924

GRACE PERIOD

Western Literature Series

A NOVEL

GRACE PERIOD

GERALD W. HASLAM

UNIVERSITY OF NEVADA PRESS / RENO & LAS VEGAS

Western Literature Series

University of Nevada Press, Reno, Nevada 89557 USA

Manufactured in the United States of America

Design by Carrie House / HOUSEdesign LLC

Library of Congress Cataloging-in-Publication Data

Haslam, Gerald W.

Grace period : a novel / Gerald W. Haslam.

p. cm. — (Western literature series)

ISBN 13: 978-0-87417-679-7 (hardcover : alk. paper)

ISBN 10: 0-87417-679-4 (hardcover : alk. paper)

1. Cancer — Patients — Family relationships — Fiction.

2. Physician and patient — Fiction. I. Title. II. Series.

PS3558.A724G73 2006

813'.54 — dc22 2006002134

The paper used in this book meets the requirements

of American National Standard for Information

Sciences — Permanence of Paper for Printed Library

Materials, ANSI Z.48-1984. Binding materials were

selected for strength and durability.

FIRST PRINTING

15 14 13 12 11 10 09 08 07 06

5 4 3 2 1

For warriors lost: Dorothy Overly, Jeannie MacGregor, Lefty Osell, Ellie Nishkian, Sally Ewen, Carol Brandner, Mike Madick, Ellie Black, Ron Schiff, and Marje Epp . . .

For warriors still fighting: Traci Lech, Les Cohen, Joe Alzugaray, Martha Molinari, Diane Romaine, Redmond Kernan, Bonny Meyer, Ray Zepeda, and Tim Staples.

And for all the others who will one day battle cancer.

Even now

I know that I have savored the hot taste of life

Lifting green cups and gold at the great feast.

Just for a small and a forgotten time

I have had full in my eyes from off my girl

the whitest pouring of eternal lights . . .

from "Black Marigolds" by Chauras

(translated from the Sanskrit by E. Powys Mathers)

PROLOGUE

We'd enjoyed only three casual dates before that event in the Student Union at UCLA*, but we'd hit it off long before, since the first day of our chemistry class. The professor had assigned lab partners alphabetically: I was Martinez and she was Minata, so we were paired. As it turned out, we were both jocks — I was wrestling at 165 pounds, while she ran track and cross-country — and both serious students, too, so we soon became pals.*

Two-thirds of the way through the semester, me like nearly every other guy scrounging for dates with the campus queens — or the pushovers — it occurred to me that I might go out with someone I actually liked, so I asked Nancy to attend a basketball game with me, then maybe a frat party afterward. She agreed, and we cheered for the Bruins (who lost), danced, talked together, and schmoozed with mutual pals.

The following weekend, we shared beer and pizza, then a dull foreign film, and later coffee with friends. We talked easily, each finding the other interesting, and I learned a lot about her: She told me, for example, that her family had been interned during World War II, and that her dad had never forgotten or forgiven. She had finished fifth in the state high school cross-country championships her senior year and had medaled in the two-mile in the state track meet as a senior, too. She didn't eat red meat, but loved Mexican food — stuff like that. Later, she spared me the embarrassment of the mandatory sexual groping by delivering a sweet good-night kiss; it seemed just right for a second date.

On our third date, she invited me in, and we ended the night smooching in her dorm's parlor. I think I was already hooked. Something about our restrained intimacy made me feel we should always be together. And we could laugh together and figure out how to solve the world's problems. I even liked the way she stood, the way she crossed her ankles when she sat, the way her hand massaged my arm every once in a while, letting me know she was happy to be with me. I was falling in love, schmaltzy as that sounds.

What happened in the quiet lounge on a Thursday before class was a moment I've never, never forgotten. Remembering it can still warm my eyes. Anyway, I was sitting in one of the oversized chairs going over German vocabulary when Nancy wandered in wearing running shoes, shorts, a T-shirt, and her cross-country warm-up jacket, and I have to admit that my eyes for a second locked on her beautiful legs.

"Hey, sexist," she smiled.

"Hi," I grinned, raising my eyes.

Then she walked over and, to my surprise and delight, sat on my lap, curled there as though she always had and always would, then said, "I've been thinking about you."

The quiet lounge wasn't a big make-out spot, but you could neck a little there as long as you didn't get too hot and heavy and bother other folks, so I wrapped my arms around her, kissed her cheek — she smelled spicy — and said, "Hey, lady, how's your day?"

She was warm and firm — absolutely right, in fact — and she leaned her forehead against mine and said, "You really have been on my mind, interrupting my study time." I swear I thought I'd swoon like one of those fops in British novels. She sat angled away from me, with her head turned to face me, and the back of one of my hands rested lightly on her left breast. She did not protest, but I moved my hand as soon as I realized where it was — that took a few seconds. I was breathless.

Physically, our intimacy didn't progress further that afternoon, but that was far enough, and by the time we stood and walked hand in hand to class, something between us had changed. We were a real couple, not just pals dating.

I married Nancy two years later, shortly after our graduation, and the three of us — Nancy Minata Martinez, Martin Carlos Martinez, plus a secret third party nestled in his mother's tummy, Douglas Ichiro Martinez — became a family.

BOOK ONE

1

Two years and nine days after my son's funeral, one year and three days after my divorce became final, one year and two days after my daughter told me she would never speak to me again, I tried to kill myself.

I remember the period leading to that as my hibernation. It began shortly after we buried Doug, then Nancy moved out of the house. His slow death from AIDS had torn our marriage apart, leading to what I'd hoped would be an amicable divorce. Fat chance. Our meetings with an arbitrator had immediately turned tense as financial settlements snipped the ties Nan and I had built in nearly thirty-four years: I would keep our tract house in south Sacramento; she would receive the cottage on the upper Sacramento River, plus a settlement from my retirement plan; we would divide our son's effects.

Nancy's attorney was a thoroughly competent young woman named Sandra Brieger, who seemed to me to be perpetually angry. Mine was Jim Flynn, a guy I'd worked out with at the gym for years. Since this was going to be amicable, I'd figured why not give good old Jim some business. Against the formidable Ms. Brieger, however, he seemed always to be rocking back on his heels like a fighter who'd caught a Sunday punch.

Sitting with the arbitrator that first day, for instance, Jim had genteelly referred to his counterpart as "my dear." Her flint eyes had snapped his way, then she'd addressed the arbitrator: "Please inform Mr. Flynn that I will *not* be patronized. He *will* address me as a fellow attorney. Is that understood?"

"Mr. Flynn?" said the arbitrator, a young, modishly dressed man — probably one of those so-called Sensitive Males who've learned the new rules for pleasing ladies.

Jim, his plaid vest askew, had smiled, bowed slightly, and sought to charm his way out of it: "I was only trying to extend common courtesy to my esteemed colleague — "

"Don't extend that particular one anymore," ordered the arbitrator, and I saw my attorney blink. That's how our "amicable" divorce got started.

Nancy fled from my life as soon as the dissolution agreement was signed, leaving with the sudden bustle of a frightened bird. There had been no talking through our problems — and, believe me, by then I was willing to talk about anything. "Nan, honey," I'd appealed in the hall of the courthouse before we signed the papers, "can't we just go someplace together and work this out? Don't do this, please."

Her eyes had softened for a moment, then she'd straightened and said simply, "No, Marty. Too much has happened."

That was that. The next day our daughter, Lea, telephoned me and said, "This is all your fault! If you'd just opened up Dougie'd be alive and Mom'd be home. Don't ever call me again! Don't talk to me! You're not my father."

A couple of weeks later, Nan's sister and brother-in-law, Audrey and Rollie Hollingsworth, had driven down to help her relocate north to the cottage. They lived in Dunsmuir, just up the road from our place—her place now—in Castella on the river. Nan and I had always looked forward to retiring there someday and being their neighbors.

Rollie telephoned me while he was down for the big move. We were fishing buddies, so I knew he meant it when he said, "This ain't exactly the happiest day of my life, Marty. Audrey feels the same way. Bad enough you guys had to lose Dougie . . . now this."

"Now this," I agreed.

"You comin' up for the openin' day of trout season like always?"

"I don't think so."

"You could stay with us," he offered. "Your ex-wife won't even have to know you're up here."

I'd never before heard Nancy referred to as my "ex-wife," and it daggered me.

Once Nancy had departed, I went to bed and mostly stayed there, enveloped by a somnolence dense as clay. I had nearly two years of sick leave accumulated at the newspaper where I'd long worked, plus the possibility of unpaid leave after that, and I took advantage of it in order to get my life together, or so I told the managing editor, Ned Schmidt. He was sympathetic, although he tried to tempt me back into the fold: "Listen, Martini, there're rumblings about that Senator Bearheart murder again. Your coverage of it was terrific; I'd sure like you to take another look."

"Can't," I replied.

For a long moment neither of us spoke. Ned seemed to be waiting for some kind of explanation; finally he said, "Well, listen, a dean at Sac State supposedly said in a staff meeting, and I quote, 'I couldn't hire a top-flight Negro professor if I trolled a watermelon.' If true, that ought to make a juicy story."

"Not interested."

After another pause, he asked, "What's wrong?"

"I don't feel well," I said, then hung up and slept—dreamlessly—a man drifting through dark plasma, unable or unwilling to focus. Except for what seemed to be sudden urgent urinations, I just drifted, placing Doug and Nan and Lea as far from my mind as I could, without memories or interests.

When I ate . . . well, I don't remember eating much. Certainly I was as slim as I'd ever been. And I didn't exercise. I bathed infrequently, and hardly shaved. Occasionally I must've telephoned out for groceries, but I don't remember much about that either. During the first few days, I did occasionally answer the phone, but Nancy never called, Lea never called, and Doug couldn't, so I unplugged the damned machine.

Before that, Jim Flynn reached me a couple of times: The dogged Ms. Brieger was demanding this or that alteration of the agreement. "Jeez, that little gal sure seems pissed off at the world," he observed. "She got that dollar-a-year clause in there and I think she'd like to bleed you white. Whatever's wrong's all your fault as far as she's concerned. She acts like she hates you."

"She doesn't even know me."

"She knows men, or thinks she does."

She also knows divorce law, I thought but did not say. I was sleepy. "I've gotta sign off, Jim."

"Listen, when're you coming back to the gym? There's nobody there I can beat at anything anymore."

"My back . . . ," I lied.

"Oh, yeah."

Then I swirled back into sleep. Let the pugnacious Ms. Brieger have all the little edges. I didn't care. My family was gone and, in a way, so was I.

Nights I found myself waking with darkness and stalking the halls and rooms of our house, my eyes burning as I gazed at the photos of my wife and kids and me that lined the walls. Mostly I remained in bed, flopping from side to side, staring into darkness, desperate to once more doze. When I arose, I often didn't turn on any lights but instead wandered through gloom. I tried those nights to avoid everything that reminded me of who was missing, but the kitchen Nan had remodeled just before Doug came home that last time mirrored her efficiency and her creativity. She'd left her spices and many of her cooking tools—just enough of her to make me yearn.

I couldn't bring myself to remove her photographs from the walls either, although I tried not to study them: our wedding pictures, the framed mélange of snapshots from our European tour, that sequence of Christmas photographs along the hall. Nancy remained a presence in our house as in my life.

So did Lea: a shot of her junior high cheerleading squad; her high-school graduation portrait; her soccer-team photo; and my favorite, a gap-toothed second-grade grin.

Our son was on those walls, too, of course: our baby, our little boy, our young man, our splendid scholar, our army officer, our young professor.

In the den hung a blowup of the snapshot taken the day I had led him up his first ten-thousand-foot peak with a Sierra Club group. We stand there, me in jeans with a plaid shirt open to my chest, a red bandanna around my neck, a white painter's cap on my head; my arm encircles Doug — nine years old — in jeans and a plaid shirt, with his own red bandanna and white cap, proud to be dressed like me. Behind us, clouds cross a startling sky. So, so long ago . . .

After his death, I found that small white cap tucked into one of his drawers. He had kept it all these years. And I had the cap, damp from my tears as often as not, but I didn't have Doug. He had said to me shortly before he died that we would in some mysterious way see one another again. That, he believed, was Christ's promise, but I could not bring myself to embrace it, much as I wanted to. No, there had been one chance, and I had blown it.

Roaming the darkened house, too, I occasionally glimpsed someone askew — hair wild, eyes haggard, face slack — and I'd jump like a man encountering a ghost, then realize it was a mirror or a reflecting window. I'd move aimlessly up and down the halls, until, near dawn, merciful sleep usually claimed me.

■

It would have gone on longer except that one evening I realized that I was sitting in the backyard with a can of gasoline and a box of matches. I didn't know how I'd ended up there, but I could damn sure figure out what my next move would have been.

As soon as the sun came up, I fought sleep and telephoned the newspaper's health-plan coordinator to find a psychiatrist or psychologist, but she gave me the name of a Dr. Miranda Mossi, a family practitioner who was our plan's "gatekeeper." I tried to explain that I desperately needed psychological help, but I was told I had to visit Dr. Mossi first.

God, I could hardly organize myself to dress or shave, but I called the number I'd been given, only to be told that the physician was booked solid that day. I tried to explain my problem to the receptionist, but began weeping. Only a moment later, it seemed, another voice said, "This is Dr. Mossi. How may I help you?"

"I'm sorry to be a bother . . . ," I choked.

"You're not a bother — Mr. Martinez, is it? Tell me what's wrong."

Somehow I couldn't keep from crying as I explained briefly what had happened, with only an occasional "Yes" or "That's understandable" from the physician. When I finished, she said, "All right. I'll make an appointment for you with a psychiatrist colleague of mine, Dr. Len Molinaro, for as soon as possible . . . tomorrow morning, if I can. Meanwhile, I can squeeze you into my schedule today at . . . at four fifteen. Also there's a drop-in group at the county mental health service if you need help sooner."

All I could say was, "Thanks. I'll come in to see you."

I thought four fifteen would never come, but it did at last, and the doctor turned out to be a large, handsome woman, about my age. Her first words after greeting me were, "We tried to call you to tell you that Dr. Molinaro said he can see you at five this afternoon."

I was still somewhat dazed by all that had happened that day, so I stammered something, then finally managed to say, "Thanks so much, Doctor, I've really been low. Where's Dr. Molinaro's office?"

"Just at the end of the block. You can walk there from here."

I said nothing because I felt tears again welling.

"You're doing the right thing in seeking help, Mr. Martinez," the physician told me, patting my shoulder. "I'm not qualified to make a psychiatric diagnosis, so I won't, but I know you're on the right track. Are you feeling any better?"

I clouded once more, but managed to smile and say, "I'm aware that I'm trying to get better, but can I ask you a question? Why did I have to call you before I could call a psychiatrist if I'm having a breakdown of some kind?"

For a moment, her dark eyes flashed. "Don't get me started on the absurdities of modern managed health care." She shook her head, then smiled and said, "I always tell my patients when they're under stress that the three Fs — family, friends, and faith — are cornerstones of good health."

"I've lost contact with my friends . . . and my daughter doesn't speak to me anymore."

"Your wife?"

"I'm divorced."

She crossed her legs, then asked, "Have you spiritual support?"

"Spiritual support?" I asked.

"Church? Temple? Mosque? Lodge? Maybe just a special pub?"

"I used to be a Catholic, but I fell away years ago. I used to hang out at a journalists' bar, but I've been out of circulation there for quite a while, too."

She smiled again then. "You're a journalist. Are you *that* Martin Martinez, with the *Express?*"

"Yes," I nodded, flattered that she recognized my name.

"Well, Mr. Martinez, let me tell you candidly that I'm a Catholic myself, and divorced, too," Dr. Mossi said, "but the Church remains my great solace. You may have quit *it,* but I'll bet *it* hasn't quit you. A few years ago, I was diagnosed with a life-threatening illness. I received a blessing for the sick and it soothed my soul. Don't underestimate the power of the spirit."

She stood then and said, "It's about time for you to stroll over to Dr. Molinaro's office. Do keep me posted on your progress, won't you?"

Dr. Mossi's words buoyed me. My mom used to say, sort of apologetically, about any large girl, "She's robust, isn't she?" Dr. Mossi was indeed robust, and well proportioned, too, plus she had a lovely smile and, as near as I could tell, a personality to match. I even glanced at her left hand to make certain she wore no wedding band . . . then chuckled at myself, big-time lady's man who couldn't keep from crying. But it was good to feel that way again, if only briefly.

As I walked to the psychiatrist's office, I realized that had been the first time I'd noticed a woman in that way since Nancy'd left me. I guess my slight elation was false, though, because I began weeping as soon as I started telling Dr. Molinaro about my family. When I'd finally finished that sad tale, the youthful psychiatrist said, "You feel guilty for your son's death, don't you, Mr. Martinez?"

"I sure do."

"When something that terrible happens, we frequently feel like we have to assign or assume guilt," he explained, "but you shouldn't. His homosexuality and his lifestyle choices almost certainly were out of your, and likely his, control."

"I wasn't much of a father." The corners of my lips tugged downward, and I was yet again fighting tears.

"That's worth regretting, but don't beat yourself up over it." He gazed at me over fingers entwined before his face. "It sounds to me like you *did* learn your lesson, and that you became his good friend when he most needed you. When crunch time came, you were there for him, Mr. Martinez," he said slowly. "But you've had other messages about that, haven't you?"

"My wife and daughter . . ."

"Who are honestly concerned but by no means objective, and are almost certainly subconsciously deflecting their *own* senses of guilt."

I shook my head and said, "They're hurting."

"Not more than you, I'd guess," the psychiatrist observed. "You lost your son to AIDS, then your wife left . . . and your daughter became estranged, too?"

I nodded. "That's about it."

"There'd be something wrong with you if you *weren't* at least somewhat depressed by those events. That's a normal human response."

I had to smile slightly. "Then I'm normal," I said.

"If you ever had any doubt about that, don't," he said. "Everything I've heard from you says 'normal,' except that you've experienced clinical depression almost certainly triggered by those sad events, and likely by your biology. We can balance the latter with a prescription, I'm sure."

"I'll go for that." I hadn't mentioned my suicide attempt.

"Listen, let me ask you something else . . . unrelated," said Dr. Molinaro.

"Sure." This calm young man had me feeling better.

"You've had to urinate three times during this appointment," the physician said. "Do you always have to go so frequently, or is that just doctor's-office nerves?"

"That's become my pattern."

"Hmmm. Have you seen a urologist?"

"I haven't seen anyone for long time."

"Having to pee that often's got to be a real drag. Why don't you see a urologist? He'd probably be able to prescribe something to relieve that urgency."

"I don't know anyone."

The young man stood and walked to his desk. "I'm not in the urological referral business — that's Dr. Mossi's bailiwick — but my dad goes to Jack Solomon. He has an office right across the street here in the medical complex. He's a nice guy. If you'd like, I'll have Candace call Dr. Mossi and get you a referral. You want to try him?"

"Sure." I liked this kid. He was all business.

He spoke briefly to his receptionist over his office phone, then smiled. "Back to my own specialty," he said, "let's arrange to talk once or twice a week for a few weeks, depending on how you feel. We'll see how the medication works to alleviate your depression, but I think you need to talk through the pain you're feeling. You don't have anyone else to do that with, do you?"

"No."

"How about if we get together next week at this time? And, of course, you can call anytime . . . day or night."

"Sounds good." I realized even as I spoke that I was trying to sound chipper — a male's automatic denial of problems.

He handed me a prescription, walked me to his receptionist's desk, said good-bye, and greeted another patient who had been sitting in the waiting room.

Candace telephoned the urologist, then said, "I talked to Dr. Mossi's office and to Dr. Solomon's too. Would day after tomorrow at one be okay, Mr. Martinez?"

"Sure."

After stopping at a nearby pharmacy, then taking my first pills, I felt better than I had in . . . well, in months at least. I knew it was too soon for the medication to be working, but I was breathing again because I realized that Doug and I had indeed become friends, close ones, at the end of his life; somehow I'd managed to forget that. Since his death, then Nan's departure and Lea's estrangement, I'd really had no one to share my feelings with. I was amazed what one conversation could accomplish. I wanted to call Nancy and tell her, and to tell my daughter, too.

Instead of driving directly home, I headed north out old Route 99, where agricultural fields and bursts of trees awaited me. It had been a long time since I'd done that—since the last day when my ill son and I had cruised here. He'd loved the open country as much as I, and what I saw reminded me of him: great flashing flocks of birds, farmers selling roadside produce, mallards and coots dipping into flooded rice fields, tongue-lolling dogs in the beds of pick-ups. I even noticed one couple—kids, not much more than fourteen or fifteen—walking hand in hand into a small rural store. It all reminded me of the Merced area when I was growing up, of the boy I once was and of the boy I had lost.

On those jaunts after he was ill, my son and I had begun to engage in what I remember as the first real conversations we'd had since . . . maybe ever. His perspectives were always a bit askew of mine, so I was intrigued. One day, for instance, as we drove back toward Sacramento on I-80, with downtown buildings shimmering through heat waves rising from the supine landscape, he said, "Have you ever thought about the city being the capital of the most populous state, and it's really a kind of island right in the middle of this incredible agricultural valley?"

"An island? In what sense?" I'd asked, my journalistic curiosity piqued.

"Hey, Sac's full of slicks who don't have a clue what's going on around it. Just look at it up ahead, all those buildings above the plain even *look* like an island." He'd grinned and added, "I'll bet most of those guys strutting around the capitol in their silk suits and Italian shoes don't even know where they are. These farms really could be an ocean, for all they know."

"Well said for a Sacramento boy," I grinned.

He chuckled at himself, then added, "It's just that there's not a lot of connection between the rural places we drove through today and the city we live in, let alone with the capitol itself, but you and Mom always took Lea and me into the country or down to Merced, so at least we grew up knowing there *was* country. We knew tomatoes came from someone's hard work, not supermarkets."

From that point on, our long rides had become forums, and I found myself consistently impressed with the playfulness of his observations—something I'd never taken the time to notice before.

2

A couple of days later, after signing insurance forms in Dr. Solomon's office, I was shown into an examination room that featured large, not altogether fetching posters of the male and female urinary systems. Only a few seconds later, a matronly nurse slid in the door and handed me a clear-plastic cup. "Can you give me a urine specimen?" she asked pleasantly. "Well, not for me personally." She smiled. "It's actually for the lab. That's the bathroom. Just leave the cup on the shelf in there."

Since I had been about to ask where I could relieve myself, I quickly complied with her request. Back in the examination room, I plopped onto a chair just as the hall door opened and a bald, compact man entered. "Mr. Martinez," he announced, "I'm Dr. Solomon." We shook hands.

"What brings you in?" he asked pleasantly.

"Frequent urination," I told him, "plus urgency. When I've got to go, I've *really* got to go."

"When was your last PSA test?"

This was a new term for me. "PSA test?"

"Prostate-specific antigen. It's a blood test."

I shook my head. "I've never had one — that I'm aware of."

He nodded. "Well, we'll do one today as part of your examination. Please take off your clothes except your shorts and climb into one of these lovely gowns." He extended what looked like a folded blue bedsheet. "Just open the door when you're finished changing, and I'll be back to examine you."

So far, so good, I was thinking as I tied the gown closed. This pleasant man seemed unalarmed by my problem, so I remained calm about it too. Nothing he did as he inspected my body — stethoscope, blood-pressure cuff, "say ahhh . . ." — revealed any tension. "Drop those shorts, and I'll examine your genitals," he directed, and I complied. "Okay," he said after a moment, "if you'll turn and bend over the table there, rest on your elbows, I'll check your rectum and prostate."

It had been quite a while since I'd had one of these digital rectal exams, but I hadn't entirely forgotten how uncomfortable they could be. This one was no exception. As he at last withdrew his gloved finger, he said, "Don't worry about that bit of urine you squirted. That's a normal response, especially if the prostate is enlarged, and yours is. Let's do an ultrasound."

The nurse wheeled a machine with a viewing screen next to the exam table, and she remained to operate its various dials and knobs. As I lay there, Dr. Solomon spread gel on my groin, then began slowly rubbing a metal knob over that area, saying "hmmm" several times, and reciting some figures, which the nurse wrote down. He turned the screen then so I could view my own innards.

"Your prostate's a bit large — not uncommon in men your age — and that's probably what's causing your urgent urination."

"Why does it enlarge?" I asked.

"Well, the common clinical reasons might be an infection in the gland, or a condition called benign prostatic hyperplasia, and, of course, the older man's curse, prostate cancer. Probably, we just live too long."

"Prostate *cancer?*" Maybe my emotional cushion was still thin — I experienced a spike of fear.

"Whoa," he said. "Don't assume the worst, Mr. Martinez. We'll do that PSA test and see what it tells us.

"Janis here will draw blood, and we'll send it to the lab. We should have results by tomorrow afternoon. I'll give you a call then. Go ahead and dress. We can schedule one more consultation after we get results."

■

I took the urologist's advice: He'd said there was no reason to assume the worst, so I didn't . . . much, anyway. Then again, maybe that was the effect of the antidepression medicine. In fact, I began to feel pretty good. When Ned Schmidt, my editor, next telephoned me I was delighted to hear from him. After pleasantries, he said, "We've held your job for a long time, Marty. When do you think we can expect you back?"

"This is good timing for me, Ned. Believe it or not, I'll be back soon. It turns out I've had clinical depression, and I'm on a drug now that already has me eager to get to work. Let me finish a little business — maybe another week — and I should be in."

"Great," he said. "Our coverage of rural stuff has really fallen apart without you." Unlike most of my colleagues, I had not aspired to cover state politics and capitol happenings; the Great Central Valley, with its vast stretches of farmland and churning communities, had been my bailiwick. Few other writers at the paper had focused long term on that unglamorous region.

"I have to tell you that the high powers have been putting a lot of pressure on me to replace you," he added, "and I don't want to do that. Your fans have been writing to the paper wondering when they'll read your stuff again. I just hope you're really feeling okay."

"I am," I said, and I was, except for missing my son, my wife, my daughter. I also harbored a kernel of concern over my damned prostate.

I was about to sign off when Ned added, "Oh yeah, the Bearheart rumors have died down again, but if I hear anything more on that I'll let you know."

"Good."

I busied myself around the house, principally attending to the large box of unopened mail I'd earlier avoided. Sure enough, I'd somehow missed a note from Nancy that had arrived last month. I devoured its brief text:

Dear Marty:

I'm writing to remind you that Lea's 30th birthday is coming up the 20th of next month (you never could remember dates). Because of what's happened, be sure to at least send her a card.

Sincerely,
Nancy

"Sincerely"—that word dominated, that and the assumption that I wouldn't even send a card.

It also dawned on me that Nan wouldn't remind me of Lea's birthday, then forget it herself. My calendar read March 18, two days before the day. What the hell, I thought, then dialed Lea's telephone number. After the fourth ring, she answered. I said, "Hi, Perico, this is Dad."

"Yes?"

"Happy birthday."

"My birthday's not until day after tomorrow."

"I know, the twentieth."

"Well, thanks for calling," she said and hung up.

■

Dr. Solomon's call came the next afternoon. "I'm sorry to report that you have an elevated PSA, 8.7," he said.

"I *do?*"

"I've had men in here with PSAs literally ten times that high, and they're still walking around," he said. "Don't let the possibility of cancer panic you. I do need you to come in for a biopsy, though. How about tomorrow afternoon at . . . at three?"

"Okay." I was too stunned to say anything else.

Lying alone in the darkness that night I thought about cancer, dread creeping into my body as though an ice-water IV was at work. Was this some kind of punishment? I might soon be dead, insensate, gone . . . but only after my bones had been invaded, my spine collapsed . . . gruesome knowledge picked up from my coverage of the prostate-cancer death of a local politician. When that notion progressed to terror, I lurched, literally shuddering the bed.

And I began to think of my mother, who'd trusted me and who'd asked for me at her bedside, and whom I had so terribly failed. I knew I deserved this cancer—my Purgatory.

No! A malignancy that hadn't even been diagnosed and might not exist had nothing to do with me being a bad son, a lousy brother, a disappointing husband, a thoughtless father . . . It was just cells gone wild, a rational, scientific problem.

Still, I could not will the guilt away or think it away or curse it away. Instead, I curled there and recalled what my son had endured. Then I remembered something Doug had said to me: "When it gets too bad, I just pray."

I'd been a cultural Catholic all my life rather than a spiritual one; I'd certainly never been much of a Christian. My kids were baptized, but not confirmed in the Church. To my surprise, though, Doug had become a devout Catholic while in college, long before he was sick. After he was ill he had explained to me, "I just let go and pray, Pop, and guess what . . . I feel *so* much better."

"Why hasn't God cured you?" I asked, unable to hide my skepticism.

My son had looked at me for several moments, then replied, "The Bible says, 'God's ways are not man's ways.' God's about healing me, not curing me. Has it occurred to you that God might have to let my body die to save my soul? I'll take that trade."

He might take it, but I wouldn't. I wanted my boy to live.

"Prayer works, Pop. I'm sick, but I'm not afraid."

He'd added in response to a question he accurately divined I was thinking: "No matter what some idiots might say, homosexuality isn't a sin. Homosexual *acts* may be sinful, but the state of homosexuality is just a challenging condition."

That memory helped my mind, but my belly did not let go of the cold fright that lumped there; nausea threatened and I started to rise from bed, but hesitated and said, "Our Father, who art in heaven . . ." I thought it would come right back to me, but I grappled to remember the words. "Hollow"? No, that was how we had parodied it as kids. "Hallowed be thy name. Thy kingdom come, thy . . . will be done . . . on . . . earth as it is in heaven."

Then the rest was suddenly there: "Give us this day our daily bread, and lead us not into temptation. Forgive us our trespasses as we forgive those who trespass against us, and lead us not into temptation but deliver us from evil. Amen."

By the time I'd finished the entire prayer, then concentrated to say it all once again all the way through, I'd for a moment at least forgotten about the cancer and my belly was calm. When I realized that, I also realized Doug had been right.

■

The next afternoon the urologist worked on me. There was no reason to be prematurely frightened, I kept telling myself, but I was. I lay on my side on the table in the examination room at Dr. Solomon's, and my silent "Our Fathers" were interrupted by occasional "oofs" as he maneuvered an ultrasound transceptor, like a king-size dildo, up my rear and fired a tiny harpoon into my prostate gland to remove a stab of tissue for biopsy.

The first time he triggered it, I was jolted by a sharp pain amidst the general discomfort. With each succeeding stab, I became more tense, jerking in spite of myself. "Try to remain still," he cautioned. "We'll be finished soon."

Easy for him to say. Under my breath I continued mumbling, "Our Father . . ."

After we finished, the physician showed me what appeared to be half a dozen strands of red thread floating in a bottle. "I'll send these over to the lab, and we should have the pathology back by day after tomorrow. Why not make an appointment for late afternoon on your way out?"

"Sure."

"And relax, even if there turns out to be malignancy, your prostate isn't terribly large or lumpy." He added, "A couple of years ago, mine was larger than yours, and it wasn't malignant. I had to have a TURP—a roto-rooter." He smiled.

I couldn't help imagining a worst-case scenario. "I'd like to read about the disease. Can you recommend anything?"

"Why not wait until we know for certain what's going on? We should hear no later than tomorrow afternoon."

I nodded, but wasn't satisfied. On my drive home, I stopped at a bookstore and picked up a book on prostate cancer. Reading it that evening, I found precious little to cheer me.

3

"I've got cancer?"

"I'm afraid so," Dr. Solomon responded. "Are you okay?"

How can I be okay if I've got cancer? I thought. "I'm shocked."

"I would be too," he said. "What you've got is a mid-range—Gleason score of 6—adenocarcinoma of the prostate, but it doesn't appear large or out of the capsule, so we should be able to treat it successfully."

"Oh," I gulped. I'd read about the Gleason score and knew it was a grade of aggressiveness based on how regular or irregular the cancer cells were.

"There's no single, unambiguous treatment for this. After you go through the staging process, we'll have a better idea of what we're dealing with."

"And 'staging' means . . . ?"

He smiled and said, "I can tell you're a journalist; you ask lots of questions. That's a good habit when it comes to health. It's a series of tests designed to show us how far this has progressed and exactly where it's located."

I started to interrupt, but he continued, "We can treat the cancer even if it's spread, but only palliatively. We don't know how to cure it once it escapes the capsule."

"Well, what I want is the treatment that will definitely eliminate the cancer and minimize side effects."

"Mr. Martinez," he said, "you've chosen the wrong cancer for that."

As I departed, the receptionist handed me a packet containing a booklet on prostate cancer, a flyer about the local support group, a list of services offered by the American Cancer Society, and a small bundle of appointment cards. "Dr. Solomon said you can be free this week and next, so I went ahead and scheduled you for exams right away. Okay?" She spoke brightly, as though we were discussing a luncheon date.

"The sooner the better."

I sat in my car in the parking lot for several minutes before starting the engine, saying to myself, *I've got cancer.* Everything had changed, but I didn't know exactly how.

■

At home I found the light on my answering machine blinking, so I pushed the button and heard my daughter's voice asking me to call. That was followed by my ex-brother-in-law, Rollie, saying he'd call back. The third message was from Ned Schmidt asking me to call. A fourth caller clicked off without saying anything.

Despite my situation, I was embarrassed when I telephoned the editor. "Ned," I said, "you're not going to believe this . . . I'm not sure I do. I was just diagnosed with prostate cancer."

After a long silence, he gulped, "Jeeez, Martini. How bad?"

"I don't know. I'm going to undergo more exams next week."

"You know, you're the third guy I've talked to this month with that damned disease. It seems like it's everywhere." After a short pause, Ned said, "Listen, would you consider writing a piece or even a series about what you're going through? We've carried all kinds of stuff about breast cancer, but not much at all about prostate cancer."

"I don't know about that, but . . ."

"Do you remember when Mark was sick?" He cut me off. "He kept it quiet, but he had prostate cancer, and he treated it with radiation . . . went in every morning for a couple of months. Anyway, he kept working. He took a little time off for a nap each afternoon, but otherwise he didn't miss a beat."

"Until he died, anyway," I responded. "I'm ready to get back to work, but I need to get my mind off this."

"You're about out of sick leave."

"How about unpaid leave?"

"I don't know if the higher-ups will go for that."

"Okay," I said. "As soon as this staging is done—a couple weeks—I'll decide."

"Keep me posted. I've got a load of possible assignments waiting for you beside rumblings on the Bearheart thing."

"I'll think about writing a piece on prostate cancer," I replied absently. Newspaper assignments didn't seem important.

"Good. Oh, listen, I almost forgot," he added. "You'll be receiving some stuff in the mail that might influence what's going on now. The corporation's offering a golden handshake for employees over fifty. If you accept, I could still hire you for special projects, pay you a little spare change that way."

"Okay."

The next morning I underwent abdominal X-rays and extensive blood work at the local hospital. The following day my bones were scanned—"hot spots" showing up in my right leg (broken in a high school football game), my left shoulder (injured wrestling in both high school and college), and my jaw (*TMJ* problems); otherwise, the radiologists told me, I was clear.

I had a pelvic *MRI* the next morning in what felt like a sausage machine. My breath suddenly tightened and panic welled in my throat. I started to call the technician, but instead squeezed my eyes shut and muttered a tight Our Father, then another, then another . . . until the noisy exam was over. The scan revealed no metastasis.

Throughout the whole staging process, I remained surprised at how quickly the appointments had been made and the results had been returned. I was also surprised that the Our Father had become a virtual mantra for me. Although I drove by St. Apollinaris Church daily, I never felt comfortable enough to stop in.

■

I had just settled in front of the computer the evening after learning of my *MRI* results when the phone rang. "Dad?" My daughter's voice from the speaker had a shrill, almost panicky edge. "Daddy?"

"Lea, what's wrong?"

"Mom hasn't called in over two weeks. She calls every day but she hasn't now for *weeks.* I'm afraid something's happened to her. I don't know what to do."

"Okay, calm down," I said soothingly. "I'll see if I can chase her down. Your mother's pretty resourceful."

"Do you want to come over and talk? We could order pizza in or something."

I staggered at that unexpected invitation. "Come over? Sure, I'd love that."

I drove there immediately. Lea wasn't quite as warm in person, but she did give me a quick hug and offer a cup of coffee. "I really want to talk to Mom. I *need* to," she said. "Don't you have any idea where she is?"

"Aunt Audrey mentioned Mom being interested in something called the Madre Maria Society. Has she mentioned it?"

"No," my daughter sighed, then her chin began to quiver, and she approached me. "Oh, Daddy," she suddenly sobbed, "I'm so unhappy. Everything's just falling apart; Trevor told me he's moving back to Australia without me after all our plans. Now Mom's in some *cult* or something. I just don't know what to do."

Sad to say, I wasn't surprised to learn that the core problem was her love life. My daughter had a knack for choosing losers, but that didn't make her pain any less real. "We don't know for certain what Mom's doing, Perico," I told her, "so don't assume the worst. Think about what would make you happy and we'll work toward that."

"I want to start again," she said, her voice high and childlike. "I just want us all to be together again — you and Mom and Dougie and me."

"Me, too, Perico. That's what I want, too. But . . ."

She buried her head against my shoulder and moaned, "But we can't do that, can we." It wasn't a question.

"No, we can't," I said. "But Mom will turn up."

"Can things get any worse?" she sighed.

I almost stopped myself, but instead I said, "Lea, I have cancer." There was no good time to share that information.

She pulled away from me and stared at my face. "That isn't funny," she said.

"Tell me about it. I really do have prostate cancer. I just learned about it this week."

She collapsed then into a kitchen chair and buried her face in her arms. "Oh God!" she cried.

■

The next morning I completed a computer search of the Madre Maria Society, finding more than four hundred listings. I read the organization's Web site and learned that it had been founded by an Austrian priest in 1934 after he'd had a vision, and that its mission was "to promote a return to traditional Catholic morality and life and the evangelization of all society." That seemed standard enough to me.

The founder, Gerhardt Gollinger, had migrated to the United States in 1939 to escape the Nazis and had founded a retreat. He had died in 1969, and his followers were lobbying for beatification. The new "primary prelate" was a priest named M. Arthur McIntyre, who also claimed to have visions. He had no parish but operated something called a "personal prelature."

I telephoned Brian Cohn, the religion writer for the *Express*, and asked him about it.

"This Madre Maria bunch is ultraconservative," he told me. "It runs some orphanages in Mexico and Guatemala, but on the downside supposedly all mail to and from members is monitored, and members supposedly have to take a vow of secrecy, stuff like that. It's not very big in the United States, but it's got plenty of followers in Europe and Latin America."

He laughed then and added, "But don't worry — it won't take over the world because it requires celibacy even of its lay members, so there'll be no second generation."

"That's comforting," I replied.

"There is one more thing," said Brian. "It's been implicated in some attacks on abortion clinics and porn theaters and that kind of thing, but nothing's ever been proven. Some guy wrote a letter about it that was published in the *Washington Post,* claiming that McIntyre may have actually sanctioned the killing of particularly egregious sinners, but the evidence was soft, so it didn't go anywhere."

That's great, I thought. Nancy hooked up with a bunch of religious nuts.

■

I called Rollie and Audrey to ask if they knew what Nancy was doing, only to be swept into what sounded like a conversation about our late father-in-law that snapped my mind from my problems. "Hey, Beaner, did ol' Kenji ever warm up to you?" he asked.

"Warm up? No, but he tolerated me, which is about what I'd hoped for from him."

"Hell, you're a professional man and I'm just an Okie mechanic. I'd've thought he'd favor you."

I had to laugh. "You're a rich Okie mechanic who owns his own shop. To him I was just non-Japanese, and he was outraged when Doug was born so soon after Nancy and I married."

"Hey, at least you guys *got* married, didn't you? Hell of a lot didn't. Me and Audrey had Vivian about . . . what? . . . eight months after we got married. We were *all* pregnant in those days. Like it or not, that's what young folks do. What he should've been concerned about is good kids and good marriages. He sure raised a couple dandy daughters far as I'm concerned."

"Me, too," I said.

"Remember how he'd say he wasn't prejudiced, 'but think of the children.' One time I said to him, 'Kenji, who exactly's mean enough to discriminate against innocent little kids because they're mixed, except racist nuts. Are *you?*' He got sore as hell at me — which was okay, since I was sore as hell at him."

Our father-in-law was often sore at Rollie, who despite his lack of formal education had always been not only smart but something of a rabble-rouser. I'd never had balls enough to challenge Kenji the way he did.

"Anyways, my kin were tickled as hell anybody'd have me a-tall," he chuckled. "They fell right in love with Audrey. Who wouldn't? I had one old aunt to call her my 'China doll,' and she never figured out the difference between Japanese and Chinese. She loved Audrey just the same."

"I thought Okies were supposed to be racists?"

"You bet. My kin didn't much cotton to 'Nigras' — which is the way most of 'em said it — and they'd never even seen a Basque or a Filipino or an Armenian before they come to California, probably hadn't even heard of 'em. It was all pretty exotic. But my mama, she read in the Bible how Moses he married this Ethiopian woman, so that made it okay for me to marry Audrey. And then some Japanese boys from our little town, they served and won medals overseas during W. W. Two; that was all it took for my daddy and uncles to accept 'em, because they were veterans.

"And you know, I never heard one word of talk from my family about my kids being mixed. That daddy of mine, he just loved little Vivian; she was sure his favorite. Oh, he loved Estelle, too, but he thought ol' Tommy was a blister."

"He *was,*" I said.

"Yeah, I guess he was an ornery little turd," Rollie said with what sounded like pride.

"Well," I told him, "my family'd already been mixed for about three hundred years when I married Nancy."

I heard Audrey's voice in the background saying something, then Rollie said, "What'n the hell'd you call for anyways? My little bride wants to use the phone."

"I've forgotten."

"I believe you've caught that old-timer's disease. *CRS.*"

"*CRS?*"

"Can't remember shit!"

His laugh was a high "Yip!" as usual, and I realized how long it'd been since I'd heard that, let alone engaged in a silly conversation like this. "Listen, have you guys seen or heard anything from Nancy?"

"'Fraid not. She told Audrey she might be goin' on some religious deal . . . a pilgrimage."

"Religious pilgrimage? Do you know where she is?"

"Maybe in North Carolina with this outfit she was gonna join up with, the Mother Maria or somethin' like that."

4

The Sacramento Prostate Cancer Support Group met each Wednesday, or so said the flyer I'd been given at the urologist's office. There was an information number listed, too, so I dialed it. After three rings a voice said, "Morton O'Brien, attorney-at-law. Tony speaking."

I hesitated, then said, "I'm calling about the prostate cancer group."

"Just a moment."

"Hello, this is Mort," said a deeper voice.

"Mr. O'Brien," I said, "this is Martin Martinez. I'm calling about the support group."

"Have you been recently diagnosed?"

"Last week."

"Not a pleasant experience, I know," he responded. "How'd you hear about us?"

"Dr. Solomon."

"He's one of the good ones. Some urologists really resent our existence. What're your numbers . . . Martin, is it?"

"Marty." This was too personal a question for me. I replied, "What're yours?"

Mort chuckled. "You don't want mine. I was diagnosed with a PSA of 61 and a Gleason of 7. All I could do was go on intermittent hormone therapy . . . been chemically castrated for nearly five years . . . growing breasts, having hot flashes, but alive."

This kind of candor from a guy I'd never met shocked me, so I felt obliged to say "My PSA's 8.7 and my Gleason's 6."

"Have you been staged?"

"We're doing that now."

"With those numbers, you're apt to be clear. What therapy are you considering?"

"I'm not sure. That's one reason I want to attend the meeting."

"Good decision. There'll be one other new man that I know of tomorrow night, so we'll give you two a chance to hear about treatment options from survivors. See you at seven."

That word "survivor" caught my attention. "Right," I responded a moment later. "At seven."

"And Marty," Mort added, "don't let this eat you up. We've all been there and we'll all do our best to help you." He sounded like an old chum.

■

The next morning I felt as though I was holding my breath in the urologist's office until Dr. Solomon began talking: "There's no evidence of spread beyond the prostate capsule, Mr. Martinez. Your lymph nodes appear normal, and your bones are clear. That's the good news. There *is* more tumor mass in the left lobe than I'd anticipated. Still, you've got some therapeutic options . . ."

"Didn't I read somewhere that surgery's the gold standard?"

Dr. Solomon chuckled. "Well, it's the gold standard of us surgeons, anyway," he said, "but there are other treatments — external-beam radiation, brachytherapy, cryotherapy — and all have different side effects." He took off his glasses and absently wiped them on his white jacket, waiting for me to say something, I guess. When I remained silent, he added, "Staging is an imperfect process, Mr. Martinez, so if it were me I'd assume the worst and take the most aggressive approach despite the side effects. If we don't kill the cancer, none of the rest will mean much. Dead men don't worry about impotence or incontinence."

"Well . . ." As tense as matters already were, I was about to complicate them, so I cleared my throat, then said, "I've read that I should get a second opinion on all this. Can you recommend someone I should see?"

"With a straightforward case like this appears to be, I'd talk to a radiation oncologist, do some reading, and join a support group to get some input from survivors."

"I've already contacted the local support group. Why don't you give me the names of local radiation oncologists?"

"Fair enough. But, Mr. Martinez" — he placed a hand on one of my shoulders — "don't drift away on this. Some men, especially if they're asymptomatic, just go into denial and wait too late. Adenocarcinoma is a relatively indolent malignancy, but at some point it *will* metastasize if you don't treat it. Once that happens, we won't be able to do anything but palliate. If I'm ever in your position, I'll do exactly what I've just recommended to you," he added.

■

After receiving the bad news about cancer, I'd called Dr. Molinaro's receptionist and asked for the first appointment that he had. There was a cancellation, so right after lunch that day I sat in his office, and he asked, "How are you with it? How's your anxiety level?"

"High enough," I replied.

Dr. Molinaro smiled. "I'll bet, but you say you've had positive contact with your daughter?"

"Yes."

"That's one less stress to have to deal with."

"My biggest fear when I heard that word, 'cancer,' was that I'd die alone, estranged from my daughter, divorced from my wife, rejected by my family. At least my daughter's back, but let me tell you why . . ."

When I told him about Nan's disappearance, he gazed at me over the top of his reading glasses and said, "I guess the medication's really working, because you're dealing with enough problems for both of us. Try to put stress aside; it will weaken your immune system. Most of all, don't assume the worst."

Then he added, "You have problems with your extended family, you've said. Can we explore that a bit?"

I gazed at my hands, soft now after all my years as a journalist, and thought about my father's *manos,* hard as manzanita, and of my mother's pride when I'd earned the white-collar job that would soften me. I remembered how she deflected the smart-assed remarks in the neighborhood about me not doing a real man's work. And I thought about how I would later let her down. "I'm not ready for that just yet."

"Fine. Anytime you *are* ready, I'm here. Let me ask you another question: Do you meditate?"

"No, but I pray," I said, a little astonished at my own answer.

"Does it help?"

"Sure does."

"Then by all means keep doing it. Have you always been religious?"

I had to shrug and say, "I'm a foxhole Catholic, Doctor. Hard times have forced me back."

"As long as it works," he responded.

■

I arrived fifteen minutes early for the prostate cancer group's meeting, and the conference room was nearly empty. A large, balding man about my age was sitting at the head of an oblong set of tables pushed together. He looked up and I said, "Mort?"

"Yes." He smiled. "And you're . . . ?"

"Marty Martinez."

"Good to meet you, Marty," he said as we shook hands. "You're early. We can get a little acquainted. I'll get you a name tag, too. By the way, are you the Martinez who used to write for the *Express?*"

"Yep."

"I liked your stuff. That series you did on pesticides was terrific."

"Thanks."

"Most of the guys'll be trickling in right at seven, that's their pattern. We've got a couple of hundred members, but only about fifteen or twenty attend the weekly meetings. It's not the same fifteen or twenty each week, though, since the old-timers mostly come once in a while. Here's a list of members." He handed me four sheets of paper stapled together. "Fill in this card and I'll add you to the list. And do feel free to call any of us to talk about your illness."

"I'm encouraged that there *are* old-timers," I said as I scribbled my name, address, and phone number on the card.

"Well, you'll by no means be the sickest guy here — or the healthiest. That's part of what makes the group interesting."

Just then two middle-aged men walked in together and approached. The larger said, "Mort, this is Bill Kennedy, the old pal I told you about. We went to high school together a hundred years ago at Grant. He's just been diagnosed."

"Bill," said Mort, extending his hand, "glad to met you." Then he grinned. "Any friend of Red's can't be all good.

"Red, Bill, this is another new member, Marty Martinez." We all shook hands. "Why don't you two new fellas sit up here near me when the meeting starts?"

A few minutes later, as latecomers hustled in and picked up name tags from a small table near the door, Mort theatrically rustled a sheaf of papers and said, "Let me read you this." He grinned broadly. "Three rules for men with prostate cancer: One, never pass a urinal. Two, never trust a fart. Three, always use an erection . . . whether alone or with someone."

The laughter was genuine, and I guess I was a little surprised; I'd expected a grim conclave.

Mort followed his joke by reading announcements: A seminar on alternative therapies for prostate cancer would be held at California Pacific Medical Center; the American Cancer Society invited the group to assemble a team for the Relay for Life; a new issue of *Prostate Cancer Exchange* had arrived and was available in the oncology center's library. He followed that by asking for any announcements from the membership.

A heavyset man—"Art"—raised one hand and said, without waiting to be called on, "It hasn't been in the paper yet, but Rich Haslett died last week down in Palm Springs. His wife called me."

"Rich died?" grunted a small man whose name tag said "Bob."

"I heard his cancer had come back hard and fast," Mort explained.

A familiar-looking man seated across from me—"Al"—said, "Yeah, I heard his cancer'd turned refractory, and that the chemo they tried just wasn't working, but I didn't know it was so bad." That gruff voice clarified my memory: He was Al Royster, a physician I'd interviewed years before when I was writing a feature about emergency rooms. His hair hadn't been white then.

"Rich's wife said there'd be a memorial service up here in a couple of weeks," Art reported. "The cancer collapsed his spine, and she saw him suffer something awful. She said the doctors wouldn't give him enough painkiller."

Bob, making notes of some kind, asked, "What were his initial PSA and Gleason?"

"In the thirties, I think," offered the man across the table.

"Hmmm." Bob nodded. "Mine was 42."

I'm thinking, 42? Mort said his was 61. Mine is 8.7, and my biopsy showed cancer in both lobes of the gland. Bob and Mort must have it from their knees to their chests.

"And his Gleason?" Bob asked.

"His Gleason? Oh, high. Nine, I think," replied the man across the circle. "He was diagnosed by a local urologist up in Chico, and he said the guy had him scheduled for surgery and never even discussed options. Of course, the post-surgical pathology was bad, and things just seemed to get worse and worse for him."

An old man wearing shorts and golf shirt—"Ralph," read his tag—sputtered, "I'd never let a *G.D.* doc cut on me. The urologists aren't telling us the truth about brachytherapy. Those radioactive seeds are the ticket, but urologists hate 'em. They're just concerned about their *G.D.* bottom line." He addressed Bill and me then: "You new guys mark my words. Brachytherapy!"

"We're gonna take up a collection and get Ralph some assertiveness training," commented Mort, "and to help him develop some strong opinions. He's too wishy-washy now."

"We might buy him some good sense, too," said Dr. Royster.

General laughter followed, with Ralph himself joining in, and that seemed to break the tension. Then Mort added, "We'll send Mrs. Haslett a card and flowers, and Art, can you get us the time and place for the memorial service?"

"Sure thing."

"We can all do our best to be there." Mort paused, then said, "Well, we have two new members here tonight. Marty Martinez and Bill Kennedy. Marty, would you like to tell us something about yourself and your condition?"

I summarized my situation as best I could, and the group listened thoughtfully. Once I'd finished, Mort said, "Before anyone speaks up I just want to warn Marty—and Bill, too—that dang near everyone in this group turns into a medical expert, and that most of us sway our comments so that our own therapeutic choices seem like the best ones." He said this with a smile, but I could see that he was serious.

The experts started in immediately, and before long Mort interrupted, saying, "See what I mean? If it's new and supposedly less damaging it's got to be better."

A man near the back of the room said, "Well, brachytherapy certainly doesn't produce nearly the morbid side effects that surgery does—like impotence!"

Mort grinned when he responded, "And what will you do with a hard-on in the cemetery? Leave it sticking out of the ground for a little tombstone?"

Guffawing, a large man on whose ID badge was printed "Jake," chortled, "You might could get lucky and all the old maids'll play squat tag on it!"

Before the laughter subsided, Bill Kennedy spoke up for the first time. "I was just diagnosed yesterday and I— I—" His chin began to quiver and his eyes filled. "Isn't anybody else here scared?" he asked, barely controlling his voice.

"We all are, Bill," responded Mort. "We all are."

5

My good luck continued that week—or I thought it was good luck, anyway. I was able to schedule a late-afternoon appointment with a radiation oncologist named Paul Nimitz at the University Medical Center. I was beginning to believe that when it came to cancer, physicians found time even on busy days.

The doctor was another kid—to me, at least—cordial without being effusive. I got right to the point, asking, "You've read my file. What regimen of treatments would you recommend for me, Dr. Nimitz?"

"Well," he said, smiling slightly, "first of all you have to understand that Dr. Solomon and I are like two salesmen: He's selling a Cadillac and I'm selling a Lincoln. We both believe in our products, and both can be winners or lemons.

"But if you were my father or brother, given your numbers, I'd recommend a course of 3-D conformal radiation. I'd also recommend concurrent hormonal ablation for at least six months. I have a hunch your cancer *might* be out of the prostate on the left side, in which case heavy-duty radiation, plus blocking your testosterone, could kill the malignancy without destroying too much surrounding tissue."

When I asked him why he thought the cancer might be out, he explained, "To me your prostate feels lumpy on that left margin. I'd play it safe if I were you."

I left Dr. Nimitz's office more unsettled than I'd been when I entered it.

■

As I was wheeling home, I began to say an Our Father, then realized I was driving by St. Apollinaris Church. Almost without thought, I swerved my car into the parking lot.

I hadn't been inside a Catholic church since my son's funeral Mass, but I immediately knelt before a large statue of Jesus, sighed, then said simply, "Please help me with this decision," and began saying an Our Father. From there I launched a nearly flawless Hail Mary, then a flawless Glory Be, and I realized that I was relaxing. I said the same three prayers again, this time for Doug.

Much relieved, I blessed myself and stood just as a young man wearing a bright golf shirt emerged from the sacristy. "Hi." He smiled.

"Hello."

"I'm Father Tran," he announced, "the assistant pastor," and he extended his hand.

"I'm Marty Martinez," I said as we shook hands. I recognized him as a priest who had once visited my son.

He didn't seem to remember me. "Are you a parishioner?" he asked.

A little embarrassed, I said, "No. I've been away from the Church for a long time. This is my first visit in several years."

Father Tran's smile was genuine. "Welcome home," he said.

■

When I arrived at my house, there was a message from Ned Schmidt on my answering machine, so I dialed his number. "How's your health, Martini?" was his first question.

"Shitty," I replied, then explained as well as I could what was going on.

After I finished, he said, "I really hate to add pressure, but I need to tell the high powers when or if you'll be back. Have you considered my suggestion about early retirement?"

That lump of stress in my gut seemed to swell: cancer, Nancy, job . . . what next? "Ned, I really will decide about all this within a week, okay? I thought I knew what I was going to do, but I keep getting conflicting information from doctors."

"Your health is most important, but this is important, too. Let me know as soon as you can, Martini."

"Okay. Have the office send me a personal retirement assessment, will you, so I can figure out exactly how much money I'd receive on the pension plan."

"I'll do it today. Take care, Martini. Listen, do you mind if I let people here at the office know what's up? There's already a rumor out that you're at death's door."

"Tell them," I replied.

"Oh yeah, our Fresno guy just wrote about a big irrigation district down there that's trying to bully its way to lining a natural channel that provides groundwater for several local communities. Sounds like your kind of story."

"Yeah," I said, too concerned about my own problems to care.

■

Later that afternoon, I wandered into the kitchen and warmed coffee in the microwave, then sat at the dining room table. Time to call Lea, but another thought came to me: Why not telephone Dr. Royster from the support group?

A woman answered the phone and I said, "Hi, this is Marty Martinez. Is Dr. Royster available?"

"Just a moment, Mr. Martinez," she said.

After a short pause, he said, "Hello there, Marty."

"Hello, Dr. Royster—"

"Al," he corrected.

"Al," I said. "I'm having real trouble choosing a therapy. Why am I deciding when I haven't any medical training?"

I guess my voice betrayed upset, because Dr. Royster interjected, "Calm down, Marty. All any physician should be is an advisor. You should *always* make your own health decisions, based on your doctor's recommendations."

"Okay." I accepted his admonition, although I'd been raised in a family that treated doctors like priests or wizards.

"What're your PSA and Gleason scores, again?" he asked.

"I'm an 8.7 with a Gleason of 6."

"My numbers were just a tad higher, and I had surgery because I've never really trusted radiation, since way back when it was used for everything . . . acne, adenoids, you name it.

"I'm also a physician, so the pathology report was damned important to me.

I'd recommend that a surgeon remove you from it, and put it in a bottle where it can't hurt anyone."

I asked, "How about side effects?"

"Remember that I'm seventy-four now, probably about ten years older than you, right?"

"Right."

"Since the surgery, I wear a pad for stress incontinence, especially late in the day. When I play golf, a good swing usually leads to a good squirt. So does a bad swing.

"As for sex, I use a penile pump. It sort of works. My wife and I've been lovers for a long, long time, so we've figured out what to do.

"There *is* one more thing that influenced my decision," he added. "If you have surgery and the pathology report shows local spread, as mine did, adjuvant radiation is usually more successful than salvage surgery is if primary radiation fails."

"Okay."

"Make a decision about therapy and don't look back or you'll drive yourself nuts."

I thanked him and hung up, feeling somewhat relieved. Maybe surgery *would* be the best route for me.

■

Not long after the call, I heard a knock at the front door, then it opened before I could respond. "Daddy?" my daughter called.

"I'm in here!"

Lea entered the kitchen and asked, "What did the doctor say?"

"The surgeon suggests surgery and the radiologist suggests radiation. I just talked to a doctor who's in the support group and he said he'd chosen surgery."

"Are you going to have surgery, then?"

Once, years ago when I was a kid standing on a bridge over the Merced River, I saw a drowned body being slowly tumbled downstream by the current. That's how my life was beginning to feel, tumbling slowly away from my control to wherever a current carried me.

"Daddy?" Lea's voice was distressed. "You look so strange."

"Yeah," I replied. "I'll probably have surgery. What did you find out about Mom?" She had told me she was driving to Davis, where an acquaintance said he might have seen Nancy.

"It wasn't her," Lea responded. "When I showed him the snapshots in the album, he said the woman he'd seen was heavier and younger — and he wasn't even sure if she was Asian — maybe Latina. He hit on me, though," she added. "Maybe that's why he really called. He'd heard I was unattached again."

"How'd he know you were looking for your mother, anyway?"

"I just sort of passed the word around to other servers, and I e-mailed everyone in my address book and asked them to pass the word. I've had a bunch of calls, but mostly just to sympathize."

"We'll find Mom, honey. And a good-looking woman like you is bound to attract men, as you know by now."

"Thanks for the compliment, but the wrong kind are attracted to me," she said.

■

Uncle Rollie, who'd earlier telephoned to ask if he could bunk at my place the night before his regular cardiac exam, arrived in time to see Lea, who was departing for work. "Hey, Muffin!" he called as he strode up the front steps. "I brought your favorite dog for a visit."

His pooch, Jimmy Dean — named for the famous sausage maker — was a formidable wurst producer himself. He lifted his leg against the mailbox support, then scratched a considerable number of divots in the surrounding grass. How such a small pooch could kick up so much sod was an enduring mystery to me. "What kind of dog is that anyway?" I asked.

"Ol' Jimmy? Why, hell, he's a pureblood Tasmanian spaniel. One of the rarest breeds there is. Use 'em to hunt kangaroos."

Lea was giggling at our old routine, but she was also edging behind me, since Jimmy Dean was also a heroic Tasmanian leg-humper. "Does he have papers?" she asked.

"You bet." This was another old joke: When Rollie and his wife had picked up the puppy at the local dog pound, Audrey had innocently asked the man in charge if the mongrel came with any papers. He'd handed her a roll of toilet tissue.

Lea left for work and I telephoned for Chinese food, then while we drank a beer and waited for the food, I told my ex-brother-in-law what was happening with my health. "Boy, that's a pisser," he grunted, then laughed at this own choice of words. "Why can't they just tell you what the hell needs to be done, then do it? I'd purely hate bein' up in the air like that."

"I thought you Okies always just said, 'Cut it off.'"

"You bet, but only when we're talkin' about Mex'cans." He grinned. "Slice you chile peppers up is what I say." He sat across from me in the family room with Jimmy Dean at his feet.

"What the hell is that dog licking?" I asked.

Rollie was suddenly chuckling, then he said, "You hear about the ol' boy that seen a dog doin' that, so he turns to his buddy and says, 'I'd like to be able to do that myself'? His pal, he says, 'Hell, pet him. He'll probably let ya.'"

I guffawed as much at Rollie's yipping laughter as at his joke. We were still chuckling when the doorbell rang, so I hustled to the porch to collect the food. While we were eating, I told my brother-in-law that Lea was searching for Nancy.

"Good luck," he said.

"Are you sure there wasn't a guy involved?" I had to ask. "I mean, most of the disappearing acts I ever looked into for the newspaper turned out to have a sexual angle."

"Naw, it was that religion deal."

The phone rang before I could say more, so I picked it up. "Hey, Champ," I heard, "this is Johnny O. Long time no talk."

"Hey, Johnny. How are you?"

Johnny O was Johnny Orozco, an ex-prizefighter who'd been my pal since grade school. "Johnny's okay, Champ. You?"

He was just checking in, so we made small talk until he signed off. After I hung up, I turned to Rollie and said, "That was your old sparring partner, Johnny O."

"That's another chili bean's lucky I never got around to workin' him over. I was pretty rough mysownself."

Since we knew Johnny could have whipped us both—together—I chuckled and said, "You might've needed that dog to help you."

"Ol' Jimmy, he's rough cob, too." The pooch now snored on Rollie's lap, looking like a small toy.

"At least we'll be safe tonight . . . with a watchdog and all."

"You bet."

6

After Rollie left for his medical appointment the next morning, I decided to telephone Father Tran. My ex-brother-in-law's humor—and the beer we'd consumed—had allowed me to escape my problems for a few hours, but I had awakened tense, and I remembered that the young priest had said, "Welcome home." I also recalled that doctor, Miranda Mossi's, story about the blessing of the sick. If it was good enough for a physician, then it ought to be good enough for me.

The priest answered the phone, so I said, "Father, this is Marty Martinez. We met the other day at the church. You gave me your card."

"I remember. How are you?"

I cleared my throat, then said, "Well, not too hot. I have prostate cancer. I wonder if I could come by for a blessing."

"Of course. I can come to you, if you prefer."

"I'm not bedridden or anything, Father, just troubled. I've almost decided to go in for surgery."

"Well, you and your doctor heal your body. God will heal your spirit, but don't bargain," he advised.

"I'm in no position to bargain, Father. I know that."

"Let's set a date to get together," the priest said. "How about tomorrow at ten o'clock?"

"See you then."

"Put your trust in God, Marty. It'll be okay."

The placebo effect, or whatever it was, worked again. I felt much better after that short conversation, but I had another call to make.

■

Dr. Solomon wasn't available when I telephoned, but his nurse took the message and told me he'd call back. Rollie was going out to lunch with an old pal after his visit to the doctor, so I fixed myself a Dagwood sandwich and ate it with a few chips and a beer. I read through the *L.A. Times* and the *San Francisco Chronicle* as I ate, on the prowl for news stories I might be able to develop into features. Just as I finished, the urologist returned my call. "Sorry I'm late, but I'm working my way through messages during lunch."

"Thanks for getting back to me. I've decided to go ahead with the surgery. Can you do it?"

"Sure," he responded. "Just a second — I'll check my hospital schedule." After what seemed to be a long time, he returned to the phone, saying, "Okay. I wanted to make sure Bill Frazee would be available to assist. How about the morning of the twenty-ninth next month? That gives you time to begin donating autologous blood. Can you go to the local blood bank tomorrow afternoon at four to begin that?"

"Sure, but why do we have to wait so long?"

"We need three units of your blood — just in case — donated a week apart, and you need time to rebuild your strength after that. With your numbers, a month shouldn't make a difference. I'll have my receptionist schedule the blood appointments, and an appointment to come in here day after tomorrow so I can give you all the information about the surgery and the University Medical Center — the business side of the equation."

"I'm ready to get going on this ASAP. One other thing, though. The radiation oncologist said he had a hunch it might be worse. Extracapsular, he said."

For a moment the urologist did not reply, then he responded, "Well, I've seen the results of all the tests, and there was nothing there I could see . . . and neither did the pathologist."

After we hung up, I telephoned my daughter and explained what I'd done. She said, "Just get it out, Daddy, before it spreads. That's the main thing."

■

The young priest opened the door to the rectory at St. Apollinaris and said, "Come on in."

As he led me to his small office, I said, "You ministered to my son a few years back."

"I remember you and him," he said, "but I didn't when we met in the church the other day. You're the journalist and your son was a professor."

"Yes, at San Francisco State."

"How've you been since his passing?"

"Not really well," I admitted. Before I talked about myself, though, I had a question that I wanted to ask. "Father, this is off the subject, but what do you know about the Madre Maria Society?"

"You thinking of joining?"

"Not likely," I replied.

"The Madre Maria Society? Well, I don't know much. It's an ultraconservative, ultra-traditionalist sect, pretty militant about abortion and pornography and other hot-button stuff. It works at the boundaries of the Church, just like a lot of ultraliberal groups . . . and ultraliberal priests, like me." He smiled at that last revelation.

"It's not nutty?"

"Any organization on the extreme attracts nuts, but no, the group's not inherently nutty as far as I know. I think it's got some nutty ideas, though."

"But it's legitimate?"

"As legitimate as Republicans . . . or Democrats," he smiled.

"That's not much of an endorsement," I said, then added, "I think my ex-wife might be involved with it."

The young priest said, "God bless her."

The Anointing of the Sick carried me back to the mysterious religion of my youth. Although it was conducted in English in an office, the cadence of the prayers, the priest's voice, and the anointing with blessed oil stripped years of skepticism from me. I felt much stronger when the brief rite was finished. Only a vague shadow of inquietude lingered.

"God will give you strength to deal with whatever you have to face," said the priest. "But you still look a little troubled. What's up?"

"This is a big bite for me, Father," I said. In fact, I hadn't consciously thought about it before, but I sensed this was an opportunity to deal with something deeper and more painful even than the cancer, something erupting like a boil. "I haven't been much of a Catholic, but I'm suddenly devout now that I'm scared."

"Hey, if it brought you back—"

"But I think I'll need to go to Confession soon. I *know* I will. But I'm scared of what I have to think about."

He nodded, saying, "Well, I understand that. It's not easy for a priest to confess either, but I also understand that you can't get past whatever's bothering you if you don't confront it. You've been away for a while, so let me tell you it's not 'Confession' anymore, it's 'the Sacrament of Reconciliation,' about getting rid of what's most troubling your soul. If the process is an ordeal, not a relief, then something's wrong with it, because that isn't the intention, no matter what some think.

"If you're ready for the sacrament, we can do it right now, in the privacy of this office, face-to-face—no dark box."

That made me squirm. I wanted to, but it would take me days to dredge up *all* the bad stuff. When I told him that, Father Tran nodded, then said, "If it's really been years, just confess the most painful things, the ones you can't get clear of, and let God forgive you and help you move on. You can always mention others that trouble you later as they occur to you, and you'll be in a state of grace in the meantime." He added, "Not a bad bargain. Want to give it a try?"

His enthusiasm and openness tempted me, but I realized that I couldn't speak about my worst sin, not yet anyway. In fact, I could barely bring myself to think about it . . . but I could never really forget it, either, In fact, it seemed so heinous to me that it invalidated anything good I might've done. "No, not today, Father. I'm not ready, not yet. I've got some serious thinking to do . . . an examination of conscience."

"I understand, but don't think yourself into knots. It isn't reasonable to expect to remember everything."

What I couldn't bring myself to tell him was what I *could* remember.

"Don't be too hard on yourself," the priest added. "God will forgive anything you're truly sorry for, even things you can't forgive yourself for — maybe especially them."

I thought of mealymouthed excuses of why I couldn't confess now, but finally just repeated the truth. "I'm just not ready yet. Words are my business, Father, and I have to figure out how to say what I have to say."

He smiled, then said, "A confession doesn't have to be perfect, just perfectly sincere."

"I'm sure I can manage sincerity and imperfection." I smiled back. "But let me think about it."

"Of course. God's patient even if some pushy priests aren't. The essential message of Christ's life is forgiveness."

As he accompanied me to the parking lot, making small talk, a husky older man walked out the back door of the rectory, and Father Tran said, "Marty, let me introduce you to the pastor, Monsignor Kelley."

We walked over and I was introduced to the monsignor as a new parishioner. "Father Tran says you're the boss here," I said.

The white-haired priest replied with a wink and the hint of a brogue, "I don't think anyone is *this* independent young man's boss, but I do *try* to restrain him a bit. You're new to the parish, then, Mr. Martinez?" He wore a golf sweater with the sleeves pushed up to his elbows, and his forearms looked like Popeye's, knotted with muscle.

"Yes."

"Well, welcome. We've a lively group here, if I do say so myself. I'm off for a doctor's appointment, so pray for me," he said. "Then a bit of golf . . . pray for me again." He grinned this time. "I hope to see more of you, Mr. Martinez." We shook hands and he strode away toward a late-model Honda.

■

After the monsignor departed, Father Tran asked, "Where're you off to today? More doctors' appointments?"

"No, actually, I'm just headed home."

He smiled and said, "Candidly, I'm trying to recruit more members for a group I convene here at the rectory every Wednesday morning . . . it'll start in fifteen minutes. It's based on a book about Catholic practices, and it's for anyone trying to figure out what's really going on in the contemporary Church. There are no men in the group — other than me, I mean. I'd sure like some masculine support."

I really didn't want to add an obligation to my life, but I was feeling indebted. "I can try it," I finally said, "but no promise that I'll stick. I'm not much of a joiner, and I'll be going back to work soon — or I hope I will."

"This should be a perfect class for you." He kept selling. "I won't take back the anointing if you don't return next week."

"Okay, I'll give it a shot."

A group of women, mostly older than I, were seated around a long table in the rectory's conference room when I walked in with Father Tran. "Hello, everyone," he called.

They greeted him and examined me. The priest motioned for me to sit next to him, and I did. "This is Marty Martinez, who'll be joining us for a while. Marty, this is Mrs. Marquez, Mrs. Marcou, Mrs. Donati, Mrs. Tynne, Mrs. Banducci, Mrs. O'Reilly, Dr. Mossi, Mrs. Acuña, and Mrs. Stoltz."

Dr. Miranda Mossi smiled in recognition and nodded at me.

Father Tran caught that and asked, "Old friends?"

"New ones," said the physician, and I liked that. She didn't refer to me as a patient.

The class surprised me. An organization as large and as old as the Catholic Church has many nooks and crannies. I didn't know, for instance, that it was called "catholic" because in the days after the death of Jesus it had allowed non-Jews to become communicants; the idea that *anyone* could join was radical at the time. Because of Catholicism's history of anti-Semitism, it was hard to think of the Church as a Jewish invention.

Father Tran read from the text, stopping frequently to allow for questions and comments, discussing a chapter about apparitions. I've always been fascinated by stories of the Virgin Mary's face appearing on a tortilla or a dish towel.

Anyway, after the priest read about the difference between a weeping statue of the Virgin Mary in Sicily in 1953, an event declared "worthy of belief" by the Church, and an unendorsed event in Virginia in 1992, Mrs. Marquez declared firmly, "There are many, many secret apparitions and signs to the devout that Holy Mother Church doesn't know about. Some people don't reveal them."

Father Tran smiled and said, "A lot of apparitions and signs are *claimed,* anyway. I suspect that most aren't reported to the Church because they would be investigated."

Dr. Mossi's eyes were twinkling when she asked, "The book said that the tears of the weeping statue in Sicily contained the complex proteins and salts and trace elements normally found in human tears, didn't it?"

"Yes."

"Who did the analysis?" Her tone was pleasant, but I sensed skepticism —which I shared.

Father Tran responded, "Well, the Church is *extremely* reluctant to accept those kinds of events, since they're claimed constantly. Everybody seems to have something with the Lord's imprint on it, so the Church employs a sophisticated scientific team with a wonderful lab. Remember, Miranda, there are literally hundreds of thousands—maybe millions—of Catholic scientists and physicians like you, so a highly qualified group can be assembled to investigate every claim. *At least* ninety-nine times out of a hundred, they reject the occurrence. For example, the one in Virginia turned out to happen only when a certain person was present; no one else ever saw the statue weep. They found puddles of so-called tears—which I seem to remember turned out to be tap water. It was a no-brainer."

"Before the Mass was changed to English and the altar was turned around," said Mrs. Stoltz, "there were more signs because the people were closer to God the way Jesus intended."

With a tone so pleasant that he seemed to be praising her, Father Tran asked, "Did you miss the week we read the chapter on rites? Here—" He fanned the book's pages, then read: "The 'old' Mass was only about three hundred years old. It followed forms established by the Council of Trent. . . . The Mass we see today is actually more like it was in early Christian times than the Mass of Trent was." He shrugged and added, "There it is."

"When they changed to this English Mass," Mrs. Marquez said, "the statue of Our Lady at St. Mary's parish began to weep. I have a picture Mrs. Ricomini took and you can see the tears just spilling."

Father Tran lowered the book and said softly, "One of my professors in the seminary used to say that events like that always seem suspiciously self-serving. When was the last time you heard someone say 'Jesus appeared to me and told me that my ideas were screwy'? I've never even heard of anything remotely like that, have you?"

No one responded, but I saw some hard squinting. This debate society sure wasn't the Catholic Church I remembered.

Finally Dr. Mossi smiled and kept her tone light when she said, "In a world where children are abused, where there's homelessness and starvation and gangs shooting each other right here in town, I doubt that Our Lady's values are so superficial that she'd weep over the change in a ceremony."

"Me, too," added Father Tran. "I don't doubt your friend's sincerity, but I do doubt if that particular occurrence was ever investigated."

Mrs. Marquez's face was stony when she said, "Mrs. Ricomini doesn't lie."

“I’m sure, but she can certainly be mistaken,” said the priest. “Even if the statue really did weep, how could your friend know why?”

Before any of the other ladies could answer, Dr. Mossi said, “Amen. People can believe anything and claim anything. But remember the logical fallacy of reversing the burden of proof? It isn’t up to the Church to disprove anything. It’s up to the claimant to prove it.”

Some icy faces around the table told me that not everyone remembered that fallacy, or liked it very much.

To my astonishment, I’d actually enjoyed the meeting. This seemed to be a far more accessible organization than the ominous one I recalled, and just hearing controversies discussed openly intrigued me. I thanked Father Tran afterward, and he asked, “Will you be joining us?”

“As my time allows, sure. I won’t make it every week, but I’ll make it when I can.”

I turned to Dr. Mossi, who stood near us, and said, “You and Father Tran are the liberal wing, aren’t you?”

Both of them laughed. “The truth is that we represent the view of most parishioners far better than the conservatives do,” the physician said, “which I suspect is why they can be so adamant. They’re fighting a rearguard action.”

I chuckled, then said, “Let me tell you a story that didn’t seem appropriate in class. When I was a young reporter, some man out in West Sacramento reported that the image of Jesus appeared on his stucco wall each time it rained. I was assigned to cover it because lots of people were gathering every cloudy day.

“Anyway, on the day after my story appeared in *The Bee,* I got a phone call from a woman who said, ‘That isn’t the face of Jesus appearing, it’s the face of John the Baptist.’ I said, ‘Oh? How do you know?’ She said, ‘Well, Jesus came to my house yesterday and he told me.’ That tickled me, so I said, ‘Are you sure?’ and she said, ‘Would Jesus bullshit me?’”

When we stopped laughing, Father Tran said, “That’d make a great title for a homily: ‘Would Jesus Bullshit Me?’ I’ll see you two,” he said. “I’ve got a house call to make.”

As Dr. Mossi and I walked toward the parking lot, I said, “Tell me, Dr. Mossi—”

She interrupted me to say, “Miranda. Call me Miranda, please.”

“Miranda, do you attend every week?” I asked.

“Yes,” she said with a smile. “I take every Wednesday morning off for Mass and this class. It’s one of the little luxuries I’ve been granting myself since I was ill a couple of years ago. Life’s too short . . . and all that.” She smiled again.

I grinned, perhaps a bit sheepishly. “Are the meetings always so contentious?”

“Oh, no. This was an unusually hot one.” Dr. Mossi’s—Miranda’s—tone didn't change when she said, "I understand that your biopsy was positive. . . . Dr. Solomon's office forwarded a copy to me as your primary-care physician of record. How have your staging appointments gone?"

Despite the physician's presence, I'd completely forgotten about my cancer during the meeting. "I guess the cancer is contained, so I'm going to have surgery at the University Medical Center, and I've joined the local support group."

She responded, "Good. The surgical team there is first rate. A support group is important, too." Then the doctor said, "I'm a breast cancer survivor myself, Mr. Martinez."

That revelation shocked me, but I said only, "Marty."

She smiled. "Marty—and I attend a support group, so believe me, I know." She smiled again and said, "See you next week?"

"Sure." I was troubled to learn that she, too, had cancer, but I tried not to let that show when we shook hands and said so long.

As I watched the large, attractive lady walk away, I realized that my battery had recharged in her presence.

7

I attended theology classes the next three weeks primarily to see Miranda Mossi. More than once she placed a hand on my arm as we chatted, and I was half tempted to ask her to lunch, but the circumstances didn't seem right. Each Tuesday evening I attended the support group, and on Thursdays I gave a unit of blood for my surgery. Sunday Mass completed my social life.

I ran into Miranda after church on that third Sunday and, as we stood near our cars in the parking lot, she showed me snapshots of her grandchildren. "It's my sworn duty as a grandma to make certain everyone sees them."

"I look forward to meeting them."

"I look forward to introducing you."

"Hey, we should hit it off," I suggested, "since we may *all* be wearing diapers."

She laughed, then said, "You are a character, Marty Martinez."

"Thank you," I said.

"One question." Her face turned serious and she asked, "Do you know a prayer called the Anima Christi?"

"I don't think I've ever heard of it."

She smiled. "It's a prayer, a powerful one. It's the one I began saying when I was diagnosed. It gave me strength. I want to share it with you." She handed me a card decorated like a small scroll.

I glanced at it, then said, "Thanks," feeling a bit awkward.

"I say that daily," she explained, "and I can't tell you how much comfort it brings me."

The idea that I'd receive a prayer rather than a prescription from a doctor struck me as odd. In fact, I was surprised to hear that a physician relied on a prayer to aid her own health.

"I also say it for all my friends with cancer," she continued. "I'll say it for you, too, now."

"Thanks. I was really shocked when you told me you were a cancer survivor."

"I'm a survivor for now, at least," she said, then told me how she'd endured a radical mastectomy, radiation, and chemotherapy and was so far clear of recurrence. "There's more. I always thought I was a compassionate doctor before, but afterward has been a whole new ball game for me. I lightened my practice up and tried to spend more time with my kids and grandchildren, and with friends too, and I'm volunteering at La Clinica de las Mujeres at Guadalupe Church. I'm also a silent partner with a friend, Kathy Mettler, who's also a breast cancer survivor, in a small boutique at the cancer center. It's mostly for breast cancer survivors—merchandise like wigs, prostheses, flattering clothes. We run it at the lowest possible margin, and we let the word out early that we wouldn't turn anyone away even if they couldn't pay, but we almost break even."

I could only shake my head. This woman amazed me.

Before I could say anything, she added, "Best of all, I have those two grandchildren, and one of my daughters-in-law is pregnant again right now."

"I hope to have a grandchild someday."

"I hope you do, too. I can't tell you how much fun they are. I just wish mine lived nearby."

Later that day when I glanced at the card she'd handed me, one line jumped out at me: "From the malignant enemy defend me." I taped the prayer on my bathroom mirror and determined to recite it each morning while I shaved.

■

Although I explained to my daughter what the priest had said about the Madre Maria Society being legitimate, she kept beating the bushes trying to find out what was going on with her mother, but mercifully she left me out of it, not wanting to add stress to my life, I guess.

Without necessarily intending it, Rollie did that too, because he said at one point, "Well, I think that whatever ol' Nancy's up to, she knows what she's doin' and she doesn't want us involved, hard as that is for Audrey and Lea and maybe for you to accept. She's always kinda kept her own counsel."

My ex-wife had indeed always been resourceful and determined. When we had married, my mother had said that Nan was too private: "Still water runs deep, *mijo,*" she had said in a tone that suggested a warning. There may have been deep water in our family, but none of it was particularly still, so Mama was troubled. I really didn't know what she was talking about: Nancy always seemed warm and open to me. She could damn sure take care of herself, too, or at least I thought she could.

Besides, I guess I'd always kept my counsel as well as she kept hers, since I'd never even told my wife and kids why the break between my Merced family and me had occurred. So when Lea suggested, "Shouldn't we at least call Uncle Manuel and tell him about your surgery? He could tell the others." I hesitated, then said, "No, I don't want them to worry about me. That word 'cancer' really scares people." Her eyes told me that she knew something else was wrong, but she didn't push.

I did, though. I had to admit my guilt to God before I underwent surgery, so I was editing the words of a confession in my mind, going over and over them. Heaven and Hell might not be rational concepts, but I was living in an increasingly nonrational space, where primal fear warred with spiritual comfort. If I died in surgery, I wanted to have a chance to see Mama again, to apologize, so at last I telephoned Father Tran and arranged to drop by for Confession. The words on the phone came easily, but the drive over was tough; part of me just wanted to point the damned car down the freeway and drive away from cancer and Confession and ex-wives who joined cults. But I didn't.

The priest greeted me with a smile and handshake at the rectory door and we walked into his office, where he sat in one chair and pulled another near. "Sit there, won't you, Marty?" After placing a stole over his shoulders, he said, "Ready?"

I sighed. "Yes. In the name of the Father and the Son and the Holy Ghost. Bless me, Father, for I have sinned." I hesitated then, as Father Tran incanted the words of greeting. Finally, I whispered, "I want to tell you something terrible I did. I want you to help me beg God for forgiveness." I fought to control my shaky voice, and the priest touched my shoulder, saying, "No hurry. Let yourself work your way through this."

After several moments, I took a deep breath and said, "On the night my mother died, I was with her at the hospital. She'd had a stroke and was unresponsive and I just sat there, feeling awkward, maybe even embarrassed, and ... I don't know what. It had gone on for so long ... in and out of the hospital, up and down the highway ... and, oh God, I hate to tell you this, but I just wanted everything to end. After a couple of hours, I got up and told the nurses not to call me and went home. I don't know why, but I did it. When I telephoned them the next morning, she was dead . . . my mother was dead. She died alone in that hospital while I was home in bed with my wife. My mother died alone."

I paused, but Father Tran said nothing, so I continued: "My brothers and sisters had trusted me. They thought I was on duty, but they found out what I'd done and none has ever spoken to me since, and I don't blame them."

Father Tran didn't look up. His chin seemed to rest on his chest and his eyes fixed on something across the room. "Why did you leave? Can you answer that now?"

My eyes remained half shut and through the lashes I noticed the silhouette of a bush moving in the wind outside the window behind him. "I think I was so. . . so scared. . . so cowardly. . . so afraid of death's reality. . . I don't know the words, only the feelings. I wanted out and I didn't . . . grasp . . . that you're never out of your family. Can God forgive me? Can Mama?"

Silence stretched between us, a dark canyon, and I waited for him to chastise me, but finally he said, "You're a parent. Is there anything you couldn't forgive your children for if they were truly sorry? Anything at all?"

"No."

"Then how can your mother, let alone your Divine Father, not forgive you if you're sorry? And you are, aren't you?"

Tears slid down my face as I murmured, "Yes."

"Then you're forgiven. God forgives you and your mother, who is with God, does too. Forgiving yourself will be more difficult. I'm going to give you general absolution now, and I want you to begin a process of healing yourself. It was a terrible sin, but not an unforgivable one. Weep, gnash your teeth, do all those things it says in the Old Testament, but do them privately in your sorrow. Find a way to help others as you should have helped your mother . . . maybe join a ministry for shut-ins at the church.

"Your Purgatory will be the process you endure learning to forgive yourself. You need to reconcile with your family, so ask for God's help. He'll see to it. You may endure some terrible times, and it might take the rest of your life, but it will be worth it."

I already well knew the terrain of Purgatory.

The priest fell silent and seemed to gaze far away again, then he said, "For your penance say one Our Father from the depths of your heart. Now let me offer you absolution. . . ."

I sat there, knowing that God and Mom had forgiven me. And I knew that the priest was exactly correct. By the time I walked into the church to say my penance I was exhausted.

■

Nancy's brother, Toshio, called the evening before I was scheduled for surgery and surprised me.

"What's up, Tosh?" I asked.

"Nancy was here," he said. "She had lunch with Janine and me."

My heart swooped. "Is she okay?"

"She's fine, and you were right, she has gotten herself involved with some religious group, but it's not a cult or anything. She comes and goes as she pleases.

"Janine told her about your surgery. She — Nancy, that is — sends her best wishes."

Her best wishes. "Thanks, Tosh."

"Listen, old guy, we're all pulling for you, too. Masako and David said to tell Uncle Marty they'd say a prayer for him."

"Thanks." Everybody, it seemed, was praying for me, everybody but my daughter who didn't believe in God. "Listen, Tosh, can you do me a favor?"

"Sure."

"Call Lea — or have Janine do it — and tell her about Nancy. She's really worried about her mother."

"I'll call," he assured me. "And we'll come up to visit you this weekend. Okay?"

"Okay. See you then."

Rollie telephoned an hour or so later as I was finishing packing for the hospital and stumbling about aimlessly, wishing I could go right in and get things over with. "Me and Audrey and ol' Jimmy Dean we're pullin' for you, Beaner," he said, "but if you don't make it, leave me your *Playboy* collection, willya?"

I replied, "Screw you." Then, to keep things light, "Is that dog of yours smart?"

"Ol' Jimmy Dean? Shit fire and save matches, that dog could launch a rocket! And by the way, let me remind you that if you let that damn cancer kill you, I will personally have to kick your Mex'can ass."

Grinning, I said, "I'll keep that in mind. I've got some news for you guys. Tosh called. He said Nancy showed up and had lunch with Janine and him down in Modesto."

"No shit? Did he say what's up with her?"

"Only that she's involved with that Madre Maria bunch, but I don't think he talked to her about it. Janine probably did. Have Audrey give a call."

Uncharacteristic silence followed, then Rollie asked, "Listen, Marty, would you mind if me and Audrey and Jimmy Dean drove down to be there tomorrow?"

I felt my eyes warm, and I said, "Naw, come on down, but don't feel like you have to race to the hospital early enough for the start of surgery. But I think

Lea could use some support while she's waiting. That'll be the worst part."

"You bet. We'll be there. Hey, Audrey wants to say a little somethin'. Hang in there, chili bean."

My sister-in-law's voice was faint. "Marty?" she said.

"Hi, dear."

"I just want you to know that I'm praying for you." She was obviously close to tears, and that reminded me that I was indeed dealing with a life-threatening situation. "I know things'll be okay," she added.

"Thanks, Audrey. Believe me, I'm praying, too, dear. I'll see you tomorrow."

■

Lea drove me to the medical center before sunrise, agonizing over her mother's visit to Toshio and Janine. "I just can't figure out why she'd go there and not stop by to see us."

"Me either."

"It just seems like something strange is going on."

"But didn't Aunt Janine say she's okay?" I asked.

"She said Mom seemed the same as always."

I signed in, then waited while others scheduled for early surgery did the same. Lea clung to my hand, and I examined everyone in the room with a reporter's curiosity—people sick enough to require surgery, and maybe some in for optional treatments. Most were my age or older, more women than men, most busily gazing at magazines or newspapers, obviously trying to keep their minds off what was to come, but one young woman, not much out of her teens, I'd guess, sat wide-eyed in a family cluster, and none of them even tried to feign nonchalance.

Before long, I was escorted to a prep room where, after stripping, I slipped into a gown, then thigh-length stockings meant to keep blood clots from forming in my legs, and finally booties with rubber grippers. Only after I'd passed a nurse's inspection was Lea allowed to join me.

"You look cute in those white stockings, Daddy," she said, but she looked even more scared than I felt. In fact, I had begun to feel primed, like a guy ready to play a big game.

"You should see the black ones I wear at home," I said.

Lea tried to laugh, but couldn't.

I took her hand in mine, and said, "Don't be afraid, Perico. This is a good day. We're doing something about the cancer. A bad day would be if we *couldn't* do this. I'm not afraid, so don't you be."

Her chin came up, and she said, "Okay, but I wish Mom was here."

"So do I."

The nurse returned and said, "Do you need anything?"

"How about a mug of coffee?"

She laughed and winked at Lea. "Not this morning. If you're ready, sit in that wheelchair and I'll push you over to pre-op. Your surgeon should be ready anytime now."

She wheeled me, Lea walking alongside, with a hand on my shoulder. At a large double door, the nurse stopped and said to Lea, "We'll have to leave you here. The waiting room is just through those doors."

"All right," Lea replied, and her hand squeezed my shoulder.

"How about a good-luck kiss, Perico?" I asked.

Lea searched my face for a moment, then kissed my lips. "Thanks," I grinned, and gave her a thumbs-up, my love for her suddenly palpable as breath. "See you later, Perico. Don't worry, it'll be okay." I wasn't going to let her down by kicking the bucket.

The nurse wheeled me past clutches of nurses and others in surgical gowns, most holding paper cups of coffee and conversing with a frivolity I didn't share. I found myself thinking, as I often did with airline pilots, I sure hope they slept well.

Pre-op turned out to be a large, brightly lit room, empty in the middle but with chairs lining the walls. In those seats sat several of the people I'd seen in the waiting room, all wearing stylish gowns like mine. Since a couple of the ladies had been rather expensively dressed and made up, it was interesting seeing them in this democratic drabness. The young woman I earlier noticed was not yet among us.

I'd no sooner seated myself than two nurses entered and began talking in hushed tones to one of the older ladies. After a moment, one of them left, then returned with a wheelchair, and soon the three of them were gone. Just as they departed, another nurse wheeled the young woman in and seated her on a chair near me. She appeared terrified, so I smiled and nodded. She tried to respond, but could manage only a tight nod.

"Mr. Martinez?" said a young man in scrubs. "Dr. Solomon's about ready. Let's go on into the operating room."

I stood and hesitated, assuming that I'd have to sit in a wheelchair, but he merely smiled and said, "This way."

I followed him into the hall, grateful to be on my feet, and as I walked across it a voice stopped me: "Marty?" I turned and there stood Dr. Miranda Mossi. She wasn't wearing scrubs. "I just stopped by to wish you luck," she said. "It'll all go fine. It was worth getting up early to see you in that outfit."

For some reason, I extended my right hand, but she chuckled and said, "This visit is worth a hug," and she did just that. "I'll see you in recovery," Miranda said, smiling.

I was smiling back when I said, "See you there, Miranda. We can discuss theology."

In the operating room, I mounted the surgical table, and the nurse asked, "Are you a friend of Dr. Mossi's? We don't see her around the surgical pavilion often."

I said simply, "Yes."

Around me, half a dozen people were working at this task or that one, all very businesslike. No sooner had I been positioned than a dark young man said, "Hello, Mr. Martinez. I'm Dr. Patel. I'll be your anesthesiologist. We need to get this IV set up, then I'll put you under. This will be the easiest experience of your life—or so other patients have told me. Ask any question you have while I'm working. This isn't secret."

Inserting and taping the needle was virtually painless. I had no questions. "Dr. Solomon will be with us shortly, so I'm going to put you under now."

I nodded just as Dr. Patel was saying, "Mr. Martinez? Mr. Martinez? Can you hear me? It's all over. You did just fine."

I vaguely recognized the physician amidst the warm syrup in which I seemed to be floating, then another, more familiar voice said, "Marty, you came through without a hitch. I met your daughter and your in-laws in the waiting room. I'll go tell them you're awake." One of Miranda Mossi's hands touched my cheek, of that much I was certain. Then she was gone.

8

The next day, despite discomfort in the area of the incision—mercifully muted by pain medication—as well as the unfamiliar sensation of a catheter in my urethra, I felt relieved. The cancer was out and I could begin to live again. Lea seemed to have moved into the room with me, sitting in the chair next to the bed and quietly reading most of the time. "The surgeon said everything went fine," she said at one point. Rollie and Audrey, without their dog, stayed for most of the morning, while Tosh and Janine were there all afternoon, but I slept so much I virtually missed them. Dr. Mossi stopped by, too. I remembered that.

When Father Tran visited on the day after surgery, Lea was downstairs in the cafeteria. The priest said he had brought me Holy Communion. I at first stammered, then told him that I needed to continue my ongoing Confession.

"You've been absolved of everything," he said, "but if you need to talk things out beyond Confession, no problem. Do you need to examine your conscience for a few minutes?"

"Yeah."

"And remember we want you to see the Sacrament of Reconciliation as a comfort, not an ordeal. As much as people love to judge others, only God can really do that. My job is to offer the certainty of forgiveness."

"Let me go over what I need to say, then let's do it."

"I'll go visit another parishioner up the hall so you can think about it. I'll be back in . . . say . . . twenty minutes. And Marty," he added, "don't tie yourself in knots over this."

"I'll be ready."

After Father Tran left, I lay back on my pillow and tried to review my transgressions. Some sins were easy to identify: I had frequently coveted, if not my neighbor's wife and goods, then just plain other women and other stuff, especially the former, but I hadn't committed adultery or stolen anything. Beyond that, things thickened: I could say over and over again that I hadn't been as a good a father as my son and daughter deserved and that it now grieved me, or that I had sometimes taken offense over trivial or even imagined slights by my wife. I'd never really shown my wife and kids how much I loved them. I'd been a successful journalist, but hadn't done much for other Americans of Mexican descent. I just wasn't very proud of my life, despite my apparent success.

When Father Tran returned, he asked, "Ready?"

I nodded.

"Remember, this is an imperfect process, Marty," the priest assured me before I could begin speaking. "If you forget something that comes up later, don't feel bad. We all do that, and it doesn't invalidate anything. Just keep digging until what troubles you is purged."

"Okay." This whole approach was so different from my frightening memories of youthful Confessions that I wondered if it was the same sacrament. I had been intimidated in grade school by a nun who said—at least I *think* she said—that if you didn't mention every single sin, your Confession would be sacrilegious. Now, as an adult, I realized the impossibility of that, so the new approach made sense to me. And maybe Sister didn't even say that; maybe I just inferred it.

The young priest intoned the familiar words, and I responded—involuntarily lowering my voice to a whisper—with the equally familiar "Bless me Father for I have sinned. Father my last confession was . . . what? . . . a week ago. It would be easier to tell you the commandments I haven't broken, than the ones I have . . ."

"That's fine."

"Well . . . I haven't killed anyone. I haven't stolen anything. I haven't committed adultery. But I think I made hash out of the rest. I was a successful journalist, but I didn't tell my family how I felt about them; readers knew more about my feelings than my wife and kids did. And I *have* been a disbeliever. My son became a practicing Catholic in spite of my example, not because of it, and my daughter is an agnostic. I just wasn't a very good father or husband."

"Intentionally?"

"It feels that way to me now. My son died of AIDS . . . my wife divorced me. I think I was just so self-centered . . ."

"But did you intend those things?"

"No, but I probably did intend the thousands of slights that contributed to those results."

The young priest's face was serious when he said, "You're a sensitive man. I suspect that makes you vulnerable to subtleties that many don't even notice, and you hold yourself responsible for many sins. But God is far more complex still, and He will understand and forgive them, all of them. You have to build your future having learned from those mistakes. Think of specific events that evoke guilt, then purge them."

He paused, then added as he gazed directly into my face, "You'll see your mother in Heaven, Marty, and I'll guarantee she's long since forgiven you and is praying for you, just as I'm certain your son is. Maybe that's why you're back."

Irrational as it was, I believed what Father Tran said was true, and I was indeed sorry, so sorry, for everything that had happened, and grateful for this moment. My eyes welled: This young guy must think I'm a champion blubberer.

Father Tran sat quietly while I regained control, then he said, "God forgives you. For your penance I want you to say a rosary when you return home." He uttered the formal words of absolution then. Just a moment later, he said, "Prepare to receive the body of Christ."

After Communion and the final prayers, the priest tapped my shoulder and said, "Well, I've others to visit, but I'll stop by tomorrow."

Just then Lea returned. "Oh," she said, startled, "excuse me."

"I'm just leaving," said the cleric, then he extended his right hand. "I'm Father Tran."

Sounding more quizzical than cordial, my daughter replied, "Lea Martinez, Marty's daughter."

The priest excused himself and left. "What's up with that?" Lea asked.

I was still smiling when I said, "He's a priest, I'm a Catholic, so he visited."

"I thought you'd left the Church."

"I've returned. I told you I was going to Mass again," I said.

She didn't pursue it, and neither did I. I was feeling fine and I didn't want to lose that in a dead-end argument.

Miranda Mossi dropped by every morning for a few minutes, making small talk, telling me the religion class had missed me and wished me well. She hugged me at the close of each visit.

On his rounds, Dr. Solomon examined my stitches. "I was able to spare that right nerve bundle, so with luck you won't be impotent. We'll have your pathology in a couple of days," he told me the second day. "Remember, when it comes to where the tumors are located, a millimeter of good tissue is worth a mile."

"Let's hope we get that millimeter."

"I'm confident we will," he said.

Nurses seemed to check me every few minutes, and one bathed me in the morning, then walked me around the hallway. Although I felt okay, my legs were shaky when she first helped me out into the hall with Lea in tow. My appetite returned by the third day.

After one of those walks, Lea asked, "Is this Dr. Mossi your doctor or what? She seems *real* concerned about you."

It was a legitimate question, but I was temporarily discombobulated by it. Finally, I explained, "She's a general practitioner I consulted. Now we're in the same religion class at St. Apollinaris. She's also a cancer survivor, so we've become friends."

"Well, I think she hopes you'll be *more* than friends." My daughter's tone told me she disapproved. Then she said something that made me laugh aloud: "I didn't think you liked large ladies. Mom's petite."

"I don't think I do—as a class—but I do like Dr. Mossi. I guess I just like nice people." But I was thinking that being *more* than friends with Miranda Mossi might not be too bad.

Lea ignored that remark and asked, "Why did you start going to church again? I thought that was ancient history."

"Fear and the memory of what Dougie told me when he was dying drove me back to God."

Lea jolted, probably at the mention of her brother's death, and she fell silent for a moment, then said, "Daddy, do you really think going to church will help you? Do you *really* believe in God?"

"Yes, I believe in God, and God has already helped me, giving me strength to deal with whatever comes up." Even as I spoke, I realized that this was an extraordinary conversation for us. I had always been a professional communicator, but never much of one at home. I don't think I'd ever had more than a couple of talks like this with my kids, and those were as much booze-fueled as heartfelt. On this day, though, I answered as honestly as I could.

"And you *believe* that? How do you know it wouldn't have happened anyway?"

"I don't *know,* honey, I *believe.*"

We fell silent then, and I suspect that my daughter left that exchange with a deeper knowledge of me, just as I left it with a deeper knowledge of her.

An hour or so later, Dr. Solomon entered the room and began examining my sutures. "You're healing nicely. I think we can release you tomorrow, but I've got bad news." He glanced away from me toward the window, and I sensed immediately that I might be in deep trouble. "The pathologist found cancer in one seminal vesicle, plus on the margin of the apex. That really shocked me, especially the seminal vesicle involvement; it changes your prognosis, and not for the better. He also found that your Gleason score is 7, not 6 — 4 and 3."

I'd read enough to understand what it all meant: My cancer was locally advanced and more aggressive than we had believed. It had reached a stage that wasn't often cured. "What do we do next?" I asked.

"We'll schedule adjuvant radiation as soon as you're healed from the surgery . . . in about three months."

"Sounds good," I replied. In fact, it sounded horrible.

As soon as the physician departed, my daughter asked hoarsely, "They didn't get it all?"

"No, but they'll clean it up with radiation."

"But they *can* clean it up, right?"

"Sure," I replied, hoping I was correct.

"Isn't that what they said about the surgery, they'd get it all?"

"That was their hope."

Lea was nothing if not outspoken. "It looks like your church didn't heal you after all," she said.

"Hey, I don't pray to the *Church,* Perico, I pray to God. My soul feels fine even if my body's in trouble," I told her, a little startled that it was the truth. "I'd bet that God heals the part that most needs healing. In my case, that was the soul. Besides, I didn't pray to be healed, I prayed to be given strength to deal with whatever I faced. I'm dealing with it."

We left it there.

9

I'd heard horror stories about catheters, so I was a little concerned about the one in me. Once I returned to the house with a tube extending from my bladder through my penis to a bag strapped to my leg, though, I found it no worse than a nuisance. The device sure *looked* horrible, but I could hobble around, and I was grateful for that. By late afternoons, however, my urethra became sore and I felt like doing little more than lying still.

The second morning I was home, the phone rang. I was alone, so I shuffled out and answered. "Hello, Marty," said Dr. Mossi. "Can you use some company this afternoon? I'll be in your neighborhood, and I'd like to stop by for a visit."

That question pleased me. "You would? Great. But you've heard of bad-hair days?" I asked.

"Sure."

"Well, I'm having a bad-catheter day. You may not want to be around me."

She said, "I can stand it if you can. Would three o'clock be okay, or will you be resting?"

"I'll set the alarm and put on a fresh peignoir." As we spoke I was playing with unopened get-well cards that I'd piled on the counter. I hated them because I hated being sick, although God knows I'd sent plenty just like them in the past.

"Do that," she said, laughing. "See you then."

I'd no sooner hung up than the doorbell rang. When I opened the door, there stood Father Tran. "Are you supposed to be out of bed?" he asked, extending his right hand.

"Yep," I replied. "Come on in and excuse the mess."

"You're absolved. You should see my apartment at the rectory. The monsignor's about given up on me."

We plopped in the living room, the priest having said no to my offer of coffee. "So, how are you feeling?" he asked.

"Physically okay."

"Bad news?"

I nodded. "They couldn't get all the cancer. I've read enough to know this is the long-term beginning of the end."

"Well," he said, "God will decide. But you've already begun to heal your soul."

"I've heard famous born-agains say you should just give your problems to Jesus . . ." I was still framing my question when he responded.

He smiled. "We Catholics think Jesus — or God — gives us problems," he said, "plus the grace to deal with them, of course. How we handle that has a lot to do with our personal salvation. There's little about our religion that's passive."

I'd never before heard it framed that way, and I had to think for a moment before I responded, "Well, I'm praying for strength. That's what keeps me from falling back into depression, that and friendship . . ."

"With Dr. Mossi, may I ask?" He smiled.

"Yes, definitely. I've been really lonely."

"So has she, I suspect. She's a fine woman. It may not be very priestly for me to say this, but her husband was a jerk. A rich jerk, but a jerk nonetheless."

This young guy never ceased to surprise me. "She mentioned that he's a doc and that they're divorced and annulled," I said.

He nodded.

"Another good thing seems to have come out of this mess," I told him. "My daughter, whom you met, is back in my life."

"Wonderful," he smiled. "That must be worth a great deal. Could it be that a plan beyond our reasoning is at work here?"

"Don't trick me, Father." I smiled. "Of course it can."

"And don't give up on your chances of survival, Marty. Amazing things can happen. Does your daughter live nearby?"

"Yes. She has a condo over near the capitol."

"Is she married? She's a very attractive woman."

"Yes, she is — attractive, I mean — but I'm afraid she's attracted more than her share of the wrong kind of men. She's had several failed relationships and she's not married."

"She didn't look very happy when I met her."

"She was a rebel, and when she was just out of high school, she announced to her mother and me she was going to move in with her boyfriend — who turned out to be a drug dealer, by the way," I told him. "I said, 'Okay, that makes it easy for me to tell you something Mom and I've hidden: We were never married. We just moved in with one another back in the sixties and never got around to it.'" I couldn't help grinning as I told this story.

"Well, I didn't get any farther than that. She went nuts. I was lying, of course," I added.

Father Tran was shaking his head. "You're an evil guy," he laughed. Then he said, "One of my sisters lived with her boyfriend for nearly four years, but when she got pregnant, he left. Her baby lives with my parents now, down in Westminster, and my sister's back in college. The grandchild is a wonderful little girl, a wonderful gift, but the situation isn't wonderful."

After a few moments I said, "Lea's not too keen on the Church either. When her brother was sick, she started taking him to Mass. One Sunday the old monsignor — McCarthy, was it? — just happened to say from the pulpit that homosexuality was a perversion and a sin. Lea challenged him on the steps after Mass and has never been back since."

"She did the right thing," the young priest said. "Homosexuality isn't a sin at all. It's a condition . . . and a challenge. *Fornication,* whether heterosexual or homosexual, is a mortal sin."

"Doug was a faithful Catholic," I said.

"Then he's in Paradise — and Monsignor McCarthy, I should tell you, is in Mojave now."

"Good riddance," I said. Mojave was about as far from Paradise as I could imagine. I felt better than I had all day after learning of the monsignor's new address.

Miranda Mossi hugged me when she arrived later that afternoon. I was mincing about, because of my sore urethra, and she asked, "Does that catheter bother you?"

"Oh yeah," I grunted.

"You'll only have to put up with it a couple of weeks."

"How much do I owe you for the consultation?"

"Well, how about lunch someday when you're feeling better?"

I smiled as I replied, "You're on. But — " I hesitated, then said, "You know I'm going to have to see you professionally before long, don't you? I'll need your advice on radiation."

"I want to talk to you about that," she replied. To my surprise she took one of my hands in both of hers, then said, "Don't laugh, but I'm going to refer you to a colleague."

That shocked me, since the sense that my doctors were my friends comforted me. "Why?"

"Marty," she said, her eyes gazing directly into mine, "this may be a one-way street, but I can't ethically treat someone I'm . . . I'm *involved* with, and I'm becoming involved with you."

"You are?" For a moment I sat stunned in my pajamas and robe, my thin hair wiry, my chin sloppily shaven, and this wonderful woman was telling me that she was becoming involved with me. "It's not a one-way street, Miranda."

Something else immediately occurred to me: She's a doctor and she knows we've both got cancer. Hers could be worse than mine, for all I know, and mine isn't good. Maybe we're on a different clock than folks who are well. Maybe we need to move faster if we're going to have anything together at all.

She sat back and said, "I really enjoyed meeting your two sisters- and brothers-in-law at the hospital."

"Those folks are my *ex*-sisters- and *ex*-brothers-in-law."

"Yes, your *exes*. Do you have brothers and sisters?"

"Two brothers and two sisters, in the Merced area." I didn't want to go into that story, so I added, "None of them could get away that day."

"Too bad," she replied. "Your daughter didn't seem too charmed by me."

I shrugged. "Lea's had a tough time since her brother died, then her mother and I divorced, then her own personal life fell apart — and not for the first time."

"I understand." Miranda nodded. "My youngest son, Robbie—I've mentioned my three boys?—well, he's really struggled with the divorce. His older brothers seem to understand."

"To tell you the truth, Miranda, I'm not sure I've really accepted what happened in my life." I was embarrassed to admit it. "I guess that in some ways I still love Nancy, or at least our memories." Feeling free to tell her that made me realize that this was a new kind of relationship for me. "Our son's death just seemed to rip us away from one another, and I've never really understood why."

"Those situations are all so different and so difficult," she responded. "My husband was a philanderer, so our marriage came apart a piece at a time over a period of years. It had started with mutual need and friendship when we were in medical school, but there had never been any deep passion, so maybe the end was inevitable.

"By the time he was gone I was just relieved, and I guess I poured myself into work to escape. I was on automatic pilot until you walked into my life. But let me ask a serious question." Her expression changed as she said, "Can you ever love another woman?"

"I didn't used to think so," I replied. Then I leaned forward and kissed her.

We were still in a semi-clinch when the doorbell rang. I had to take several deep breaths before I answered it. There stood Johnny O in his customary sleeveless T-shirt, sinewy arms exposed. He held a bouquet. "I heard you was sick, Champ," he said, his eyes moist. Like so many tough guys I knew, Johnny was openly emotional; he responded with a hug when I embraced him.

"It's not really cancer, is it, Champ?" he asked.

"It's really cancer, Johnny," I said, "but it won't get me right away."

"Any organ you need, Champ—heart, lung, liver—you got it. You stuck with Johnny when he went broke. Johnny don't forget."

"All I want's your friendship, Johnny."

A tear began sliding down his cheek when he responded, "You got that, Champ. You always got Johnny's love." Then he noticed Miranda and quickly removed the soiled baseball cap he wore and wiped his eyes. "'Scuse me, ma'am, Johnny never noticed you. Did I interrupt?"

"Johnny, this is Dr. Miranda Mossi. Miranda, this is my old buddy from Merced, Johnny Orozco. He used to be the number one welterweight contender. He fought for the world title twice. When Johnny says he'll give you a lung, he'll really give you one . . . but it might not be his."

Even Johnny laughed, saying, "Awww, Champ."

"I've got to get to the hospital for rounds, Marty. So nice to meet you, Mr. Orozco," said Miranda, extending her hand.

The ex-pug took it and said, "Call me Johnny, please, Doctor."

The physician shook his hand, saying, "If you'll call me Miranda, Johnny."

"Deal," he said.

"Deal," she responded. At the door, Miranda said to me, "You've got my number. If you have time, please call me tonight."

"Deal," I said, then I pecked her cheek.

Once more that smile engulfed me. "Deal," she said.

The door had no sooner closed than Johnny O said, "You got lipstick on. You been kissin' the doc?"

"Looks like," I answered.

"Still an operator after all these years." He winked.

■

The phone interrupted my conversation with Lea that evening. I answered when I heard Ned Schmidt's voice on the machine. "Martini, how're you feeling?" my editor asked.

"Okay, Ned. Not good, but okay."

"Are you *really?*"

"Yeah, I'm okay," I told him. "The surgery wasn't pleasant, but I'm coming back from it."

"How're you doing on your prostate cancer piece?"

I was accumulating too much experience to go with the information I'd gathered by reading, but not yet writing. "I've haven't started, but I'm glad you've prodded me."

"I'll tell you, Martini, I've done a little reading about this prostate cancer, and, man, I had no idea! It's an epidemic. It kills just about as many guys as breast cancer kills gals, but it hasn't got anywhere near the same attention. I don't see many runs for the cure or marches for research for this like I do for breast cancer."

"Yeah," I agreed, "I've noticed. Guys seem to hunker down when they should do what the AIDS community does, act up. They should demand proportional funding for research."

"Say that in the piece you write. Chew guys' asses for not taking the gloves off."

"Right," I said.

"There's no hurry, but we can run it on a Sunday with a front-page breakout, then continue on an inside page. Or we could do the Sunday spread, then revisit the story at some interval as time passes."

"I like that better — the updates, I mean. It'll really personalize the disease," I said.

"Okay, Martini, I'll send Bob Wolfe over to take a few shots later this week, so have your hair done."

"I'll get my catheter polished."

"Too bad we can't take a picture of that. That would damn sure get guys' attention."

Lea looked troubled when I hung up, so I asked, "What's wrong, honey?"

"Daddy, promise me you won't get involved with this Dr. Mossi who was at the hospital. We need to find Mom."

"I'm not sure Mom's lost, Perico," I replied, "but I *would* like to hear from her."

"But this doctor woman . . . ?"

My daughter was sort of fiddling at the sink as she spoke, so I took her hand, then said, "Lea, I've been terribly lonely since Mom left. *Really* lonely. Miranda Mossi is only a friend. We've a lot in common, and I feel as though I can talk intimately with her."

"You can talk to me. Besides, how can Mom ever come back if you're . . . *dating* . . . this doctor woman?"

"Mom can come back anytime she wants, but I've been alone long enough. I'm not looking for a wife, but I am looking for someone to pal around with — a companion." I'd never thought I would use that word to describe a lady.

"I'll be your companion until Mom comes back. That doctor's taking advantage of you being lonely," asserted Lea.

"Hasn't it occurred to you that she might be lonely too?" I smiled, but I was thinking that I truly hadn't realized how hard the divorce had hit my daughter. I knew *she* was lonely, and I knew, too, that her own record of failed relationships was shaping her vision of Miranda and me.

"There's really not going to be anything left, is there?" Lea finally said, her eyes glistening.

"Of what?"

"Of our family. It used to be so much fun when Dougie and I and you and Mom did things together . . . you know, had picnics at the river or went to concerts or whatever. Now it's all gone."

My heart swooped as she spoke. "Things change," I responded, "but they can only fall apart if we let them. You and I have to stick together, but not by placing limits on one another's lives. I want you to find someone and be happy. I want the same thing for myself."

She replied: "I only want to find Mom."

"Lea, no one will ever replace your mother in my life; I'll always love her. But I can't stop living because we split. What Nancy and I had no one can ever take from us, but it's over, as nearly as I can tell. And if I can love someone else, I will." As the tension mounted, my urethra began aching, my sutures grew sore, and my innards throbbed, so I checked my watch and was telling the truth when I said, "I need to take some pain medication."

She left shortly thereafter, unhappy with me, but with a promise that she'd return tomorrow. I found myself hoping she'd find a new topic by then . . . or find a decent boyfriend for a change . . . and lighten up on me.

10

The next week, whiz bag strapped to one leg, I returned to the prostate cancer group. Mort greeted me warmly before the meeting, then said as soon as the guys assembled, "Welcome back, Marty. Do you want to talk about your surgery?"

"I'll pass," I said.

"Okay, fair enough, but we're all delighted to see you," the leader added, and a couple of voices chanted, "Hear! Hear!"

As soon as the leader finished his announcements, Dr. Royster addressed me: "This is my usual lecture to postsurgical guys," he said. "Once those nerve bundles are cut in surgery, you cease having spontaneous nocturnal erections. So if you're impotent, get a penile pump and begin using it every day to create an erection, or your penis will atrophy.

"If your doc prescribes a pump, your insurance will likely pay," he added.

"What bothers me with the pump is that me and my wife, we lost the . . . spontaneity," interjected a fair-skinned African American man who wore no name tag. "When I was diagnosed we were past that quickie-on-the-table stage, but we *did* have an occasional happy shower. Man, we sure miss them."

I telephoned Dr. Solomon the next day and asked about a pump, and he agreed with Dr. Royster's advice. "After your catheter is out and we're sure you've healed inside, I'll give you a prescription for one. Meanwhile, give your willy a good massage a couple of times a day, certainly every time you shower. Get some blood in there, but wait a bit on the pump," he added. "You've still got some healing to do."

■

Later that morning I carried a cup of coffee into the den, catheter bag swishing against my leg. When I sat at my computer to write about prostate cancer, the words came fast. I was really rolling when the ringing telephone interrupted me. I'd nearly forgotten how good it felt to spin a story. "Yeah?" I said when I answered.

"Hey, Beaner, how you doin'?"

"Hey, Rollie. I'm feeling okay, but I wish this catheter was in your dick, not mine."

"Oh hell, that little thing wouldn't fit gear big as mine. They'd need a fire hose for me. Listen, I heard that takin' out that catheter deal is a pisser."

"Nice choice of words." I had to laugh. "Anyway, I hope you're wrong, because I'm sure looking forward to getting it out."

It went on like that for a while, with nothing of consequence discussed. After Rollie hung up I returned to the prostate cancer article. I'd just begun to assemble my writing process again when the phone rang once more. "Yeah," I said into the speaker.

"Martín?" My full name pronounced with what sounded like a self-conscious Spanish accent. "This is a voice from the past, Eduardo Rivera."

It was indeed a voice from the past. Eddie Rivers had been a high school classmate of my brother Raul's, a half-Anglo kid who'd tried to hide his Mexican ancestry. A few years ago I heard he'd changed his name and become 100 percent Mexican, a political force on the local college campus, where he'd landed in the Chicano studies program.

"I'm teaching a course on the history of our people, Martín, and wondered if you might be able to visit my class and make a presentation."

"Thanks for asking, Eddie, but I just had surgery, so I'll be out of commission for a while."

"Nothing serious, I hope."

"Prostate cancer."

"*Oh God.* I'm really sorry to hear that, *ese.*"

"You're no sorrier than I am. Listen, Eddie," I felt compelled to ask, "you've always called me Marty. What's with all this *Martín* stuff?"

"It's time to return to our pure Mexican roots, Martín," he replied.

I suppressed a chuckle. "I always thought Mexican meant *impure* in the best sense . . . mixed."

"You miss my point," he hissed with a condescension he had likely honed on campus liberals. "California is ours! *Aztlan!* We intend to take it back. You can help us."

"Good luck with that, Eddie." He and I had read different history books. "But I don't know of any evidence that there was any particular Hispanic presence here in the Great Valley before the Treaty of Guadalupe Hidalgo. If there was, I'd've written about it long before now."

His voice lost its cultivated edge. "Where do you think all those names come from, man—*Merced, Mariposa, Modesto* . . . even *Fresno?*" He pronounced the words with that exaggerated Spanish accent.

"From explorers passing through, not settlers — or that's what my history books say. Spain controlled California for a little over fifty years, Mexico controlled it for twenty-five, and the U.S. has controlled it since 1848, over a hundred and fifty years. Who has the best claim?"

"Our Indian brothers controlled this land for . . . ah . . . maybe ten thousand years!" he sputtered.

"Ours? You used to be white. If you want to give it back to the Indians, then you should start the process by leaving."

"You won't talk sense!" He hung up and I was relieved.

I settled back at the computer and began considering where I'd go next in the prostate cancer article. Wouldn't you know it, that damned phone rang again. I decided not to answer it and sat through seven rings. Finally it stopped. I exhaled, then began to reread the text on the monitor's screen in order to get back in the drift, but the phone once more began ringing.

I reached over and lifted the receiver. "Yeah?"

"Marty, are you okay?" asked Miranda. "I called a minute ago and you didn't answer. I was afraid something was wrong. Or am I interrupting something?"

"No," I said. "I'd rather be talking to you." I wasn't lying.

■

Shortly after the removal of the catheter — not a big deal at all, just a momentary pinch and it was over — I visited Dr. Solomon's office once more to talk about using a penile pump. I hoped I'd soon have a use for an erection.

To control the postsurgical urinary incontinence, I was doing enough kegel exercises to qualify for the *Guinness Book of World Records.* I felt as though I was finally beginning to govern that — unless I sneezed or unexpectedly stepped off a curb. I'd had no hint of an erection, though. When I massaged my penis while showering, there was never a sensation. But in the presence of Miranda Mossi — the focus of my sexual thoughts anymore — excitement caused my limp business to tingle and feel as if it might be rising. It never was, though.

Dr. Solomon's nurse finally called my name, and I followed her into a treatment room. The urologist entered immediately; he told me he'd rarely had a man ask about a penile pump so soon after surgery. I again explained what I'd heard at the support group, and he laughed, saying, "Well, Al Royster always was a troublemaker. You're not bleeding or anything? Do you have any discharge from your penis at all?"

"Plenty of involuntary urine."

Dr. Solomon grinned and said, "Okay, Mr. Martinez, loosen your trousers and lie down on the table. I'll inject you with alprostadil to make sure your penis responds."

"You'll do *what?*"

His nurse entered the room after I got into position on the table, while the doctor deftly tore a hole in what looked like a paper towel, then slipped it over my penis. A moment later, the nurse handed him a hypodermic syringe, and he said, "This will tell us if your penis will still enlarge." Then he plunged the needle into my organ.

I gasped.

"That didn't hurt as much as you expected, I'll bet."

Since I hadn't expected a needle at all when I'd made the appointment, I could only respond, "It hurt enough."

He smiled, and said, "I'll be back in a few minutes. If you develop an erection, I'll prescribe a pump. Keep your fingers crossed."

I was willing to cross more than my fingers.

Ten minutes or so later, when he returned, I had a full-fledged but aching erection. "Okay," he said. "I'm happy to report that I'll prescribe a pump."

It was the best news I'd had in a while, so I responded with a hearty "Thanks."

On my way home, my penis still aching, I picked the device up at a drugstore. As soon as I arrived, I read the instruction booklet and viewed the video. It all looked easy enough.

Later that evening, after my chorizo had recovered from the injection, I assembled the pump—sliding a large, clear-plastic tube onto a thick handle that enclosed an electric motor into which I'd placed three batteries. I fitted a thick, soft rubber band onto the open end of the large tube. Then, as the video instructed, I lubricated that end and positioned the clear cylinder around my penis, flush against my body.

When I pressed the button atop the handle, I heard a buzz as the motor pulled air from the tube. After a few seconds, I felt it tighten against my body as a vacuum developed, and moments later my penis began to fill a bit. The instruction booklet advised that I periodically stop and release the vacuum for a few seconds. When I pressed the button again, once more the vacuum pulled blood into my penis—it filled more this time—then I again released it.

I continued the process until the organ lifted from the bottom of the tube and I had an erection. Amazing. Less amazing, I also had a somewhat uncomfortable penis . . . not exactly painful, but tingling from the pressure of the vacuum, so I released the vacuum. I pressed the button again, but stopped just before real discomfort set in, and this time I had an erection without distress. As I looked at my swollen penis in that clear plastic pipe, I felt like saying "welcome back." I then proceeded to the next step, gradually working the rubber band toward my body so that it would close around the base of my penis and keep the blood in it so the erection would endure for a while.

When that band actually popped onto my shaft, though, I jumped; it didn't exactly hurt, but like so much since this cancer had entered my life, it was a nuisance.

■

Miranda picked me up for the religion class the next day, and Father Tran was clearly delighted to see me walk in the door. "Hey, you look great, Marty," he said. "We've missed you." The various ladies seemed to agree with him until he added, "We've needed another liberal voice."

"Not really," said Mrs. Marquez, though with a smile.

It didn't take the liberal and conservative sides long to disagree that day. No sooner had my welcome been completed than Mrs. Donati mentioned that she'd read that some Protestant churches believed that Jesus had brothers and sisters. "How can that be if Mary was ever-virgin?" she asked.

Father Tran explained, "Well, the King James Bible says Jesus was Mary's firstborn, not that he was her only child."

"That *can't* be true!" Mrs. Marquez snapped.

Several of the other ladies expressed such dramatic disapproval — everything from heavy sighs to rolled eyes — that I had to cinch hard to suppress laughter.

"Of course, in some cultures," added the priest, "you would be called the firstborn even if you were the only child. More interesting, maybe, is that according to one Jewish tradition, Joseph was a widower with several children when he married Mary."

"I've never heard that before," said Sylvia Marquez.

"There's about as much evidence one way as another when you investigate that story. Could be, but it's by no means a sure thing."

"But that *couldn't* be either, Father!" insisted Heidi Stoltz. "Saint Joseph had to be *pure* to be chosen to care for Jesus and Our Lady."

"There's nothing impure about sex in marriage, Heidi," Father Tran responded mildly, "let alone about being a parent. Somewhere along the way, some Catholics seem to have gotten the idea that only celibacy is pure." The youthful cleric paused, then added, "I can tell you that the assembled bishops of the Church have formally declared that no lifestyle is superior to marriage . . . including their own."

"They *did?*" gasped Mrs. Stoltz. "My mother told me religious life by far was the highest vocation. It broke her heart when I married Mr. Stoltz and didn't become a nun, but I was young."

Lucky Mr. Stoltz, I thought.

Mitzi Banducci raised a hand then — something almost no one else ever did before speaking — and the priest nodded at her. "As a practical matter, I think it would be better to have married clergy."

Father Tran responded, "We already have some — widowers, mostly, or priests from other rites who've joined us. Not a great many, but there are fathers and grandfathers saying Mass."

"Good," said Mrs. Banducci. "I can't imagine anyone who's been in a long-term, loving relationship not understanding that there's more than passion involved in sex; there's comfort and caring and communication. Sex as an expression of love can't offend God."

"Monsignor McCarthy said only to have babies!" snapped Mrs. Marquez.

Before Father Tran could respond, the usually silent Mrs. Donati spoke up: "Why are we talking about *relations?*" Her voice cracked. "What's that got to do with God? Is everything sex in America now?"

The priest gently responded, "God ordained sex, but to answer your question, I'd guess life's about as sexual now as it ever was, but we've broken with the taboo on speaking candidly about it."

"Sex is the curse of Eden!" asserted the woman.

I whispered to Miranda, "I'm glad I'm not Mr. Donati,"

"I'm glad you're not, too," she replied.

Mrs. Marquez scuffed her chair across the floor then and said, "I suppose we'll endorse evolution next!"

Before Father Tran could answer, Miranda said, "Well, as someone trained in human biology, I believe that theory is an imperfect description of God's plan, yes."

The priest nodded.

Outside a few minutes later, I asked Miranda, "Want to go for a hike and talk about Charles Darwin?"

"Are you really up to a walk?" she asked.

I could only smile, sore urethra or not. "I'm desperate for one. My son taught me to enjoy the river trail across from the university. Game for a stroll?"

She glanced at her watch. "How long will it take?"

"Five minutes or five hours, more like the former for me right now, but whatever we want to spend — plus fifteen minutes to drive over."

After a moment, Miranda responded, "Sure, let's go. But I warn you that I've never been an outdoorswoman."

"You'll love it."

11

We parked, then strolled over a dirt levee onto the small grassy area in front of the riparian forest. A paved trail ran there, one used by everyone from bicyclists to joggers; I'd even seen an electric wheelchair buzzing along it. Below that, more wooded and closer to the river, lay a dirt horse trail that my son and I had tended to walk, since in our experience equestrians were a rarity there.

Miranda and I strolled the dirt path that day, wandering among cottonwood and willow thickets near the stream, where wild grapes draped from high branches and berry bushes blocked access to the frigid current. From within those thickets we could hear the scurrying of rodents and birds. "This forest is one of Sacramento's wonders," I said.

"You're right," Miranda said. "This place really is remarkable. I had no idea . . . and to think we're in the middle of the state capital."

I nodded and smiled, pleased that she liked it, then said, "A Fish and Game officer told me mountain lions have always traveled through the Valley along these riparian forests where there's cover. I know there're plenty of deer in here, plus a zillion possums and rabbits and joggers, for them to eat."

Miranda raised her eyebrows and said, "That's reassuring" just as we heard a shrill voice — "Fluffy! Muffin!" — then saw a stout man restraining two tiny poodles on a tandem leash walking toward us. We nodded at him as I said, "Speaking of cougar bait — "

"Which?" she said, and I had to laugh.

Not far behind the man, a runner about my age — all sinew and sweat — was struggling toward us, his face crimson, his arms pumping. He panted grimly past without looking up, and I said, "He reminds me of a guy on my high school track team who used to run too long in the same place. But at least he's doing it."

"Or overdoing it," she amended. "I'm glad I'm not his physician."

"Or mine," I said. "I'm starting to droop. Time to go home."

Miranda stopped and held both my hands when she said, "Thanks, Marty, for introducing me to this place. I'd heard of it, of course, but just never got around to visiting. It really is splendid."

I started to say, "So are you," but couldn't squeeze the words out.

When we finally reached the car, Miranda once more said, "This place is a treasure. Let's come back."

"Let's," I said, happy as a man with a grim prognosis could be.

■

The letter from Nancy I found in the mailbox that afternoon read,

Dear Marty:

I have found peace with the Madre Maria Society at the New Hope Community. Father McIntyre is our leader and he is a great man of God. He has healed my soul. I want you to know this because Janine told me you have been concerned about me.

I hope to visit Medjugorje to see the Virgin Mary. My soul is ready for the journey.

I also want you to know that I forgive you. Nothing we do will change what happened to Dougie, so we must both move on. I am praying for everyone.

Yours in Christ,
Nancy

I felt like asking "Nancy who?" She'd never been deeply religious, so this letter seemed out of character. Besides, what did I need her forgiveness for? I was imperfect but so was she . . . so was everyone. Maybe I hadn't been demonstrative, but I'd loved my wife and kids. After several moments, though, I was softening, admitting how much I missed what we'd had.

Unable to reach Lea, I left a message on her answering machine telling her I'd heard from Mom. I told her no more, assuming that she likely knew far more than I about what was going on.

That evening, Miranda and I dined at Bobby Leong's, a trendy spot near the church. We talked about our failed marriages, each of us seemingly anxious to get that stuff out and dealt with. She acknowledged that her husband had early on veered from her to other women, although he continued for a time to want the respectability offered by their marriage. She'd finally kicked him out and had avoided him since their last day in court. "Good riddance," she summarized with restrained heat. He had already gone through another marriage and was now, she had heard, dating his young receptionist.

I told her about my breakup, and she listened with apparent interest to my very different story. "You lost a child," she said. "I can't think of anything worse. Then your marriage . . ." We moved past the subject of Doug pretty quickly, since I really didn't have the heart to discuss it and she seemed to sense that.

When I finished by telling him about Nancy's letter, Miranda's smile remained unchanged when she said, "It must be a relief to have that settled — her whereabouts, I mean."

"Yeah, it is. I do still worry about her."

Miranda reached across the table and took my hand. "Of course you do," she said. "And you should."

I could only nod.

"Well, a small part of me still wonders about my husband, but I had to move on and I have. The scar is there, though, for me just like for you."

I didn't really want to talk about Nancy . . . or Miranda's ex-husband, for that matter. After a few moments of silence, I gazed at her and said, "Getting to know you has been wonderful, Miranda, the best thing that's happened to me in a long, long time." We were holding hands, so I reached across the table with my other hand and covered ours. "You've been a terrific support in this mess I've let myself get into."

She flashed that smile again and said, "That's what doctors are for."

"Not as a doctor, Doctor, but as a woman . . . a friend, a special one, I hope."

She squeezed my hand and said, "Thanks for that, Marty. There was a time after my own surgery when I wondered about the woman part."

"May I kiss you, Dr. Mossi, right here in front of God and the world?"

"You may," she replied.

We leaned across the table and our lips—hers warm, soft—touched and lingered, then parted with mutual smiles.

Miranda dropped me off that evening with the promise that she'd see me tomorrow. After a sweet good-bye kiss, I hummed as I walked toward my house, only to be confronted on my porch by my daughter. "Dad, you *kissed* that doctor!"

"I kissed that woman, Lea. Her profession has nothing to do with the attraction."

"That's just semantics. What about Mom? She's trying to reestablish contact, and you're . . ."

"Lea, sit down," I ordered after we entered the house, and to my surprise, she did. "Mom and I are *divorced.* We're no longer married. I really wonder what she's doing in that commune or whatever it is, but I'm not going to stop living."

My daughter started to speak, but I raised a hand to stop her and said, "That's number one. Number two is that my private life is private, just as yours is and Mom's is. I've let you say more than I should have because I know you've been worried about your mother and, frankly, because I haven't wanted to say anything that would cause us to become estranged again. You're my daughter and I love you, Perico. I want you in my life."

She sensed an opening and interjected, "If you really love me, you'll—"

"No!" I snapped. "That's not fair. There can't be conditions in this except that we not try to manipulate one another. We both want to make sure your mother is okay, but my personal life is mine. Period."

I thought she might bolt then, but instead she began weeping softly, saying, "There's really nothing left, is there?"

"Oh yes, there is!" I objected. "There's my love for you and for your mother, and for your brother; that will be there as long as I live. There're our wonderful . . . and sad . . . memories. And I think there's your love for all of us, or you wouldn't be so concerned about these things.

"I'm just asking you to trust me the way you asked your mother and me to trust you all those years ago when you declared your independence and moved in with George."

Her head snapped up and she said, "You were right about George, he was a jerk — and I think I'm right about this doctor." She looked at that moment like a little girl begging.

"You don't even know her, honey," I replied. "You've met her, what? Once? This isn't about abandoning anyone. Love isn't like that — a tank of gas that can be emptied. It can be infinite. I don't love you less if I begin to love Miranda . . . you know that."

"You can only love one person at a time, romantically, I mean," she asserted.

"I think you've been listening to too many song lyrics. What about the time you were agonizing over Rob and Howie?"

"That was different!"

I smiled. "So is this."

"You love her, then?"

"I'm not certain," I said, "but if I ever do, I'll want your support. I'll never unlove your mother, but our relationship has changed. We've all got to accept that.

"Besides," I added, "nothing in your mother's note to me sounded like she was yearning for a reconciliation."

"She *wrote* to you?"

I handed her the note, and she calmed a bit. To my surprise, she didn't bring up her mother again, so I brewed us some tea. We talked about visiting Rollie and Audrey as soon as I felt like traveling. I urged Lea to return to the community college and finish her associate's degree, telling her I'd gladly pay for tuition and books. I finally invited her to lunch with Miranda and me soon. She declined, but left the door open, saying, "I'm not ready for that yet."

"Let me know when you are," I said, and I kissed her cheek.

■

I used my new penile pump again the next day, managing to develop a full-sized erection; that was a great way to prepare for a date, I mused, since I was picking Miranda up for dinner.

We dined at Sinaloa, the only Mexican restaurant nearby that offered *frijoles entiros* instead of lard-filled refried beans, as well as some meat-free, dairy-free entrées. As I'd been advised at the prostate cancer group, I had removed red meat and dairy products from my diet, which sometimes made eating out a problem, but in this restaurant the sauces were so rich that not even my diet could ruin their savor.

Over beer, chips, and salsa, I summarized for Miranda my earlier conversation with Lea. She nodded, saying, "I understand. My youngest son, Robbie, watches me like the proverbial hawk. He, and your daughter too, are adults, but they act like kids, especially when it comes to Mommy or Daddy."

"How about your other boys?"

"Oh, James and Nick are married, not living in Sacramento, and involved with their own lives and careers. Robbie isn't; he's going to junior college on and off. I think the older boys would be happy to see me happy. They're also a little more savvy than their baby brother about what their father did to precipitate the divorce. They don't blame me. Robbie was still in school when that happened, though, and it's really stuck in his craw."

When Miranda dropped me off at home that night after dinner, I kissed her, then said, "Can I entice you in for a drink, or maybe some smooching?"

"Well," she said, smiling, "I'm not thirsty."

"Then come in by all means."

Inside, I lowered the lights and started the stereo — Frank Sinatra — real bachelor-pad-of-the-'60s atmosphere. I felt more like an infatuated kid than a swinging single, though, with my fire intensely rekindled when we kissed.

Although as tall as I was, she somehow managed to position her head a bit lower than mine there on the couch. I mentioned that to her; she smiled and said, "It's a skill large girls learn." Necking with a woman other than Nancy required reschooling; it had been a long, long time. Miranda was larger, and her lips were fuller, so soft and warm that they seemed to engulf mine wonderfully, and her tongue played lightly with mine — both different from Nancy but decidedly pleasant.

As we moved deeper into passion that evening, I began to lightly stroke one of her breasts. After a moment, she breathed into my ear, "Wrong side."

It took me minute to understand. Wrong side?

She kissed my ear and deftly moved my hand from her left to right bosom, and I immediately felt the difference, and sensed that she did too. I also became acutely aware that my penis was tingling, almost throbbing, but that it remained soft. My breath surged ever faster, and my ambitions were as prurient as they'd ever been, but that night—on one level at least—I gave in to the sad sense that I was damaged.

■

I continued using my pump each day, and Miranda and I necked each of the next several nights, but I ended up frustrated and even a little angry. Dr. Solomon had talked vaguely about the possibility of me regaining an erection, but I gathered it was perfunctory reassurance, because everything I'd heard at the support group suggested that urologists tended to overestimate the chance of retaining potency after surgery.

I had to talk to someone about this, so I telephoned Dr. Royster.

"Hi, Marty. What's up?" he asked.

"It's what's not up that bothering me." I explained to him a little about my relationship with Miranda.

"So you've got a lady interested, but you can't perform. Has she complained?"

"We haven't talked about it."

He said, "You ain't a kid, Marty, and neither is she from what you say. I'll bet you'll be able to do enough—even without an erection—when the time comes. Guys tend to overestimate hard-ons. You've got a tongue, toes, fingers, and ingenuity. Try various positions. You say she's a doc? Then she's apt to know things you won't because she'll have heard about them."

"It's just frustrating," I admitted.

"Let me tell you, too," he added, "I was only good for half an erection *before* I got sick, but my wife and I've carried on. Your situation isn't unusual, so don't become one of those feel-sorry-for-myself types. Get on with life. If your lady friend loves you, it won't be your erection she cares most about. And if your erection comes back, that'll be a gift. If it doesn't, you two'll figure out how to satisfy one another."

I finally gave in. "Okay, okay," I said. "I'll spend more energy on figuring out how to do what I can and less feeling sorry for myself."

Al chuckled. "Ah, you got my message. How's your PSA?"

"The same."

"Then you'll need more therapy before long, so don't get too comfortable."

"Not much danger of that," I said.

12

When I telephoned Father Tran to tell him that my professional life had progressed to the point where I'd no longer have time for his religion class, he was understanding. "No problem. I'm delighted to hear you're back at work. But if you find time to drop in occasionally, please do."

In any case, Miranda reported that we had become the subjects of concern at the class. Some of our colleagues seemed worried that these two divorced Catholics, whom they had grown to like, might stumble into scandal. Sylvia Marquez and Heidi Stoltz in particular seemed concerned over our possible moral decline and they urged that we join the seniors' singles group at the church. We did attend one potluck sponsored by that organization . . . a collection of desperately friendly widows and divorcées, mostly.

In truth, I guess I'm a born monogamist, and my social life had expanded about as far as I wanted it to, farther in fact, since I was attending only about half the gatherings of the cancer support group. Most evenings, Miranda and I just hung out together — dinner, a movie, a snuggle, that kind of stuff.

Meanwhile, my articles on prostate cancer had been well received, so I was being invited to talk at civic and service clubs. I'd also published a piece in which I attacked the sheep and cattle ranchers in the foothills who were lobbying for a return of 1080, the deadly poison they liked to use on coyotes. I pointed out that sheep and cattle, not coyotes, were ruining the environment, and that the use of 1080, now that the foothills were being populated by commuters and retirees, would be insane. I received lots of letters on that one, too, mostly from sheep and cattle ranchers, one of whom called me a "goddamn commie," a label I hadn't received for a long time.

I was working now on a piece about irrigation and the fuss caused when some water previously available to farmers was returned to local streams to protect salmon and steelhead populations, and wondering what the next batch of letters might accuse me of, although I could probably guess. I was also casting about for yet another project to follow that one. Remaining busy made it easier to forget I was sick.

I slid past my three-month checkup with a PSA still hovering at 0.3 and feeling fine, but Miranda pointed out, "It's over three months, Marty. The hiatus is over. It's time to get started on radiation. If you have *any* PSA left, the surgery failed. We need you to see Paul Nimitz again."

I simply nodded and said, "Okay."

By then I was past the incontinence that had plagued me after the operation; on my daily walks, I'd leave only a small spot on my pad. Although impotent, I was again plenty sexual.

My relationship with Dr. Mossi had progressed to about the heaviest petting possible. If I hadn't been so damaged, I'd have pushed for more, but my shame over my inability to perform acted as a governor. My penis hadn't been much of a factor, but my heart had been: I was falling in love with a woman I thought I could happily marry, and I sensed that she was ready for a deeper union, too. We might never have coital sex, but we could have real love, and I determined to let her know how I felt about her . . . but somehow the words wouldn't come.

■

On the Friday afternoon after I made an appointment to see Dr. Nimitz, I dropped by Miranda's place for lunch. We shared sandwiches, glasses of wine, and small talk, the stereo playing Ella Fitzgerald in the background. After dining we settled on the couch, and I took a deep breath, then said, "You've complicated my life, Dr. Mossi, because I'm . . . I've fallen in love with you."

Those wonderful dark eyes glistening, she responded, "Mr. Martinez, you have uncomplicated mine, because I love you, too." Her smile, as usual, dazzled me.

I kissed her, then kissed her without breath, then kissed her again without anything but the usual sensation of always wanting to kiss this woman. One of my hands entered her blouse. A moment later I felt my zipper being pulled down, and I was suddenly embarrassed, wanting her to stop because there was virtually nothing there for her to fondle, and I was afraid my pad might be wet. But another part of me—remembrance, I guess—wanted this all to continue so that I could make love with a woman I loved.

When her hand finally caressed my penis, though, I felt I had to halt what we were doing. Finally, she asked softly, "What's wrong?"

"I'm afraid . . . I'm afraid I might leak . . ."

"You won't." She lowered her head and kissed my penis—I shuddered with pleasure, but my hands extended toward her head, not quite touching: I had to stop her. I could feel my penis filling, filling, filling . . . then everything released in a surge of pleasure, but I was sure the worst had happened.

A moment later she whispered, "You came, didn't you?"

I managed to gasp, "Yes. Are you . . . okay?"

"I'm fine." She kissed me there once again.

I'd never had a dry orgasm before and it was . . . well . . . different. It hadn't felt quite as good as the old fluid ejaculation—or at least I didn't think it had—but it sure felt better than anything else I could think of.

We retired to her bedroom and I kissed her where and how I never had and she, too, crested, then slumped sleepily. We napped, and when we'd both awakened and were sharing coffee in the kitchen, Miranda said, "I don't want to embarrass you, but let me explain something, Marty. Early in the day before fatigue sets in, you aren't apt to leak much. I wasn't in any grave danger." She smiled. "But you were. I felt like eating you up."

She walked me to the door and we kissed once more. "I really do love you, Miranda Mossi," I murmured as I kissed her ear. "I want to marry you."

That stopped her. "And I love you, Marty." She smiled sadly. "Life for both of us would have been so much simpler if we'd met one another first. But we didn't."

I started to respond, but she added, "I told you that my husband had our marriage annulled after I divorced him?"

"Yeah, but you guys were together for what, nearly twenty years? You had three kids? How can that just be *annulled?*"

Miranda sighed. "Well, I told you that in retrospect we married more to support one another in medical school than for love." She smiled and added, "He called me 'Carmen.'"

"Carmen?"

"Carmen Miranda . . . it seemed cute at the time. Anyway, there was just a kind of mutual need between us and lust, of course. Then as time went on I did come to rely on him—ironically just about the time I came to distrust him.

"One priest, who was an attorney, told me that a marriage was like a seed; if it didn't grow and flower, then perhaps it should be annulled. Ours certainly didn't flower, so it was annulled." She shrugged. "The tribunal bought that argument."

"Are you sure he didn't buy the tribunal?"

She shook her head at that, but I was serious. The whole Catholic annulment process, as I understood it anyway, smacked of cronyism and influence to me.

"Did you ever consider it?" she asked.

"No, and I don't think I could. I'd feel like I was dishonoring my kids and their mother. Nancy and I are apart now, but she was a good wife for most of the years we were together. And our kids were . . . well, *our* kids."

For a moment I saw a shadow cross Miranda face, but she smiled a second later and said, "You're a good man, Charlie Brown. One reason I love you is that I know you're loyal. You'd do the same thing for me, I know. I'll take what I *can* have."

"I can give you my love," I said, and we embraced once more, but I was amazed that I kept declaring feelings so openly, something I'd rarely done with Nancy. "I can give you what's left of my life. I'll marry you tomorrow if we can."

"We can't—not and remain Catholics. Let's both think about what marriage would mean. I'm sure God would forgive us, but we'd be denied the sacraments," she said, almost to herself.

We kissed once more, then she opened the door for me and I almost ran into a young man, athletic-looking and dressed expensively, with dark hair and a slightly olive complexion like Miranda's. He scowled at me.

"Oh, Robbie," said Miranda, "I'd like you to meet my friend Marty Martinez."

I extended my hand and, after a moment of hesitation, the young man gave me a dead-fish handshake and didn't smile. "'Lo," he said without making eye contact.

"This is my youngest son," Miranda said, patting his back.

"Your mother's told me about you," was all I could manage in the face of his obvious scorn.

"Yeah?" he grunted.

His mother raised her eyebrows at me. Robbie obviously didn't want to talk to me, so I said to Miranda, "I'll see you for dinner," and she winked at me.

Miranda had warned me that her youngest son wasn't charmed by the idea that she was dating anyone, so his behavior was no shock. It didn't please me, though.

■

When I arrived home, Johnny O was sitting on my front porch in one of the chairs. "Hey, Champ!" he called. "Johnny just came by to see how you're doin'?"

"I'm doing great, Johnny. Want a beer?"

"Yeah, sounds good."

I walked into the house and fished two longnecks from the fridge, then carried them to the porch and sat next to him. "So how's your life going, Johnny?"

"I got too many wives and not enough money, Champ." He grinned. "And none of 'em likes me."

He wasn't lying about the wives. Johnny had married five times that I knew of and fathered a dozen kids, and he lived alone now in a single-wide trailer. All the money he'd made boxing went to his various families, and I had no idea how he made ends meet working at the truck stop, plus bouncing for a bar on weekends, but he'd never asked me for a loan, or any help at all.

"You know my kid Gabe—he's Paula's son—he's gonna go in the Golden Gloves this year. He's a welter. I'm gonna work in his corner with Jimmy Muñoz."

I didn't say anything, but I was saddened to hear that. In many ways, Johnny's kids seemed to still live in the world their father and I'd grown up in, the one we'd escaped. Gabe had to have better options than getting his brains beaten to mush in order to be somebody. A couple of Johnny's other sons had done time for gang violence, and none of his kids that I knew of had finished even junior college.

The phone rang, and I excused myself and went inside to answer. Miranda said, "Robbie's coming over to talk to you. It'll probably be a what-are-you-up-to-with-my-mother speech. Be kind."

"I've had kids," I replied. "They're treasures when they aren't being pains in the ass."

She laughed, then added, "Oh, yeah, Robbie said he thinks you're awfully dark."

"Johnny O's over here having a beer with me. If your son sees us together, he'll think I'm light."

After I hung up, I returned to the porch, and Johnny asked, "What do you hear from Manuel?"

"Nothing," I had to admit. My older brother hadn't spoken to me since our mother's funeral.

"I always thought Manuel shoulda turned pro. He could really fight. You know, right after Johnny won the Nationals in Chicago that year, I came home to Merced and got into it with that damn Manny. Your brother, he hadn't read Johnny's press clippings, I guess, because he sure didn't know how dangerous Johnny was." He laughed.

"Man, that first punch he landed busted my nose—blood and snot all over my face. Never got hit harder in my life. And he could hook off a jab! I knew pros who couldn't do that. Anyways, we musta fought for an hour. Johnny was just hangin' on, Champ, then Johnny landed some nice combinations, but Manuel never even went down." The ex-boxer's eyes flashed with excitement as he told the story, and his body bobbed and weaved, his arms throwing phantom punches. "If the cops hadn't broke it up, Johnny might've died. Manuel, too."

Johnny might've died, but I knew he wouldn't have quit, and my older brother wouldn't have either.

"Soon as the cops left, your brother Raul, he showed up and he came after Johnny because I'd fought Manuel. But before he could land anything, Manny told him to butt out, this was between us. Well, Raul, he argued with Manny and pretty soon those two were fightin'! You Martinezes were the fightin'est damn family in Merced. If somebody fought one of you, he had to fight all of you! Your sisters, your mother and father, your grandparents, your dogs, even your chickens!"

I well remembered that epic battle between Johnny and Manuel, although I'd not been present. Everyone in town talked about it for years; in fact, old-timers were probably *still* talking about it. Johnny had been a junior middleweight then and Manny had been bigger, a cruiserweight maybe, or a small heavyweight, but street fights aren't arranged by weight classes.

We were still chuckling when a sports car roared up in front of the house and Robbie emerged, then stalked toward the porch. I stood to greet him, welcoming a chance to talk to the kid. He stopped a couple of steps from me and growled, "You stay away from my mother, dude."

I glanced at Johnny and his eyebrows went up. "This is Miranda's son, Robbie," I explained. "He seems to have a problem with me."

"You damn right I do. You just stay the hell away from my mother, dude, or *you'll* have the problem."

Johnny shook his head and asked, "Marty, is this boy always so nice?"

"Mind your own fucking business," snapped the young man, and Johnny's eyes locked on him.

The old fighter slowly stood and I saw his heavy shoulders loosen, his long arms relax. "What'd you say to Johnny, son?"

"I'm not your fucking son," the kid hissed, turning his eyes toward my pal. Robbie probably only noticed white hair and wrinkled face, not the tight body beneath them, because the kid moved a threatening step toward Johnny.

And in that instant I realized that I'd have to jump Robbie to keep him out of the hospital, because Johnny, who had a trigger temper, was about to damage him. Before Miranda's son returned his gaze to me, I grabbed him and easily maneuvered him into a hammerlock. He was on the lawn, immobilized, before he realized what I'd done.

"Let me up, you sonofabitch! You blindsided me!"

"In your dreams," I shot back, suddenly angry myself because he'd placed me in this position. "What's your problem?"

"You're doin' my mom!"

"What business is it of yours?"

"You better stay the hell away from my mother!" He lurched with all his strength so I returned the favor, all but dislocating his shoulder, and he gasped, "Ahhh!"

"I'm going to tell you this once, *Robbie.*" I spat his name. "I understand that you love your mother and that you want to protect her. Okay. Well, I love her, too, and I want to protect her. There's nothing casual about our relationship, but there's plenty private about it. Her private life is none of your business, and neither is mine."

"My dad said — "

Aha! I thought. There's the instigator. "Your dad doesn't know *squat.* He lost a good woman and I found her. He may still want to control her, but he's out of the loop. You might want to think about who abandoned your mom. I didn't."

He struggled again then, and gasped, "He said you're using her because she's white."

At that instant I almost really hurt him. Instead I replied, "I love your mother because she's a wonderful woman."

From across the street, Bill Watson, an elderly neighbor, hollered, "You want me to call the cops, Marty?"

"It's under control, Bill," I grunted back. Then to Robbie I spat, "I'm going to let you up now, and when I do, you're not Miranda's kid anymore as far as I'm concerned. I'll treat you like a man starting a fight with me, and I'll *hurt* you. But that's better than what Johnny might do. He'll *maim* you."

I released the young man and stood, suddenly aware of how exhausted I was; my legs were shaky, my heart was pounding. Still, I squared my shoulders as Robbie slowly rolled to his feet, unable to lift his right arm. He swayed in front of me, eyes still feverish.

"You tell your dad to come face me himself if he has the guts. And I want you to come back and talk to me, too, when you've cooled off and grown up a little."

He ignored my comments and spun toward his car, then burned rubber as he sped away.

"That your lady's son?" asked Johnny. "Boy, I hope he grows up real fast. He might get hurt."

"I think he's already been hurt, Johnny, that's the problem." Only then did I realize that I'd wet my pants while struggling with the kid.

Johnny didn't seem to notice. "He better not try to hurt you, brother. Johnny won't let him."

"He won't, because I won't let him either."

The old boxer grinned then and said, "For a guy that's sick, you can still do the dance — a real Martinez."

"If it's a short dance," I puffed, still winded.

After Johnny left, I picked up the empties, then walked into the house, my legs shaky from the encounter with Robbie, my heart still pounding. I changed trousers and shorts, put on a Depend, then lay down for a nap. I was getting too old for that stuff.

13

After our first deep intimacy, I felt married to Miranda — not only my heart but my body was hers and hers was mine. I put the disturbing encounter with her son out of my mind and sat at my desk dreaming of her like a lovestruck teen. I snapped out of that reverie when I realized that the light on my answering machine was blinking. I pressed PLAY and after a beep, Ned Schmidt's voice said, "Martini, I need to talk to you. Call as soon as you can."

He sounded strange, so I immediately dialed the editor's number. "Schmidt here," he barked.

"Ned, this is Martini. What's up?"

His voice lowered, and he said, "This isn't for publication, but you aren't going to believe what's happened. After your series on prostate cancer, I went in for a PSA test. My *GP* didn't want to do one; he said it gave false positives. He just wanted to wave his finger up my ass. Anyway, I told him you'd said that the digital gave false negatives, and he got angry, so I left and went to a urologist." He paused and seemed to take a deep breath, then said, "Anyway, my PSA came out at 18."

"Crap!" I said.

"Then on Monday I had a biopsy, and it was positive."

"What was your Gleason score?"

Ned replied, "4 plus 4. 8."

I paused to control my voice because 8 was dangerously high. This was an aggressive tumor. "Are you being staged now?"

"Yes."

"Listen, Ned, ask your doc to knock out your testosterone with hormones while you're deciding. That way the cancer stops growing and you can take your time to make a decision."

He sounded dubious. "Well, the urologist said this was a slow-growing malignancy. He said I could take as much as six months."

"Eight's a high Gleason score. With hormones you can relax."

"Martini, he's a doctor, and I *am* relaxed."

He sounded plenty tense to me. "Hey, Ned, they're just like journalists: some good, some bad; some right, some wrong. At least get a second opinion, and come with me to the prostate cancer support group. Listen to guys who've already been there, then make up your mind."

"I don't want to listen to a bunch of old farts talk about being sick. I'll trust my doctor."

"Those guys in the group are fighters, Ned. They're confronting their illness. They're not in denial."

"I'm not in denial," he snapped. "Besides, the doc said I could take my time. People can live *years* with it."

He wasn't hearing me, so I said what I shouldn't have: "Well, keep notes on what your doctor says, because you might need them at the malpractice trial."

"Talking to you's a fucking comfort," he spat. "A fucking treat!" He hung up.

I stood there shaking my head, angry at myself and at him because I had not been able to impress on my old pal how serious his problem might be.

■

Despite all the other things going on in my life, Miranda dominated my thoughts. I wanted to marry her, so I decided to take the initiative and telephoned Father Tran to ask if I could come over for a talk. He said yes, he'd be free after the daily nine o'clock morning Mass. Since my radiation appointment with Dr. Nimitz wasn't scheduled until eleven thirty, I could do both.

I drove over, and the priest welcomed me to the rectory, ushered me into his office, and offered coffee. I declined and got right to the point: "I want to marry Miranda, Father. Her earlier marriage was annulled, but mine hasn't been —"

"Are you considering annulment?" he interrupted.

I hesitated before saying, "No . . . not really."

"That complicates matters."

"I know."

"And you won't?"

"I don't think so. It wasn't a bad marriage, Father, it just sort of came apart. I didn't think I could ever love anyone again, but I was wrong. I love Miranda."

"Well . . . if your relationship has grown that strong, then you probably should be married," he said. "This is dicey stuff, because you're both pretty well known in the community, so it's better for you to be married and not give scandal by cohabiting, if that's the option . . ."

"It might be."

He seemed to contemplate what I'd said, then continued: "Unfortunately, you can't be married in the Church, and that will separate you from it to a degree. The Church believes that contracting a new union creates a situation of public and permanent adultery. That doesn't mean marriage will separate you from God, though. Only God can know about that. You can still attend Mass, of course, and you should, but you can't receive Communion. You can take advantage of the Sacrament of Penance if you're truly contrite about whatever sins you confess. Best of all, you can still pray and maintain your personal relationship with God."

"We wouldn't be excommunicated, then?"

"No. That happened in the bad old days. Today we want everyone to partake of Mass and to persevere seeking grace to live the best Christian life they can." He smiled then and added, "You two wouldn't be alone. We have more than a few parishioners in similar situations."

"The Church has meant a great deal to me since I've been sick," I admitted.

"And I think Miranda coming into my life has been a Godsend, literally, so I don't want to be estranged from her or it."

He nodded. "You don't have to be. I don't want to be invasive, but could you two consider a chaste marriage?"

"We could," I agreed, "and we might have to because of our illnesses, but not willingly."

"It's between you two and God," he said, "but whatever you decide, you'll still be my friends."

I smiled and admitted, "We're counting on that."

■

I sat in Dr. Nimitz's waiting room later that morning, nervous again because I knew he would give me a candid prognosis, and I wasn't certain I wanted to hear it. The room was nearly deserted, but across from me in the oncologist's office I noticed a young woman, probably Lea's age, slim but not pretty. Her clothing, clean and neat, nevertheless seemed to indicate that she hadn't much money. She held a magazine, I noted, but obviously wasn't reading it.

As I returned my gaze to the *Sports Illustrated* on my lap, I became aware of a strangled sound, like an animal in distress, coming from the hall that led to the treatment rooms. At first I was baffled, so I strained to see what was going on, then realized the sound was a voice. Soon a young man, strand thin, his skin yellowish and bruised, shuffled to the receptionist's desk and rasped something.

Finished there, he turned and made his way slowly toward where the young woman sat. She stood and walked to him, then took him in her arms, and led him to the chair next to hers, where he plopped. She immediately put an arm around him and laid her head on his shoulder, while he closed his eyes and rested his head against hers, appearing exhausted. After several moments, she whispered something to him, and he managed a smile. They stayed that way for what seemed to be a long while. Finally, the woman kissed the young man's cheek, then stood and helped him to his feet, wrapped both her arms around one of his, and they slowly shuffled out of the office.

My face heated as I watched them. He was clearly dying, but he was also clearly loved. And I had been feeling sorry for myself because I couldn't manage an erection.

A second later a nurse called me into a treatment room. After the usual prelims—weight, temperature, blood pressure—the oncologist tapped at the door and entered. "Mr. Martinez, good to see you again, though not under these circumstances. I've read your file and I've talked to Dr. Solomon. It looks as though you've got a moderately aggressive, locally advanced cancer. I think we need to hit it as hard as we can with external-beam radiation — I'd like to go to 6,500 rads — seven and a half weeks — since recent studies show that the more rads you can take, the better the chance we can stop this thing. I'd also like to put you on concurrent hormonal ablation."

One thing about this guy, he didn't beat around the bush. I liked that. "Yes," I agreed. "I've read that hormones might help."

He smiled. "Of course you have. I've been reading your series in the *Express*. It's first rate."

"Thanks. What's my prognosis?" I asked, not wanting to beat around the bush either.

Dr. Nimitz replied, "Not great, not horrible — as I'm sure your reading has forewarned you. For some reason, we don't cure a lot of these locally advanced cases, and we don't really know why. I suspect that as soon as the cancer escapes the capsule, micro-metastases are loosed into the body, but no one knows for certain. What we do know is that with seminal vesicle involvement, the ten-year rate with recurrence is about 80 percent."

My belly chilled. "I've read that, too. I was hoping it was wrong. And when the cancer comes back?"

"Hormones, which last a couple of years on average. Then matters get pretty desperate because chemotherapy hasn't worked well for prostate cancer. I think those figures for how long the hormones last are probably wrong, though, based on starting the therapy too late. I recommend starting before PSA is above 10. There's a small but compelling body of evidence that says the effect can last *much* longer if you do that."

"I've read that, too."

He paused and seemed to gaze at me, then said, "Did you read that you're not a statistic? Don't let those figures throw you. Every case is unique, including yours. This course of treatment will give you the best shot at beating the disease."

"Okay."

"I'll examine you today, then I'll schedule you for tomorrow to begin measuring to define the target and set you up for the treatments — daily, five days a week. Today I'll give you a prescription for Casodex and an injection of Zoladex."

"I know most of what you've told me, but my information doesn't seem to have cured me."

The oncologist smiled then and said, "It seems like there's a sort of natural hope that enough knowledge will suppress the disease. Unfortunately, as you said, it doesn't seem to work."

■

Because of the change in my situation, I attended the support group that night and asked who there had undergone adjuvant radiation. A guy named Shields, who was evidently a longtime member but who had not attended since I'd joined, immediately snapped: "That's all the damned oncologists know: surgery, radiation, chemo. Well, I've been going to a holistic healer and she tells me that my real problem with this cancer is that I've got too much mercury in my system. She examined my hair and said that I needed to have my old fillings removed, eat lots of cilantro for a week or two, then take an herbal compound she'll give me, and the mercury will be purged."

Mort asked, "Did you do that, Shields?"

"Oh yeah."

"And what's your PSA now?"

"I don't do PSAS anymore. I just watch my diet. And look at me, strong as a bull almost three years after I was diagnosed. Can you believe I'm sixty-seven years old? I still got a hard-on that can etch glass. I keep my wife happy. How many of you can say that?"

"I hardly know your wife," said the leader, but Shields didn't laugh. Then, ever the politician, Mort said, "That's probably the right course of treatment for you, then, Mike, but Marty here's got a far more advanced and aggressive cancer than you."

He turned toward a tall, younger man I'd also seen only rarely at the meetings and said, "Pete, your situation was like Marty's. Why don't you tell him what you decided to do?"

The young man cleared his throat. "Well, after my surgery it turned out that I had involvement in a seminal vesicle, plus some spread on one side, so I went over to Stanford. The doctors there put me on six months of hormone therapy and they radiated me for seven weeks. They also said that micro-metastasis had probably escaped, so it would recur eventually and I'd have to go on hormones. I'll hate that."

It was a variation of all the guys' fear, and he didn't have to say more; none of us wanted to be chemically castrated.

Shields scoffed, "Oh hell, what do doctors know! Cut, burn, poison, that's what. Cut, burn, poison!"

Pete's eyes snapped toward the older man, and he said evenly, "Look, just because you're barely sick and even some nutcase *healer* can't hurt you doesn't mean the rest of us are. Exactly how many men with advanced prostate cancer have been cured by cilantro?" His tone was not kind.

Shields suddenly stood and said, "This group is getting too damned touchy. Now you see why I don't come anymore," and he stomped from the room.

"Well," said Mort, "that got us going."

Jimmy Molinari, most notable because his pants were seldom zipped, seemed to have dozed through the exchange. He looked up then and said, "What the hell's going on, or am I just having a senior moment?"

Mort said, "Jim uses Chinese herbs and he's as bad off as I am, or worse. And they've dropped your PSA, haven't they?"

"Sure have," the octogenarian responded, "but my balls have shriveled up to the size of peas. Of course they weren't much bigger to begin with."

"It's important to believe in whatever therapy you choose," Mort pointed out. "That decision is an act of faith."

As the meeting broke up, a husky young guy I didn't recognize slid up to me and grinned. "What tickles me is all these old guys talking about sex in the present tense."

"You a grammar teacher?" I snapped.

"Hey," he said, "I was just kiddin'. You don't have to get salty." He spun away, shaking his head.

I stood there watching him, a little ashamed that my temper had flared, when two older men approached to tell me they'd had adjuvant radiation after failed surgery. Both were now on hormones, they told me, but Curly, the bald one, added, "It was worth it. Hell, you gotta take your best shot, Marty. That's all any of us can do. I'd've never forgiven myself if I hadn't at least *tried* to beat this thing."

14

I awoke next to Miranda and for what seemed a long while lay there smiling at my good fortune. At breakfast she could have talked me into anything, and I agreed to attend the theology group with her. Once we arrived, though, I stepped roughly off the curb and felt a squirt, and realized immediately that my penis had somehow slipped from behind my pad and I'd wet myself. *Great.*

I immediately placed the sweater I carried in front of my fly, then veered into the restroom. A blotter's blossoming appeared on the right side of my zipper. I repositioned my leaking tool behind the pad, then did my best to sop up the damp spot on my trousers with paper towels.

I walked out with my sweater in front of my fly and sat at the table around which we assembled in the meeting room, confident that the suntans I wore would quickly dry.

Everyone greeted me cordially, but no sooner had I settled next to Miranda than I heard Sylvia Marquez say, "Father, at one meeting a while back you said that homosexuality wasn't a sin. Well, I just read an article in the *Monthly Visitor* that said it's an abomination unto the Lord."

Father Tran replied, "Sin is an abomination unto the Lord, Sylvia. What I said is that homosexual acts are sinful but homosexuality isn't. It's just a state of being."

"This article said those people are an *abomination!*" She seemed to like that word. "God hates them."

Miranda whispered, "See all the fun you've been missing."

Instead of moving on, the priest said pleasantly, "You know, there are likely many celibate gay priests, just as there are many celibate straight ones . . . and there are some of each orientation who break their vows. The ones who break their vows are sinners. The ones who live up to them aren't."

"Gay priests?" gasped Sylvia.

Miranda pushed her chair forward, then said quietly, "In a world where real love is rare and people just go through the motions in marriage, I doubt if God looks much askance at anyone fighting to remain chaste, no matter what their sexual orientation. I suspect He views them with greater affection than He does loveless heterosexual couples who stay together because they find it socially convenient.

"Besides," she added, "if God hates homosexuals, why does he create them?"

For a moment everyone seemed to stop breathing, until Sylvia snapped, "They create themselves. They *choose!*"

"Not likely," said Father Tran. That again silenced everybody, then the priest added, "Hate the sin but love the sinner."

Mrs. Marquez and Mrs. Stoltz locked eyes momentarily. Both stood. "I can't stay and let sin be condoned," Sylvia announced, and she left the room, Heidi close behind her. I wondered who would follow, but no one did.

Father Tran appeared stunned. He stood as though to follow and call them back — me thinking, Don't do that, Father — then he sat back down and scratched his head, saying, "What in the world was *that* all about?"

"Something personal, I'd bet," suggested Miranda.

"Well, I guess we've got a new topic for today," he said.

After class, Kathleen Tynne stopped Miranda and me as we entered the parking lot. "You were right about it being personal, Dr. Mossi," she said. "Sylvia is estranged from a gay daughter, poor woman."

■

After lunch we drove to the river trail for a walk, strolling hand in hand like young lovers — or an old married couple — over the dusty horse trail amid the riparian forest. We talked for some time about the strange scene at the scripture class. Finally, to change the subject, I said, "Tell me about that boutique you own."

"Co-own, actually, with my friend Kathy Mettler," she corrected. "There's not much to tell. Kathy's another breast cancer survivor — she had a double mastectomy about the time I had my single, and she had even more trouble than I did finding suitable prostheses. Anyway, we just decided that when we got better we'd provide that kind of service for local women, and now we sell those, plus wigs and hats and scarves and lingerie and clothing and you-name-it."

"Well, if you carry a penile prosthesis, let me know. I sure need one."

Miranda's face softened, and she asked, "How are you with this new therapy, Marty?"

We were weaving in and out of serious subjects like slalom skiers. "I guess I'm afraid of being emasculated and of dying, of course. You've given me so much to live for that I can't pretend it doesn't matter."

A chubby guy in a sweat suit shot by us on a scooter, one leg working hard to propel his weight. "We've given each other something to live for, Marty," Miranda said.

"Let's whip both cancers."

We hugged and kissed lightly, then I said, "I talked to Father Tran about us marrying."

"I know." Miranda smiled. "I talked to the monsignor."

I looked directly into her eyes and said, "Marry me, Miranda . . . please. I want to spend the rest of my life with you. It can be a chaste marriage, if that's what it takes, but I don't want to be alone anymore. I want to be with you, to take walks like this one and to debate theology and maybe one day to share each other's grandchildren."

She pulled back and looked directly into my eyes, and asked, "And you can accept being limited by the Church?"

"We wouldn't be excommunicated."

Miranda nodded. "I know that, too," and she fell silent, pausing so long that I was afraid I'd lost her. Then she said, "It would be better if we were married. I wish things were different, simpler, but this is where we are. Let's do marry, Marty."

I could only choke, "Thanks."

"A *real* marriage," she responded.

I got her meaning.

■

That afternoon, clad in a fetching gown that exposed my hindquarters to the breeze, I endured the usual indignities while Dr. Nimitz figured out the exact focus for radiation in my groin, then tattooed tiny dots — radiation targets — on each side of and just above my pubis. Finally he escorted me to a table under a vast machine and introduced me to a young woman named Vonda, the radiation tech. Chatting pleasantly the whole time, she positioned me, explaining that she would take an X-ray to help target the prostate bed, then give me my first treatment.

Vonda talked constantly, which was in many ways a relief because I didn't have time to think about what was happening. I had assumed that Dr. Nimitz would operate the machine and perform the treatment. This would be the beginning of the next stage in my loss of control over what was left of my life.

The actual zapping was painless. Vonda positioned the machine around me — above, below, left side, right side — disappearing each time into a radiation-screened area before turning on the machine while I, lying on the table, heard a buzz but felt nothing. Still, I recited the prayer Miranda had recommended, "From the malignant enemy defend me." Finally the nurse said, "That's it," and placed a footstool beneath me. It had not taken more than ten minutes, with most of the time spent aiming the machine or positioning me.

"See you tomorrow," Vonda added. "And" — I heard her giggle — "if you pull that flap on the left side of your gown you can cover your bottom — unless you're trolling for a date, that is. If you are, it's too late. I'm married."

I had to laugh. "Rats," I said. I liked her.

Tugging the flap until my rear was covered, I returned to the alcove with its changing rooms and eight chairs. It had been empty earlier, but now two women and a man, all in gowns, were waiting for their treatments. I said hi and everyone smiled. "New?" asked the seventyish man.

"My first day," I admitted.

"May I ask what for?"

"Prostate."

"Mine started in the lung," he told me, "but it's in my brain now. That's what Vonda's shooting. She says the target's really small." He chuckled, and I thought: This guy's got cancer in his brain and he's *joking?*

"Anyway," the old man said, "I'm Herb and this is Julie and that's Mabel. They've both got breast cancer."

"Julie," called Vonda, and the younger woman — she didn't look much more than thirty — stood and smiled at me as she walked past. She filled her gown rather well and I was tempted to glance at her walking away to see if *her* bottom was showing. Then I immediately felt guilty.

Herb was grinning when he said, "Welcome to the club. The uniforms aren't great, but you do meet some nice folks here."

"And some smart alecks like Herb," winked Mabel, who also appeared to be in her seventies.

I slipped into the changing booth, feeling more confused than anything else. Those people were probably sicker than I was, but they were upbeat, while I was frankly scared and more than a little uncertain when I stripped away my shield of conviviality.

■

At home I found a tense message from Lea on my machine, so I telephoned her immediately. "Daddy, how do you feel?" she asked.

"Okay."

"Has your hair started to fall out?"

I laughed to myself. "Honey, if that happens it'll be much later. I've got over seven weeks of this to deal with. I'm sure there'll be some changes in my body."

"As long as they get the cancer." She suddenly bawled; I could hear great sobs for several seconds, my heart plunging.

"Perico, we'll get it. We'll *get* it, baby. It'll be okay," and I felt like bawling with her, not because of the cancer but because my daughter loved me.

"I'm sorry," she sniffled, then she said, "Randy says to hang in there."

"Tell him thanks." One of the best things that had happened to me recently was that Randy Lozano had entered Lea's life, so now her mother and I were no longer her focus. He seemed far more substantial than the slicks she'd been hooked up with before, a single father trying to raise a three-year-old son after a doper ex-wife had divorced him. I had the feeling he'd long since seen enough of life's flash—as I'm sure Lea had—and that he wanted a stable relationship. For my daughter's sake, I sure hoped he did.

"Perico, I've got something wonderful to tell you."

"What?"

"Miranda and I have decided to marry."

She did not reply.

Finally I said, "Lea?"

"How can you do this to Mom?"

I didn't feel as though I was doing anything to Mom.

After my daughter finally hung up, I changed clothes, then slipped into my office to brainstorm a new feature story for the paper. As I sat at the computer, I heard the doorbell ring but decided to ignore it. The ringer was persistent, and I remembered that I'd told Miranda's son to come back, so I answered the door. There stood Ned Schmidt. "Martini," he said, "I want to talk to you about that story of yours about farmworkers down in Huron."

What the hell was he doing here? In all the years I'd known him, he'd never come to my house. I said, "Do you like the idea?"—wondering all the while what the real idea was.

"Yeah. I think you're right. The big landowners out there are trapping whole generations in peonage. You're right about that. Where'd you get that statistic about only 11 percent of local kids graduating from high school?" His voice was hard, yet somehow tremulous.

"The Institute for Rural Studies. Coffee?" I asked.

"Sure."

As I poured, he said, "This is some of the toughest stuff you've ever written."

"I don't have to worry about being fired by anyone anymore," I said, smiling, "so I'm less careful."

He chuckled. "This one'll probably piss off the publisher. Can you prove all the stuff in here?" he asked.

"Piece of cake," I responded as I handed him his coffee.

"You'll need to, because the publisher will want this fact-checked to the bone."

We fell silent for a period, sipping our coffee, then I broached the topic I suspected he really wanted to discuss. "How's your treatment going?"

"I haven't decided which one to do yet."

He'd been closemouthed with everyone, so I really didn't know what was happening in his life. I'd been afraid he'd say something like that, though. I asked, "You're on hormones while you decide, though, aren't you?"

He looked up, obviously irritated. "No, my urologist said this is slow-growing, and I don't want to put up with the side effects of hormones."

My heart sank. His health was presumably as bad as or worse than mine, yet he was diddling around. One reason I hadn't contacted him about this topic was that talking to him about it was so frustrating; he truly seemed to be—and I hated this trendy term—in denial. He didn't want to learn from my mistakes, and he wouldn't let me help him, yet he still wanted something from me . . . assurance, maybe.

I sat down and looked away from him for a moment, then said, "Look, Ned, this is serious business, deadly business. You should come to the support group—"

He cut me off. "I already told you I'm not interested."

I plowed ahead. "And meet guys who've been where you are. Have you gotten a second opinion yet?"

"I'm happy with my doctor."

"Come on, Ned! What if he's wrong? What if it's more dangerous than he knows? You can't gamble on him. What if he hasn't had time to keep up with the most recent developments? Is he a urological oncologist?"

"He's my *doctor.* He does these surgeries all the time. He knows what he's talking about. I like what he says."

"And with a Gleason of 8, he didn't recommend that you go on hormonal ablation to stop the cancer's growth?"

"It's 9. They reexamined the biopsy."

"Nine! Oh, shit, Ned, you've got to get on hormones right away!"

His mug crashed, all but broke as he slammed it onto the counter next to him. "Damn it, Martini, you act like you're a damned doctor yourself! You're *not.* You're a journalist just like me. I came over here to ask you about your treatments and the side effects, I didn't come for a fucking lecture!" His eyes were filling with tears, and I was certain it wasn't only rage. He was scared, like all of us with this cancer.

I stood and raised my hands in supplication in front of my chest, saying, "Look, Ned, you're my friend and I'm afraid you're getting into deep shit like I have. But I've said all I can about it, except that I can't understand why you won't at least go to one support group meeting, listen to some survivors. There are lots of differing opinions in the group, and you can talk personally to men who've had every therapy you're considering— "

He was looking away from me, breathing heavily. "I already told you I'm *not* interested in that."

"Okay," I said, feeling defeated, as though my old friend was committing slow suicide. "What do you want to know?"

15

Mondays I had what Dr. Nimitz called the "well-baby checkup." For me that first Monday was only my fifth day since I'd started radiation, but a nurse drew blood, then escorted me into one of the treatment rooms. A few moments later the oncologist joined me. "Any ill effects?" he asked.

"Not so far."

"Well, with any luck, you won't have any. These new machines aim much more accurately than the old ones. It would be a good idea if you began taking a little psyllium with juice every morning to stabilize your bowels in case they get irritated."

I nodded.

"When do you see Dr. Solomon for your first Lupron injection?" he asked.

"This afternoon."

"Good. That and the Casodex pills are important adjuvants to the radiation. They should shut down your testosterone and stop the cancer for now. Any questions?"

"Just one so far. My daughter asked me if I'll lose my hair."

The physician grinned and replied, "Just think about which area we're radiating. I don't think she'll notice your baldness."

I had to smile.

Vonda chattered at me again while she worked that day, at one point saying something about "going for a cure." I guess that shocked me — as many things in the cancer world had — so I said, "I thought you were always going after a cure."

She replied with surprising candor, "No, not really. We do a lot of palliative work, especially with bone lesions to reduce pain. Usually when someone's in for several weeks of treatment we're trying for a cure. If it's just two or three weeks, we're radiating to palliate. We *wish* we could always go for a cure, but that isn't reality."

"Oh," I replied, immediately wondering if my seven-plus weeks was long enough to be going for a cure, but not wanting to ask just then.

After being treated that day I returned to the alcove and found Julie sitting with a small girl on her lap. "Where is everyone?" I asked, since all of our appointments were scheduled well in advance.

"Oh, Mabel went in first today. She beat me here for a change. Herb's in talking with Dr. Nimitz."

"And who's this?"

Julie smiled and said, "This is April, my daughter. Say hello to my new friend Marty, April."

The little girl glanced up at me through blond bangs and grinned — her front teeth missing — as she said, "Hi, Mr. Marty."

For whatever reason, only then did I realize that Julie wore a wig, and that she was even younger than I'd realized. Her face was drawn and sallow, so she was probably much sicker than I'd realized, too. "Hi, Miss April," I said. Then to Julie, "Would you like me to watch April while you're being treated?"

"Mabel's got dibs," smiled the young woman. "I'm only coming in for a few more days. They're radiating a bone lesion on my hip, trying to stop it, so I didn't bother to arrange for a long-term sitter. Most days April stays with my mom while I'm here."

"Ah," I said, understanding that this young woman had just told me that her cancer had metastasized to her bones. Vonda wasn't able to go for a cure. "Well, lucky Mabel if she gets to play with April," I added, thinking to myself that the whole definition of lucky changed in this room. A few weeks without pain, or perhaps living long enough to see your daughter start school . . . or long enough to say good-bye . . . all could now be lucky.

I drove home sad that day.

■

"How was the injection?" asked Miranda as we sipped cream sherry for dessert.

"One more way station on the journey," I responded.

After a moment, she said, "I've been thinking about another one—our marriage."

My heart suddenly chilled: She'd changed her mind.

"There's no reason for us to dally," she said. "We don't know how much time we have, so let's take advantage of this grace period."

Suddenly giddy, I asked, "Do you mean period of grace?"

She didn't laugh. "That, too," she said. "Being together's been a blessing."

That sobered me. "It has," was my only reply. I embraced her, kissed one of her ears and inhaled her fragrance.

We hugged for what seemed a long while, then as we separated, she said, "Let's have a small ceremony—just immediate family—out at the river parkway. And I'd like a Christian minister to celebrate the ceremony, not a civil service."

"When?"

"Soon," she replied.

"How will your kids respond . . . especially Robbie?" I hadn't spoken to him since the day when I'd saved him from Johnny O.

She smiled, "Well, James and Nick, the older boys, will support us. They don't know you yet, but they love me and they want me to be happy. Robbie will hate it, I suppose . . . even though his father is living with that receptionist. How about Lea?"

I had to smile. "You know, she's amazingly inconsistent about all this. She really does like you, I think, but deep inside she's still hoping that somehow her mother will come home and that we'll all be family again. Nancy's life seems pretty bizarre to us now. I really don't know."

"When I was in high school in Piedmont," Miranda said, "the parents of one of my girlfriends broke up, and she had a nervous breakdown. I really thought about that when John and I were splitting. I didn't want my sons to suffer."

This conversation was moving into territory I didn't enjoy traversing, so I asked, "How'd your family end up in a ritzy town like Piedmont?"

"Because my father's family came from the Piedmont in Italy. After he made it big in banking, he couldn't wait to buy a fancy place up in the Piedmont Hills."

"Your mother?" I asked.

"Oh, she married above herself—according to him. She was from Rome."

This time I grinned, asking, "What does a sack of shit sound like when it hits the ground?"

"I know. I know." She shook her head. "Wop!"

"A little Merced humor. After high school you went straight to Stanford?" I asked.

"No, I did my B.S. at Dominican College in San Rafael, then went to medical school at Stanford."

"And how'd you end up in Sacramento?"

"My ex-husband's an endocrinologist and there was a need for one here. I could practice general medicine anywhere. At first I didn't like this area. The weather was too hot in summer, too foggy in winter—but it's home now."

"I've never loved the weather here," I admitted. "One time when I was working for the Bakersfield newspaper, my mom and dad drove down for a visit. I thought she'd complain about the heat, but she said, 'No me gusta Bakersfield. Hay demasiado Okies.' After that, whenever my family got together one of my brothers or sisters would look around at the in-laws and say, 'Hay demasiado Okies'—an in-joke."

Miranda chuckled, then said, "I missed having brothers and sisters, but I was sure treated well as a result."

"Spoiled rich girl?" I asked.

"You might say that . . . if you're insensitive." She smiled. "What's kept you in the Valley? We both know that once affirmative action came into play an accomplished journalist with a Spanish surname like you could probably have gone anywhere."

I could only shrug. "Well, I really think this is a remarkable region. I can go to Bakersfield, one of the world's major centers of country music, attend a cockfight with a hundred Filipinos at Delano thirty miles up the road, listen to world-class poets read in Fresno, see a Hmong exorcism in Merced, and maybe go to a Juneteenth celebration in Allensworth—all in a day or two. To me this is far more interesting than L.A. or the Bay Area."

"I'm sure you'd get some argument from lots of people."

"No doubt. Feel like a nap?" I asked.

"I thought you'd never ask."

Later, as we lay in bed smooching, Miranda whispered, "I've thought of something we can try."

I was so aroused that I could only choke, "Sure," wishing I'd brought my pump.

She maneuvered our bodies into a position like an L, with me on my side and our legs entwined but open enough to position us flush against one another. She reached down and rubbed lubrication on my soft penis, then positioned it and said, "Try pushing now." I did and at first felt only the titillation of pressure. But a second or two later, after a slight adjustment, my penis seemed to slip just a bit into her and I heard her sigh. It had been a long time, but I remembered what to do, beginning with micro thrusts, slowly, then faster, my breath deeper, my sensations deeper, then deeper still until . . . until . . . until I realized that I wasn't going to be able to orgasm. It just wouldn't happen, but we were actually having sexual intercourse, without an erection, without orgasm, but with love. Our first time with one another, and because of my strange new circumstances, it felt like my first time ever.

■

I spent a couple of hours the next morning at Sacramento State University's library looking for fresh material on California's multiethnicity. I intended to write a piece on the state now being home to more nonwhites than whites, having a minority majority, as it were, and I'd just found some publications from New California Media when I heard, "Martín?"

Turned and saw the gray ponytail and Pancho Villa mustache of Eddie Rivers.

"What brings you to campus, *vato?*" he asked, adding, "I've been meaning to call you."

"Just doing a little research," I said without much warmth.

"Well, I want to thank you for writing about the exploitation of our people. We need prominent Mexicans like you speaking out for *la raza*—"

"Wait, Eddie," I said. "I've told you before, I'm not a Mexican, I'm a Californian—just like you. My grandparents were Mexicans. The kids who cross the border today are Mexicans. But *this* is my country. What I wrote about the oppression and exploitation of Latinos I'd write about anyone."

"Wetbacks!" Eddie hissed. "Remember the Okies in high school called us that? Wetbacks! Why do you deny your *raza?*"

Anger flared, but I swallowed it and said, "Name another journalist who's been so unambiguously of Mexican descent. But I'm an *American* of Mexican descent, not a Mexican. Eddie, you play into the hands of every racist in this state when you say you're a Mexican, not an American. They *want* us to be Mexicans, not Americans or Californians. They *want* us to identify ourselves as *others.*"

"We *are* others, the cosmic race, *la raza cosmica!*"

He sounded so melodramatic that I had to chuckle. "Yeah, well, Mexico isn't the cosmic country . . . it's chaotic."

"Because of how America exploits us!"

"Where do you get that 'us'? You're a Californian like me."

"True Chicanos don't abandon their heritage!" he snapped.

"You seem to think there's only one way to be Chicano — "

He cut me off. "California *is* Mexico! This is *Aztlan,* yet we're forced to work the fields — "

My patience had evaporated. "Eddie, your dad was a plumber. As far as I was concerned, you were one of the rich kids at school. Now you're forced to teach maybe three days a week at the college. That must be tough for a campesino like you."

"I just wanted to thank you, Martín, but you can't accept that," Eddie hissed. "You Martinezes always look for a fight!" He spun away, ponytail flying.

16

The morning before my next-to-last checkup with the radiologist, I noticed blood in my BM. Since I was also once more abundantly leaking urine, I really didn't need bowel problems, but I had them. That brought out the hypochondriac in me, and I couldn't help wondering if the radiation had triggered colon cancer or something worse . . . whatever that might be.

I was still doing my workout walks each day and lifting weights — light weights, of course — but I wasn't very frisky. I needed a nap every afternoon. On the other hand, despite taking those testosterone blockers that some of my prostate colleagues claimed had caused them to balloon, I remained only a little heavier than my college wrestling weight. Of course, that weight wasn't distributed exactly the same way it had once been.

Dr. Nimitz said, "You're doing exceptionally well, Mr. Martinez. Really. You've had few side effects, from what I can determine."

"How about that bleeding?"

"It's not from your bowels. You had a small incipient hemorrhoid. The radiation has irritated it. We'll take a good look at your bowels six months down the road, but you really do look fine."

"How about the PSA?"

"Not so fine. We can't seem to drive it below 0.1, even with the hormones. I can't tell you why, but the reason is probably genetic. A few men don't seem to have the immune system to resist this cancer as well as others do."

"If the books I've read are correct, that means my PSA will be rising fairly soon. The cancer will recur quickly."

Dr. Nimitz nodded. "It could. Let's wait and see what the next test shows. You've got seven more days of radiation, plus four more months of hormonal ablation. We really don't have to completely cure it. If we knock it for a loop, you can live your normal life span and die from something else while this is still in your body."

"Great," I said, half meaning it.

A whole new cast had joined me for the midmorning radiation — Herb and Mabel were gone, and Julie was dead . . . the saddest funeral I've ever attended. My new colleagues were a large woman named Jimmie Sue (an aging ex-waitress with breast cancer), Salvador (a young physician with a brain tumor), and Buster (an aging salesman with prostate cancer). I had become aware that they, like the guys in my support group and Miranda, were my real peers, because we all faced illness and endured the dehumanization of what Salvador called patienthood, an "ethnicity" of the ill.

A week or so before, gabbing before our treatments, we'd all agreed that we didn't ever want another nurse to call us "sweetie" or to ask if we had to "go potty." As if on cue, Vonda's assistant, Mona, stood in the doorway and called to Dr. Sal, as we called him, "It's your turn, sweetie."

"There's something I need to talk to you about," he replied.

■

Miranda's question startled me, since it came out of the blue. "What do you pray for most of all, Marty? A cure?"

I hesitated, started to say that I prayed for our situation to work out, but realized that another, even deeper need drove me. "I pray to be reconciled with my family. And I pray that you and I can marry. A cure is in third place."

Miranda nodded, then replied, "You'll get your second wish. Your list is about like mine. I don't want to probe, but what happened with your family? I've heard enough stories from you to know you were really close once. Why did it come apart?"

I'd never discussed this with Nancy or Lea. Until I fell ill, I didn't even allow myself to think much about it. If there's something even more intimate than sex, for me this secret was it. After a long pause, I sighed, then said, "A few years ago when I was full of myself because I was successful — winning awards and stuff like that — I did something terrible." I told her the story.

Her response didn't surprise me: "You've got to learn from a mistake like that, because you can't undo it." Before I could speak, she added, "My other favorite prayer, one I say all the time, is simply, 'Oh God be merciful to me, a sinner.' I say that because I know my God *will* be merciful if I ask."

"That's one I need to say, then," I replied. "I really am sorry about all the mistakes I've made along the way, all the people I've let down, and I don't know how to put things back together. I also don't understand why I've been lucky enough to find you, Miranda, but I don't ever want to lose you."

"You won't," she said, and we embraced.

■

Lea had directed more and more of her attention toward Randy, but I wasn't entirely out of her loop. "Daddy," she said when she called that evening, "how did your checkup go?" She knew when those were scheduled, so she always telephoned to find out what was going on.

I hesitated, not wanting to upset her, but not wanting to lie either. "Well, the PSA's almost zero," I said. "One more week ought to do it."

"Are you still feeling okay?"

"Just those minor problems I told you about, Perico. You can't radiate an area without some problems, but mine are minor," I said, thinking that the most important one, the PSA, was not minor. To change the subject, I said, "Have you thought any more about having lunch with Miranda and me? Maybe you and Randy both could join us — double date."

"I'll talk to Randy about it. I think it's time you got to know him better." She paused, then added, "Tell me honestly, how serious are you about Dr. Mossi?"

"I really am going to marry her."

Lea seemed to stop breathing, then said, "I think you need to . . . to *reconsider* what you're doing. You're real vulnerable with all this bad stuff going on."

That comment made me want to laugh or cry, but I responded only, "I'll want you and Randy with us when we say our vows."

"And you don't think she's taking advantage of you?"

"Lea, do you know how sick Miranda is? She's lost a breast to cancer, and she's not out of the woods any more than I am. It could come back anytime."

Silence, then, "I didn't know it was that bad."

"She and I are on different schedules than most people. Our time together might be pretty limited."

"But what if Mom needed you?"

"I'd respond, of course, but Miranda Mossi is the woman in my life now. Mom is a dear old friend."

"Oh," she said.

■

Later that day, I sat at my computer and began assembling thoughts on California's mixed population and its cultural consequences. I had some fairly clear ideas about what I wanted to write, but the phone rang. I decided to simply listen to my answering machine.

After the beep, I was stunned by a voice I hadn't heard since my mother's funeral: "Marty, this is Chava."

I immediately picked up the receiver, delighted that my youngest brother Salvador had called me. It was the first I'd heard from any family member since Mama's death, so I was momentarily giddy. "Hola, Chavito," I finally said, my voice unable to hide my joy. "Que paso, vato?"

"Manny's had a stroke, a bad one," he replied in a flat voice. "The docs don't think he's gonna make it. Gloria asked me to call and tell you."

He added that last, I knew, so I wouldn't think that he'd forgiven me. I wanted back into my family, but not this way, not with my older brother sick and my younger brother calling only as a favor to Gloria.

"Where is he?" I asked.

"At County."

"When can I visit?"

"Anytime, but do it soon. He can't talk or anything, but he'll know you're there. He's in intensive care, and they've got him on a ventilator."

Manny had been my hero ever since I was a kid; he had been a great football player in high school, a soldier, and a father figure after Papa was killed. He'd also been the one who'd cut me loose from the family after I'd failed Mama. I couldn't let him die without telling him how sorry I was and how much I loved him. "I'll drive right down," I said. Chava hung up without saying good-bye.

I was to meet Miranda after work that evening as usual, so I called her office and told Katharine, the receptionist, what was happening, feeling like my life had become a series of phone calls. I left a message for Lea, too, packed an overnight bag just in case, then headed for my car.

■

I hadn't driven down Highway 99 from Sacramento to Merced since before Doug's death, and I was surprised at how much property south of Sac had filled with houses. The afternoon was unusually clear, and most foliage was dry, with trees clustered around farmhouses in the remaining open land, but by the time I reached Lodi, then Stockton, then Manteca, then Modesto, it seemed that a linear city was sprouting along the old highway, with only brief rural breaks, the state's agricultural heartland appearing to grow houses more abundantly than alfalfa or corn.

Past Turlock, though, the landscape opened and not only farms but ranches could be seen, especially far to the east where grassland rolled and cattle grazed. My brothers and sisters and I had worked on farms around here, and in packing sheds, too, when we were kids. We weren't poor, since our dad had been the foreman for the Alves Dairy, but Papa didn't believe in allowances for teenagers. Those jobs had provided us with respect — you were treated as an adult if you could do adult work — as well as spending money. After my father's death, we all turned our checks over to Mama to help support the family.

My older brother, Manuel, came home from the army and found a full-time job at the Caterpillar agency to help Mama keep the rest of us in school. He eventually worked his way up to manager of the service department, where as far as I knew, he was still employed. He was probably the smartest of our bunch, and certainly the hardest worker.

I was second oldest, and both Raul and I had graduated from college, but Raul had been killed as a second lieutenant in Vietnam. My two sisters had completed at least two years of junior college, both had good jobs and enduring marriages; only Manny had wed a Latina, his high school sweetheart, Gloria Villanueva. Strange to me, all my siblings remained the Merced area.

Merced. Mercy. I hoped my family would be merciful to me.

A light rain began falling as I entered my hometown. I couldn't help thinking about my family, about the high school football games I'd played here, the proms, the speech tournaments, the wrestling competitions, the heated nights smooching by the river — and about how proud Mama had been of me when I was salutatorian of my class at MHS. Of how I'd failed her.

I drove around town on my way to the hospital, past my family's old house across the tracks from the railroad depot — a Hmong family lived in it now, I noticed. Raul and I used to play catch by throwing a baseball clear over the roof, each trying to guess where the other would toss it . . . until one of Raul's flings accidentally beaned old Mr. Ortega and we were ordered never to do that again. I swung by Engine Company 4's firehouse, where my little brother Chava was now a captain, then past the old movie theater, where I'd necked with girlfriends more than once. I couldn't help noticing just down the street the duplex in which Manuel had confronted me and kicked me out of the family after Mama's death. So, so many memories, but that last one was too much: I had to pull into the park near the courthouse and breathe deeply in order to assemble my emotions as I gazed at the grand old building through the dappled windshield.

I knew I could only pray that my family indeed would have *merced* on me. I didn't need them to punish me for failing Mama; I was doing that on my own. Despite being forgiven by God, and surely by my mother, I was torturing myself every time the memory returned, which was often. This surely was Purgatory.

I said, "Oh my God have mercy on me, a sinner," then restarted the car and drove through a light rain to the hospital.

17

My family clustered in the waiting area outside the intensive care unit. No one seemed to notice me until I was practically amidst them, and the nieces and nephews—young adults mostly now—greeted me with hugs and kisses. None of my siblings made a move toward me, so I asked them as a group, "How is he?"

Chava, my baby brother, whose face was now lined and whose dark hair was streaked with gray, shook his head at me and said, "Not good. You better go in right now. Gloria's waiting."

For a moment, I found myself wondering if I would only recognize how old I'd become by looking at my aging brothers and sisters. None made eye contact, although their spouses smiled. "Okay," I said. "What's the procedure to get in?"

"Push that buzzer next to the door," my younger brother said. "A nurse will ask you to identify yourself through the speaker. We've already told her to expect you."

I followed those orders and entered a brightly lit arena, a half circle of alcoves with beds surrounding an elaborate, bustling nurses' station. My sister-in-law was sitting with her back to me at a bed about halfway around. In front of her lay Manuel, with tubes and wires connected to him. For a moment I stopped, stunned by the scene—my strong brother flat on his back—just as a nurse approached and said, "Mr. Martinez?"

Gloria looked up, then stood and walked toward me, hesitated, then continued until she hugged me and kissed my cheek, saying, "Oh, Marty, he's bad, real bad. The doctor says Manuel's had a brain-stem stroke. He said the brain's still swelling, so things will probably get worse. He said that if we take him off the ventilator, he'll die. I'm afraid we're gonna lose him."

Despite having had seven children, my sister-in-law was still a pretty woman, a bit heavier than in her prime but looking far too young to be the grandmother of five. Her own younger three kids were still in school—two at the junior college, one at Stanislaus State. Looking at her, I thought it didn't seem possible that we were in our sixties now, in this hospital, talking about the imminent death of my brother.

"Can't we take him to some place like Mayo Clinic?" I asked, my desperation unhidden.

Gloria squeezed my arm. "You can talk to the doctor, but he said there's nothing anyone can do."

Manuel looked like a splice, he had so many tubes and wires running into and out of him, and that ventilator tube in his mouth dominated. He lay unmoving on the bed, covered only by a sheet. His hair had whitened considerably since I'd last seen him, but he still had that muscular, athlete's body. His head didn't move as Gloria returned to his side and stroked his brow. "Honey," she said softly, "Marty's here."

No response.

"Hi, Manny," I said, trying to sound normal although I was close to tears. What could I say next?

"He drove down from Sacramento to be with you, honey," my sister-in-law continued. I saw tears welling in her dark eyes. It must be wonderful to have been loved by her all these years.

My brother lay there, unresponsive as clay.

"Jesus, Manny," I finally blurted, "I'm so sorry you're sick," and I reached over and put my hand on one of his thick arms. Then I noticed his eyes following me, and I knew then he was alert in that ruined body.

"Manny, if you can hear me, look left."

He looked left.

"Can you move your eyes right?"

He moved them right.

"Okay," I said. "It's left for yes, right for no." I'd seen this in a movie a long time ago. "That way we can communicate."

I sighed then, knowing what I had to say. "Manny, I know I let you and Mama and everyone down when I didn't stay with her that night, and I want you to know there hasn't been a day since that I haven't been sorry. I've prayed for God's forgiveness and for Mama's, and I know they forgive me. I hope you can, too, but even if you can't, I want you to know how much I love you . . ." I could no longer hold back tears, so I quit trying. "And how sorry I am. You've been the best brother a guy could've had. You sacrificed your education so the rest of us could go to school.

"I'll see that your kids will have the same opportunity to finish school that you gave me. That's a blood promise, *carnal,* a *blood* promise. May God curse me to Hell if I fail you again."

His eyes never left me.

"Besides Papa, you're the most important man I've ever known. You were always my hero. I don't want to go to my grave without your forgiveness. If you can forgive me, look left. Please look left."

Gloria was weeping, too, one arm around my shoulders.

His eyes darted left, and I embraced him, kissed his bristly cheek. "Thanks, Manny. Thanks so much. I've lost Dougie; I've lost Nancy. I lost Raul and Papa and Mama. I almost lost Lea. I couldn't stand losing you, too. I just couldn't live."

Gloria bent and softly kissed her husband's forehead, saying, "You did the right thing, honey. We've got to keep the family together."

Sadness hung in the room like a shroud. My brother had always been an upbeat guy, so I decided to try to lighten this sad, tough conversation. I said, "Hey, Manny, maybe I should tell Gloria about that time when I was in junior high and the Mejia brothers chased me home from school."

I turned to Gloria, who I assumed had heard this story many times. "Remember those three? Two were in high school, and they cornered me in the parking lot at the railroad station, not too far from home. Tony and Joe were kicking my ass, then for some reason the big one pulled a switchblade. But Manny heard the ruckus and came outside to see what was happening, and he lit into them. He hit Richie, the big one, so hard he lifted him off the ground, then all of a sudden it was the two of us chasing Tony and Joe back down the street." I couldn't help smiling at the memory. Merced had not been a soft place to grow up, but it had been interesting.

Out in the waiting room Gloria and I walked directly to my brother and my sisters, Esperanza and Alicia. "I apologized to Manuel about what I did to Mama," I told them, "about letting the family down. He forgave me. I've confessed my sin and God has forgiven me. I believe Mama has, too; she knew I was imperfect all along. Now I beg all of you to give me a chance. I can't be separated from my family anymore."

Gloria said, "Manuel just forgave Marty."

"How *could* he?" demanded Chava, his chin out.

"Are you calling me a liar?" my sister-in-law snapped.

Chava shrugged and said, "Of course not. I just didn't say it right. *How* could he?"

I assumed that he simply didn't want to believe me, that he'd carried the anger around so long that he was comfortable with it. Gloria explained what had happened, then Alicia and Esperanza both hugged me. Their husbands shook my hand. Chava simply stood back and said nothing, but his wife hugged me. It wasn't much, but it was a start.

My younger brother soon disappeared down the hall, so I asked Gloria, "Shall I relieve you?"

"No, I'm staying with him. But maybe tomorrow afternoon."

"Okay, I'll be here then." I decided to drive all the way back to Sacramento that night so I could have my final well-baby meeting with Dr. Nimitz the next morning, and to pack a larger bag. I said good-bye to my sister-in-law and the rest of the family, then walked into the dark parking lot. The light rain had stopped and I was feeling as relieved as I had after Confession when I opened my car's front door, only to hear my younger brother's voice.

"Marty."

As I turned I was jolted by a punch, my head snapping back, my arms automatically coming up into a defensive position. I almost lost my balance on the wet pavement. A second punch grazed my face, and I blocked a third, though I was still dazed from the first one.

Chava was popping me. What the hell was going on? Then I heard him cry as he launched his fists, "Why'd you do it, Marty? Why'd you *do* it?" All the Martinez boys had been raised to fight, so I guess hitting was the only way he knew to express emotions as strong as he was feeling. There'd never been anything subtle about my little brother.

I made no effort to punch him back, but I did dodge and block his efforts as best I could. A fireman, he stayed in good shape and I wasn't fully recovered. I was afraid he'd wear me down and really hurt me. Then, as suddenly as the punches started, they stopped and Chava embraced me, sobbing. "He's gonna die, Marty. Manny's gonna die."

"It's okay, Chava," I said. "He's in God's hands. He's in God's hands."

I glanced about the parking lot, but no one seemed to have noticed the quick fray. Good, since I assumed that Latinos caught fighting in Merced were still put in jail without much discussion.

Once he calmed, I explained to him that I had a doctor's appointment early the next morning. He wanted me to spend the night with Cindy and him, but he understood. I didn't mention cancer. I did promise that I would return to the hospital the next day, then I gave him another long hug.

I drove home, one cheek icy where Chava had connected, but I was happy. If punching me purged him and helped him forgive me for what I'd done, it was well worth it. They could all punch me.

■

When I finally arrived home late that night I telephoned Miranda, but there was no answer; then I remembered she was on call and was possibly at the hospital, so I didn't worry about not reaching her. I left my daughter a message about Uncle Manuel, and left one on Johnny O's machine, too.

Before brushing my teeth and turning in—my heart churning over all that had happened—I stretched out on the floor to do sit-ups and push-ups. I felt myself squirting urine with each effort: small, warm bursts. I snapped for a moment, cursing—"Damn! Damn! Damn!"—and pounding the floor. I seemed to be losing the urine battle, no matter how many kegels I did, no matter how many cinches. I had less and less urinary control as the radiation wore on. I'd been told to expect this, but I still hated it. Radiation was burning everything in my groin, but what choice did I have? And my brother was dying. Sometimes I felt like I was losing control of everything ... feeling sorry for myself again.

What the hell was I thinking? I was lucky to have a brother, to be back in my family, to have a wonderful woman in my life. I pulled tightly into myself and began a prayer of thanks: "Our Father ..."

■

The first thing I remembered when I awakened the next morning and staggered into the bathroom was that I had neglected to use the penile pump the previous day. I would pump up after I showered, but first I'd have to mop the urine off the floor around the toilet. I was getting up to pee every hour or so all night, stumbling more asleep than awake into the bathroom and missing the toilet about as often as I hit it. I guess one good thing was that no one but Miranda, who understood, saw the embarrassing puddles I mopped up most mornings.

As I drank the single cup of coffee I allowed myself, I telephoned her and explained what was happening with my family. I told her I'd try to drop by in the evening, but that would depend on my brother's situation. I'd call in any case.

"Marty," she said just before hanging up, "I'll pray for your brother."

"I'll miss you ... *more than you know, more than you know.*" I broke into burlesque singing because it was easier than revealing the surge of emotion I was feeling.

"You nut." She laughed. "Call me."

"For sure." As I hung up, the doorbell rang. There stood Johnny O. "Johnny's gotta go to work, Champ, but I brought this card for Manny. Give it to him, please. Tell him Johnny loves him, Champ, and that he's prayin' for him." His voice broke as he handed me an envelope.

"Sure," I said. "Have you been in a fight?" A nasty bruise blackened one of his eyes.

"Naw." He grinned and said, "Johnny took a nose dive at work the other day. What happened to *you*, Champ?"

"Chava popped me."

"He did? You duke his ass?"

"Naw. He's just upset about Manny."

"I hear that," he muttered. "Tell Chava Johnny says hi." That I'd been hit because my brother was upset didn't surprise him; he was from the same neighborhood.

"Okay. You want a cup of coffee, Johnny?"

"Thanks anyway, Champ, but Johnny's gotta go to work. My son Javier — he's from Nina — he's gonna meet me. I'm gonna loan him some money for a down payment on a car."

"Okay." I smiled and patted his shoulder. "Tell Javi I said hi."

Just then a name occurred to me. "Hey, Johnny, is Lester Jackson still a minister?"

"Yeah, ol' Lester he's got that little Baptist church."

"Do you have his phone number?"

"Sure, Champ. What's up?"

"I'm getting married," I revealed.

"To the doctor?" Johnny asked.

"Yep."

"She's a good lady, Champ." My pal dictated the phone number, then hurried off.

I checked my watch. It wasn't too early to telephone Lester. He was another ex-boxer whom I'd known casually over the years, and he responded cordially to me. We made small talk for a bit, discussing Johnny and some bouts we'd both seen, then I finally moved to purpose of my call. "I'm going to marry a lady named Miranda Mossi, Lester. Would you perform the ceremony?"

"Of course. It'd be an honor, brother. Is that *Doctor* Mossi, by the way?" he asked.

"Yes."

"A fine lady. Dr. Mossi treated my daughter-in-law Arletha when she had that terrible infection, and some of the poor families in the church, they go to her. She let 'em pay what they can or she doesn't charge at all if they can't pay. She hand out drug samples so they don't have to buy expensive medicine, too. She's a special lady. She might not remember me, but I talked to her last year at the ecumenical breakfast."

"We'd like to be married down by the river, maybe across from Sac State near the pedestrian bridge."

I heard the ex-boxer chuckle, then he said, "You gettin' old for a hippie weddin', brother, but it's your ceremony—yours and your lady's and God's—not mine."

"Miranda'd prefer that setting."

"So be it. You're a lucky man, brother."

"Don't I know it. I'll tell you, Lester, I keep learning new things about that woman. To me she's a jewel."

"Seem like."

Lester and I arbitrarily set the wedding date for two weeks from the next Saturday. I assumed it would be no tux-and-matching-pink-dresses affair, that we'd keep it as casual as possible. I knew that Kathy Mettler would be Miranda's maid of honor and I was going to ask Chava to be my best man.

I telephoned my daughter after talking with Lester, but again only managed to speak to her answering machine. Maybe she and Randy were out of town.

18

My appointment with Dr. Nimitz went quickly. He offered only one admonition: "The radiation will keep working for months after we stop, so as a precaution I advise that you carry extra pads and underpants when you travel." He noticed my eyebrows raise, I guess, because he quickly added, "It's what I'd do if I were in your situation, Mr. Martinez . . . in case of temporary bowel problems."

Great, I thought. What next?

As soon as I left his office, ready to drive to Merced, I remembered one more obligation. Near the parking lot, I found a booth—thinking it was time to buy a cell phone—and called the newspaper to tell Ned Schmidt that I'd have to have an extension for the feature on irrigation I was writing. He hadn't been talking to me much lately, and all I got was his answering machine, although I was certain he was monitoring it.

When I thought about Ned's health, I was almost more worried than when I thought about my own. I knew I should insist that he listen to me, but . . . Answering machines and the way they were used made me uncertain that technology had done much to improve human communication, but I didn't have time to worry about it right then.

It had rained off and on throughout the night, so the day was crystalline as I got on the road. Below Turlock I again gazed at fields in which my siblings and I had worked. To the east, the Sierra Nevada loomed, blue with snow-crusted peaks, while the streams the highway crossed were swollen by rain and snowmelt from those distant mountains. When we were kids, Manny would assemble the whole gang of us and drive us in his jalopy to the river outside Merced to fish and swim. "This water comes all the way from Yosemite," he told me once, but I — a know-it-all eighth grader — hadn't believed him. I'd heard of Yosemite, of course, but had never seen it. To me it was like Disneyland — just some rich person's invention.

Only years later did Nancy and I actually take our kids to Yosemite Valley. Sure enough, right down its core flowed the Merced River. Once more Manuel had been right.

Near my hometown, empty fields surrounded the highway — or apparently empty fields. Actually, they were as developed as a Los Angeles parking lot: agriculture without many farmhouses. Once, riding Amtrak to Bakersfield, I'd heard one matron say to another: "Look at all that land and no homes for people. What a waste!" I'd been tempted to ask exactly where she thought her food came from, but kept my mouth shut. Now, around Merced and nearby towns, houses were indeed replacing agriculture, and that same question remained: "Where will our food come from?"

When I arrived at the hospital early that afternoon, my younger brother's face told me all I needed to know. "Manuel?" I asked, and Chava grasped me, hugging hard as he said, "He's brain-dead. Gloria's still in there with him, and so are Esperanza and Alicia and Cindy."

"He's *dead?*"

"He's brain-dead. The priest has already been here, but the doctors still have his body hooked up. They want us to donate his organs. Gloria doesn't know what to do. She wants to talk to you."

"I brought this for Manuel, a card from Johnny O," I said. "I called him last night and he came by this morning with this."

Chava grunted. "Johnny O. He was one tough *vato.* He and Manny almost killed each other that time."

"He has great respect for our brother. He told me Manny was the toughest guy he ever fought." We fell silent then, each caught in our own thoughts, our own memories, until I squeezed one of my brother's thick arms and turned for the door into the intensive care unit.

As soon as I'd greeted my sisters and sisters-in-law, Gloria asked them to leave us alone so she could talk to me. They complied without a blink.

Gloria all but collapsed as soon as they departed, sobbing, "It's like my heart's been torn out. Why did God do this? We've been together since high school. Forty-six wonderful years."

I tried to soothe her. "God gave you forty-six years, dear. More than my mama and papa got."

She was shaking her head, tears streaming down her cheeks. "I don't know how I'll live without him. I don't think I want to. It just feels like it's all ending so soon."

"You'll live for the kids, Gloria, and for the grandkids, because Manny would want you to. He'll be with you, and he'll be waiting for you in Heaven. I really believe that. Live with his memory the way you'd live with him. He'll be there."

She gazed at me then. "And with all your education, you really do believe in that, in Heaven, I mean?"

"I really do, Gloria. The same way I know Dougie's still with me."

She paused and wiped her eyes with a handkerchief, seeming to consider what I'd said, then choked, "Marty, I don't know what to do. Now the doctors want to cut him up and take his organs. They make me feel like I have to."

"You don't have to do anything, dear. You tell me what you want, and I'll deal with the doctors for you."

"Manuel always made all the decisions for us. I'm not even sure how much money we have for his funeral. He didn't tell me. He just gave me money each month to run the household."

I was embracing her lightly, rubbing her back, and I said, "Don't worry about money for his funeral. I'll take care of it, and I'll help you straighten out the family finances. My brother would never leave you without resources. It's just a matter of finding them."

We sat then in the chairs next to Manuel, who looked about the same, except that his eyes were closed, and that machinery still buzzed, still pumped. I suddenly felt myself drifting toward rage: This was a kind of torture for Gloria and me and the rest, my brother dead but kept here like a mummy in front of us.

"I don't want them to cut him up, Marty." My sister-in-law began sobbing once more.

"Okay, then that's that."

"But that doctor he told me Jimmy Aparicio's grandson needs a kidney, and that Manuel could help him."

This stopped me. Suddenly it wasn't just an abstract issue of organ donation, it was the grandson of a neighborhood pal. "What's wrong with Jimmy's grandson?"

"I don't know. He has to go on a machine all the time to clean his blood."

I suddenly puffed like a winded horse. "Okay, let me talk to the doctor and to Jimmy, find out what's really going on. If this is life and death, let me have you talk to a friend of mine, a doctor named Miranda Mossi. She'll tell us the truth."

"And you trust this doctor?"

"I'm going to marry her, Gloria."

My sister-in-law's eyes registered that.

I had no luck reaching anyone at the Aparicio house, but my conversation with Dr. Nguyen, the youthful resident, confirmed that one of the people in town who desperately needed organs was Buzzy Aparicio, the grandson of a guy I'd gone through school with. "You know," the young physician added, "we seem to have an inordinate number of young people killed around here, mostly in traffic accidents, but the immigrant families simply won't donate organs. They seem to equate it with witchcraft or something. My family is that way," he added.

My next question seemed to startle him. "Is this a for-profit situation?"

"You mean do we charge?"

"No, I mean is there a company involved that's harvesting organs, then selling them back?"

The question seemed to shock Dr. Nguyen. "Of course not," he sputtered. "Where'd you get that idea?"

"I'm a journalist with the *Sacramento Express,* Doctor, and I can tell you that California has more than its share of companies operating that way."

"Well, we work directly with the team at the UC Davis Medical Center in Sacramento. There's no intermediary."

"Okay. I'll see if I can talk my sister-in-law into donating. My brother would've wanted to help Jimmy's grandson."

Before talking to Gloria again, I alerted Miranda — who was home that day, thank God — that I might need her to talk on the telephone to my sister-in-law about organ donation. Then I presented my opinion to my brother's grieving wife, ending with "Manny'd want you to help that boy."

Gloria said she wanted to help Buzzy, too, but she didn't want her husband cut up.

Finally she agreed to talk to Dr. Mossi. I wasn't privy to what was said between them, but Miranda convinced Gloria and soothed her, because once she'd hung up, my sister-in-law said to me, "If the kids agree, I'll let the doctors help Buzzy."

Then she added, "I like your friend, Marty. I invited her to Manuel's funeral. If she's going to join the family, we might as well meet her now."

■

Late that afternoon the clan assembled in the meditation room down the hall from intensive care. Dr. Nguyen told them about the request to donate organs, then I spoke, then Gloria. Most of the kids were better educated than their mother and father had been, but this was their father's body, so masks of resistance froze their faces. When their mother talked about Buzzy Aparicio, though, one daughter—Allison—gasped and said, "He's in school with my Lisa," and the masks began to soften.

Manny and Gloria's oldest son, Tom, used the term "cut up," but Dr. Nguyen, who wasn't much older than my nephew, said gently, "This is done like all surgical procedures, with care and precision. We don't just harvest organs. We know what's at stake for families. I'll perform this procedure the same way I would if I was transplanting an organ from my own father."

He reached into his pocket and pulled out a wallet. From it he removed his driver's license and turned it around so we could all see a pink card. "That's my donor's card," he said. "It gives permission to remove usable organs from my body after my death. I want all of you to know that I'm committed to this."

I had almost without thought signed up for the same program when I last renewed my license. Somehow, throughout this difficult afternoon, I had forgotten about it, but I removed my license from my wallet and held it out for everyone to see.

That seemed to quiet all opposition, and Dr. Nguyen hugged Gloria, then said, "Your husband will save at least one life."

Chava spoke up then. "That's how he lived, Doctor. That's how my brother lived."

I telephoned Lea from the hospital, actually hearing her voice for a change. "I've got sad news. Uncle Manuel's dead."

"What happened?" She sounded stunned.

After I explained as carefully as I could, Lea said, "Oh, Daddy, I'm so sorry." Her voice swooped. "When's the service?"

"Saturday at eleven at Our Lady of Mercy."

"How's Aunt Gloria?"

"Not good, and neither are the kids." I explained all that had gone on to my daughter, all except the punch-out with Chava, and she agreed that donating her uncle's organs was wonderful.

Finally, I said, "Lea, you should call your mother. She was fond of Manny, and he sure liked her."

"Why don't you?"

"You should call her, honey. I know she won't be able to come to the funeral Mass, but she should know, and it's better if she learns about it from you."

"Better for who?"

To deflect her attention, I almost said, "For *whom.*" Instead I told the truth: "For me."

■

For some reason, I was embroiled in a sexual fantasy as I awakened that next morning, sweating and tangled in my sheets, sensing that my penis was miraculously erect. When I groggily reached down and felt, though, it was a flaccid nub, but tingling. The experience had been as real as life, but still my body couldn't respond. Chemical castration sure wasn't killing my memory. I needed a shower — a long, cold one.

Miranda and I picked up Johnny O before we drove south to Merced and the evening Rosary service for Manny. "Oh, hi, Doctor," said the boxer as he climbed into the backseat.

"Hi, *Miranda,*" she said. "Remember?"

He grinned. "Johnny never called a doctor by his name before."

"I'm not a his," said Miranda.

"You're sure not," agreed my homeboy, still a ladies' man.

We talked about Manuel and the Martinezes and various neighborhood pals as we drove to Merced, and Miranda more than once looked at me with some wonder; these were new stories to her. "Oh yeah," Johnny said at one point, "don't let this guy fool you, Doctor Miranda. He was another one of those battlin' Martinezes. He kicked some ass, lady, I'll tell you that."

Miranda grinned at me and said, "I thought you were a *student?*"

"I got good grades."

"And . . . ?"

This time I had to grin. "Well, if I took any crap and didn't fight back, my older brother would've beaten me like an omelette, so I always fought back."

Johnny added, "He fought good."

"You *guys,*" said Miranda. "My father was a banker, and I don't think I ever heard of any of my cousins having fistfights. How'd a roughneck like you become a journalist, Marty Martinez? Punch your way in?"

I had to laugh. "Nothing so dramatic. I started writing sports for the high school newspaper because a good teacher encouraged me, old Mr. Lister — remember him, Johnny?"

"Ol' Listerine? Yeah, he was a good guy."

"Anyway, I got pretty good at it, so the local newspaper hired me to cover sports while I was still in junior college — I even wrote about some of my own wrestling matches, and I always sounded like a real champ in those stories." I laughed. "Anyway, when I went away to the university I majored in journalism. I went to work for the Bakersfield paper after I graduated, and the *Express* eventually hired me because my name's Hispanic—that's what was going on then—but I proved I could write and dig up facts, so I'm still there after thirty-one years."

"This guy, he won a bunch of writing prizes," Johnny interjected.

"I know," Miranda said. "He makes me look at the certificates hanging on his walls every time I visit."

Johnny was laughing and I was about to reply when my bowels suddenly, urgently bubbled. I thought I was about to pass gas, so I cinched—did a tight kegel—but I could barely resist the urge. Oh, man! I began searching desperately for a rest stop, a service station, a park—anyplace with a bathroom.

"Are you okay?" Miranda asked.

I hated to reply, but I said, "My incontinence just kicked in. I've *got* to stop."

Her hand gripped my forearm and she said, "It's okay, Marty. Do what you have to do. Johnny and I are grown-ups."

I don't think Johnny understood what was occurring, at least not until he saw me pussyfooting to the restroom of an Exxon station. What he couldn't see was me thanking Dr. Nimitz for advising that I carry spare underpants and pads.

The cleanup required that I wash myself with wet paper towels in the locked men's room, throw away my soiled underpants, then simply take a deep breath or two. I had to pull my trousers up and troop out to the car to grab that clean pair of shorts, plus another pad, from the trunk. After returning to the restroom and clothing myself, I finally went back to the car.

Miranda had explained to Johnny what was likely happening to me, so my old buddy simply patted my shoulder after I returned to the driver's seat, saying, "Hang in there, Champ."

Miranda placed her hand on my thigh as I pulled back into traffic, and she said softly, "I love you."

When I'd finally calmed down, I asked her quietly, "What causes a bowel explosion like that?"

"Most likely you've developed radiation colitis. With any luck it'll pass as you get over the effects of the radiation."

"And if I don't have luck?"

"Carry spares," she said.

■

The Rosary for Manny was held that evening at the church in which we Martinezes had all been baptized. It seemed to have shrunk, but it wasn't much changed since the last time I'd attended Mass there—a Christmas midnight service with the whole clan the year before Mama died.

My family gathered in the first two rows, and an old priest whom I didn't know led the incantatory prayers that soothed us: "*Hail Mary, full of grace, the Lord is with thee . . .*"

We responded, over and over, "*Holy Mary Mother of God pray for us sinners now and at the hour of our death, amen,*" until the response became a chant and the chant became our breath. I was on automatic pilot by the time the service ended.

Before returning to the sacristy, the priest shook hands with everyone in the family section, saying to me as he grasped mine, "We'll certainly miss Manuel. He was one of the parish's stalwarts."

There was an interesting assemblage on the darkened parking lot after the prayers, but I was too tired to much enjoy it. An old classmate named Jaime Doyle did pull me aside and whispered, "Marty, I just want you to know that Luz is in a nursing home now. She's got that Alzheimer's deal."

"Alzheimer's? Luz? Jesus, she's so young. I'm really sorry to hear that, Jaime." His wife had been a classmate of Raul's, a cheerleader whose leaps had seemed bionic.

His eyes were watery when he said, "She always liked you and Raul." Then he swallowed hard and added, "She don't know me or the kids anymore. She don't know no one."

Emotionally exhausted and physically pooped, too, I could think of nothing more to say, so I hugged Jaime, said I'd remember his wife and him in my prayers, then turned toward Miranda and said, "Let's go."

Johnny had already slipped away to spend the night with his cousin Consuela and her family, but I had to tell my own insistent kin that my physical condition made it impossible for me to feel comfortable in someone else's home. "Oh, come on," Esperanza argued, insisting, "Bob and I have plenty of room. Don't we, hon?"

Her husband, Bob Mardikian, who Rollie once proclaimed "wouldn't say shit if he had a mouthful," grunted, "Yep."

Miranda replied simply, "He's right. There are medical reasons for him not to."

"Oh," said my sister. End of discussion.

On our way to the motel, I said, "You know how to use that M.D. when you have to."

"It has its advantages," she said. "Are you okay, though?"

"Tired and sad, but okay."

"There was sure a gang of people wanting to touch base with you . . . and with Johnny, too."

"Johnny took care of them," I said. "I'll feel more like socializing tomorrow when I've rested."

As we pulled into the parking lot at the Best Western, Miranda asked, "What was that cluster of men — Mexican men, I'd guess — all wearing cowboy clothes? There were some women and kids, too, but those men with those boots and jeans and hats with tassels really caught my eye. They were like a group within the group. What was that about?"

"Alicia told me Manny'd been coordinating an outreach program for the church to help undocumented Mexicans who worked around here. He was trying to help them with legal status, but with other things, too, like finding them groceries when they were hungry. I'm sure that's how those people knew him."

"He must have been quite a man," she said.

19

Manny's funeral Mass at Our Lady of Mercy was like a multi-year reunion of Merced High School. We Martinezes — counting aunts and uncles — spanned nearly fifty years there, and now various nieces and nephews were students at the school, so the church was overflowing with mourners. Manuel had been cremated and his ashes privately buried in the family plot, but Johnny, Chava, and I were honorary pallbearers, along with Al Rocha, Junius Peppers, and Ben Gonsalves — guys Manny'd played ball with in high school.

Throughout the ceremony, Jimmy and Josefa Aparicio hovered on the edge of the crowd. As soon as the priest invited everyone to join the family for lunch in the parish hall, though, the Aparicios sought out Gloria and embraced her. Manny and Gloria's kids were quickly involved, with many tears, and I heard Jimmy say to my sister-in-law, "Anything you ever need from us, Gloria, just call. *Anything.* Our families are one now." Jimmy and Josefa were driving to Sacramento to visit their grandson in the hospital, so they couldn't stay for lunch, but Jimmy grabbed me just before they departed and said, "Don't worry about Gloria or the kids; we'll be here to help them."

"Thanks, Jimmy."

"No. Thank *you.*"

■

The party that followed in the parish hall would have delighted Manuel. While Miranda got to know my sisters and nieces, I joined the old-guys table. Al Rocha noticed the bruise on my face, and said, "Don't you Martinezes ever quit? Hell, I ain't had a street fight since I was fifty." That broke everyone up, and Johnny said, "Rocha, you couldn't fight when you *could* fight!"

"I'll tell you what, *vato,* you're lucky I didn't turn pro and knock you out." That gave everyone a big laugh, since Al had always been a clown, not a battler.

As it turned out, he had married one of my old high school girlfriends, Margarita Bernal, so he said to me, "You made it real easy for me, Marty. After a pug-ugly like you, I looked real good to her," and everyone laughed once more.

I saw Jaime Doyle eating at a nearby table, so I walked to him, put my hand on his shoulder, and said, "I'm sorry I couldn't talk last night, Jaime. I didn't feel well."

"That's okay, Marty."

"I just want you to know how sorry I am about Luz. She's a wonderful gal, a great mother. If there's anything I can do . . ."

His eyes began blinking and he whispered, "Pray for her."

I squeezed his shoulder, saying, "And for you, buddy."

A husky young man sitting next to Jaime said, "Dad?"

"Oh, Marty," my old friend said, "this is our son, Ernie . . . we call him *Torito.* He's a linebacker for the Bears." He turned toward his son and said, "Marty here played safety when I was on the team."

"Were you guys any good?" *Torito* asked with a smile.

"Everyone's favorite opponent," I replied.

That was the tone, a gathering of old friends sad to have lost Manny but delighted to have known him and to be together. Johnny O, who rarely returned to Merced, said to me, "Man, there was some sinners takin' Communion for Manuel today. Johnny oughta know, because he was one of 'em."

An Okie classmate named Archie Young said, "I'm gonna join this Catholic deal if it's so easy it'll take you two jokers."

"*Pendejo* Holy Rollers!" Johnny winked. "No wonder all the Martinezes used to kick the shit out of you."

"In their fuckin' dreams," snapped Archie.

"Remember that night we all got drunk and went swimming in the big canal?" Rocha said. "This Okie"—he nodded toward Archie—"he took off buck naked with a machete hacking the branches off trees in the orchard across the road. He's lucky he didn't cut off his chorizo!"

"Sheee-it, dick's too small a target, man," laughed Junius Peppers, the huge black man who now coached track at MHS.

"Ask your mama!" Archie snapped and everyone broke up.

Suddenly Johnny O dropped his plate. No one bumped him, so it was a surprise—as much to him as to us.

"Hey, man, paper plates don't break," advised Chava. "Go get a refill. We pay a Mexican kid to clean up."

I laughed at my brother's words, although I knew what he meant. I said, "Hey, Chava, I thought *you* were a Mexican kid." My younger brother had briefly been a foot soldier in *el movimiento* a couple decades before.

"This kid's a *real* Mexican, smart-ass," replied Chava, an edge creeping into his voice.

We were all laughing, but Johnny did what my brother advised, loaded another plate. I noticed a baffled look on the ex-boxer's face.

"Hey," Junius said, grinning, "you remember when Johnny and Manuel put turpentine on that dog's ass and let him loose in the assembly at the school? You guys got swats from old Mr. Gilman, didn't you?"

"Yeah," Johnny said. "He tried to make us cry, but Johnny and Manuel didn't. Gilman, he couldn't hit all that hard. Remember, Manny used to call him Mr. Bozo because he had those red cheeks and that red nose?"

Junius shook his head. "He was a racist motherfucker, too. If you were a Blood or a Chicano, you didn't have to do much to get swats from him. White dudes like Gonsalves and Young here could shit in the hall and get home free."

Big Ben grinned and said, "Hey, my old man told me Gilman'd done the same thing to Portugee kids in the old days. He'd been there forever."

"Why didn't anybody knock the hell out of him?" I asked.

Johnny answered, "Because he was vice principal. Gilman was nothin', but vice principal was a big deal. Besides, if I'd've duked him, my papa would've killed me."

Ben added, "Today, some kid might shoot his ass."

"You got that right. It's a different world today, man," said Junius. "It's a cold-blooded world."

While the beer flowed and the stories continued, I noticed off to the side of the room that Gloria had joined Esperanza, Alicia, Cindy, and Miranda. I don't know what was said, but soon the four were talking animatedly, then my sisters-in-law and sisters were introducing Miranda to various cousins and aunts and uncles.

Chava pulled me aside and asked, "What's up with Johnny? It's like he's clumsy all of a sudden. Is he punchy or what?"

"Johnny? Naw," I replied. "He still talks okay; he still thinks okay. He delivered a hell of a lot more punches that he ever caught."

"He sure doesn't move the same way," Chava said.

"I know."

Hugs and tears and kisses finally saw us off. As soon as we pulled onto the road, Miranda smiled and said, "You have a wonderful family, Marty. Every color of the rainbow. And Gloria's so gracious."

Johnny chimed in, too. "You know, I never met Marques, Alicia's husband, before. He said he fought in the Golden Gloves back in Louisiana. How'd she meet him?"

"He was stationed at the air force base."

"He's a good guy. He looks a little like Sugar Ray."

"Yeah, he does. Chava told me Marques and Manny got to be real close," I added.

"Marques says that oldest daughter of theirs is a volleyball star at the high school now," Johnny went on.

"You know, if they'd had girls' sports in the old days like they do now, Alicia might've been a star. She was a great athlete, and so was Esperanza."

"What's this?" asked Miranda as I rounded a corner near the train depot.

"I want to show you the place where we Martinezes were raised," I said as I slowed the car. "Right there." I pointed at the small stucco house with its grassless yard and burnished chinaberry tree. "It's funny, but I haven't lived there for over forty years, and my family's been out of it for nearly thirty, but this is still home . . . It still grips me."

"We had some good times there, Champ," said Johnny.

"Yeah, we did," I agreed as I turned the car toward Sacramento.

We dropped Johnny off at his mobile home in the early evening, then I drove Miranda to her place. Both of us were fatigued; it had been a long, emotional day. As we embraced to say good night, I heard myself say, "Miranda, thanks for being you."

She pulled back for a moment and eyed me, smiling. "Marty, come in with me. I don't want to be alone tonight. I don't want you to be alone either." She smiled and kissed my cheek. "Come in and hold me, dear," she said. "That's all I ask. Don't worry about your libido."

■

Lester Jackson conducted a brief wedding rehearsal at the river. Kathy Mettler was there, as was Johnny O, standing in for Chava, my best man, who couldn't get off fire duty for the practice. Miranda's oldest son, James, scheduled to give her away, was flying out from Denver, so he missed the rehearsal too. No big deal, since this was to be a relatively informal ceremony. To my surprise, though, Lea showed up and stood to one side looking nervous after greeting us.

Just as the rehearsal ended, we heard the multi-toned calls of geese approaching. "Canadian honkers," said Reverend Jackson, shielding his eyes with one hand and searching the sky. "Coming this way." We all gazed upward, since the birds sounded closer each moment, but the trees surrounding us obscured our view until those calls grew loud indeed, then a ragged wedge of fliers — perhaps a dozen — passed above us. The geese were so close that we could see their heads panning slightly as though searching the terrain.

"How wonderful," Miranda said, and she squeezed my arm. "I love that sound. It's a good omen."

The minister smiled and said, "That was a treat." Then he added, "Tomorrow I'll bring this little arbor deal I've got and put it up right here. It'll give us a place to focus on. A couple of my boys will help me haul it over."

"That'll be a nice addition, Reverend Jackson," said Miranda. "Now let Marty and I take you all out to lunch, won't you?"

He smiled, "Why, thank you."

"Everyone," Miranda said, "let's meet at Cafe Michoacán on I Street over near the university for lunch."

As we walked toward our cars, I said to my daughter, "Do you want to drive over with us?"

She hesitated, then said, "Sure."

We three traveled silently toward the restaurant until, just as I pulled into the parking lot, my daughter said in a strangely froggy voice, "Miranda, can I ask you something?"

I thought, Oh shit! Lea's going to start trouble.

"Why are you marrying my father?"

Miranda turned and smiled at my daughter, who was riding in the backseat. "Because I won't have to change the monograms on my underwear," she said.

"*Excuse me?*" My daughter blinked, suddenly fighting back tears when she responded: "I'm *serious.*"

"Because we love one another, Lea, that's why," Miranda replied softly. "Because we need one another."

"Oh," said my daughter.

■

A white arbor was in place when Miranda and I, along with my brother and sister-in-law, arrived at the riverbank for the wedding. Reverend Jackson awaited us in his vestments, and he sure didn't look much like an ex-pug. Two handsome young men who resembled him stood on either side of the arbor, supporting it. Somebody, likely Lester's family, had sprinkled flower petals on the ground around it. The whole arrangement looked more formal than I had imagined it would.

"Getting cold feet?" asked Miranda.

"Not likely."

Lea and Randy arrived shortly after we did, and so did Kathy and Nick Mettler, as well as Chava and Cindy. Johnny O trailed in soon after they did, as did James and his wife, Cynthia, and Miranda's middle son, Nick, and his pregnant wife, Loni, plus Miranda's grandchildren. Robbie had also been invited, but, to quote his oldest brother, "He's still acting like an asshole." That was the wedding party.

"Shall we start?" asked the minister.

We nodded and assembled at the arbor. No sooner had Lester begun reading the ceremony, than we heard buzzing and loud talk coming from the paved jogging path a few yards away, then a gaggle of Rollerbladers whizzed by, talking loud enough to be heard over the whir of their skates. The minister shook his head, then carried on.

Behind us, on the trail, an older couple stopped and watched the ceremony. Then a disheveled young man carrying an old sleeping bag in a clear plastic sack paused and watched too. Just as we reached the "I do" part, a group of joggers struggled past, conversing loudly about the collapsing marriage of Justin and Briana, whoever they were.

As I kissed the bride, another gang of joggers puffed by, and a long-haired kid called, "Good luck, dude and dudette!"

I laughed. "We really picked a romantic spot."

Miranda smiled and said, "It's romantic enough," so I kissed her again.

"Chava," I said then, "give that homeless guy this, will you?" I slipped him a twenty.

My brother took the bill and said, "If I'm ever on the street I'm coming up here. You're easy." Then he walked to the man and handed him the bill. The recipient at first looked shocked, then he smiled and waved thank you to me. I gave him a thumbs-up.

It seemed like a perfect wedding.

■

We awoke late the next morning. Actually, I roused first and I lay there watching her sleep—those full lips, those heavy lashes, that wonderful nose. She shrugged and the sheet fell from her chest, exposing not only her full breast but the large scar where tissue had been folded closed when her other breast was removed. I'd never really examined it because that absence of one breast didn't interest me nearly as much as the remaining one did. I wanted to devour her, but merely watched and watched and watched until her dark eyes fluttered open. I gave in then and kissed the inside of her left arm.

She smiled sleepily. "Give me a second," Miranda said, and she rose so gracefully that she reminded me of the river, and disappeared into the bathroom. A few moments later, she returned to bed, extended her smooth arm and said, "Now, where were we?"

"Here," I said, as I kissed the crook of her elbow.

After much smooching and petting, Miranda said breathlessly, "Let's try something else." She straddled me and after some manipulation, began to gently rock on my full-but-soft penis, slowly at first, then faster and with greater intensity, her eyes closed, her lips tight, her breath hissing. I knew what was happening, so I did my best to keep my penis flush against her until, with a great gasp, she relaxed and collapsed over me, her hair covering my face.

We remained that way for what seemed a long while. Finally, she asked, "Did you come, dear?"

"No, that's out for now, but you did. That's good enough for me."

"I sure did," she said.

BOOK TWO

20

I moved into Miranda's house after we married; that left my place empty, but not for long. My daughter, who seemed to accept my union cordially though not joyously, had moved into Randy Lozano's apartment, and soon they were talking about marriage and even kids.

Instead of renting the old family house to strangers, I stunned Lea and Randy, who I knew were just scraping by financially due mostly to credit-card debt dating to their old relationships, when I offered them free use of it. Randy stammered, "We couldn't do that, Marty. We've got the condo . . ."

My daughter sounded almost offended as she gasped, "Daddy!"

"No rent," I said, "but I'd want you to put some money away for your little boy's education each month, Randy. I'd trust you to do that."

"Okay." He sounded dazed.

"But Daddy . . . ," said Lea. Then, after catching his eye, she said to me, "Randy and I have to talk this over."

I'd expected that, since she had to talk everything over. "Honey," I said, "the house is going to be yours anyway. I'd rather you two got your finances in order right now so you can enjoy life. Not paying rent should help you do that."

I wasn't entirely philanthropic in this, by the way, since the thought of sifting through years of accumulated papers and junk in order to clean before renting was daunting indeed. This way, I could seal my junk in my old den, or perhaps the garage, then dip into it occasionally as I deemed necessary. I had, after all, many file cabinets full of notes and research I'd always intended to use someday—which I had come to understand meant that my survivors would one day have the task of throwing it all away. Being a pack rat, I kept it anyway.

Following a few more starts and stops, Lea and Randy came to their senses and accepted. After they moved in, my wife and I occasionally lunched with them and Tyler, Randy's three-year old, a bright little redhead . . . who in turn gave me the pleasant illusion that I was a grandfather. Randy himself, as I got to know him better, seemed to be a good, hardworking kid who, like Lea, had gotten on a wrong track early, been through the mill, and was now ready to settle down.

Although I really wished that they'd marry if they were serious, especially about having children, I kept my mouth shut about that. Besides, if Lea had married her earlier live-ins, we'd all be less happy today. Anyway, letting them have the use of the house gave me the feeling that I'd done something good.

I was happy, most of all, that my daughter and my wife seemed to get along. That was much better than Miranda's situation: Robbie hadn't spoken to his mother since before the wedding. Fortunately, though, her other two boys were gems.

■

Miranda suggested that we celebrate our second wedding anniversary at a fashion show sponsored by the boutique she and Kathy Mettler owned at the hospital, but that we keep it quiet — a party just between the two of us while we enjoyed the company of friends. That sounded fine to me.

The American Cancer Society became a cosponsor and soon announced that an unnamed "special celebrity guest" would appear. I asked Miranda who it was, but she wouldn't tell me. "What makes a secret guest important is that he or she is really secret — even from you."

"Give me a hint: animal, vegetable, or mineral?"

"No way."

"Boy, you're tough," I said. "I ought to cut you off."

"Don't you dare." She smiled, kissed me, and pinched my rear.

I called to ask if the *Express* would allow me to write a piece on the gathering for the local feature section. The mystery of the special guest added glamour, and Bob Romaine, who'd replaced the retired Ned Schmidt as editor, went along with the idea, mumbling something about "public service." After a moment, he added, "Oh yeah, the corporation just sent out a new executive editor."

"Who?"

"Some young hotshot from back East named Roswell Gilbert."

"*Roswell?* Boy, with a name like that, he's lucky he didn't go to Merced High School. He'd've been pantsed." I laughed, then added, "I'll get started on this story right away, Bob."

I wrote the piece, and it was published the next Sunday morning in the Sacramento Life section, along with a photograph of the two boutique owners. "This should really help attendance," Kathy told me, "and bring in some money for the ACS. Thanks, Marty."

■

A week before the fashion show was scheduled, Johnny O called. "Hey, Champ," he said, "do you think Dr. Miranda would mind if Johnny went to see her? My boss, he wants me to have a checkup. He's gonna pay."

"Mind? No, she'd be happy to see you. You sick?" I asked.

"Me? Naw, I just need a checkup because I been droppin' stuff. No big deal."

"When you call the office for an appointment tell the receptionist that I told you to call. That might sneak you in today if there's a cancellation."

"Okay, Champ. Thanks."

I all but forgot that conversation as the day wore on, but when Miranda returned home that evening, she said, "Johnny was in today. I'm sending him to a specialist. I'm troubled by his symptoms."

"Too many punches?"

"Could be," she said. "Muhammad Ali's not the only ex-boxer with brain damage."

"Could it be something else?"

She shrugged, "It could be a zillion things, including just age. He's no kid. That's why I'm sending him to a specialist. I want to be certain."

There was something guarded about her behavior the rest of that evening, and I suspected she was even more worried about him than she'd shown, but I said no more.

■

Meyer Hall, adjacent to the hospital, was jammed for the fashion show, and all the guests seemed to know my wife — she was either their physician or in their breast cancer support group or something. Only a few recognized me, so I enjoyed examining the room and the crowd. I'd visited here many times before for various meetings, but tonight it was decorated with bunting and full of people holding glasses of wine and nibbling snacks, a heterogeneous group that included several local politicians and many women wearing colorful hats or turbans. The audience was largely female, but plenty of men were in attendance too. The mixture wasn't as white or as affluent as I'd expected, definitely not the usual high rollers.

That shouldn't have surprised me, though, since the boutique was noted for not turning anyone away. "Cancer is a great leveler," my wife had said to me, "and a pretty good bullshit filter, too." She had a way with words.

After the refreshments, Kathy Mettler mounted a large platform surrounded by folding chairs at one end of the room and spoke into a microphone. "Ladies and gentlemen, please grab those refills and join us at the stage. The show is about to begin."

Taped music had been softly playing over the sound system throughout the cocktail hour, largely unnoticed amid the room's din, but it began to be heard as couples and singles and groups quieted and found chairs or stood behind the seating area. Lights flashed over the platform, then dimmed, and a lavender-tinted spotlight soon focused on a stunning white woman, perhaps thirty-five and bald, with what appeared to be a butterfly tattooed over her left ear. She wore tights and a T-shirt and filled them well indeed. "Look at the figure lines of Kylie as she models — under her clothes, of course — the new Signature prosthesis bra from Elantra," Kathy read from a script. "Kylie has had a double mastectomy, but there's still a lot of lady left!"

The young woman twirled, stopped, and posed her hips in a move Mae West would have envied. The crowd burst into applause as she strutted to the other side of the stage. "All right, sister!" shouted a female voice. I found myself thinking, All right, sister, indeed. I didn't know what I'd expected, but I certainly hadn't anticipated anyone as striking as Kylie.

"That lady's a knockout," I said to Miranda.

"She's also a miracle, diagnosed at stage four nearly three years ago. She's every bit as spunky as she looks. After chemo she shaved her head because she likes the look."

The next model was a heavyset, gray-haired white woman, who wore a purple cocktail dress. "Mona's wig is a new model from our Ascent line," Kathy read from her notes. "Her gown and prosthesis foundation are both from Mode O'Day."

Mona was followed by a middle-aged black lady wearing orange shorts and matching halter. She also sported a wide-brimmed straw hat pulled rakishly over one eye. Before Kathy could read her script, a deep male voice called, "That's my baby. Lookin' good, too!" and the crowd laughed, as did the model. "Kinesha's summer apparel is from the new Laguna Collection. She wears a single-breast prosthesis from Spring Associates . . ." Kathy paused while Kinesha swept the hat from her head to unfurl a large, orange-patterned scarf tied pirate fashion. "And a silk scarf from the Lautrec line."

"Whoa! She's another beauty," I said.

"She has seven kids and is deep into chemo for a recurrence, but what you see is what you get: a wonderful woman."

The parade of models continued—and it really was the models, not their outfits, that intrigued me—a diverse group including a young Asian woman who removed a wig of long black hair, a sixtyish white matron who appeared hand in hand with two small kids—grandchildren, I supposed—as well as a rotund black lady who boogied across the platform and exchanged risqué comments with the audience. I'd spent enough time in the cancer world myself to understand that patients who were open about their illness tended to be feisty; this joyful evening certainly confirmed that.

The final model, I assumed, would be our celebrity guest. I didn't recognize her, but she was a petite, stunning young white woman who appeared onstage sitting on the shoulders of a large, muscular black man.

It took me several moments to realize that he was Reggie James, a retired 49ers linebacker.

"Wow," I whispered to Miranda, "so he's the celebrity. He looks like he could still play."

"Ladies and gentlemen, we're pleased to close with Edie and Reggie James," Kathy announced. After the applause subsided, she said, "*Reggie* is a breast cancer survivor."

The entire room seemed to gasp, as the large man carefully lowered his tiny wife to the floor. Behind me I heard a male voice hiss, "No shit!"

I found myself thinking, Why didn't I know about his illness? Why didn't all of us know?

Kathy handed Reggie the mike. He surveyed the crowd then said, "Edie and I want to thank all of you for coming out tonight and supporting breast cancer research. I underwent a lumpectomy and chemotherapy when I retired from football two years ago.

"I want all you guys in the audience to check your nipples for lumps. This disease kills men, too, because so few of us ever examine ourselves. If you won't do it, ask your sweet lady to. Make it part of your love play. Make it part of your life.

"My wife found the lump that led to this." He shrugged off his golf shirt to reveal a chiseled body with a pink scar where his right nipple should have been. The crowd once more gasped, then fell silent.

"My wife saved my life," the ex-football star added, and his voice suddenly deepened. He embraced her then, and they kissed—a real kiss, not a peck—and the audience rose to give them a standing ovation as all the other models were returning to the platform.

Sitting there, I felt my nipples. No lumps. I saw several other guys doing the same thing. "Why has this been kept a secret?" I asked my wife.

"It hasn't, but newspapers didn't carry much about his surgery at all. It was easy to miss. Maybe he just wasn't famous enough."

■

The following afternoon my wife said, "Sit down, please." She took my right hand in both of hers and an icicle of fear pierced me: I was certain her cancer was back. "There's no easy way to tell you this, Marty," she said. "Johnny has amyotrophic lateral sclerosis."

"He has . . . ?"

"ALS."

"Lou Gehrig's disease?" I asked, hoping I'd misunderstood.

"Yes, Lou Gehrig's disease."

"My God!" That horrible news immediately put my own situation in context, since I still had efficient treatments open to me, while the few proven medications available for amyotrophic lateral sclerosis were much less effective. That evening, I telephoned Johnny and he said to me, "Well, Champ, looks like Johnny's in a new fight."

I told him I was praying for him and he said, "That's good, Champ. Johnny needs prayers because Johnny's gonna go the whole fifteen rounds! The bell's just rung."

I knew he wouldn't quit. He'd accept this battle the way he finished the fight with Mendoza back in '63, with a broken jaw and two broken knuckles on his right hand, but still exchanging punches as the final bell rang, even staggering the world champion with that damaged right mitt.

21

After Ned Schmidt's early retirement to deal with his cancer, his replacement, Bob Romaine, offered me even more assignments, so my schedule heated up and I took great satisfaction in the work. It was his idea that I write something on Portuguese bullfights sponsored by various Azorean groups in the Valley. "In fact, why not write about the whole deal instead of just the bullfight? I understand there's some kind of fiesta, too."

"It's a *festa* in Portuguese, I think," I corrected. "That sounds like fun."

I telephoned my brother, Chava, long an aficionado of such events, and we made a date for the weekend after next so he and Cindy could take Miranda and me to a ring in nearby Escalon.

We met in Manteca, where we ate lunch; then we all climbed into their vast SUV and headed east toward Escalon and the bullring. Neither my wife nor I had ever seen one of the local corridas, so we were intrigued. Chava explained as we drove that he'd become a fan by attending one years ago with a classmate, Bill Sousa, whose younger brother would actually be in the ring today as something called a *forcado.* When I asked what that meant, Chava grinned. "Well, it ought to mean 'idiot' or maybe 'shock absorber.' You'll see soon enough."

My wife had said she didn't want to attend if the bull would be killed, but Chava explained, "This is strictly bloodless. It's not a fight at all, but a kind of ceremony of courage. Marty speaks enough Spanish — or he used to — to know that '*corrida*' doesn't mean 'bullfight'; that's just a screwed-up English translation. Even in Mexico, where bulls are still killed, it's not a fight, it's the ritual sacrifice of a brave animal — and sometimes of a brave matador."

I'd never personally developed much interest in the corrida, although I'd read Hemingway's *Death in the Afternoon.* It seemed too much like dumb people taunting a dumb beast, albeit a dangerous one. Images of the bull-versus-bear spectacles from California's past had stuck in my mind after I read about them. "The corrida's always seemed pretty primitive to me," I said. "I've never bought into the quasi-religious explanation."

"*Quasi-religious?* Who bought this *pendejo* a thesaurus?" my brother replied, the slightest edge in his voice. "*Muy pendaja, cabrón!*" he said to me. "That's the whole point. It's a ritual sacrifice. If the matador gets hurt, that's a screwup. It's a rite of guts and skill. It's like that bull is nature itself trying to hook the matador."

"I know blood rites exist in all cultures, but this one—" I started to say.

My brother interrupted me. "Hey, Marty, we Americans kill more people than anybody, but we act squeamish when it comes to a cultural ritual. What they do in these Portuguese corridas is retain the rite without the death. Think about standing in front of a sixteen-hundred-pound bull with only a cape in your hand, then tell me you wouldn't be scared."

"I'd be scared shitless," I admitted.

"Me, too," he said. "Even a fire wouldn't be scarier than a bull charging three inches from your nuts. Think about it, *vato.* When that matador stands there and moves that cape to make the bull just barely miss him, that's what he's dealing with."

"This is actually a three-day celebration," my sister-in-law explained. "There's a parade, a dance, a picnic, and every year they crown a queen and her princesses—Holy Ghost Queen or Dairy Queen or something. It's a big deal. Janet Fontes—you remember her, Marty?—she told me she thinks these *festas* are what remind people like her that she's Portuguese as well as American."

"That's better than having rednecks remind you that you're Mexican as well as American," I said with a smile.

■

The wooden arena bordered farmland outside Escalon. It was crowded with people, a surprising number of whom didn't fit the fair-skinned, dark-haired, dairy-worker stereotype endured by so many of the state's Azorean Portuguese. This was a relatively prosperous-appearing crowd, with many of what might be called Anglos, plus a large sprinkling of what I assumed were Mexicans—although maybe not, since the Portugees I knew were actually a varied lot. In any case, the majority, chewing on *linguica* sandwiches and drinking concession-stand beer from plastic cups, wore western clothing: boots, jeans, cowboy hats.

When the event finally started, it was heralded by recorded music blasting from speakers while mounted men, the *cavaleiros,* dressed as though George Washington was still president, entered the ring to cheers; they were followed by the *forcados,* a gang of young guys wearing what looked like knickers with stockings and bright sashes along with stocking caps and short jackets. They were greeted with more cheers, some laughter, and friendly shouts. Most grinned and waved at friends in the audience. "That big *forcado,*" my brother said, "the one in front, that's Sousa's brother. He was a stud linebacker at UC Davis." Finally the two matadors entered, a slim young man in an almost clownish eighteenth-century outfit and an older, thicker man in a similar outfit. A great cheer went up from the crowd. Chava nodded at the young one, saying, "That kid's Manuelito DeCosta, a famous matador they imported this year. He's a big-name guy in the old country, supposed to be really good. The other one's a journeyman named Ernesto Alves."

After the ceremonial introductions, a bull was released into the arena, looking more like coiled steel than flesh, apparently searching for someone or something to hook with horns from which the tips had been cut and replaced by leather caps.

"The bulls all come from Mexico," Chava said.

Soon one of the mounted men and a horse that appeared to know exactly how not to be caught by the bull were exciting the crowd. The mount swerved like a halfback as the bull again and again gave chase. Meanwhile the *cavaleiro* placed small decorated spears in the beast's shoulders. "They've got Velcro on them," my brother said, "and that's a Velcro pad on the bull's back."

"Yeah, but they have points, too," I replied. "Look at that blood."

I glanced at Miranda, but she gave no sign that she was upset.

With a final flourish, the *cavaleiro* leaned far from his saddle, and while the horse remained just out of range, he touched the head of the bull. The crowd roared. "That guy's another star from the old country—Vitor Almeida. He's been around for a while, but he's still one of the best," Chava said.

Everyone seated near us seemed on the verge of apoplexy, most shouting in Portuguese, a language that has always frustrated me because it's so close to Spanish but I don't understand more than a bit of it. Two men were jumping up and down next to Miranda, both wearing white shirts and red scarves, looking more like Pamplona than Escalon.

The mood changed somehow when the younger matador entered the ring with a slow, almost mincing gait. Willow slim, he appeared vulnerable as the bull serpentined around the arena, its hindquarters always a tick behind its head. When it spied the matador, it charged.

The man stood his ground and used his cape to direct the animal's energy past him. The *toro* pivoted immediately—those hips still a tick behind—then once more charged. Again the matador used his cape to lead the animal just out of range. After a third frantic charge, the bull stopped and apparently tried to figure out what was going on, giving the man time to turn his back and stride elegantly away.

"He looks like a dancer, doesn't he?" my wife said. "And with death just inches away."

"It's not a sport I'm taking up anytime soon."

"It's not a sport," my brother corrected.

Miranda turned toward Chava then and said, "What happens to the bull when this is over?"

"He's recycled as *linguica.*"

"So no matter how brave the animal is, he's sausage?" she asked.

"As far as I know," Chava replied.

Meanwhile the crowd was roaring "Manuelito! Manuelito!" each time the matador used the cape to lure the bull close . . . but never too close, and the two men next to us, along with most of the crowd, were on their feet. "Marty, I'm going over to the bathroom," Miranda said. "Cindy, do you want to come with me?"

"Why do women always take partners to the can?" asked Chava.

Watching the gals leave, I nearly missed DeCosta "stabbing" the bull between the shoulder blades with a sword that wasn't entirely Velcro; it had a short point and blood streamed from the animal's back.

As Manuelito made his leisurely exit, I turned toward my brother and said, "Man, if he'd've walked like that in our neighborhood, some *vato* would've taken that suit off of him."

"No lie," he chuckled.

The *forcados* jogged into the ring then and lined up, waving their arms and calling to the bull. "Are these guys going to stand there and let that bull run into them?" I asked. I'd seen something like that on television.

"You got it. Look at Sousa in front there. He's the main shock absorber."

"He's the main idiot, you mean."

Chava laughed, and just then the *toro* charged and Sousa managed to absorb the blow—a small cloud of dust exploded from his jacket with the impact—while trying to wrap the horns with his arms as he was lifted from the ground and the two guys behind him were knocked sprawling. One *forcado* ran behind the bull, apparently planning to grasp its tail, but the animal was too fast, pivoting and hooking with its blunt horns. The man just barely managed to leap out of range.

The crowd, meanwhile, cheered and hooted even louder, its connection with the *forcados* intimate, while with the matador it had seemed worshipful. I mentioned that to Chava, and he said, "These're all local guys. I think that only the matadors and that one *cavaleiro,* Almeida, are from Portugal. Being a *forcado*'s a big deal to these Azoreans. It takes guts."

"You forgot one other characteristic," I said. "They've got to be fucking nuts, too."

"That helps," Chava replied. "You notice they save this 'til last, when the bull's tired."

"I wouldn't do it unless the bull was dead."

The next charge resulted in the same outcome, so the *forcados* once more assembled. Yet again they were scrambled, and Sousa was beginning to look pretty ragged from the beating he was taking. "Do they have subs?" I asked.

"Right now they probably wish they did, but the bull's pooping out. They'll get him in a minute."

Sure enough, on the next charge Sousa managed to hold on and the whole mob leaped on the animal, while one man grabbed its tail. "I hate to say it," I told my brother, "but this is a pretty degrading conclusion for the bull, isn't it?"

"That's life," Chava shrugged. "Contrary to what books say, enough idiots can always overwhelm a hero."

On the walk back to the car, my brother said, "You know, there're bullrings all over the Valley — Gustine, Thornton, Tulare ... you name it. It's a Portuguese tradition, but it's becoming as much regional as ethnic. Out here I guess we're still living a little closer to the bone than you city slickers are."

"Slick *this,*" I said, pumping my arms.

We passed several *forcados* drinking beers and unwinding themselves from their long sashes amidst jovial groups of family and friends. My brother called, "Hey, Sousa! Good job!"

The husky man grinned, then shook his head and said, "I'm gettin' too fuckin' old for this, Chava."

22

Since our marriage, my personal life had become settled and fulfilling, so I gave little thought to either the religion class or the prostate cancer support group, spending most of my days at home writing, calling for information, or searching the Web. I wasn't doing much legwork anymore.

I certainly didn't go out mornings if I could help it. My confidence about such matters had never returned after that BM incident on the drive to Merced. I didn't leave home without having emptied my bowels, but my bladder usually seemed under control until late in the day, when fatigue set in. I always carried spare pads, spare underpants, and wet wipes, too. I felt like carrying a spare body.

That Tuesday Miranda was at work, so I was sitting at the kitchen table reading a report from the Great Valley Center about the disastrously high incidence of teen pregnancy in our region when the phone rang. Johnny O's voice slurred, "Hey, Champ, you wanna go to the fights with Johnny next week? I got a couple ducats, and this new kid from Mexico, Lopez, he's fightin' Joey Caruso in the main event. Oughta be good. Joey'll make him earn his pay."

"Which night?"

"Thursday."

"You're on. I'll swing by and pick you up."

It would feel good to be doing something normal, without worrying about chemical castration or my pal's disease. Besides, going to the fights with Johnny was a floor show: he ducked and punched, bobbed and weaved along with the contestants. He was slowing down, but he was still Johnny O.

■

An hour later, I was typing notes on the new story, when the phone rang.

"Marty, this is Mort O'Brien," I heard over the answering machine.

I picked up and said, "Hey, Mort, how are you?" I was happy to hear his voice.

"I'm okay. Listen, what's going on with you? I keep reading all those features you write, but long time no see. Are you okay? The guys keep asking about you."

"I'm okay. My personal life has sort of filled up, though."

"Well, I just thought I'd check in. How's your PSA?"

"Still steady, knock wood. How about yours?"

"Oh, about the same. When you find time, I'd like to schmooze with you—lunch, or maybe just at one of the meetings."

I felt guilty that he'd had to call me. "I'll be in to a meeting soon. It'll be good to catch up."

"Talk to you soon?"

"For sure," I replied.

After we hung up, I wondered if anything *was* up—like his PSA—but got back to work. I decided to make it a point to attend a support group meeting soon.

■

Late that afternoon, In the midst of writing possible leads for the pregnancy story, I was interrupted several times by the telephone. I let the machine answer, but when I heard Rollie's voice I gave in and picked up the receiver. "Hey, Beaner," said my ex-brother-in-law, "where the hell you been keepin' yourself? We ain't heard diddly-squat from you for a long time. Miranda keepin' you busy or what?"

What was I to say? "Yeah, she is, but I'm also working more for this new editor at the paper, and just trying to keep my life productive."

"How's ol' Schmidt doin' with that cancer deal?"

This was a topic that pained me, but I replied, "Not real well, I hear. He's on hormones. He's not talking to anyone about it as far as I know, but I saw one of his daughters at the store a couple of weeks ago and she said he's pretty depressed and just kind of holed up at his condo."

"That's some sad shit. He always seemed like a good guy."

"He was, and a straight arrow to work for, too."

I wasn't enjoying myself the way I usually did when talking to my brother-in-law, so I lied. "Listen, Rollie, I've got a guest here. Can I call you tomorrow?"

"You bet. I just called to tell you that Nancy's put your old place up for sale."

"The cabin?" That was a shock. "I thought she loved it."

"Audrey says Nancy told her she has too many memories about the place, so she's gettin' rid of it."

"How much is she asking for it?"

"It seems real high by standards up here, seventy-nine five."

Compared to Sacramento's prices, $79,500 didn't seem high at all. I could refinance my house and pay cash for the cabin; I didn't want to lose it. "Who's the agent?"

"Some new guy from L.A. Valpredo's his name."

"You have his number?"

"Naw, but I can get it."

"Okay." I paused, then said, "If you talk to him, tell him I'll give him seventy thousand cash. I want to keep the cabin. Doug and Lea loved it. I love it."

"I'll call him, then let you know what comes of it."

"Rollie, thanks." I knew he'd do exactly what he said, so I relaxed. "What kind of dog do you have anyway?" I asked.

"Ol' Jimmy Dean, why he's an Austrian Bratwurst spaniel, one of the rarest breeds . . . got little pouches like kangaroos."

■

Lea's call came shortly after lunch, and she was bubbling. "Daddy, guess what. Randy and I are pregnant. The doctor confirmed it this morning."

They had been living together for a long time, so I could indeed believe it. And I could be every bit as tickled as she was, though I couldn't immediately grasp that I'd be a grandpa at last; I'd about given up. "That's wonderful, Perico, just wonderful!" was all I could sputter, although I immediately wondered if the parents-to-be intended to marry.

"And don't worry, we're going up to Reno to get married next month. Can you and your wife go with us?"

"Her name's Miranda, and I'll check with her."

Her voice swooped when she said, "Daddy, I didn't mean it *that* way. I like Miranda."

"I know. Sure, we'll join you."

As soon as she hung up, I phoned Miranda's office and asked the receptionist to have my wife call me when she had a break.

Next I telephoned Manny's widow, Gloria, in Merced and gave her the good news. "Let everyone know, will you, dear? I'll give them each a call later."

"Of course, Marty." She hesitated, then asked, "How's your health?"

I had told the family about my situation shortly after my brother's death, and I knew that word "cancer" really frightened them.

"I'm okay, dear," I replied. "I'm holding steady."

"The kids and I light a candle for you every Sunday."

Once more I smiled; it was wonderful to be part of the clan again. "Thanks, Gloria. Give everyone my love."

I was about to telephone Johnny O, when the phone rang. I heard, "Mr. Martinez, this is Dr. Solomon," on the answering machine, so I picked up the receiver. "I hate to tell you this," he continued, "but results of your latest PSA test just came back, and it's 0.5. That could be an anomaly — sometimes these things spike — but when it's been consistently at 0.1 for nearly two years, then it begins tracking upward, well, that usually isn't good news."

My heart seemed to stop. For a moment I could think of nothing to say. I had radically altered my diet — no meat, no dairy, lots of soy and green tea, lycopene, selenium, and vitamin E — and I'd been working out daily. I'd also tried every therapeutic alternative I'd been offered. I guess I'd convinced myself that I'd be one of the 20 percent with my diagnosis who managed to resist recurrence for a long time.

I was wrong. The therapy that had killed my potency and continence hadn't killed the damned cancer. "Well, crap!" I finally sputtered.

"My sentiments, too," agreed the urologist.

"What's next?" I asked, struggling to control my voice. This fundamentally changed my relationship with the disease: All hope of cure had to be abandoned, and surviving as long as possible with the disease had to become my new goal.

"You're scheduled for your checkup next week, so I'll look closely for evidence of a local recurrence then—to find out whether any local tumors are growing. If we don't find anything, we'll have you do another PSA test in three months, see if it's still rising and how fast, then make a therapeutic decision."

"Meaning hormones again?"

"Most likely," he said. "That or an orchiectomy, but remember that for men with early recurrences those treatments can allow you to stay alive for years, and in years we'll have better therapies for this disease."

Yeah, you could kind of stay alive on hormones, I thought, but you did it chemically castrated—without testosterone, without libido, without pep, losing bone density and muscle mass every day, maybe developing breasts if you were unlucky, and again putting up with those damned hot flashes. I didn't give orchiectomy—castration—any thought; no way I'd do that.

An hour later, as I sat gazing out the front window, Miranda telephoned. "Do you want to meet me for early dinner with the Mettlers?" she asked.

I said, "Sure."

"Let's meet at Mexicali."

"Okay," I said.

"Oh, what did you want to tell me when you called?" she asked.

"Do you want the good news or the bad news?" I asked as flippantly as I could.

"I don't want any bad news," she replied.

"The good news is that Lea called this morning to tell me that she's pregnant, and that she and Randy are getting married. She wants us to travel up to Reno with them when they do."

For a moment she said nothing, then she responded, "That's not good news, Marty, that's *great* news!"

"I feel the same way. I can't wait to be a grandpa!"

"Is there really bad news, too?"

"Do you remember Emily Dickinson?"

"Of course," she said. "Even premed students took lit. She was the Amherst poet, right?"

"Right. She wrote about a snake scaring someone, 'and zero at the bone.' That happened to me today . . . without a snake." I explained what Dr. Solomon had said, and again she was silent for a moment, then she said, "Okay, when I get home, we need to figure out a strategy to deal with this. We aren't giving in."

"We damn sure aren't," I agreed.

"Why don't you have another test right away?" she suggested. "Sometimes the PSA will spike, then drop down again. We've been sexually active lately. That might account for it."

"We abstained before the test," I pointed out.

"Please, Marty, for me if not for you."

I smiled, though my throat remained icy. We had indeed been making love. We were using the pump a couple of times a week; not bad for old-timers. "Let's skip dinner with Kathy and Nick tonight, have supper in and talk more about this," she urged. "I have an idea."

■

"Once you're in the cancer world, everything's iffy," Miranda said, sipping at cream sherry after the meal. "Live for the moment, since that may be all you have."

"I've been thinking about that, too."

My wife sighed, then said, "I've been considering closing my practice, just volunteering at La Clinica de las Mujeres. I've invested pretty well, so we can afford to live without my income, or what's left of it. With medicine going the way it is, I'm really just keeping the office open so my staff can have jobs. I can give them generous separation packages, plus help them find other work . . ."

"You've been thinking about this for a while, haven't you?"

"Well, either one of us might be in big trouble tomorrow. Let's make the most of whatever time we've got left."

Her tone troubled me. "Are you okay, Miranda?"

"Of course I am . . . for now. That's why it's time to let go of some obligations. We can travel, we can play with our grandchildren, just generally enjoy life." She paused, then added, "We've probably both got some tough times coming . . ."

"I know," I said. "I know."

"But as long as we're alive and we're together, we'll be fine. Let's not let these diseases dictate our lives."

"Amen."

We rose, hugged, then wandered toward our bedroom, but my wife stopped me at the door. "No farting tonight," she ordered.

"Me? How about you?" I grinned.

She grinned back, saying, "Ladies don't fart. I just had a slight attack of the vapors."

"Man, I'd hate to be around if you had a *bad* attack!"

■

When I drove over to pick Johnny up for the fights, his condition shocked me: He'd deteriorated considerably since I'd last seen him, but his eyes glistened with excitement as I helped him transfer from his wheelchair to the car seat. At the arena, I damn near couldn't wheel him in because so many people stopped to greet him. "Hey, Johnny! Great to see ya, kid!" called one heavy guy chomping an unlit cigar. "Wanna go a couple rounds?"

"You never lasted two rounds," my pal shot back, and the heavy guy laughed and said to me, "This guy was the greatest! The uncrowned champ!"

"He's still the greatest," I replied.

"Absotively!" agreed the cigar chomper. "Absotively!"

Johnny O smiled and nodded his way past other well-wishers, back in his milieu, and although I'd actually considered canceling this date because of my bad news, I was now delighted that I'd brought him. I knew he was housebound, or trailer-house-bound, and I'd vowed to make it a point to visit him more often, get him out of that dreary setting.

Once we reached our place at ringside, I asked, "Who was that heavy guy with the cigar?"

"You didn't recognize him? That was Babe Lazarini, a good lightweight."

"*That* was Babe? Man, he's a super-heavyweight now."

Johnny grinned. "He's let his trainin' slip a little."

We sat through two four-rounders, local youngsters long on enthusiasm but short on skill. "That one black kid might make a fighter," the ex-pug said, "but he's gotta learn to use his reach. Jab, jab, jab. Hook off the jab. Johnny could show him how." His face turned sad for a second, since he probably realized that he couldn't show him anymore.

The six-round semifinal was entertaining. A Filipino bantamweight from nearby Stockton taking on a Mexican stablemate of the main eventer, Lopez. "Sal Rosario told Johnny that the winner of this bout might get a main event soon," my pal said. "He likes this Villa kid."

These two boxers were much more polished than the earlier fighters had been, moving well, their punches tight and clean. The Filipino, Villa, who had faster hands, landed more cleanly, but the Mexican boxer never backed away. In fact, neither of the warriors backed up more than a strategic step or two during the entire fight, and both threw punches in combinations.

As the bout progressed, I noticed that Johnny wasn't moving with the fighters as much as he usually did, although his face grimaced and puffed with them. "Left hook!" he shouted. "Left hook! Double it up!" In fact, he was less active and less vocal each round. Villa won a unanimous decision, and the crowd cheered both fighters and tossed money into the ring.

Johnny turned toward me after the decision was announced, and his face had become slack. "Champ," he said in a faint voice, "maybe Johnny oughta go home. He's all in."

"Sure. Are you okay, buddy?" I asked.

"Just pooped."

As I pushed him up the aisle, I stopped the wheelchair so he could respond to another friend, a large black man I vaguely recognized. Sal Rosario, the promoter, grabbed my arm from behind then and said, "We were gonna introduce Johnny from the ring before the main event. He okay?"

"No, he's not, Sal. When he has to leave the fights, he's damn sure not."

"Naw, he's not, I know. I know. I just hoped . . . Jeez, ol' Johnny." Sal slumped away.

It was all I could do to lift my pal from the wheelchair to my car's seat, since he was too tired to help much. At his trailer, I again struggled to heft him into his wheelchair, saying, "I may need someone to lift *me* when I get home."

"Sorry, Champ," he replied, "but Johnny just ran outta gas." He seemed genuinely amazed. "That never happened before."

"No big deal, buddy." I was thinking that we'd lose Johnny soon, and that didn't seem possible, but his face now sagged, hardly like the guy I'd picked up a couple of hours earlier. "I have good days and bad ones myself," I admitted. "Listen, let me come by next week — Tuesday would be good — and take you to lunch at the Squared Circle. I'll bet we run into some of your old boxing pals."

"That'd be good, Champ."

"Do you need help getting to bed?"

"Naw. Johnny'll be okay."

I patted his back and turned to leave when he said, "Marty . . . Marty, you been a real pal."

He hadn't called me Marty ten times in the fifty-plus years we'd known one another, and I had to avert my face so he couldn't see my eyes blinking and my chin softening. "See you, Johnny," I hugged him. "I'll call Tuesday."

■

When I arrived home, I discovered that Rollie'd left a message on the answering machine, so I called him back. "I called that real estate guy," he told me, "and he said he'd drop the price to seventy-seven five for cash. He said he expected lots of offers."

"Did he say he was bluffing?" I asked.

"Naw, but he was."

Rollie gave me the newcomer's name and address, then launched into a tale about how this agent had quickly ingratiated himself by transferring into the local Rotary, then leading a drive to promote the youth soccer program. "He ain't but a gander-assed kid, but he seems like a good guy. I think he thinks he's a real sharpie when it comes to business, though."

"Then what's he doing up in Dunsmuir? That's not exactly Wall Street."

"Good question," Rollie said.

"I've got other news, Uncle Rollie," I said. "Lea's pregnant. She and Randy're getting married."

"Shit fire and save matches! Don't things ever calm down at your place? Wait'll Audrey and the kids hear. When's the weddin'?"

"They're going to sneak off to Reno on their own to get married, but we'll have a big reception here for them when they get back. I don't know exactly when."

"I shoulda known you'd be too damn chintzy to pay for a weddin'. You'll probably have Mex'can food at the reception, too, bowl of damn beans and a tortilla."

"What'd you want, biscuits and gravy?" I demanded.

"That'd be damn white of you."

23

Now that my PSA was rising, I slunk back to the support group. Mort was there when I arrived, and he grinned. "Well, look what the dog dragged in! How are you, Marty?"

"I've got a recurrence."

"What're you going to do?" he asked, suddenly solemn.

"I'll decide once I know how fast it's doubling."

I slid into the chair next to his — only a few other guys were there, talking in two small clusters near the windows — and continued, "Being married again, I sure don't want to go back on hormones."

"I understand." Then he changed the subject. "Listen, I've been meaning to call you because I need an associate leader for the group here to cover for me when I'm gone. I'd like you to consider doing it."

"I thought Bob was your backup."

"Bob died."

"Bob? I didn't know."

"You wouldn't have recognized his name in the obits, because his given name was Thomas, Thomas Herndon. Bob was just a nickname. Anyway, his hormonal therapy had been failing, and he tried chemo, but nothing worked for long. It was pretty gruesome toward the end — paralysis and all that, but he did go pretty fast once it got to his spine. He was a brave guy."

I could only shake my head.

"Al Royster's getting worse, too. So is Bill, the guy who joined the same night you did. He's pretty depressed — been going to a psychologist."

I could only shake my head. "I keep hearing that this isn't a serious cancer."

"It's damned serious for about thirty thousand dead guys a year. There's no cancer that isn't serious." The room was suddenly filling, meaning it was time to start the formal meeting. Mort added, "Well, this disease isn't a hell of a lot of fun."

"You got that right."

He turned to the assembling men and announced, "If you boys will sit down, I've got a joke to open the meeting . . ."

■

I don't know exactly what I expected, but when Lea and Randy changed their minds and decided to hold their wedding on one of the riverboats anchored at Old Sacramento, I assumed we'd have a Reno-type gathering, suit and tie, with a rubber-chicken meal to follow. But when Miranda and I showed up, we discovered Randy wearing a kilt complete with all the flourishes. My daughter looked beautiful in a sleek green cocktail dress that didn't hide her slightly swollen tummy.

I asked Lea what Randy's getup was all about, since he didn't look Scottish to me. "He said that when he got married the first time they did everything by the book — tuxes, gowns, giant cake — and got way in debt, but it didn't work, so he was trying a nontraditional approach this time. Besides," she added, "he's a nut. That's one reason I love him."

"A nut. He could've fooled me," I said.

The event grew even less traditional when the minister arrived, because he wasn't a minister at all but rather an old pal of Randy's with a twenty-four-hour permit. Best of all, his name — or nickname — was Skeeter. He was a skinny kid who really did resemble a wingless mosquito; he even had a long, sharp nose. Again I pulled Lea aside and asked, "How do you know the Reverend Skeeter is legally entitled to marry you?"

"Daddy, don't be difficult. Skeeter's an attorney. He took care of everything."

"Skeeter's an *attorney?* Who'd've thunk it? He looks to me like a guy who *needs* an attorney."

Her face clouded up and for a moment I thought I'd gone too far, but then she said, "You're kidding, right?"

"Right," I replied, and I kissed her cheek.

Fifteen minutes later, just before the small ceremony was scheduled to begin,

Lea approached Miranda and me. Her face looked ashen and she said, "I've got a big favor to ask, Miranda. Melinda Woo, my bridesmaid, didn't show up. She just called on my cell and said she's been in a minor traffic accident. Can you stand up with me?"

My knees nearly buckled at the request — the wicked stepmother recast as bridesmaid — but Miranda didn't miss a beat. "Of course, Lea. I'd be honored."

On that promising note, with no more than a dozen of us in attendance, my daughter was married. Randy in his kilt looked especially proud when his five-year-old son, Tyler, as ring bearer, joined the couple up front. Reverend Skeeter remembered his lines.

Miranda and I had decided that rather than invite my large family to the ceremony on the boat, we would inform everyone that we'd host a reception at our place in Sacramento soon. Predictably, only Chava, dragging an embarrassed Cindy with him, showed up anyway. They sat with me. I found myself moved by what I saw, because I knew my daughter deserved a stable relationship and I sensed that Randy, kilt or no kilt, wanted that too. If he provided that for her, he could flounce around in a prom dress for all I cared.

My brother poked me and said, "You want my hankie?"

Afterward, while we waited outside the ladies' room for our wives, Chava said, "Man, that daughter of yours is still a knockout. Randy's a good-looking kid, too. He's got *great* legs."

I couldn't help laughing.

"Is he Mexican?" my brother asked.

"His name's Spanish," I replied. "But I don't give a damn what he is as long as he's a good husband."

He grinned. "Remember that old saying, 'La clase primero es la clase mas guero'?"

"Yeah, there used to be a lot of jokes about who was darkest. Who was that white guy at the high school who called Raul a smoked Irishman? Raul chased him clear around the gym."

He shook his head, then said, "You know, sometimes I think these young gangbangers are from a different world. Maria dated one and he threatened to rough her up if she didn't put out. She told me, and I told him if he looked cross-eyed at my girl again I'd break his fucking arms. Well, he let the word get out that he was gonna come back with his gang to take care of me, so I had Arnie Schmidt look this punk up and explain what was going to happen to him and his if anything happened to me or mine."

"Schmidt was a rough football player," I recalled.

"He came back from Vietnam even rougher. He's a cop now, and a damned hard case. He told that kid that if he so much as talked to me or my family again he'd not only kill him but he'd also ace his whole family even if he had to go to Mexico to do it. I think he tapped the kid's kidneys once or twice just to prove he wasn't bullshitting, and the kid must've got the point, because he left town right away.

"I'll tell you, Marty." He shook his head. "I used to think I was a Mexican until all these guys started coming north to work. Being around them showed me how American I am."

"Did you know that there're supposedly more Mexicans in L.A. than in any place except Mexico City?"

"No shit?" He raised a thick eyebrow.

"The border's never been sealed, so I think to them it's all one big country — Mexico and California."

"Isn't that what our *abuelo* and *abuelita* said about the border?" my brother asked. Then he added, "I see young guys standing out in front of that Exxon station by the railroad tracks — Indians mostly. I hired a couple to take out a tree. Good workers."

I heard a tinkling version of "La Cucaracha," then my brother pulled a tiny cell phone from his pocket and held it next to his ear. "Hey," he said. "Where are you?"

After a moment, he said, "In Sac with Marty. His daughter just got married."

Chava grinned, then said to me, "Junius says hi." He returned to his call. "Okay, meet you at the clubhouse at ten." He glanced at me as he closed the phone and explained, "We're playing golf tomorrow with Robles and Archie."

"I've got a question," I said. "What ever happened to *how* are you? Who cares *where* you are?"

My brother replied, "You're *so* fifties. You better get back to worrying about Mexicans."

"I don't worry about them," I replied. "I think those kids'll determine this state in the next couple of generations, but we won't know it because we're on our way out . . . 'Bare ruined choirs where late the sweet birds sang.'"

"Bare ruined *what?*"

"Just something Shakespeare wrote about aging."

"*Shakespeare?*" Chava chuckled. "How about Richie Valens? Damn, you send a chile choker to school and he becomes an intellectual. Shakespeare." He shook his head.

"I wasn't smart enough to get in shop class like you, *vato,* so I tried something else. It's called R-E-A-D-I-N-G. You ought to give it a shot."

"You oughta try E-A-T S-H-I-T, *pendejo,*" he snapped.

We were both laughing when Cindy and Miranda emerged from the ladies' room. My sister-in-law said, "What're you two grinning about? Something dirty, I'll bet. I should've warned you about marrying a Martinez, Miranda."

■

Driving home from the wedding celebration, I explained to Miranda the emotional tug the cabin in Castella still held for me. "That's understandable," she said. "I think we should buy it, but have you heard the story about the man and his wife who were trying to make love, and he couldn't perform? Well, finally he said, 'It's no good, I just can't think of anybody.'" She paused, and I raised my eyebrows; she wasn't noted for spicy stories. "I don't want you to think of anybody," she said.

"I won't," I replied, meaning that I'd certainly try not to.

"Okay, I'll go halves with you so the cabin will be genuine community property," she offered. That seemed like an unnecessary arrangement, but once I thought about it I realized that Miranda was right.

The next morning I began the process of obtaining money for my half. As soon as the real estate agent learned that we would simply write him a check and purchase the property after Rollie and Audrey inspected it, he contacted his client, Nancy Minata Martinez, and soon a deal was struck at seventy thousand dollars, including furniture. We were even able to sign the papers in Sacramento.

Lea and Randy—and his little boy, of course—enjoyed the first post-purchase visit, and my daughter came back with a list of little repairs. I told her that as far as I was concerned it was a family retreat, so she could take care of them. "Get *real,* Daddy," she responded. Randy said he'd do what he could, acknowledging that he was no handyman. That made two of us.

24

I explained to Dr. Solomon that I had decided to do intermittent hormone therapy when the time came. To my surprise he replied, "That may not be a choice you have."

"Wait a minute," I said. "When I was facing my initial therapy, you basically told me I had to choose on my own. That was tough, but I studied and did it. Now I'm much better informed, and I've decided on my own therapy."

His face tightened at my tone, but he replied in a reasonable voice: "Your health plan considers intermittent treatment experimental. It much prefers orchiectomy."

"You and I both know that castration's irreversible. And think about what that does to a man psychologically."

His response was sharp. "I'm more concerned about what the cancer does physiologically."

"If quality of life really means something to you, you need to think about both."

The urologist stood and said, "This isn't getting us anywhere, Mr. Martinez. Maybe you should talk to someone else."

"I'm not trying to be disrespectful, Dr. Solomon, but words are my business," I said. "Think about the connotations of 'orchiectomy' and 'castration.' Most folks don't even understand the first one, but they know the other's a kind of maiming."

"Wait." He sounded heated this time. "I understand that you're upset, but I'm just trying to offer you a treatment that will allow you a few more years with reasonable quality of life."

I wasn't deflected. "Castration's only the most economical treatment, not necessarily the best," I argued. "When I called UCSF to research the pieces I wrote, the oncologist I talked with said they don't often use orchiectomy there anymore. It's too inflexible a treatment — that's a quote — because new stuff is coming up all the time. Why should a guy close the door on other possibilities?"

"All right, Mr. Martinez," he said, sounding exasperated. "If you can convince your health plan, I'll do what you wish."

I telephoned Miranda when I arrived home and explained what had transpired. "Well," she said, "there's one more example of what's wrong with managed care — in its present state, anyway." We eventually agreed that if I encountered any problems with my health plan, we'd pay for the treatments out of pocket.

■

The call surprised me. "Mr. Martinez?" said a woman. "This is Melissa Dupre, administrative assistant to Roswell Gilbert, the executive editor at the *Express*. He asked me to call to invite you for coffee in his office at your convenience so he can say hello to you personally. He's been reading clippings of your work, and he's most impressed. He has an idea he'd like to discuss with you."

Well, I thought, if the new editor's so impressed why couldn't he call me himself? But I was curious about him, so three mornings later I sat on a soft leather couch in his office sipping delicious coffee and surveying the young fashion plate who sat behind a huge mahogany desk. He was dressed in what was obviously a tailor-made suit — sans coat — with bright suspenders, a monogrammed shirt and rep tie. Mr. Gilbert was a far cry from old Windy Strader, who had presided over a much shabbier version of this office for nearly three decades.

When Windy called you in, at any hour, he poured you and him a stiff jolt of red-eye to grease the conversation. He would also pour himself several others over the course of the day, but he'd managed to remain an effective newspaperman and businessman, too, until his liver gave way.

In any case, "Mr. Gilbert" — and it was clear he wanted to be called that — was an artificially cordial young guy, about the age my son would have been. "Your clippings and awards are both very impressive, Mr. Martinez. You've been a real pioneer on the *Express,* its first Chicano" — he pronounced the word "Chicayno" — "as far as I can tell."

I sensed immediately, perhaps from his dulcet tone, that he was going to let me go and was starting with the softening-up process. It took him a while to get down to business, but at last he said, "As someone who's already officially retired, your situation is different than nearly anyone else's on the staff . . . or *not* on it." He chuckled. "I'd like you to move to a new assignment. We've hired a brilliant young Chicayno" — that word again — "writer who graduated with highest honors from Harvard just two years ago, then won major awards at the *Post.* Her name is Monica Salinas."

"Where's she from?" I was thinking, if Monica's *from* Salinas she might work out.

"Harvard. Oh, you mean originally? Chicago. She was a National Merit Scholar in high school there."

"Does she speak Spanish?" I asked.

"She minored in it at Harvard."

"I mean street Spanish."

He shrugged and smiled. "Spanish is Spanish, she tells me."

Good luck, Monica, I thought. Some *vato* from the barrio will teach her a new dialect before long, and it'll sound like Chinese: *Chinga* this and *chinga* that. I knew it would take her years to understand this community if she wore Harvard as a badge. Still, all this was strangely impersonal to me, although his decision seemed dumb.

"Are you aware of the changing demographics here in Greater Sacramento, Mr. Gilbert?" I asked. "The younger population is increasingly less white, and the general population is aging, especially in all those retirement communities in the foothills."

He only smiled. "Our numbers show that there'll be a constantly renewed youthful, well-educated generation of state workers in Sacramento, plus more and more young, affluent, well-educated professionals. They're our major target audience now, the young and socially active and, frankly, well-to-do ones. This is strictly a business decision." I started to speak, but he waved me off like a pesky insect. "Candidly, we also think it's time that this newspaper became a national force, a *New York Times* of the West. I intend for us to pursue that goal."

I was impressed by his candor. "Well," I said, "on your first point, those seniors have a few bucks and some influence, too." I was about to mention the paper's relative isolation from national audiences, but he cut me off.

"Which is why we haven't forgotten you," he added. "I want to offer you a weekly column we're going to initiate. We'll call the column 'Gray Matters,' and you can write about topics of special interest to senior citizens."

I gazed at this twerp for a moment, then said, "I take it I won't be needed for my usual features? I can write about good denture adhesives and where to snag a great buy on Depends?"

His eyes snapped toward me, and mine stayed riveted on his. He apparently wasn't used to impudent employees, but he controlled himself. "There's no need to be facetious, Mr. Martinez. I don't have to show you these courtesies. I'm just trying to find a way to keep you affiliated with the *Express*."

He was lying, of course, because he knew that my work over the years had created a reader base that he didn't want to lose, so he'd rather not fire me. "Don't bother," I said, rising. "It's been nice not working for you."

"Mr. Martinez—"

The days were past when I would have wasted my breath telling this pompous prick to kiss off. I walked into the newsroom to the old stringer's desk that I'd lately been using when I came in to file my stories, picked up the phone, and dialed the number of Sacramento's other daily newspaper, the *Tribune*. I asked for Bud Hartley, the managing editor and another old pal. "Hey, Bud," I said, "the new imperial wizard of the *Express* just relegated me to a column for senior citizens, so I told him good-bye. Can you use a part-time feature writer?"

"Are you kidding? When can you start? Oh yeah, remember the Bearheart murder way back when?"

"Yeah, I covered it. What's up?"

"The new senatorial lounge is going to be named for him," he chuckled. "If I remember Bearheart, it'll be a cocktail lounge."

"Right."

I had a new job and Roswell Gilbert had unknowingly paid for the call. That felt grand.

■

Miranda seemed genuinely amused when I told her the story of my meeting with the executive editor. "He sounds a bit like a twit," she said.

"That about sums it up," I replied.

"And now for something entirely different," she said. "How would you like a little massage?"

What brought this on? I thought, but I wasn't foolish enough to ask. "Sure."

As I lay on our bed, my wife rubbed baby oil on my neck, my back, my thighs, and I slid toward sleep, but only toward it. Part of me, as much memory as passion, was being aroused. She pressed her lips to my ear, kissed, then whispered, "Turn over."

I did that and she glided her fingers between my toes, then up my feet, my calves, my thighs. I was no longer drifting toward sleep by then, feeling erect although I knew I couldn't be. But I was ready enough.

Miranda continued the massage, rubbing baby oil on my belly, my chest, my nipples. Her fingers lingered there, moving gently, then she asked quietly, "Have you been checking your nipples?"

"Not really," I replied. "I thought one cancer was enough."

Miranda nodded and said, "Most cancer victims think that way, but unfortunately that's not reality. Cancer doesn't care."

"Great," I said. "Cancer *victims*?"

"I let my emotions creep in," she said. "Cancer patients. Cancer survivors. Cancer *victims* is politically incorrect."

"Well, *victims* sums up how I feel when I think about it."

She kissed my nipples and I ceased thinking about it.

■

News that Monsignor Kelley was ill shocked the parish; he seemed to be such a picture of health. Rumor had it that he was suffering from prostate cancer, and that made his situation of special interest to me. I telephoned the rectory and found myself routed through the secretary—"I swear, he's had five hundred calls since Sunday, but he told me to put you through if you called. He read about your experiences."

"Hello, Marty," the monsignor's big voice boomed after an interval. "I suppose you've heard my recent news."

"Prostate cancer?"

"Yes, the old man's curse."

"What're you going to do about it, Monsignor?"

"Ahhh." He paused for a bit, then said, "I'm leaning toward surgery. Tim Cullen from the parish is my urologist, and he says that's the gold standard."

"Surgery is the gold standard for surgeons anyway, and it does work," I said, "but there are also some less-damaging choices: brachytherapy, 3-D conformal external-beam radiation, some new variations of cryotherapy . . ."

He said, "So many choices. Can you explain those things to me — at my level, of course, which is *Reader's Digest?*"

When I finally finished my brief lecture, Monsignor Kelley said, "Well, you've given me a good deal to think about. More than I wanted, perhaps. This isn't simple, is it?" he added ruefully. "And that book you recommend . . . ?"

"I'll drop my copy by."

"We'll talk when you do, and thanks, Marty. This has been most enlightening."

25

I guess Dr. Cullen, whom I didn't know, was the more persuasive, since the monsignor decided to go ahead with surgery. Father Tran announced in Mass that another priest would be sent to help at the parish while the pastor recuperated. A week later, an older man I'd never seen before led the procession down the center aisle to the altar as the service began. Father Tran emerged from the sacristy and walked to the lectern. "Please be seated," he said. "It's my pleasure today to introduce you to Father Michael Andrews, who will help while the monsignor recovers from his recent operation. Father Michael will fill you in on his background during his homily, but I just want you to welcome him to St. Apollinaris." The congregation applauded politely, and the older priest nodded.

Mass proceeded at a much slower tempo than Father Tran or Monsignor Kelley had ever set, with occasional long silences ("Is he still breathing?" Miranda whispered at one point). Once the Gospel had been read, the tall, stooped man moved behind the lectern and said, "I thank you all for that warm welcome. Monsignor asked me to tell you something about my background this morning. I'm a San Francisco native — St. Peter's parish — and I was ordained there in 1964."

As he continued his autobiography, Miranda whispered to me, "A priest that long? Why doesn't he have a parish?"

"Good question."

Several minutes later, just as I assumed that Father Andrews was about to conclude his story, thus his homily, he launched into a sermon: "It's important for all of you to understand that I have been sent among you to warn that the promise of the Apocalypse is real and imminent. The Second Coming is at hand. Christ will return, and among sinners there will indeed be much wailing and gnashing of teeth . . ."

By the time he finally finished, I was gnashing my teeth and in the mood to wail. Man, what a long-winded performance. As Mass continued, I noticed that the new priest used as much Latin as he could, and that he seemed to be constantly upbraiding the alter servers, both girls. Ah, I thought, a perfectionist as well as a traditionalist . . . and a windbag, then immediately regretted my mean thought. When it finally came time for Holy Communion, the new priest announced, "If any of you would like to receive Communion in the traditional Catholic manner, just wait until the lines have shortened, then come forward and kneel before the altar." A surprising number of people did that, but only a couple of them were familiar to me. He seemed to have brought a following with him, many of them women wearing scarves or hats.

I was glad he'd brought a portable congregation, because I was determined to avoid his Masses at all costs, if this one was typical. It was like observing the devolution of the Church. By the time we finally escaped, a considerable crew had gathered, awaiting entry to the next Mass. In fact, a few had entered the church, apparently thinking they were late for noon services.

As we left one man asked, "What took so long?"

"New priest," I said to him, then I soto-voiced to my wife, "And almost a new religion."

■

On Monday I went in for my recheck at Dr. Nimitz's office. Seated across from me was a couple, apparently Mexican, the woman wearing slacks, a sweater, and a large, elaborate gold crucifix. Next to her, the man wore jeans, silver-toed cowboy boots, and a straw cowboy hat with a small tassel dangling from the rear of its brim. They sat in obvious discomfort, exchanging whispered thoughts. I wondered which had cancer.

I found out almost immediately, because Vonda emerged from the hallway that led to the radiation unit and approached the couple. "Mrs. Enriques?" she said.

The woman suddenly looked distraught, glancing at the man. She clutched his hand and mumbled, "*Sí.*"

The man said, "My wife, she don' spik the English."

"Okay." Vonda smiled and continued, "I'm the radiation technologist. Dr. Nimitz wants to start your wife on treatments right away." She paused, waiting for the man to translate, I guess, but it was clear he didn't fully understand.

He mumbled something to his wife, then said politely to Vonda, "Could you talk more slower, please?"

This time Vonda's voice grew loud and she mouthed words as though speaking to an infant. That bothered me, so I said, "Tal vez yo puedo traduscar, señor y señora."

They both turned toward me, and he said in English, "Thank you, mister, please."

"Vonda," I said, "what do you want me to tell them?"

She gazed at me for a moment, as though surprised, then said, "She had lumpectomy in her left breast and doctor wants to start radiating that area right away."

My Spanish was far from eloquent, but I could say most of that, far more than Vonda had been communicating with shouts.

Mrs. Enriques listened to me, then replied to her husband. He translated, "My wife, she say radiation it hurt your longs."

Vonda appeared baffled. "Longs?" she said. "Long's Drug Store."

For a second, I thought she was kidding and my temper flared; this was no time to be funny. "Lungs," I said.

"Thanks, Mr. Martinez," the nurse replied, with no hint of facetiousness.

"She's afraid you'll burn her lungs," I explained.

Vonda turned toward the patient and said, "We don't direct the rays into the body, Mrs. Enriques. We do it like this." While I translated, she drew a sketch of a breast on the pad she carried, then drew arrows from the sides. "We shoot from the sides," she said.

"*De los lados,*" I explained.

The woman mumbled something softly to her husband. He turned toward Vonda and explained, "This lady she tol' to my wife the radiation it's not too good for you."

Vonda glanced at me, then said, "The cancer's worse. It will kill you if we don't treat it."

Mrs. Enriques looked at me and I said, "La cancer es peor. Su murío."

My Spanish was imperfect, but she got the message. "Oh," she said. Then she signed the consent forms.

As the nurse walked away, she mouthed a silent "Thank you" to me. Mr. and Mrs. Enriques both shook my hand and said thank you. They asked if I was a doctor, and when I said no, I was a patient too, they said they would pray for me. I knew they really would.

I was called by a nurse a few minutes later, but Vonda stopped me on my way in. "I didn't realize you spoke Spanish, Mr. Martinez. Your English is so good," she said innocently.

"So's yours."

She glanced at me, then her face reddened, but I smiled at her, not wanting to come on too strong. "In a lot of the world people speak more than one language, Vonda. My Spanish isn't very good at all. My grandparents spoke it really well, but that's all they spoke. My mom and dad were both raised here, so they spoke Spanish to the old folks and in front of us when they didn't want us to understand what they were saying, but otherwise English was the language at home. I picked up a little street Spanish in the neighborhood, of course, and took a couple of semesters of Spanish in high school, but I'm by no means fluent."

"You sure sounded fluent to me."

"Well," I said with another smile, "you could be as fluent as I am in about two semesters at night school. One other thing: It really doesn't help to talk louder to people who speak another language. Just speak normally, and either draw pictures or look for a translator if they don't understand. You'll be surprised at how many people speak Spanish well enough for that."

I thought she might be offended by my admonition, but she smiled and said, "I'll remember that."

This time I saw Dr. Ed DelVecchio, Dr. Nimitz's associate and a medical oncologist. As seemed so often the case anymore, he was a kid — to me, at least. "I've read your chart, Mr. Martinez," he said. "This second PSA seems to confirm that your cancer is coming back, and rather rapidly."

I nodded. What could I say?

"I think we should get going on combined hormone therapy right now, since there's a body of accumulating evidence that the earlier you start, the longer it remains effective."

I started to ask him about intermittent treatment rather than an unbroken regimen of hormones, but he continued, "There's also good reason to think intermittent hormones will be as effective as staying on them all the time, and side effects will be mitigated. I hope you'll consider that pattern."

I'd had my argument all honed, but this young guy had beat me to it. Stunned, I said, "Sure, let's do intermittent."

He injected me with Lupron that afternoon and gave me a prescription for Casodex that I had filled on the way home. It all seemed so perfunctory, but it wasn't that easy. That night when I gazed at my drooping face in the mirror before taking my tiny Casodex pill and going to bed, I acknowledged that I'd officially moved to the next-to-last therapeutic stage of prostate cancer.

In bed, I said to Miranda, "I sure hated to start hormones."

"The side effects can be unpleasant," she said.

"More than that, though, it symbolizes a losing battle."

She smiled and replied, "Well, that's one perspective. As a physician, I'd say it symbolizes life being prolonged. Without it you'd have a year or so. With it, five or more are possible, and five years from now there'll be new therapies."

"That's the promise that keeps guys going," I said.

"Well, finally we all die," she acknowledged. "There's no cure for that."

■

Yet another telephone call came just as I was about to quit my office the next afternoon and walk to the front of the house to open a beer. I almost didn't answer, but . . .

"Mr. Martinez?" said a man's voice.

""Right," I replied.

"I, uh . . ." There was a pause, then the man asked, "You're a Catholic, aren't you?"

"Yep." I had revealed my faith in more than one of my op-ed pieces.

"That's why I wanted to tell you this and not somebody else."

"Okay. Tell me what?" I must admit, he had me intrigued.

"Well . . . uh . . ."

I began to wonder if he was going to spit it out.

" . . . my son he was . . . uh . . . molested by this priest named Father Reilly at St. Mary's parish."

That caught my attention. I'd read about such cases, of course, but not in Sacramento. "Who is this?"

After a long pause, the voice replied, "Martin Pruett."

"When did this happen, Mr. Pruett?"

"Paul was eleven then, eight years ago."

"Eight years ago? Why has it taken so long for you to call me—or someone?" I asked.

"Paul he just told me last week." The man's voice was growing shaky. He stopped and cleared his throat, then continued, "He's in junior college now and he read in the newspaper about altar boys being abused down in Long Beach, then he told me that the same thing'd happened to him, that Father Reilly had . . . molested him and other altar boys, too."

I was taking notes now. "Could we meet for coffee, Mr. Pruett? I'd like to get the whole story, and if we can find some corroboration—"

"Paul doesn't lie!"

"Mr. Pruett, you must understand that before I can go public with a story like this I need significant corroboration. I don't doubt your son, but no editor worth his salt is going to print this without corroborating evidence. Will other altar boys talk about it, for instance?"

"I don't know."

"Where's this priest now?"

"He's over in Woodland. He has his own parish."

Well, I was thinking, I can make some inquiries over there, and interview some other ex–altar boys here if they're willing. "Can you give me the names and phone numbers of other possible victims in your parish?"

"Paul can, but he's real embarrassed. He might not want to talk to you."

"I can't do much if he doesn't cooperate. I wouldn't write anything to embarrass him . . . unless he approved," I explained, "but there may be no other way to expose an offending priest. That's one of the problems with sexual abuse cases: Victims are so embarrassed or damaged by what happened to them that they won't go public."

He did not reply at first, but I seemed to hear him sigh. Finally he said, "Maybe I shouldn't've called you, but when I called the diocese, I just got shuffled from one office to another, and the bishop never did talk to me. Then some guy named Osbourn who said he was an attorney he warned me against spreading the story. He said it was actionable." The father sounded as though he was on the verge of tears.

I knew that a bully attorney threatening to sue was an old, usually phony ploy, designed to intimidate the naive. "Mr. Pruett, I'm not only a Catholic, I'm also a father. My son was an altar boy." I felt myself growing angry as I spoke. "Believe me, if this guy is molesting kids, I want to nail him, but I understand the legal system."

"I appreciate that," he choked.

"Why don't we get together this week? We can leave your son out of it until I do a little digging. If this priest is a molester, then your son probably isn't the only victim."

■

That evening after I told Miranda about the telephone conversation with Martin Pruett, she asked, "Did he sound like he was telling the truth?"

"He's either a great actor or telling the truth, and I don't think he's much of an actor. He was telling what he believed was true, no doubt about it," I answered. "I'm confident it's no hoax, but I wish it were. I need to talk to his son, and maybe some others, before I can go public, but the father was sincere."

We went to bed troubled that night, both of us churning over this story and the fact that I would write it if it turned out to be verifiable. After what I'd read about similar events in Boston, I was determined not to let the local clergy stonewall me.

■

First thing in the morning, the phone in my home office rang. I heard it from the kitchen, so I walked back and picked it up. A woman's voice immediately said, "This is the office of Roswell Gilbert. Mr. Gilbert would like to speak with you."

"Put him on," I replied.

Gilbert's tone was conciliatory: "We got off on the wrong foot the other day, Mr. Martinez. My fault. You've been a valued and distinguished member of the staff for many years, an award winner. I didn't mean to alienate you, and I'm man enough to admit I was out of line.

"I hope you'll reconsider your decision to leave the staff," he said. "You can retain your position as special correspondent, write the features you like, and perhaps help Monica Salinas break in."

Monica's first couple of pieces had been well intended but laughably naive, and I'd bet that letters to the editor had told Gilbert that. In any case, the *Express* certainly paid better than the *Tribune*, and most of my established readership was tied to it, but my response was easy. "Well, I'll always be happy to help Monica or other newcomers," I replied, "but I've made a commitment to the *Tribune* now. The editor there accepted me with no reservations, so I can't back away."

After a moment of silence, the publisher said, "We could enhance your salary . . ."

The offer hung there a moment, then I replied, "It's not about money, Mr. Gilbert. It's about having to call you Mr. Gilbert, and about having been thoughtlessly reassigned, and—"

He cut me off, saying, "We're determined to bring a new quality of journalism to Northern California. You could be a vital cog in that venture."

"It's also about you not knowing the difference between Central California and Northern California," I replied. "Look at the map."

"You can be a contrary devil, can't you?" he snapped.

That made me smile. The tone of his voice told me he was growing angry—not used to rejection, I'd guess. "You don't know the half of it," I said.

"Then there's little point in talking to you."

"Very little."

"Good day!"

I stood there smiling. I don't think I'd ever heard anyone say "Good day" in that context before, except in movies. He really was a pompous twit.

26

The reality of owning the old place in the mountains hit home when Rollie called to tell me the septic system at the cabin was leaking. I asked Miranda if she wanted to drive north with me to fix it. She grinned and replied, "No, I think I'll let you deal with sewerage like the warrior you are. Besides, I've got some full days coming up." Since she was far handier than I, the irony of her message wasn't lost on me.

She added, "If you really want me to travel up there with you, though, and we can work around my schedule, I'll go."

Since Rollie'd told me the leak looked bad, and he'd already called a company in Dunsmuir, I knew I had to drive up right away, so I thanked my wife, called Martin Pruett to reschedule our meeting, then began tossing clothes into a bag. "I'll just be a day, two at the most," I told Miranda. "I want to start exploring that molestation story."

"Are you sure this trip isn't a ploy so you and Rollie can go fishing?"

"What we'll be fishing for we won't want to catch," I said with a laugh.

The next morning, I was futzing around the cabin in Castella, toting a cup of coffee while I straightened some things and rearranged others, when Rollie and Jimmy Dean drove up. "Hey, Beaner!" he called. "The cesspool crew's not here?"

"Nope. Not yet."

"Must be a buncha damned Mex'cans."

"Yeah." I smiled. "It's too complex a job for Okies."

He laughed, then said, "Listen, I got some news for you. Nancy's over at the house. She come in on the airport bus from Sacramento last night late. Her and Audrey're gonna drive down to help Lea when she has the new baby, but when she heard you're up here, she said she wanted to talk to you."

"Nancy? At your place?" I'd known my ex would return for the birth of our first grandchild, but no one had mentioned this early arrival to me. Lea had hinted that her mother was purposely avoiding face-to-face contact with me, so I immediately began to speculate about why she wanted to see me now.

"Cat got your tongue?" Rollie asked.

"How is she?"

"Looks fine to me. Come see for yourself. Audrey's makin' those cinnamon rolls you love."

I needed to think about this, breathe deeply, assemble myself, so I said, "You head on back. I'll be there before long. I want to finish what I'm doing."

"What exactly *are* you doin,' Beaner?"

"Beats the shit out of me. Now get out of here."

"You bet," he said with a chuckle and left.

An hour later I parked in front of Rollie and Audrey's large riverfront house, then walked deliberately toward the door, which was opened by him before I could ring the bell. "You smell these rolls, did you, Beaner?" my ex-brother-in-law asked.

I was too tense to come up with a snappy reply. I entered and, across the room, saw the only other woman I'd ever loved. I hesitated, my breath catching, as Nancy placed her cup and plate on a nearby TV tray and posed for a moment in front of the picture window that revealed a stretch of the Sacramento River. Sunlight streamed from behind her hair, gray now, iridescent in that setting.

She greeted me with a hug and a peck on my cheek. "How are you, Marty? You look wonderful. I'd heard your health . . ."

"I'm okay, Nan," I replied, a bit dazed. Since our breakup I'd thought of so many things to say to her, but now I was speechless. My ex-wife's face was nearly unlined and her figure was still trim. Life at the commune seemed to agree with her. "And you?" I asked.

"I'm fine. I was just telling Audrey and Rollie that I'm coaching a cross-country team for the home-schooled kids at the community and really enjoying myself." She paused and smiled, asking, "Are you ready to be a grandpa?"

"I sure am. How about you? Ready to be a grandma?"

Her eyes glistened as she said, "It's a dream come true. That's why I flew out early, just in case Lea delivers sooner than expected. I don't want to miss the birth.

"Oh." She smiled and said, "Congratulations on your marriage. I hope I can meet your wife while I'm here. Rollie and Audrey say she's wonderful."

I stood there like a man on Mars without breathing gear, as I said, "Yes, she is."

Nancy responded, "Let's take a walk, Marty."

I saw her sister and brother-in-law exchange a knowing glance as I said, "Sure."

The two of us walked out of the house and across the road to the river that tumbled and roiled. We found the fisherman's path along the stream and headed south, a route we'd strolled countless times in earlier years; it had overgrown in places, and flood debris blocked it in others. Down the trail, Nancy looked straight ahead, not at me, as she said, "We had a good marriage, Marty. I've thought about it a lot, and I know you have, too. What happened to Dougie shouldn't have ruined it."

"But it did," I said.

"Yes, but I've gained some perspective now. I know I was blaming you because I was blaming myself, and I'm sorry about that."

"Me too." I swallowed hard. "About everything that went wrong."

We walked silently for a time then, the river rushing beside us and my belly eerie with forgotten yearning. A water ouzel emerged like a feathered fish from a rill next to the main current and dipped its small teardrop-shaped body up and down several times on a rock, then plunged back underwater.

"That's where Doug caught the big trout," I said, pointing at a pool just below a small chute. "Lea cried so much he put it back, remember?"

"I remember."

Ahead I could hear the roar of one of the rapids. "Still beautiful here," I said.

"I've worked in an AIDS hospice program sponsored by Madre Maria, too, and I've seen so many boys like our Doug . . . and so many families like ours . . . suffering."

"It's good they've got you."

Nancy put her hand on my forearm and said, "Marty, I've found someone, too. A man at the commune, that's why I needed to see you. He wants me to ask you for an annulment so he and I can be married in the Church, but now—just seeing you back where we were so happy together—I can't." She seemed to take a deep breath, then said, "I didn't call you or visit before because I was afraid I'd be swept back into love with you, and too much had happened—"

"Have you been?" I shouldn't have asked, but my mouth was on automatic pilot.

For what seemed a long time, we posed there; in a movie we would have kissed. Instead, she turned and walked to a boulder under trees next to the current, and sat down. "Tell me about your wife," Nancy said when I joined her. "Audrey says she's a doctor."

"She has a family practice in Sacramento. She's our age, divorced, with three sons and two grandchildren with another on the way. She has breast cancer."

"Oh, I'm sorry." Her hands moved toward her own breasts, then she asked, "How's your health *really?*"

"Well, I'm on a slow boat. I'm taking hormone blockers—chemical castration—and that's stopping the cancer. With good luck I could last five years or even more. With bad luck, a year or two."

"Isn't there anything else they can do?"

"Not right now. Maybe in a few years they'll come up with something. I've just got to hang on."

She nodded. "Father McIntyre, who directs our community, has prostrate cancer." She hesitated. "Why're you smiling?"

"You said 'prostrate.' There's a joke among guys who've got the disease. When someone says prostrate—and it's a common mistake—we always respond, 'I wouldn't take that lying down!'"

She smiled and shook her head. "Doesn't anything scare you?"

"Lots. But I can't let that stop me. How bad is Father McIntyre?"

"He had radiation because he was too old for surgery. I guess he's okay. That part of his life is private. He says it's in God's hands."

"He's right," I agreed.

"And you've returned to the Church, I hear."

"True."

"That's wonderful." She squeezed my forearm.

"Tell me about your gentleman, Nan."

She looked down and said, "Well, Morris is a little younger than I am — he's fifty-five — and he works in the commune's publishing house. He's an ex-priest, formally released from his vows, a nice guy, Marty, very low key. I'm sure you'd like him."

"Where's he from?" I asked.

"Los Angeles. He graduated from Loyola."

The talk veered from our personal lives toward family and friends: Johnny O's health (bad), Gloria's recovery from Manuel's death (good), Toshio and Janine's daughter going to school in Italy (terrific). Inevitably, though, we were pulled back to our own personal lives: "I read that your commune is celibate. Why can't you and Morris just marry and have a chaste relationship? Let me tell you candidly that I'm impotent and my libido's gone for now at least, but it hasn't killed intimacy."

My ex-wife hesitated, then replied, "If we weren't committed to the Madre Maria way of life we could, Marty, but Father McIntyre says it would be scandalous for us to live together if we weren't married in the eyes of the Church. We'd be excommunicated."

"No, not after Vatican II."

"Madre Maria doesn't accept Vatican II," she said with sudden conviction. "I'm delighted that you've returned to the Church, but I hope the parish you're in still practices true Catholicism."

The image of regressive Father Andrews popped into my mind, but it wasn't worth getting into, so I responded, "It does." Then I moved the conversation elsewhere, saying, "Both our spouses — or potential spouses — would be happier if we annulled our marriage."

Nan's face softened again, and she asked, "Do you want to do that?"

"No. It would dishonor all that we had and it would kill Lea."

"It would kill part of me, too," she said softly, averting her eyes. Then she said, "We'd better go back."

We walked silently, upstream now, the river and the path appearing remarkably different from the downstream stroll. An osprey passed overhead, dipped, then flew on. Under cottonwoods across the street from Rollie and Audrey's house, Nancy stopped me. "I know now we could have worked everything out," she said.

"Yes, we could have."

We embraced — my heart melting just as it had the first time we'd ever done that, so many years ago. After a moment, we walked across the street and joined her sister and brother-in-law for a lunch I could hardly eat.

■

I mulled that encounter over the next day while the crew dug new leach lines for the septic system at the cabin. I realized that speaking frankly with Nancy the day before had broken some lingering cyst of pain within me. We were all right again. There would be no more wondering about my ex-wife.

During the afternoon, while the workers completed their job, I straightened this and that around the cabin, remembering Nancy and our kids, the vacations we'd enjoyed up here. In a cluttered drawer of our old desk, I found a small reel of audiotape. On it was written simply "9/24/67" and I knew what it had to be. I still remember that day, because I had placed on the dinette table the tape in the recorder I used then for interviews and punched the RECORD button just as the kids scrambled in for lunch.

They had climbed onto their chairs, chattering as usual — Doug seven, Lea five — both all angles and action while Nancy delivered tomato soup and toasted cheese "samiches." And me, leaning in the kitchen doorway, still young enough to be a little dazed that this was really my family. My parents and Nan's mother were still alive then, so we weren't yet the older generation.

Holding the small plastic spool now in the den of this empty house, I could only remember that time now gone, now lost. How many years was it that Nan and I just seemed to drift through an unchanging life — my father and mother were always there for us in Merced, and Nan's mother lived in Santa Maria; we always spent holidays with family and old friends; our children grew, but somehow we didn't seem to age, so our apprehension of the world didn't. Those were the years when we joked about growing older because it seemed such a distant, painless process: So we were twenty-five, thirty, thirty-five? So what? Our parents were still there, and all our old friends were too; even our old neighbors remained nearby, so we could still feel fresh as kids.

I took it all for granted, generations buffering us on both sides, our own lives challenging but unthreatening, my career on an upward track. It was now as unreal to me as an old movie, and I found myself gutted by the realization that I had not appreciated that wonderful interlude at the time.

I snapped the tape into a small recorder on the dining area's counter, then pressed the PLAY button. For several moments, I heard only the dry hum of the machine, followed by a crackling. A version of my own voice rumbled out, so loud I couldn't understand it; I quickly lowered the volume and heard chairs scraping and the children's laughter and, in the background, my voice echoed—giving orders as usual, so embarrassing to hear today.

"Here's your soup, honey," said Nancy's voice.

"You know . . . you know . . . you know Marcus! Marcus! Marcus!" cried Lea. "He's bad. He's a . . ."

Doug's voice cut in: "I kicked the ball in soccer. I scored a gold!"

". . . Marcus he's a bad boy, know why?"

"Why?" asked Nancy.

"He . . . he called me a name. He . . . he called me a . . . a . . . he called me a . . . piggy."

"Shame on him," said Nancy, and I could hear her smile.

"And Rosellen, she's the goldie, and she ate some paste, and the teacher told her not to," Doug almost shouted.

"Use your indoor voice," admonished his mother.

My voice: "Did you try some?"

"I didnunt try some," he replied.

"I didnunt try some," echoed his sister.

"Why don't both of you try some soup," urged their mother.

"Maybe it tastes as good as paste," I suggested.

"Oh, yuck," said Doug.

"Oh, yuck," said Lea, then, "Know what? Know what? Know what, Mommy?"

Why hadn't I recognized then how splendid and ephemeral those moments were?

27

Work at the cabin took all day, so I didn't arrive back in Sacramento until late. Miranda, already in bed, was just enough awake to smile when I kissed her. The next morning, though, I told her about the interminable cesspool repair, then added, "I had breakfast at Rollie and Audrey's. Nancy was there."

"Your ex-wife?" Miranda's voice was half an octave higher than usual.

"She's out for the birth."

Miranda poured herself more coffee as she said, "I understand that. How is she?"

"She seems fine. I half expected that she'd be dressed like a nun or something, but she looked the same . . . or a little older, but the same."

"This is the first time you've seen her in how long?"

"Four years or so," I replied.

"And . . . ?"

"And what?"

"And how did it go?"

I put my own coffee down and said, "I didn't fall back in love with her, if that's what you mean."

"That's what I mean."

I smiled, then stood and embraced Miranda, saying, "You're stuck with me."

■

Martin Pruett was a small man with nervous hands, probably ten years younger than I. He sat across from me in Hoover's Coffee Shop cradling a cup of the house special. "I maybe shouldn't have called you, but I just felt helpless, and Paul, my son, he said he felt like nobody could help him. He's been real depressed. I was afraid he might do something drastic."

"You did the right thing," I assured him. "If the Church won't investigate, I will."

"Thank you."

I sipped from my coffee, thinking that this man was sincere. I could sense no guile in him. "Where do you work, Mr. Pruett?"

"At the big Ace Hardware over in West Sacramento. I mostly run the paint department."

"Been there long?"

"Nearly thirteen years. Before that I was with the utility district for twenty and took early retirement."

"Married?"

He averted his eyes when he replied, "Widowed. My wife she died of lung cancer last year. I quit smoking then."

"And you have the one son?"

"We—I—have an older boy and girl, too. They're both married and moved away."

I started to ask about his affiliation with St. Mary's parish, when he interrupted. "Paul, he's out in the car. I could bring him in . . ."

That surprised me. "Please do." The son's presence seemed promising to me.

A few minutes later, Pruett returned with a slight young man who kept his eyes on the floor. "Paul, this is Martin Martinez, the newspaper writer."

The boy didn't meet my eyes, but he said, "Nice to meet you," and limply shook hands with me, then sat next to his father.

His avoidance of eye contact bothered me because it might mean he was lying rather than merely embarrassed about what had happened to him. I had to figure out which. Well, I knew one way to do that in a hurry.

I reached into my bag and pulled out a portable tape recorder. Both of them stared at it as though I'd placed a bomb on the table. "I'm going to turn this on now," I told them, "and first I'd like you to repeat the story you told me, Mr. Pruett. When you're done, I'll ask Paul some questions."

The older man's face blanched. "A recorder?"

To put them at ease, I chuckled and said, "Hey, I'm an old guy. I hope you don't think I can remember all we say."

"But a recorder . . ."

I said, "We're going to have to trust one another, Mr. Pruett. If this priest is molesting kids, I want to nail him, but I can't do it alone."

The man's hands grew busier and he bit his lip, but finally he asked, "Is this just for your use?"

The boy looked up and his dark eyes met mine. "I'll tell you whatever you want to know, Mr. Martinez," he said.

Paul repeated essentially the same tale his father'd told me over the phone—and while he talked I was swept by a hormonal hot flash, sweating suddenly—but he didn't seem to notice, answering questions and naming other boys he was certain had been abused: "I know for sure Bill and Tony were because they told me."

"Okay," I said. "Do you by any chance have the addresses or phone numbers of other altar boys?"

"Paul made this list," the father said, and he handed me a sheet of notebook paper.

"I'll start here," I said. "After I talk to some other young men, I'll want to talk to you again. One way or another we'll stop this guy." Then I added, "There's one more thing you should think about. If we succeed and we get this pervert arrested and tried, you'll have to testify in open court about exactly what he did to you . . . not just say he molested you." I paused to let that sink in, then asked. "Can you do that, Paul?"

The young man gazed out the coffee shop's window for a long time, then he said, "Attorneys will ask me that?"

"His attorneys will. They know that young guys in particular can be too embarrassed to talk about those things."

"Well, they're out of luck. The son of a bitch played with my pecker and played with his own at the same time. I'll give them more than they want to hear about him. I wish the cops would let me kick his ass!"

That was what I wanted to hear. "Good," I said.

When I got back to my car, feeling elated by the young man's candor, I was suddenly swept by fatigue and felt like napping. I'd experienced this kind of episode a time or two previously and assumed it was the price I paid for living into my sixties — and probably for taking the hormone blockers. In any case, I really wasn't alert enough to drive, so I just closed my eyes and dozed there in the parking lot.

■

Before I could tell Miranda about the meeting with the Pruetts, she said, "Well, I may be excommunicated because I tangled with that new priest at the class today. I must be becoming a real Martinez."

"You did *what?*"

"After his usual spiel about the end-time and the Apocalypse," she explained, "he somehow got off on marital celibacy and how married couples shouldn't have sexual relations unless they're trying to have a baby. He said it was really the woman's responsibility. Well, I've heard he likes to bully females, whether it's little altar girls or the parish secretary, so I guess I was gunning for him."

"What exactly did you say?"

"I asked him if a young wife with, say, uterine cancer had to have a hysterectomy, would be banned from sex for the rest of her life. He said certainly. I said baloney.

"Well, that got Mrs. Marquez — she's back — going in his defense. She said that before she had her hysterectomy she was granted permission by her priest but that she and her husband had to live as brother and sister from then on. I said, 'So you consulted a male with no medical training and likely no knowledge of female physiology or psychology, and no experience in a marriage either, then let him tell you what to do?'

"Things went downhill from there," she said, smiling. "And by the way, the priest also invoked the Madre Maria Society as an example of true Catholicism. Isn't that the one Nancy's involved with?"

■

I was working on the pedophile priest story when the phone rang that evening, and over the answering machine a Monsignor Osbourn identified himself as the bishop's legal advisor. I picked up the receiver, and he got right to the point: "I understand that you're working on a story about Father Damien Reilly. Don't you realize how enemies of the Church will use that, Mr. Martinez? I can understand that you have a journalist's interest in such matters, but this is a delicate internal affair that His Excellency is dealing with in-house." His tone was affable. "As a Catholic yourself, surely you can understand that."

"Father Osbourn, I have a parent's interest and it's much deeper than a writer's interest," I responded. "It makes me ask why this Father Reilly got a new parish?"

"Nothing's been proven against him. How do you know this hasn't already been dealt with internally?"

"When I telephoned the diocese I got the runaround. The bishop better figure out that secrecy just makes matters worse."

"I don't think His Excellency needs your advice," the monsignor snapped.

"Well, he needs somebody's. Why does Reilly still have a parish?"

"If you want to play hardball, then why are *you* living in sin with a second so-called wife? Don't you think that's scandalous for two prominent Catholics?"

"My wife and I live together voluntarily, Father," I said. "I'm not molesting or coercing anyone."

"So you're determined to write about this matter and not let us handle it internally?"

"You've had . . . what? . . . eight years to deal with it. Now you're finally going to rein in a sexual predator?"

"You have no proof of that, only accusations."

"I now have the testimony of three ex-altar boys. I've five others to call. And I'm going to talk to kids in Woodland — "

"You'd better hope your own house is in order before you publish any of this, Mr. Martinez," he snapped, cutting me off. "You'd better hope your gay son didn't leave any stories behind."

That was how dirty he wanted to play. "You'd better hope I don't put you in the hospital, pal," I hissed, "because I will if you mention my son again. And if you've been fiddling with little boys yourself, watch out."

"Is that a threat?"

"Damn right it is. Keep your eyes on the *Tribune*, pal."

■

Monsignor Kelley was back the next Sunday, sooner than I would have expected, greeting parishioners at the church's door. "We'll have to exchange catheter tales," he whispered to me as we shook hands, and I laughed.

"And *you,*" he said to my wife as he shook her hand. "I understand you've put poor Father Andrews on the run."

"I've done my best," she admitted.

"Well, he'll be off to another parish with his little flock next week," the priest told us. "He's never quite been able to run a church. He's much better at experiencing revelations than at balancing ledgers."

"I have a question about another priest, Monsignor, a Monsignor Osbourn. Do you know him?" I asked.

He wrinkled his nose. "That one fancies himself the bishop-in-waiting, I think. How have you encountered him?"

"I'll tell you about it later; I want to talk to you about a story I'm researching."

"Fine."

The visiting priest was saying his final Mass that Sunday, and the church was only half full; his homilies had considerably thinned the attendance. He also seemed to have created an all-male pulpit crew—lector, altar servers, Eucharistic ministers—the first I'd ever seen in this parish. Miranda noticed that immediately and whispered, "Ah, it's 1952 in here again. Now if he'll just say the Mass in Latin . . ."

Father Andrews seemed to be trying to do just that. By the time we reached the homily I wondered if it would be in Latin.

"It is better to trust in the Lord than to put confidence in man," he intoned. After a pause, he repeated himself, adding "Better to put confidence in the Lord than in doctors or lawyers or professors or journalists and others too full of themselves, suffering from the grave sin of pride."

I poked Miranda, and she whispered, "He got both of us."

"That, my friends," proclaimed the padre, "is Psalm 118, verse 8: the center of the Bible, the center of God's message.

"There are 594 chapters before Psalm 118. There are 594 chapters after Psalm 118. Add those numbers up and you have 1,188. What is the Bible's center? Psalm 118:8, my friends, Psalm 118:8: 'It is better to trust in the Lord than to put confidence in man!' Notice that the Lord is in the center of that sentence, thus the exact center of the Bible."

My wife whispered to me, "There are seven words before 'Lord' in that sentence, only six after it."

It took me a second to count words myself, then I whispered to her, "Smart-assed observations like that keep you in trouble."

"The Lord must be the center of all we think and do," the priest continued. "There are other deeper meanings and signs shown only to those who see them." He moved then to warnings about the imminent Second Coming.

"This guy is a real fruit cake," Miranda whispered to me.

"There you go again."

Father Andrews touched as many bases as he could, since this was his last chance to reform us. "Education doesn't exempt Catholics from the moral precepts of Holy Mother Church, which are inarguable," he pointed out, causing me to again poke my wife lightly in the ribs. The unstated message was, of course, that we didn't pursue real Catholicism in this parish. Too well educated. Too skeptical. Too unwilling to listen to him.

When Miranda and I walked out of Mass, Father Andrews was surrounded by that throng of strangers who had followed him to our parish—women in long dresses and hats, men in suits and ties.

"I wonder where he'll go next?" I said.

"Who cares?" my wife replied.

"Hey," I pointed out, "he's made us appreciate the priests we have."

"He's certainly done that."

28

Miranda walked into the den holding a folder, and asked, "What's this?"

I glanced at it, then said, "A long time ago I thought I could be a novelist. That's about as far as I got."

"Hmmm." She began reading the first page aloud: "*West of the Sierra Nevada, near the exact center of California in a valley as large as England, thirty-one dark-skinned men bent over a field covered by sprouting green. Two fair-skinned men—one on horseback, the other standing next to a team and wagon—watched the workers.*

"*'I'll tell you, Mr. Mitchell,' said the wagoner, 'this war with the Kaiser ain't all bad: look at the way them Mexicans work. We'd a never had 'em here if it wasn't for the war. The government wouldn't never have let 'em in if all our boys wasn't gone.' He drew a long sip from a canvas canteen.*

"*'True, Rumsen,' agreed the horseman, 'and this is about as good a crew as I've ever hired. Silveira down the road's got Filipinos and Japs and he says they're good, too, but I'll settle for these Spics anytime.'*

"*Far above the field a lone raven pumped toward western foothills, and to the south two whirlwinds flitted. The sun hung above like a crematory flame.*"

She glanced up at me and asked, "Where'd you get this story?"

"It was inspired by things my grandparents told us about coming here. Most of it I just thought up."

"I like the way this starts. Why didn't you finish it?"

I hadn't read or thought about that manuscript for well over a decade, and it sounded unfamiliar. "Oh, I showed what I was doing to the book editor at the paper — he was an aspiring novelist — and he said for me not to quit my day job."

She shook her head. "Did it occur to you he might have been full of bull, and maybe jealous, too? What's he had published?"

"Nothing that I know of."

"I'd really like you to finish this. You're not the kind of man who's afraid to take chances."

I had to examine my own feelings before I answered. "I guess the literary world's too subjective for me, too trendy. I like straightforward writing, and he said I wasn't a stylist."

"You didn't break his nose? This is another side of you," Miranda said, "a vulnerable one."

"This is different than journalism — it's sharing of your deepest self. When it's rejected . . . well, you lose confidence."

"I'm going to read the rest of this, but I think you should finish it, assume the book editor was loony. You're a strong writer, you know that."

"Yeah, but am I a novelist?"

■

A phone call from Randy announced that Lea was in labor. By the time Miranda and I arrived at the hospital that evening, the parents-to-be had already settled in at the birthing center. The old maternity ward was long gone, and so was the waiting room that had palled with smoke in the old days.

Miranda and I had to be buzzed into the new area by a pleasant woman seated at a desk behind what looked like bulletproof glass. Lea's birthing suite was commodious and hotel-like, with medical equipment and hospital bed on one end, while comfortable chairs, a table, and a couch dominated the other one; the entryway, a bathroom, and something that looked like a kitchenette separated those two segments.

Lea, hooked up to a monitor and an IV and attended by a small woman in green scrubs, lay on the bed; Randy sat in a chair next to her, holding her hand. A small group of visitors clustered at the far end of the room, but Miranda and I walked directly to my daughter, who smiled and said, "Hi, Daddy. Hi, Miranda." First my wife, then I, embraced and kissed Lea. While I was shaking Randy's hand, I heard Miranda say, "Oh, hi, Joyce. I wondered who'd be on duty. How's it look?"

"Fine so far."

Miranda took my hand then and said to the other woman, "Have you met my husband, Marty Martinez? He's Lea's father. Marty, this is Joyce Shapiro. She's Lea's ob-gyn."

"Nice meeting you, Joyce."

"Are you ready to be a grandpa?" the physician asked as we shook hands.

"I sure am."

"I'll bet," she smiled. "It'll be a while. I want to give your daughter plenty of time to dilate. Our motto is 'Safe Mommy, Safe Baby.'"

"I agree."

When Miranda and I turned to join the group clustered at the dimly lit opposite end of the room, I immediately spied Nancy. Rollie and Audrey, Toshio and Janine, and a younger couple I didn't recognize were there too. Although I had anticipated this meeting with my ex-wife, I was briefly nonplussed. Nancy, who must have seen us as we entered, stepped forward and took both of my wife's hands in hers. "You must be Miranda," she smiled, "I've heard so much about you. I'm Nancy, Lea's mother."

Those two stood for a moment, then embraced. Meanwhile, Rollie was shaking my hand, asking, "How you doin,' Grandpa?" He slapped my back. I embraced Audrey, then Janine, and shook hands with Tosh and the young couple, who turned out to be Randy's brother and sister-in-law. By then my ex-wife had disengaged from my new one and moved in front of me. "Hi, Grandpa." Nancy grinned. "Did you ever think this would happen?"

I could feel Miranda watching us as I replied, "I sure hoped it would."

"Me, too." Nancy smiled again, then kissed my cheek.

Eventually we all settled in at the far end of the room, exchanging tales about this birth and that pregnancy. Several young women and one more young couple — all friends of Lea and Randy — passed through, offering best wishes.

"Where's Chava?" asked Toshio. "He wouldn't miss a dogfight, let alone a birth."

He certainly knew my brother. "He's on duty."

Meanwhile, my wife and my ex-wife seemed determined to get to know one another, so they chatted privately while the rest of us gabbed.

From the other end of the room I heard occasional moans, plus reassurances from the attending physician ("You're doing just fine"). Randy appeared a little ashen to me, and when I mentioned that to my wife, she said, "Go over and buck him up. You've been through this, and I know you're pretty keyed up too."

She was correct, of course, except that I'd not sat in on the birth of my two kids because fathers weren't welcome then. All this had me a bit scared.

Shortly after midnight, I heard one of the nurses who'd relieved the obstetrician say sharply, "I'll page Dr. Shapiro. We're about there."

Miranda's head snapped up.

Suddenly, it seemed, another nurse and the physician appeared. Miranda took my arm. "Say a quick prayer," she urged. "It'll make you feel better." I did that, and we paused there while Lea moaned and the doctor worked.

"That's it, just a couple more," urged the physician.

I could hardly breathe. My little girl was having a baby.

Then I felt my other arm being grasped, and Nancy leaned into me just as Dr. Shapiro announced, "You've got a boy!" and we heard a little "Wahhhhh!"

■

As we were driving home from the hospital, Miranda said, "You and Nancy did very well for first-time grandparents. Have the kids settled on a name for the little guy?"

"Douglas, after my son, and Miguel, after Randy's father. Douglas Miguel Lozano, a good name . . . another Doug in the family." My eyes teared as I said those words.

Miranda squeezed my thigh. After a long pause, she said, "Nancy still loves you, doesn't she?"

That stopped me, but I finally responded, "She loves some memory of me, I suppose."

We drove for several more minutes, her head resting on my shoulder, then she said, "Marty, if you should ever feel . . . trapped in our relationship, just tell me." She quickly added, "I pray you never do, though."

"Save your prayers, Dr. Mossi. To repeat, you're stuck with me."

"I hope so."

■

The pain that awakened me that night was like the worst indigestion I'd ever endured, accompanied by discomfort radiating into my jaw. I arose from bed and wandered into the bathroom, where I quaffed several antacid tablets. They had no immediate effect, and that ache remained behind my breastbone.

"What's wrong?" Miranda asked. She stood in the doorway in her nightgown, eyes sleepy.

"I've got indigestion — too many snacks, I guess."

"Where exactly does it hurt?"

I showed her.

"Any radiation?"

"It hurts in my jaw a little."

"And it's lasted how long?"

I told her.

"Okay," she said, her voice unambiguous. "Get dressed. We're going to the emergency room."

"The emergency room? But—"

"Hey, don't give me your male denial, Marty Martinez. Right now, I'm a doctor, not your wife, and I want to be certain this isn't a heart attack."

A heart attack? I was lean; I stayed in shape. How could I be having a heart attack? As my wife drove us to the nearby hospital, I began thinking, I've got cancer . . . surely I can't be having a heart attack too.

But I was.

"Don't tell Lea," I instructed Miranda after I was settled in the cardiac care ward. "After we know exactly what's going on we can let her know. She's already got plenty on her plate."

My wife nodded, then said, "Dr. Singh says he thinks this has been a small attack, to the extent any heart attack can be small; it didn't even show up on the EKG, but the blood chemistry revealed it. Are you sure this hasn't happened before?"

"Not that I recall. I've had discomfort there before, even in my jaw, but antacids always relieved it." I lay there with oxygen tubes in my nose and an IV taped to my hand dripping nitroglycerine solution into me.

"Well, Dr. Singh will do an angiogram tomorrow to determine the where and how bad of this, but with luck we'll be able to treat it with diet and drugs."

I had to shake my head. "This is one hell of a way to welcome my grandson into the world." After a moment, I asked, "Can you have a priest visit me?"

"Of course," she said, then kissed me, and I thought I saw her blink back tears, which almost made me cry.

The chest pain was gone when I awoke the next morning in the hospital. Maybe further testing wasn't necessary. When I mentioned that to Miranda after she arrived, she smiled tightly and said, "No chance." Well, if this situation scared a pro like her, who was I to fake nonchalance?

A lady from the parish, someone I hadn't previously met, arrived then, and she said, "Mr. Martinez? I'm Cynthia Ryan. I've brought you Holy Communion."

"Good," I replied, then introduced my wife.

"Both Father Tran and Monsignor Kelley send their best. The monsignor's saying Mass this morning, then doing a funeral, and Father Tran's taking the third grade at the school because Mrs. Madsen's sick."

"Tell them those're flimsy excuses," I said, and for a second the woman registered shock, then she noted my grin and smiled back.

The angiogram that morning—threading a slim fiber-optic-tipped tube into my coronary artery via the femoral artery in my groin—was virtually painless. I had been ready to suffer. "How's it look, Charles?" Miranda asked the cardiologist.

"So far, so good," he responded. "I'll take a look with ultrasound now."

I heard several "ums" from him. "Well, I think you've been lucky, Mr. Martinez. I suspect that you had an occlusion of a small vein, and that the blockage was cleared by the nitroglycerine. I'd call this a damned serious warning. *Damned* serious."

One night ago I'd kissed my first grandchild. Now I lay a floor below him while the cardiologist sewed shut the small opening in my groin. Miranda repeated how lucky I was, but I didn't feel very lucky at that moment. I felt shocked and scared and sad.

Back in the cardiac care unit, my wife asked me if she should telephone Lea with the news, but I said no. "She's still recovering from the birth," I explained. "Let's let her rest at least until everything's settled."

Dr. Singh entered the room then and offered me a detailed explanation of what he'd discovered, complete with photos of the ultrasound's findings. None of it was enchanting. As he'd said, the heart attack had occurred in a small, peripheral vessel; it appeared to have resolved itself once blood thinner had been dripped into me.

"We'll get you on medication and monitor your lipids and diet. Do you exercise regularly?"

"Yes."

Dr. Singh glanced at my wife, who said, "He really does. I'll keep a close eye on his diet, too."

The physician looked back at me and said, "A lot of men lie about that. I want to keep you here for another day to make certain everything is stable. Okay?"

"Sure," I said. I was in no position to argue.

■

That evening Lea visited. I could see in her face how awful I must look. "Oh, Daddy," she cried, "are you in pain?"

"No, honey, I'm really not—just tired."

"Why did this have to happen?"

I had no answer for that except, "I guess I chose my genes wrong . . . or maybe my lifestyle."

"But you've always worked out. When I was in high school the girls all said you were a hunk."

I chuckled. "Hunk of what?"

Even Lea smiled at that. I asked, "How's that little *vato* doing? He talking yet?"

"He's asleep with Randy. Oh, and Randy says hi and get well soon."

"Give Dougie a kiss from Grandpa."

Lea looked away from me as she said, "Mom flew home yesterday, before Miranda called about your heart. She didn't know you were sick. She was really shocked when I called this morning."

"I was, too — shocked by the heart attack, I mean."

"She sends her love and her prayers." My daughter's voice swooped a bit when she told me that.

"Good," I replied. "I can use all I can get."

29

The next week a home-visit nurse named Tim walked with me around the yard, then listened to my heart, recorded my blood pressure, and handed me my meds. "It's a good thing you've stayed in shape, Mr. Martinez," he said. "You'll come back much more quickly than folks who've let themselves go."

I didn't feel like I was in any shape or coming back at all, just shuffling around like an old geezer, vaguely afraid of my own heart. The attack had damaged me psychologically as much as physically. I was only sixty-seven and didn't consider myself a senior citizen or anything like that. In fact, I had been insulted when clerks gave me senior discounts without asking my age.

But I didn't feel very lively now. I flopped on the couch for a nap, but no sooner did I lie back and close my eyes than the phone rang. A moment later Tim asked, "Do you want to talk to a Johnny Orozco? He says he's a friend."

I smiled. "Yeah, he's a friend. I'll talk to him." I'd been bombarded by phone calls, but had answered only the ones from family and close pals.

"Hey, Champ." Johnny's voice was so slurred that I could hardly understand him. "What're you doin'? Wasn't that cancer enough?"

"It was enough," I replied.

"What happened?"

I explained the events that had led me to this, and he said, "You was always in good shape, Champ. I don't get it."

"Me either. My dad died of heart disease, my mom of cancer. I seem to have inherited them both. How're you doing, brother?"

"Johnny's okay," he responded, although his weak voice and foggy words told me otherwise. "Johnny's still in the fight."

That much I believed. As long as he breathed Johnny would be in the fight.

"We're a pair, aren't we?" I said.

I heard what might have been a chuckle . . . or a sob. Then Johnny replied, "They ain't counted us out yet, Champ."

Chava and Cindy showed up right after I hung up. I'd actually requested no visitors for a while after I returned home, but my brother, as usual, interpreted that as "no one but us." Chava had his biweekly break from work, so he and his wife pulled into our driveway. They entered through the back door, then found me resting on a recliner in the family room.

"Hey, Marty, you look like hell," my brother said, after his wife had hugged and kissed me.

"Guess how I feel," I responded, then added, "You've got the same genes I do, *ese,* so you'd damn sure better watch your diet. Remember what happened to Papa."

"I remember one strike and out for him," Chava replied. "I have my heart checked every year when I take my department physical. Once you pass fifty, they do an EKG." My brother grinned then and added, "Besides, Aunt Herlinda used to say I had the ice-man's genes, not Papa's."

"I hate to tell you this, but my heart attack didn't even show on the EKG while it was happening, so have them do a stress test," I advised. "You don't want a zipper on your chest."

"You got that right."

The phone rang again. A moment later, Tim asked, "Do you want to talk with a something Osbourn? I didn't catch his first name." I had to scramble a moment before I remembered who Osbourn was — I swear, the medications had erased some of my brain cells — then I said, "Sure."

Chava said, "We'll go in the kitchen and grab some coffee."

I said, "Hello," then heard, "Mr. Martinez, the bishop has authorized me to warn you that he'll take legal action if you falsely implicate any clergy in the story you've threatened to write."

As far as I was concerned, the bishop could blow it out his ass. "So?" I said.

I thought I heard him sigh. "Hasn't it occurred to you that your considerable health problems might be a message from God?"

That was stretching it, but how the hell did he know about my health? "No," I responded.

"Well, you should consider that this may be a warning."

"Monsignor, I've talked to eight boys — young men now — and their parents here in Sacramento. Now two families in Woodland want to talk to me. Maybe *you* should consider *that* a warning."

Osbourn replied, "I'm authorized to tell you that the bishop has removed Father Reilly from his parish duties pending investigation, and reassigned him for counseling and meditation. We're capable of handling problems of this kind in-house. I don't know what more you'd expect of the diocese."

"Father Osbourn, I don't have time to mince words. I expect Reilly to go to prison if he's guilty of molesting kids, and I think he is. I also think people who allowed him to continue preying on kids for years should to go jail with him, even if that includes you and the bishop. Is my position clear?"

"I suppose you equate these incidents with the horror of abortion!" he snapped.

It was a non sequitur, but I replied, "I sure do."

"I'd hate to carry your conscience, Mr. Martinez," he spat. "You play into the hands of every enemy of the Church — "

I cut him off. "No, Father Reilly did that, and you do it too, and so, apparently, does the bishop. I'm just reporting Reilly's actions, as you or the bishop should have long ago if you knew about them. That's on your conscience, not mine. People like you are destroying the credibility of the Catholic Church. I'm trying to salvage it." I slammed the receiver into its cradle.

"Are you okay?" Tim asked.

"Just a little upset," I told him. I decided that I had to finish the story about the rogue priest as soon as I could. The longer I took, the more loopholes the bishop's boys would find.

"What's wrong?" my brother asked.

Once I'd explained what was going on, Chava shook his head and said, "Now you see why I don't go to Mass anymore."

"You'd think someone would figure out that whatever they're doing isn't working," I said. "Instead, what I get from the diocese is stonewalling. They've got a mouthpiece, that monsignor who claims he's an attorney, and he's more interested in controlling me than in controlling the offenders."

"Hey, the answer's obvious," said Chava. "Don't donate any money. As far as I'm concerned, that Church is just a business and the bottom line is all it understands."

"Right," I said.

"Enough of that crap," he spat. "I've got bad news."

My belly knotted. What now?

"You remember Junior Holloway who was in Raul's class at the high school?" he asked.

"Sure."

"Well, he killed himself last week and—get this—the newspaper said he never really got over Vietnam."

"Oh, man . . ."

"We've sure lost some buddies to that war, *vato.*"

"They got the privilege of defending democracy for the rich chicken hawks."

"Chickenshits, you mean."

■

Lea brought Dougie over to see me the next afternoon. He was still a little red squirt with a shock of fine black hair. "What do you think?" she beamed.

"Well, he's small, but he might be a keeper," I said. "He really does look a little like your brother, doesn't he?"

"As a matter of fact, Randy says the baby looks like you."

"God forbid!"

Her eyes grew damp and she said, "I really want you to be around to see him grow up, Daddy."

I took her hand and said, "Believe me, I want that too, Perico. The cardiologist didn't find any other problems. Now I've got to concentrate on controlling the cancer."

"It *can* be controlled, can't it?"

"Sure," I said without adding "for a while."

She seemed ready to cloud up, then she asked, "How do you really feel?"

"I'm alive." As much as I hated my health problems, I accepted them as dues for growing older. Lea was still young enough to consider them unjust.

■

My wife and I cuddled lightly on the couch that evening. She asked the question I'd been hearing all day, "How're you feeling?"

"The truth?" I said.

"The truth," she replied.

"Wellllll . . ." I stretched the word. "A little horny."

"Only a little? What a surprise . . . but speaking of that, have you been using your pump?"

As a matter of fact, I hadn't. Somehow all the heart rehab and medication, plus the compulsion to write the story of the rogue priest, had dominated my time. Most of all, I felt like each day was full of little obligations that my strength wasn't quite up to fulfilling. "No," I answered.

"Well, do. Don't give up on the good things in life just because something's gone wrong," she advised. "It doesn't take long for anything to atrophy, so keep yourself in shape. Don't let the illness win."

She was correct, of course.

■

It was time to talk to Monsignor Kelley and Father Tran about what I was writing, but I kept postponing that, not wanted to jeopardize my relationship with them. I finally decided to telephone the young priest first. He immediately asked about my health, adding, "You've been in my prayers. Are you okay?"

I explained what had happened, and he said, "You're the last person I'd figure to have a heart attack."

"Too much grease when I was a kid," I told him.

Once we got past that subject, I disclosed what I working on, and he said, "I'd heard rumors that you were onto something like this . . . from the clerical gossip line. You know, pederasty's a terrible embarrassment. I feel like not wearing my collar when I read about priests like the ones in Boston or Santa Rosa."

"This one's right here, a Father Damien Reilly."

"Reilly—yes, I've met him. He's out at Woodland now, isn't he? A hail-fellow-well-met, as I recall."

"Yeah, he's at Woodland now," I replied, "but he was associate at St. Mary's when he supposedly molested boys. Eight of them have communicated with me so far."

For a long moment Father Tran said nothing, then he responded, "How solid are the accusations?"

"Pretty solid, I'm afraid. The boys are all young men now. Some haven't seen one another in years, but their stories are consistent. And some parents and boys from Woodland have called and asked to talk with me too."

"That's horrible."

"I need your help for background on the story," I said. "Is there anything in the training of priests that might predispose some of them to act this way?"

The young cleric cleared his throat, then said, "Well, I'd already finished college—I had a master's degree in psychology— when I entered the seminary, so I was one of the older guys. To be candid, I think most seminarians I met were too young and inexperienced when they entered the training process. Some of the Irish priests told me they were just kids when they started their training in something called the junior seminary. I'm not sure all of them were sexually defined when they entered the program. I don't see how they could be at—what?—twelve, thirteen, fourteen.

"What they taught us was all too abstract, I thought, mostly about scripture, theology, and canon law, but far too little about psychology and counseling and virtually nothing about sexuality."

"I'd've thought psych and counseling would be a major emphasis," I told him.

"It should be. I also knew seminarians who had personal problems, some about their sexuality, but who were afraid to mention that to seminary authorities because they thought they'd get the boot and they'd always wanted to be priests."

"Did you mention that to anyone?"

"I tried, but administrators there were like bureaucrats everywhere — not very open to suggestions from the peanut gallery. They'd always done things one way, and that was the way they intended to proceed."

"Do you think celibacy contributes to the problem?" I asked.

"Sure, it contributes, but only in a small way, I think," the priest responded. "I spoke to a classmate last summer — he's an ex-priest now and married — and he said that most people can't really imagine how a man can be celibate, but that he hadn't really imagined what married life would be like when he was celibate. He wasn't certain which was the greater challenge."

"How about gay priests?"

"If my reading is accurate, the overwhelming majority of abuse against kids is committed by non-celibate, heterosexual adults, often parents — another group that likely needs better training. Gays can be celibate too."

"Touché," I replied.

"Priests do need to be mature and sexually settled," he added, "the same way non-priests do. Some men simply can't achieve that as celibates, so they don't belong. It's a challenge, but most of us accept it in that spirit."

"You've been a big help, Father. I'm going to have to expose this Reilly, but you've given me some valuable perspective. I'll be careful with my generalizations."

"You always are from what I've read," he said.

30

By the following week, I was strolling an hour a day and feeling stronger. I'd also finished writing the piece on Father Reilly and sent it to Bud Hartley at the *Tribune.* He was on the phone the next day. "Can you prove this stuff, Marty?"

"You want me to bring in the documentation, Bud?"

"Your word's good enough for me, but do keep it handy. Some guy named Osbourn, who claims he's an attorney for the diocese, called to say he'll turn us every which way but loose if we publish your story."

"He's bluffing," I said. "The bishop and his circle are worried because they didn't stop that priest who turns out to be a child abuser. One of the parents told me the bishop's representative offered a settlement in return for silence and charges not being filed. He showed me the note, and I quote from a photocopy, 'The matter of your concern is being examined and a suitable pastoral decision will be made.' Notice the language keeps it as abstract as possible? The problem could be parking tickets.

"I can't tie the bishop directly to knowledge of what Reilly was doing, but I guess it was 'suitable' to move him to another parish where he had a fresh set of boys to molest."

"It sounds like you've got some unspent ammunition and a little anger," the editor said.

"I sure as hell do."

■

The day before the article was to be printed, I was considering exactly how to handle the unused material my research had revealed. It wasn't a happy picture. The cover-up especially angered me.

When Monsignor Osbourn called yet again, his tone was conciliatory. "The bishop has asked me to inform you that he has initiated a rigorous inquiry into the actions of Father Reilly. He asks only that, as Christian charity, you suspend publication of further material until the diocese has completed its own scrutiny of him."

"Too late," I replied. "The bishop should have done that years ago. You can't keep the lid on this; that's what I've been trying to tell you. But I will add to the article that the diocese is now investigating."

"His Excellency is trying to respond to the questions you've raised," he pointed out.

"Has he looked into the activities of a Father Martin Cole or a Father John Kinney? Both of their names came up more than once in my investigation."

After a moment's hesitation, the priest answered, "Not that I'm aware of. Cole and Kinney . . ." he said, writing down the names, I assumed.

"Well," I told him, "I'll be looking into their activities next. As for Father Reilly, I believe he's guilty of a long pattern of abusing boys and I'm afraid the bishop may have been an unwitting accomplice. I'll let readers decide."

"Father Reilly hasn't enjoyed due process."

"I don't think he *is* going to enjoy it much," I snapped, "but I'll be delighted to see him in court. Meanwhile, I've offered him a chance to have his say, but he hasn't responded. As you know, the bishop enjoys the same offer."

"The bishop says he'll agree to report sex crimes if accusers agree, but he wants to protect the privacy of the youngsters involved. Let me remind you, though, that no priest from this diocese has ever been convicted of any crime."

"How many 'accusers'—call them what you will—has the diocese paid off?"

"Our dealings with accusers are privileged information by mutual agreement."

"What bullshit! If the church buys accusers off and imposes gag rules when it pays, how can you possibly expect your explanations to be taken seriously?" I demanded.

"Nevertheless, no priest has ever been convicted—"

"Well, I'm one of many Catholics who're going to attack at the purse strings. When you're out of money to buy off accusers, we'll see if the record remains so pure. Why not let the priests take their chances with a jury of their peers?"

"They have few real peers in the general population and far too many hidden agendas are at work there. Surely you know that many people have axes to grind against the clergy."

"The only way to defuse that is to make the whole process transparent rather than opaque, Monsignor," I replied.

"And you really believe that?"

"I do."

■

"Marty, this is Monsignor Kelley," said the familiar brogue on the phone. "I've just had a call from Monsignor Osbourn in the bishop's office about a story you're writing. He wants me to reason with you."

I was shocked that the monsignor would get involved in this, so I explained, concluding, "For some reason the diocese has been covering for Reilly, moving him from parish to parish."

"I know who he is. Is this a sure thing?"

"Absolutely. I wish it wasn't, but absolutely."

"Then go to it," he said. "Root out the rot, boyo. You're doin' God's work."

I don't think I'd realized how emotionally involved I had become in this case, but after the monsignor hung up I stood next to the phone with damp eyes. Thank God for clerics like him.

■

My piece on Reilly ran as a front-page break-out in the *Tribune* the next weekend. Letters to the editor and phone calls immediately poured in, everything from gloating atheists to defensive Catholics. I didn't pay attention to any of them, except the handful who reported that their own kids had also been abused.

Although I had an unlisted home number, some people managed to reach me, and since all of them were pro-bishop and anti-Martinez, I assumed that Osbourn or someone in the diocese might have passed my number on. Mostly women called, but one guy, after a long, bombastic tirade that he seemed to be reading, concluded with "You had best hope you do not find yourself in my presence, sir!"

That sounded like a badly written romantic novel, so I responded, "Well if I do, *sir,* I'll knock the shit out of you." Of course, I couldn't knock the shit out of anyone. My body was weak and my confidence was even weaker; I was still taking the hormone blockers to hold off cancer. I tried to keep that disease out of my mind, but I was certain that it, not my heart, was more apt to kill me.

When my brother visited that next weekend, he said, "Where're your shoulders, Marty? And didn't you used to have biceps? Man, you're a skinny *vato* now. You look like Papa got to looking—" He caught himself before he finished.

"Thanks for sharing, *pendejo,*" I replied. "I thought I looked like Ricardo Montalban."

"You look like the north end of his horse heading south."

Three days after the *Tribune* carried my story on Father Reilly, a version of it authored by Monica Salinas appeared in the *Express,* and the lid was really off. Local radio and television were soon blaring their versions.

■

"Marty?" said the voice on the answering machine. "This is Mort. I heard through the grapevine that you had a heart attack. The guys in the group and I really are concerned about your health. Let me know how you are, will you? I can drop by, but I'll leave that up to you. I'm not sure I'd want visitors if I was recovering.

"Oh, and I liked that good piece about the bad priest."

I decided to pick up the phone. "Hi, Mort. How are you?"

"How're *you?* Rumors are pretty wild."

"I had a mild heart attack," I told him. "The damage doesn't look major."

"You seem to find plenty of time to investigate and write," he said. "You really nailed that priest—and the bishop too."

"I started that story before I got sick. It was a sad task, Mort, those poor kids betrayed by that priest."

"Aren't you a Catholic yourself?" Mort asked.

"I sure am, that's why I had to expose the abuse."

"You know, I was raised Catholic," he told me, "but I just sort of drifted away when I was in college. The political positions seemed goofy and inconsistent to me, and the medieval church structure — with bishops and pawns and rooks, or whatever — just didn't make sense. Anyway, I've never looked back."

"Catholicism's my way of accessing the sacred, Mort," I explained, "and I believe the sacred is unknowable but real, so I'm in it for good, and that's why I want to expose any corruption."

"Well, you seem to be doing a good job of that!"

■

It wasn't a question I'd anticipated or much wanted to discuss, but sitting at the dinner table that evening, Miranda asked, "What do you think death is like?"

"Apropos of what?" I asked.

"Apropos of reality," she replied. She smiled then and added, "I don't think you're on your last legs or anything, but I found myself wondering about it — for the zillionth time — after one of my patients, Mrs. Sandrini, died this morning. She was ninety-seven, I should add."

"Well . . ." I sat quietly for a long moment and thought about it, or I should say thought more about it, since I'd asked myself the same thing more than once, "I'm afraid death's just like anesthesia — nothingness — not negative or positive, just blank." Then I quickly added, "But I hope there's something real in the Christian promise."

"I have the same fear," she said. "But I truly believe that our minds are barely evolved and not nearly capable of imagining all that's possible, so that keeps me believing that there's something beyond death that we can't conceive."

"Me too," I said. "When I was in college I read a piece by an astrophysicist, named Haldain, I think, and he said something like, 'The universe is not only queerer than we imagine, but queerer than we *can* imagine.' I think existence is queerer than we can imagine, so I really think there's no reason not to hope for more.

"I want to spend more time — or non-time or whatever it is — with the people I love: you and the kids and that new grandson. You and I got a late start."

She didn't immediately respond, so I asked, "Have you ever had a patient who had a near-death experience — you know, came back from death with memories of what happened?"

She smiled. "Well, no one comes back from death. By definition, it's permanent. People do come back from comas and shock and unconsciousness, but not death." She sipped thoughtfully from a glass of sherry, and I said nothing since it was clear she was thinking about what I'd asked.

"As for near-death experience," she continued, "the light, the bliss, and all that—I think that's the brain protecting itself under great stress. It's similar to reports of drug experiences, and I suspect it's a chemical response."

I started to speak, but she continued. "There *is* another intriguing possibility . . ."

"Which is?"

"That the whole nervous system enjoys a kind of consciousness, so when the brain isn't operating well, we become aware of those other levels of cognizance."

"I've never heard that before," I admitted.

"It's only a theory."

"So what about the Christian notion of life after death?"

"Unknowable," she responded. "We accept it on faith."

I smiled back. "That's not very scientific for a doctor, but it's admirably human. You usually don't bring your work home, so I know when you do something tough's happened." I moved behind her chair and began rubbing her neck and back.

"Mrs. Sandrini was lovely, a sort of mother to everyone she met," Miranda explained as I massaged. "She had half a dozen life-threatening illnesses, but pneumonia took her. We're all going to miss that lady.

"Nice massage," she purred. "You're a lively invalid."

■

Shortly after Miranda left for the office the next morning, the phone rang and, as usual, I decided to monitor it before answering; I was still receiving crank calls about my pederast-priest article. The voice of my ex startled me: "Hello, Marty?" she said. "This is Nancy." Then she said in a burlesque tone, "Remember me? I'm the one who loves you?" and laughed. "I just wondered how you're doing . . ."

That was a crazy way to start a call. I picked up the receiver and said, "I have a vague recollection of you. I'm doing much better, thanks."

"Oh, that's wonderful. I'd've contacted you sooner, but Lea said you didn't want calls while you were convalescing."

"I'm pretty well back to normal," I told her.

"You're in my prayers, Marty. I think about you every day."

That sounded too intimate, and I didn't need that complication, even if I had opened the door to it with my question up in Dunsmuir. I responded, "Thanks for you prayers and good thoughts, Nan," then I veered the subject away from us. "You should see that little grandson of ours, he's a pistol. He looks like a red chile."

Her laughter tinkled over the phone, and she said, "Lea says he looks like you."

"That's what I said, like a red chile."

"I can't wait to get back," she said, "but it'll have to wait . . . for a bit, anyway."

"Are you going to be married soon?" I asked.

She was silent for a long moment, then said, "Morris and I have decided to put that on hold. He wanted me to get the annulment, and I told him I couldn't. Besides, I have some other things to think about.

"How's your heart, really?" she asked.

That question startled me, since I thought I'd already answered it. "It's healing."

"Mine isn't," she said. "I realize that I need my family back together again."

I could say nothing to that, so we both fell silent for a bit, then I finally managed, "We need to support Lea and the baby. The rest will take care of itself."

"God willing," she replied.

■

Father Tran called late that week. "Your exposé has had a big effect," he told me. "There's going to be a meeting of all the diocese's priests to discuss sexual abuse and how to handle it. Something good has come of this, even if it's only candor."

"I hope so," I replied. "I'm just afraid that there's more dirt and more cover-up to be exposed."

The young priest responded, "God, I hope not, but if there is, let's get it out and over with."

"What I've had to wonder in the light of the cover-up I've encountered is whether this has always gone on and always been shielded by Church authorities." I hated what I was telling him, but I needed to get it off my chest. "I read in a magazine just the other day an assertion that secrecy and silence have always characterized the Church."

"There's always been an element of secrecy, yes. Mystery has traditionally been important in the Church's persona. It's a part that has had to change faster in America, where Catholics are better educated and more skeptical and used to an open society. Democracy does that to people; blind obedience fades. I for one think that's a good thing, if we really believe in God and free will."

"I read in the paper that some ayatollah said, 'Democracy is the enemy of the Muslim faith.' Some Catholics seem to fear democracy, too," I told him.

"Well, they're wrong. The stories my mom and dad told me about their lives in Vietnam — especially under the French — really make me grateful to be an American."

31

Miranda and I attended the 7:00 A.M. service the following Sunday, and we seemed to be able to worship anonymously, but a well-dressed, nervous-looking man I didn't recognize hovered just outside the door when we emerged. "Mr. Martinez?" he said. "Can I talk to you?"

"Sure," I said. "What's on your mind, Mr. . . . ?"

"Leary, Mike Leary," he said, and we shook hands. "I've been reading your work in the *Express* and the *Tribune* for years and I've always been an admirer of yours, so I just can't see why you're attacking your own church now." His voice cracked with emotion and his eyes were watery.

"Explain to me exactly how I've attacked the Church, Mr. Leary."

It suddenly seemed he might weep — or perhaps erupt in rage. "You've held the bishop, the whole clergy really, up to scorn," he responded. "You've given every enemy of the Church ammunition."

"Hasn't it occurred to you that sex abusers are the villains in this terrible affair, they and anyone who harbors them?" I asked.

"You medias are all alike. I suppose you mean to accuse the Holy Father himself!" His tongue stuck out and curled.

"I mean to accuse anyone who protects child molesters, Mr. Leary. Anyone."

"Who gave you such power?" he demanded.

"The Constitution of the United States," I snapped. "It's called freedom of speech."

"Aren't you a Mexican?" he demanded, then curled his tongue.

"I'm an American, bozo. What're you, an Irishman?"

He retreated a step, seeming to gnaw his lip as Miranda took my arm, saying, "Let's go."

We started to walk away when Leary raised his voice: "You're destroying men of God for your own personal gain."

I turned and asked, "If Father Reilly was a Baptist or a Mormon, would you still favor protecting him? If the abused children were yours, would you protect the abusers?"

"You're not even a true Catholic," he spat. "A divorced man!"

I took a step toward him, but my wife again grasped my arm, saying, "Marty, your heart. Don't do something stupid."

By then a small crowd had gathered, and I heard one voice ask, "Is that the one who wrote those things?" as Miranda and I walked away.

Driving home, I said, "I wonder if I'm going to have to put up with characters like that every time I go to Mass."

"We'll just go to another church if that happens," Miranda said. Then she added, "I know you grew up fighting, so I'm proud of the way you controlled yourself."

Although shaken, I said, "I couldn't fight my grandson right now. Besides, maybe you're civilizing me."

"Someone had to," she said and smiled.

"By the way, what was going on with that guy's tongue?"

Miranda turned toward me, saying, "His tongue?"

"He kept sticking it out and twisting it."

"I didn't notice. I was too busy refereeing the battle."

■

I awakened that next morning still troubled about the confrontation at church, so I lay there for a while, breathing deeply to clear my mind. Miranda stirred next to me and rolled onto one side, and her pajama top pulled up enough to reveal the smooth skin covering her ribs.

I rolled her way and placed my hand on her body, then lightly caressed her side, her tummy, her breast, then her tummy again, all warm.

"Mmmmmm," she purred.

I snuggled against her back and kissed her ear, running my index finger gently around her nipple. "Does your pump still work?" she asked sleepily.

"I hope so," I said, then kissed her ear, her neck, her shoulder. "Don't go anywhere," I said.

She laughed sleepily.

I rolled out of bed and walked into the bathroom, where I pulled the pump from its drawer. I had an erection when I returned to the bedroom. "Sorry that took so long, but pumping just didn't go well. So much for spontaneity."

My love smiled. "Worth the wait."

We smooched like youngsters, except that I couldn't achieve orgasm. Just when I felt myself approaching it, the tension refused to crest. It was more than just frustrating, but I could tell how much Miranda was enjoying herself, so I continued performing as best I could until I felt her gasping, shuddering, then relaxing. During the entire time my chest didn't bother me at all; in fact, I forgot I had a chest.

She was asleep again when I arose to remove the band from my penis and to dress. I wandered then into the kitchen to make coffee. This was one of Miranda's days off, and we planned to hike along the river. I made us each a peanut-butter-and-jelly sandwich, then tossed a couple of apples, a bag of low-fat chips, and two canned soft drinks into the bag: gourmet fare.

Then I went into my office and began to check my e-mail, only to be greeted by a long list of spam. I stopped, and typed onto a sheet, "I love you, Miranda. You've given meaning to my life." I signed it, folded it, then put it in the lunch bag for her to find. It had been a wonderful morning.

■

We parked in front of a large house near the river, and as we were walking to the access route for the trail, we noticed gardeners — a man, a woman, and a boy, apparently a family — working on a nearby lawn. While we watched, the father, using a scoop shovel, filled a large plastic barrel with leaves. He then put the little guy into it, and the boy enthusiastically stomped down the load, while the mother, raking nearby, gazed at the youngster and beamed. I found myself fondly remembering working with my dad when I was a kid, and even began drifting toward richer visions of family bonding when the father grasped his nose with one hand and shot a large oyster of snot onto the ground.

Miranda said, "Let's not walk over there."

We wandered to the levee and onto the hiking trail that paralleled the stream, the riparian forest open here so we could see the river's chilly main channel rushing by. "This rotten priest story of yours seems like it's turning into a book," she said as we strolled.

"It feels that way to me, too," I admitted. "I really wish it'd end. I'm not enjoying learning about the abuse or the cover-up."

"Are you still getting those wonderful phone calls?"

"Oh yeah. Some nitwit yesterday said my work was the Antichrist. I said it was the anti-pervert, and she hung up."

"She? Talking to strange women, eh?"

"Strange is right. I may pull the plug on the story, though. It's wearing me down."

"Do what you have to," she said. "Are you hungry?"

"I'm getting there," I replied.

Miranda looked around, then said, "Let's sit over there and eat," and she walked to the trunk of a fallen cottonwood. We sat on it and she reached into the lunch bag, then pulled out the note. "What's this?" she said. She unfolded it, then read.

When she looked up at me, her eyes were glistening. "Did you bring the pump?" she asked with a smile.

I was still laughing when she kissed me.

After eating, we walked silently for a bit, hand in hand, then veered onto a side path that took us to a sluggish backwater that branched from the river's channel; it was separated from the main stream by a wooded spit, and in it I saw something dark near the bank just upstream. "Look," I said. "What's that?"

We approached slowly, but the thing didn't flee; it remained in the shallows until we were virtually over it. That's when I realized that it wasn't a single creature at all, but an assemblage of tiny black catfish. "Look at them," I said. "Amazing. They're gathered into a shape that looks like a big fish—probably to scare away predators, don't you think?"

"I guess," Miranda said. "I've seen things like this on television, but it's always ocean fish." We stood and watched the gathering as it moved slowly along the shoreline, apparently eating microorganisms, or at least that's what we decided.

Leaving the fish, we hiked through a dense forest of cottonwoods with hanging vines of Oregon grape, then entered a meadowlike section of the parkway with few trees. A breeze was picking up, and tall yellow grass stalks waved over a ground-hugging fur of fresh green sprouts. "That's beautiful," Miranda said, and we stopped to watch the dancing grass.

"It's like the fur on a grizzly, guard hairs and undercoat," I said. "This used to be prime bear habitat, but when American settlement started they were in the way. They didn't last long."

A little farther up the trail, a middle-aged female power walker puffed past, and I said, "Let's head back. You wore me out in bed this morning."

"You just need more training," she chuckled.

"Okay."

We retraced our steps, but when we arrived at the backwater where the small catfish had schooled, I saw a wake near the far shore. "Look," I said. "Is that a muskrat?"

As we strained to make out what was swimming across the way, a river otter's head suddenly popped from the water, then another, larger one emerged perhaps twenty feet in front of the smaller. "Wow!" I said. What a day this was turning out to be.

"Look at the size of that big one," Miranda said. "Is that male and female, do you think?"

"I have no idea, but they're amazing."

Swimming only fifty or sixty feet away from us, the otters seemed not to notice us at all, continuing on their way until they suddenly disappeared into a side channel.

■

I had to talk Miranda into driving by Lea and Randy's apartment on the way home. "Shouldn't we call first?" she asked.

"Naw," I replied. "Grandpa's privilege."

After tapping at the door I heard considerable bustling, then my daughter opened it. Little Dougie was in her arms, wrapped in a towel and squirming. "Hi, Perico," I said. "We just dropped by to see *changito* there on our way home."

"*Changito?*" She grinned. "Where'd that come from?"

"Family resemblance," I replied.

My daughter shook her head. "Is big *chango* there supposed to be out, Miranda? What about his heart?"

"It's okay."

Lea carried her son back to the bassinet and toweled him off vigorously. Dougie looked a little less like a plum with eyes and a fright wig than he had the last time I'd seen him, and his little pink arms and legs worked vigorously. "It looks like he got all the Indian blood on both sides of the family," I said.

"He's a quarter Japanese, too."

Miranda laughed and said, "Don't let this grandpa fool you, Lea. Your son's about all he can talk about anymore."

"Hey," I observed, "you didn't have him circumcised." There had been a sharp disagreement about that at the hospital, with my daughter favoring the procedure, but Randy adamantly opposed. "Good," I added.

My daughter turned toward me and asked, "What if he gets penile cancer?"

Before I could reply, Miranda said, "Believe me, Lea, there's really no medical reason for circumcision. We've known that for a long time. Sad to say, I had my own sons circumcised because their father insisted. It's really a cultural, not medical, imperative, and a brutal one."

"But what about penile cancer?"

"Next time you're over to our place I'll let you read about the actual incidence of that disease among circumcised and uncircumcised males. It'll ease your mind."

Although I had no medical knowledge, I was delighted for my grandson, intact little devil that he was. I hoped he'd eventually be able to use that little uncircumcised thing for a long, long time.

32

There was a message on my machine from a Melissa Cole when we returned home; she left a number and said it was urgent that I call her. The name didn't register, so I assumed it was yet another message about priests as I dialed the number. A woman answered, saying, "Hello?"

"Melissa Cole?"

"Yes."

"This is Martin Martinez. You left a message for me."

"Yes, I did." The youthful voice immediately swooped toward tears. "My father is Edward Schmidt." Ah, I thought, Ned's younger daughter. "I just want you to know that he's real sick and he wants to talk to you. He's staying at my place, my husband's and mine, 711 Eighteenth Street."

"I can come over right now if you'd like."

"Daddy'd really appreciate it."

Less than an hour later, I tapped at the door of 711 Eighteenth, and a large young man opened it. I was taken aback for a moment because I had not expected an African American. "Mr. Martinez?" he said before I could inquire if I was at the right house. "We've been expecting you. Come on in. I'm Melissa's husband, Glen. She's at the store with the kids." We shook hands.

I assumed that Ned had never mentioned his son-in-law's color to me because he didn't consider it important, and I was momentarily ashamed of myself for having noticed.

"Grandpa's in here," Glen directed as he led me to a nearby hall door. I'd not only never heard my old pal referred to as "Grandpa," but had never thought of him that way either. The young man showed me into what was obviously a child's room. Ned was sleeping on the lower bunk of a bed, a SpongeBob pillowcase crumpled beneath his head. His once dapper dark hair was now an uncombed shock of streaked gray, and a shaggy white beard covered that once clean-shaven jaw. The only arm I could see was thin and so blotched it appeared to be decorated. His deeply lined face was yellow.

"Grandpa's using the boys' bed," explained Glen, then he called softly to the sleeping man. "Dad, your friend is here."

For a moment I thought the ailing man didn't hear, but then his eyes blinked open and he lay there gazing at nothing. After a moment he said in a raspy voice, "Help me up, please, Glen."

When his son-in-law had propped him on a pillow, Ned finally said, "Hello, Martini," and extended his right hand.

He had lost so much weight that his eyes popped like golf balls, their whole orb clearly outlined under the skin blotched with bruises dense as birthmarks.

Glen asked if I'd like coffee. I deferred and he said, "Dad, can I get you anything?"

"No thanks."

The son-in-law excused himself.

"How are you?" the editor asked me then, and I could only offer a perfunctory "Okay." I almost added, "And you?"

"This stuff's about got me." He spoke slowly, as though reaching for each word. "I'm a little vague because of the pain medicine the hospice ladies are giving me."

Ned had always been something of a dandy. Now he had managed to sit on the side of the bed in T-shirt and pajama bottoms, his body almost incorporeal, his neck all cords. Amidst the bruises on one arm was the small tattoo he'd had inscribed as a young soldier, the one I used to tease him about because it seemed so out of character.

"I should've listened to you when I was diagnosed," he said. "I just couldn't believe it was happening, so I put it off."

"Aw, Ned, shoulds and woulds don't mean much in our situation. I wish I'd found a way to . . . what? . . . to counsel you then without sounding like a know-it-all, but I just didn't."

"How's your cancer?" he asked.

"It's on hold, thanks to hormones," I said.

Ned shook his head. "I waited too late to start hormones. I found a doctor who told me what I wanted to hear, and waited too late. They only worked for a year. Chemo hasn't worked at all."

"You've been a good buddy, Ned. We had some high old times back at the *Express,* didn't we?'

A smile slowly played across his face. "Remember Thorpe, the rewrite man?" he asked. "That guy could drink anything and still work. In fact he *did* drink anything."

"How about Lowder after he got hired as art and entertainment editor, and everyone assumed he was a sportswriter? He didn't know or care a damn thing about sports."

"But he was black," Ned said, "so he had to be a jock."

We continued reminiscing for an hour or so, then the editor said, "Could you get me that urinal over there, Martini, then excuse me for a minute?"

"Sure." I picked up the plastic bottle and handed it to him, then walked into the hall and closed the bedroom door. Glen approached me and asked, "How's he doing today?"

"He's slow," I said, "but his mind's clear."

"He's stage five, so he has more bad days than good ones anymore."

"Are you in medicine?" I asked.

"No, I'm a junior high science teacher over in Folsom. My wife's a teacher, too—history—but she mostly stays home with the kids and just does some substituting. Being home with them is more important."

"You've got that right."

I heard Ned's weak voice through the door: "Martini."

When I returned, he was sitting up with a Rugrats quilt over his lap. "I hate being helpless worse than dying," he said.

I noticed that a slice of his pale hip showed, as though he hadn't been able to pull up his pajama bottoms.

We reminisced a bit more, then Ned repeated, "I should've listened to you when I was diagnosed, Martini, but . . . I didn't want to have aggressive cancer. When you talked to me, it made it too real. I just stopped listening. Dumb," he muttered.

"I shouldn't have come on so strong, Ned. I've regretted it. Maybe if I'd just been more patient . . ."

He waved me off with one of those thin arms, saying, "It's about over now, anyway."

After a pause, he asked, "Can you help me stand up, Martini? I couldn't pull these damned pants up."

"Sure." I stood in front of him and he extended his arms, saying, "Lift under my armpits and I'll be able to get them." I did that and we stood there like lovers embracing, our faces close, until he said, "Okay," and I eased him back onto the bed.

My old pal slumped then, apparently exhausted by the effort. "I'm tired, Martini," he said, and I noticed that his eyelids were closing and he seemed to have to fight them back open, only to have the lids droop again.

"I'd better let you rest, Ned," I said.

He seemed not to hear, then he responded, "I guess. I guess . . ."

When I stood and took his hand, he said, "You've been a great pal, Martini. Good-bye."

"Let's make that *hasta la vista,* buddy," I said. "Until we see each other again . . . and we will."

"Hope so," he managed.

I moved to hug him, but he swooned onto that SpongeBob pillow and gazed up at me, so I reached out and took one of his hands in both of mine. "I'll pray for you, Ned," I said.

"Thanks . . . Martini."

I was certain I'd never see Ned again in this life, and I felt those weary eyes following me as I left the room.

■

"Mr. Martinez," said the recorded voice from our answering machine when I arrived home, "this is, like, Gabe Orozco, Johnny's son. My dad he's in the hospital. He asked me to, like, call and tell you." The kid hung up without revealing which hospital, which room, or leaving a number. This second grim message in a day made me think that I ought to stop answering the phone.

When I told Miranda about Johnny, she suggested, "Try University. I'm sure that's where the specialist would refer him, but I haven't heard anything about him being admitted. You want me to call?"

"I'll do it," I said. She was correct; he was at the University Medical Center, and the switchboard operator gave me his room number. I dialed it and the phone was immediately answered by the same young voice that had left the message. "Hello?"

"Gabe? This is Marty Martinez. How's your dad?"

"He's right here. You could, like, talk to him."

"Great," I said.

I thought perhaps the kid hadn't understood me because I waited for what seemed like a long, long time before Johnny's voice slurred, "Hey, Champ."

"Hey, Johnny. What're you doing in the hospital, brother?"

"Johnny couldn't swallow so he almost choked. Better now . . . I heard you been sick, too, Champ. Is it that cancer?"

My old pal's voice was difficult to understand. "No, Johnny, just that heart attack. Remember, we talked just after I got home."

"Ahhh, man . . . yeah, now I remember. Johnny's losin' it, Champ."

I explained to him once more what had occurred and then, to veer the conversation away from my health, told him about Lea's baby.

"Johnny'd like to see that grandson of yours, Champ. Johnny'd like to check out the new Martinezes."

"This little guy's a Lozano, Johnny — Douglas Miguel Lozano."

"Bet he's got a lot of Martinez in him. Tough little *vato.*"

"How long're you going to be in the hospital, brother?" I asked. "I'll drop by for a visit."

"Bring your wife, Champ. She's a nice lady, Dr. Miranda. A champ like you. You're a lucky guy." His voice was fading, making it even more difficult for me to understand.

"Yeah, I am." Because he seemed to be wearing down, I said, "I'll do my best to visit this evening." What I didn't say is that I would talk to Miranda about Johnny's health.

"Well, I think you'd better visit Johnny every chance you get," my wife replied that afternoon. "He told me he's chosen to be 'no-coded'—meaning he doesn't want to be revived or artificially supported—so in his condition he could die at any time." Miranda added, "Johnny has this terrible disease figured out, and he's going to go out on his own terms. He's tough enough not to be intimidated by death . . . That's not as common as you might think. I honestly think he isn't afraid."

I said, "You never saw Johnny fight, honey. Nothing about tough surprises me when it comes to him."

My wife stopped and gazed at me, then said, "You know, I just can't imagine him actually fighting anybody. He's such a gentle soul."

"Yeah, he really is. And brave."

"Don't miss any chance to visit him, dear, that's all I can say. He thinks of you as a brother. Tell his other friends that, too."

■

My wife drove me to the hospital that evening and said she'd meet me in Johnny's room, but first she had a couple of patients to check on. I took the elevator to the fourth floor, then found his room.

As soon as I saw my old buddy, I knew that Miranda was correct. We'd lose him soon; everything about him looked faded except those crisp eyes. "Hey, Champ," he rasped when he saw me.

"Hey, Johnny," I said, and I leaned forward to give him a long hug. "How do you feel, brother?"

"Down for a eight count," he slurred, barely intelligible. He caught on and managed that lopsided grin, then said, "Johnny's gonna have to learn that sign language, except his hands don't work too good either."

I proceeded to carry the conversation, recounting old battles, old jokes, old girlfriends who were stooped grandmothers now. "You been down to Merced, Champ?" he asked.

"Naw, but I've talked to Chava and my sisters. Nothing's changed."

"Somethin's changed," he said. "The people we knew . . . old."

I gazed at him—skin creased and waxy, hair white and thin, eyes tired, body slack—seeing myself more clearly than I ever could in a mirror. "We had our run, *hermano*," I said, "and it was good even if kids looking at us today can't imagine that, but we're on our way out now."

"You got that right, Champ."

I'd been thinking of something else on the way to the hospital, and I suddenly remembered it. "Johnny, let me ask you a serious question. When my ticker almost gave out, I was anxious to take Communion. In case the Church is right about life after death, I didn't want to dangle in Hell."

"Think it's right?" he mumbled.

"I think it might be, but even if it's not I don't figure I've lost much by believing. Besides, ever since I got back to being Catholic, I've felt better. Prayer really has helped me."

"Long time since Johnny went to Confession, Champ. Got a load of sins. Johnny'd shock the priest."

"Not likely," I said. "Why not get rid of 'em?"

"Old monsignor used to chew Johnny's ass pretty good in Confession."

"That's because you played with your chorizo so much," I said.

Johnny managed a chuckle.

"Monsignor gave me hell, too," I added. I was genuinely worried about my friend's soul, and I knew that God would be far more generous and understanding than any church. Mostly, I wanted my pal to enjoy the solace I'd had since becoming an active Christian again. "You know, brother, I'd been away from the Church about as long as you when I went back, and a young priest, Father Tran, said to me, 'Tell me what you feel guilty about that you can't forget, because that's what really separates you from God. I'll give you absolution for everything, whether you remember it or not.' And he did. It took five minutes."

"Tran? He a Flip?"

"Vietnamese, not Filipino."

"Huh." Johnny seemed to think that over.

"Shall I call the priest?" I asked.

"You really trust him?"

"I really trust him. He's a good guy."

"Call him, Champ."

■

Miranda and I decided to attend Mass that Saturday evening—unusual for us—so we were sitting with a different group than our usual Sunday morning assemblage. When it was time for the homily that evening, Monsignor Kelley announced, "The bishop has instructed that the following message be read at all Masses today: 'Recently our diocese and our faith has come under public attack for the alleged actions of a few clergy. . . .'" What followed sounded like a speech written by Father Osbourn: There was no proof of any wrongdoing; the bishop would privately deal with any problems that did arise; the recent newspaper attacks were the product of a few misguided parents and self-serving journalists; with God's help and parishioners' support the truth would triumph and the accused priests would be vindicated or, God forbid, found guilty; either way, it would be best handled within the Church. He added that we should pray for our enemies. There would also be a second collection to help pay for legal costs accruing from the recent scurrilous assaults.

As the monsignor read, I noticed more than a few people looking my way, some of them nodding, apparently in agreement with the indictment coming from the pulpit. I caught one woman pointing me out to another as the pastor read.

Once he finished the letter, Monsignor Kelley removed his glasses, then pushed his sleeves up so those knotted forearms stood in high relief, and said, "I want all of you to know that I am not in complete agreement with the sentiments expressed in this letter. In fact, I'm not in much agreement at all.

"I believe that child abuse is real and that it is a cancer in our midst. If you have cancer you don't hide it, you attack it, you excise it, you kill it. The last thing you do is tolerate it. Well, I'm convinced that the cancer of child abuse is in the process of destroying us from within, and that we must act.

"I want all of you to know that I will never hurt your children and I will not countenance anyone who would. I don't know how perverts were ever ordained, but I know something's wrong with a process if it allows them to remain in our ranks. It is time for a deep examination of who and what we are."

Miranda whispered, "Wow!"

But the priest wasn't finished. "I also want all of you to know what I said to Martin Martinez of this parish, the writer who has had the courage to expose child abuse by some priests. I told him that he's doing God's work. Father Tran and I consider ourselves fortunate to have such a man in our parish family. I can also tell you that the overwhelming majority of priests in the diocese agree with us. We don't want sexual criminals wearing the collar. We want to deserve your respect."

A sprinkling of applause followed, then it grew and grew until it seemed that nearly everyone must be clapping—but not really everyone. Perhaps twenty people rose from their seats and left the church.

I was stunned. I had mostly heard negative comments from fellow Catholics since the story broke, but now it seemed possible that more—maybe far more—of them agreed that we had to clean the mess up no matter what the cost. Miranda beamed and kissed my cheek just as the monsignor continued Mass.

■

"Mr. Martinez?" the voice from the phone said.

"Yes," I replied.

"This is Monique Leventhal, I'm a hospice nurse working with Mr. Edward Schmidt. He asked me to dial you. Can you speak with him?"

Surprised and puzzled, I replied, "Sure."

After a considerable pause, I heard that faint voice. "Martini?"

"I'm here, Ned."

"Bad now," he managed to say in what sounded like gasps. "My spine. Radiation. Didn't work. Hurts bad."

What could I say to the poor guy? "I've been thinking of you, buddy, praying for you."

After another long pause, he managed to say, "Favor . . . to ask." A long silence, then "Pills . . . in den." That was followed by an even longer silence, then, "Get them? End this."

"Jesus, Ned . . ."

"My choice . . ." Another silence, then "Can't ask . . . family." The line again fell silent, until he choked, "So . . ."—he sounded like a man drifting out of consciousness—" . . . humiliating."

"Ned, I . . ." I didn't know what to say, but legally and morally I couldn't help him take his own life.

As I hesitated, that voice gasped, "Please . . ." he begged, his voice cracking, " . . . help me." He began to sob.

Then I heard that other voice. "Mr. Martinez, this is Monique again. I've got to hang up and help Mr. Schmidt. He's upset."

I sat motionless in my chair for a long time holding the receiver and thinking about Ned—and, if the truth be told, about myself too—dying from prostate cancer.

33

I kept the painful conversation with Ned to myself, although it roiled my stomach. My visit to the cardiologist's office the next morning went smoothly. After a treadmill EKG, he cleared me for normal activity, which was fine since I'd already pretty much resumed my life. On the way home, I finally told Miranda about Ned's phone call.

She reached over and held one of my hands. "For people like your friend, it's the helplessness that's most difficult," she said. "I'm sure hospice can control the pain, but having your rear wiped by a stranger assaults everything we hold dear."

I could only say, "You never think about that part of it when you read that someone fought cancer. It's a dirtier war than anyone can imagine, isn't it?"

She nodded, "And sadder, but so many people are brave. This is horrible for your friend, but you did the right thing."

I wasn't certain of that.

We stopped to visit Changito and Tyler, so half an hour later Miranda and Lea were talking in the kitchen and I was bouncing my grandson on my knee when Randy asked, "Did Lea tell you that Grandma Nancy's coming out for a visit?"

"No. When's she coming?"

"Week after next, I think. She's got some business to handle out here, but mostly she just wants to see Dougie . . . and you, too, from what I gather." He smiled.

I didn't need my ex-wife sliding back into my life. Before I could much speculate on that, though, Randy said, "Marty, can I ask you something? How can you stay in the Church when you're writing all that stuff about those perverts?"

Like many people I knew, Randy was a "Recovering Catholic," as a T-shirt he occasionally wore declared in bold script. "Well," I replied, "after all these years as a journalist, I've come to expect human imperfection, and I haven't often been wrong. But even criminal priests can't screw up the comfort I enjoy when I pray."

"And you really believe there's a God?" he asked, not challenging but sounding interested.

"Well, I sure can't believe that human intelligence is as good as it gets," I responded. "I also *hope* that this life isn't all there is."

"This life seems pretty full to me right now," he said.

"Wait 'til you get to the end of it and realize how much you've left undone . . . or unapologized for."

"The last time she was here," he said, "Nancy spent a lot of time trying to convince me that the life I'm leading now is illusion and that spiritual life is the only reality."

"Nancy's view is different than mine. I think they're both real, elements of one existence. Both the little Dougie I'm holding in my arms and the Doug I hold in my heart are real."

Randy had more to say, but when Miranda and Lea entered the room carrying a sleepy Tyler, he let it go and took the little boy from his wife's arms.

"You didn't tell me Mom was coming for a visit," I said to Lea.

She glanced at Randy, then said, "Oh, didn't I? It must have slipped my mind."

■

Since my heart problems, I seemed to drag a bit in the afternoon, napping when I should have been working, thus not getting nearly as much writing done as I once did. I began to wonder if the depression-related somnolence was creeping back into me, but decided that I was really just burning out on the rogue-priest story. When I faced that, I knew I had to telephone Bud Hartley.

"Hey, Marty," he said.

"Bud, listen, I'm ready to move on. Why don't you assign Buzzy to the molesting-priests story?"

"I think you're gonna win some awards on this one, Marty," he replied. "It's really snowballing. Why not stay with it just a little longer?"

"Because all this misery is burning me out," I admitted. "It's so damned discouraging. If it's not some poor ex–altar boy who's been hiding a sense of guilt for years, it's some liar just wanting to get back at the Catholic Church, or it's some indignant mackerel-snapper wanting to get back at me."

Bud didn't argue. "You know I'll do whatever you want, but candidly this series has given us our greatest circulation in years. Why don't you consider just following up on the stuff you've already exposed, and I'll assign Buzzy to any new material? Think about it, okay? Give yourself a couple weeks and if you still want out, then it's done."

"Okay."

"Oh yeah," he added, chuckling. "Buzzy said some guy told him this Father Reilly you've been writing about would rather hear a fat boy fart than a pretty girl whistle."

"No doubt," was all I could say.

■

I met Babe LaFranchi late that next afternoon at the Squared Circle, a bar down the block from the boxing arena. He had gained even more weight since he'd retired from promoting fights and moved to the coast, so he looked like a vast, hairless bear sitting in the booth waiting for me. I slid in across from him, and he ordered a Chivas on the rocks for me. "Am I right or am I right, Marty? Still your favorite poison?"

I hadn't been drinking hard liquor recently, but I'd poured plenty of Chivas Regal down in the old days. "You're right, Babe. What brings you back to Sac town?" I asked.

"I had a little business, but mostly I wanted to visit Johnny O. I heard how sick he's been. I heard you been sick, too." Babe wheezed when he talked, as fat guys sometimes do.

"My ticker," I said.

"Aw, really? Me, too, Marty. I had a quadruple bypass last year." He opened his shirt and revealed a thin scar down the center of his tan chest. "The doc afterwards said to lose weight or I'd only last a couple more years. I said I'd rather live on my own terms and let the docs have those extra years."

I shook my head. "Well, Johnny's in rougher shape than either of us, but still as good a guy as ever."

"He's a sweetheart," the old promoter said to me. "The sweetest. That's why I wanted to talk to you. I was thinking I might be able to put together a benefit for him. I figure he's gotta be about tapped out."

My drink arrived, and I toasted Babe. "I'm sure he's broke. I think he's got health insurance from work — old Bob Bertolucci's taken care of him out at the truck stop."

"Bobby! Remember when Bobby fought that skinny black kid from L.A., Spider Maxwell. Jeez, Bobby had 'im beat 'til Spider landed that crazy round-house right." Babe grinned. "Bobby mighta been a real good welter if he coulda took a punch. Glass chin."

"He's been good to Johnny."

"You been good to Johnny, too," Babe said, "or so I hear."

"He's my homey." I smiled.

"I hear you're married to a doc now. Could you ask her how long Johnny's got? Is there time for me to put something together, a benefit? It'd take a couple months, three maybe."

"I'll ask."

Suddenly the massive man's eyes were damp and he said, "Johnny made me a bundle when he was fightin'. I owe him big time."

I knew that the world Babe and Johnny inhabited could be ruthless indeed, but those two were straight shooters. There were half a dozen promoters who owed Johnny big time, but only Babe — so far as I knew, at least — had come forward to help him.

"I'm going to try to start a scholarship fund for his kids," I said. "I've already written something for the *Tribune* about it, and the new sports editor at the *Express* said he's going to run something, too."

"Okay," Babe said, and he pulled a bundle of bills in a gold clip from a pocket. "Here's a G to start." He counted off ten hundred-dollar bills. "Lemme know if you need more. He's got a hell of a buncha kids, I know. How many?"

"Twelve, I think."

The big man peeled off two more hundreds and handed them to me. "There's a C for each kid," he said.

"Babe, you don't have to — "

"Johnny never once stiffed me. I owe him big time."

■

"I had a question today about Johnny from an old boxing promoter named Babe LaFranchi," I told Miranda. "He plans to sponsor some kind of a benefit, so he wants to know how long Johnny's got to live."

"I honestly don't know," my wife replied, "but he'd better plan it sooner than later. More coffee?"

"No thanks," I answered. "That's what I thought, though."

"How's your exercise routine going?"

"I've stretched the walks out and I'm weight-lifting again. It's all pretty easy, but I'm doing it."

"It's better to start gradually," Miranda said, then she added, "Nancy called my office today."

"My ex-wife? Why?"

"She wanted to know about your health, said you'd never admitted something was wrong. She wanted to know if it'd be all right for her to visit, not too much of a shock on your system."

Miranda smiled. "I told her it might be too much of a shock on *my* system."

I had to grin. "Did you really?"

"She's still carrying a torch, isn't she?"

I said, "I don't think she's *still* carrying a torch; I think she *reignited* an old one."

"It comes down to the same thing, though."

"Yeah, except that I'm happily married. I've told her that and I've told Lea that."

"Lea?"

"Just in case. She's fond of you, but she's still Nancy's girl." I stood and walked behind my wife's chair, began massaging her shoulders, then kissed her neck. "I hope you're happily married, too, lady," I said.

"I am."

■

I was amazed at how vigorously the *Express* jumped on the pedophile-priest bandwagon. Many of the cases that I wouldn't write about because of lack of evidence or corroborating testimony were exposed by Monica Salinas in increasingly livid prose. A few of the accusations really smelled fishy to me, but the *Express* plunged ahead.

Bud Hartley finally asked me about an especially inflammatory revelation Monica had run: a woman accused Monsignor Horace "Horse" McManus — a local product who had been a football and track star at Grant High School—of having raped her when she was a parishioner of his. Since Horse was an extremely popular, virile-looking guy, he made a persuasive target. The *Express* ran then and now photos of the athlete-turned-priest on the front page, a break-out summary of his life, and another break-out summary of famous sexual abuse cases involving priests nationally. This was the story they intended to use to surpass the *Tribune*'s head start on coverage.

I'd warned my editor to leave it alone, since Monica apparently hadn't discovered that Marcia Hunter, the accuser, had wanted to be a nun and had been turned down as a teen because she was mentally unstable. While living in Stockton before moving to Sacramento, she had accused her former high school principal, her family doctor, and finally her father of raping her. Local police had found no evidence of any offenses, but the local mental health department had treated her for paranoid depression.

A couple of weeks ago, the poor, sad woman had telephoned me, told me that she had "recovered memory in hypnosis" and remembered that Horse had raped her. Since the whole notion of recovered memory seemed bogus to me, I had asked some hard questions, and soon she was babbling and sobbing. I was sure there was nothing to the story but a sick woman needing help.

I telephoned Monica and warned her to be careful of Marcia Hunter and filled her in on what I knew. For several moments she was silent, then she said, "I appreciate your call, Marty, but I have good instincts about these things and I'm convinced that she's telling me the truth. Besides, this is actually more of a women's issue."

"She's psychotic. Let me give you the telephone number in Stockton of the man who treated her." I did that, and she thanked me, her voice tight.

■

Maybe it was the false charges against Horse that finally pushed me over the edge, because I again telephoned Bud and told him that I really no longer wished to write about pedophile priests. He seemed genuinely baffled. "You've broken a major story. Are you sure you're okay?"

"I'm okay," I replied, but I wasn't, not physically anyway. I was dragging around like a much older man. The people at the newspaper only saw the copy I sent in; they didn't see me slumped and dozing midday at my desk in the den.

However reluctantly, Bud gave me the go-ahead to write about anything else that caught my interest, but his voice did not hide his disappointment. The last thing he said was, "Send whatever you've got to Buzzy. He'll be taking over."

I had used the possibility of revisiting the tree-rustlers story as an excuse to move on, and Bud had laughed. "Well, talk about one extreme to another. You'll have all the gardeners up in arms, but not many other readers."

"Wait and see," I'd replied. "With the importance of agriculture in this valley — "

"Yeah," he interrupted, "but it's in this city where we have to sell papers."

We hung up and I took a nap. A couple of hours later I was at my computer when the phone rang. The message machine clicked on, and a moment later a female voice said, "Miranda, this is Jeaneve Washington. You asked me to call as soon as the results were available. They are and unfortunately the numbers aren't good. Give me a call as soon as you can, and we can review the results and talk about a course of treatment."

I wanted to pick up the receiver then and demand to know what results? What numbers? What courses of treatment would they consider? I also wanted to know who Jeaneve Washington was, for that matter; that wasn't a name I recognized.

What was wrong with my wife? I had a phone book on my desk, so I opened it and looked up Washington under "Physicians" in the Yellow Pages. There were two, Robert in pediatrics and Jeaneve in oncology.

34

"I didn't want you to worry unnecessarily," Miranda explained. "And now you're worried."

I was damned worried.

"Besides," she continued, "this isn't something we didn't expect, and there's really not enough evidence for us to be too distressed right now. My numbers haven't been good, so Jeaneve and I decided on a scan.

"I wasn't trying to keep anything secret. In fact, I'd like you to go with me for the consultation. Jeaneve will tell me what the scan revealed and we — you, me, her — will decide if it's time to begin therapy and, if so, which one. Okay? In any case, we should have some options."

"I'm going," I said. I stood and embraced her, nuzzled her hair. "I love you, Miranda. I don't want to lose you."

She kissed me, then said, "That's how I felt when you had that heart attack. I was really scared, more than I've been over my own condition. We've just got to keep snatching any happiness that's granted us."

"Tell me exactly what you think is happening."

She sat on a leather chair and I perched on its arm while she explained.

"Well, I suspect she'll tell me that the scan revealed some small metastasized tumors. It's not good, but we should be able to treat that kind of thing for a while." She smiled, maybe a little sadly, saying, "We're both just buying time anymore."

"Let's buy some more."

"That's the idea," she replied, then she smiled and surprised me by saying, "Don't look so sad, Marty. Lift up your chin. Your wattles are showing."

"Wattles? Me?"

The phone rang, and I intended to ignore it, but Miranda said, "I'd better get that. It might be Jeaneve."

A moment later she said, "It's for you, dear. Nancy."

I shook my head. I didn't need to deal with my ex-wife while I was still trying to sort out the meaning of this new stress, but I picked up the receiver. "Marty?" the voice said. "How are you?"

"I'm fine, Nancy. How about you?"

"Fine. I wonder if we can get together while I'm here visiting. Miranda would be welcome." I almost laughed aloud — my ex giving my wife permission to join us.

"We've got some tense things going on here right now," I said.

"Is it the series you wrote about the immoral priests? Lea told me about it. Immorality like that happens when we don't practice true Catholicism. Father McIntyre predicted this when they changed the Mass from Latin and let women become Eucharistic ministers. Now even priests have lost the faith."

I had no time for that nonsense. "We're in the middle of something here, Nancy," I said. "Do you want me to call you back?"

"Marty, mostly I just want to touch base with you, to talk to you. It's been too long." Her voice softened.

A long silence followed, intended, I guess, to be a pregnant pause. I moved to my favorite safe topic, asking, "What do you think of little Dougie?"

Her voice caught when she said, "He reminds me of our Dougie."

"Yes." This was too damned heavy to deal with on top of what Miranda had revealed. "Listen, Nan, we really are in the middle of something here. Let me call you back later."

"You will call, won't you?"

"You're at Lea's?"

"Yes, at *our* old house."

"I'll call."

■

I telephoned Bud Hartley immediately after opening my mail. "I've got something to give Buzzy a kick start," I told him. "Somebody sent me a back issue of a magazine called *Man/Boy* and, bigger than Hell, there's a photo of Father Damien Reilly in it—out of uniform, of course—with the caption 'Boy-lover ministers to underprivileged.' Nothing's hidden; it says he's helping street urchins in Mexico. Can you believe a priest would let himself appear in that kind of journal? What an idiot!"

"How current is it?"

"It's dated Spring 1988."

"That far back? And it came from . . . ?"

"It was in an anonymous package. I can't even read the postmark."

"Damn," Bud grunted. He cleared his throat, a smoker's habit, then said, "Buzzy's looking into some accusations against that other priest out at Folsom, and we're getting a hell of a lot more Catholic stuff from the wire services. This thing just seems to be growing. I may assign Will to it, too."

I managed what a 1930s novel might have called a bitter laugh, then said, "You know, my parish priest has always been a warm guy, the kind who'll pat your back or slug your shoulder. He told me the other day that he's stopped touching people except sacramentally. He said he even told his assistant, Father Tran, who plays on the parish's city-league basketball team, not to pat his teammates on the butt."

"You're kidding!"

"No, but I hope Monsignor Kelley was. If he wasn't, that's another angle for Buzzy—how the clergy's being changed by all this."

Bud chuckled. "It's sure as hell got crazy, hasn't it? We've gone from clergy being automatically above suspicion to them being automatically assumed guilty. If you change your mind about working on this, let me know. If not, let me know what you *do* want to work on next."

Apparently my tree-rustlers story hadn't intrigued him.

■

Miranda's cancer was back, with one small tumor confirmed in her right lung and a suspicious spot on her brain. "We have some therapeutic options," explained Dr. Washington, who turned out to be a very attractive young black woman.

"I'm sure we can radiate any mets and get you going on chemo, too. I think we have to be aggressive with this one, Miranda, since it's pretty aggressive with you."

My wife remained upbeat, though I was certain it was for my benefit, and I tried to hide how low I felt, not wanting to drag her down with me. But I hated it.

"I thought tamoxifen had your cancer under control," I said on the drive home.

"Tamoxifen isn't forever," Miranda replied to my question, "but in my case it worked quite a while. With luck, one of the new drugs will be equally effective and I'll live to die of old age, which isn't that far away, as it turns out."

I couldn't smile. "I'm planning on us growing old together," I said, "with you figuring out my Medicare strategies for me."

"Are you still taking your depression medicine?" she asked.

"I've been feeling good, so I didn't think I needed it."

"Marty"—she touched my cheek—"depression's an illness, not a mood. You know that. Treat it the same way you do cancer—because we don't need any more complications in our lives. Okay?"

"Okay."

She smiled then and said, "Let's drive over to the church, say a little prayer, then go for a walk at the park across the street, maybe stop for a latte at the used-book shop."

Miranda was trying to perk *me* up after *she* got word that her cancer was back. How could I turn down an offer like that? "Sure." I managed to smile. "Let's."

When we drove into the parking lot Father Tran, in a ball cap, blue jeans, and a logo T-shirt, was working in the rose garden next to the rectory. He waved.

We approached after parking the car, and he stood, massaging his lower back. I asked, "You trying to pass for a layman until the sex scandal blows over?"

He grinned and said, "Don't think I haven't considered it. What're you two up to?"

My wife replied, "We just thought we'd make a visit, then go for a walk at the park."

"Great day for it."

"Well," I said, "there's more to it than Miranda lets on. I hope you won't be angry, babe, but I want to tell Father Tran what's happening."

She gazed at me for a moment, then said, "Well, go ahead."

I could see that the young priest wondered if he was suddenly in the midst of a domestic dispute, but when I revealed that my wife's cancer had recurred, he quickly lost his do-I-need-to-hear-this look and took her hand. "Let me run inside and clean up a bit, Miranda," he said, "then give you a blessing for the sick while you're here."

"Thank you," she said. "We'll be in the church."

As soon as he left, she hissed in mock anger, "I can't tell you *anything*."

We walked into the church, but I still felt dreadful. Not for long, though. After saying an Our Father, a Hail Mary, a Glory Be, and an Act of Contrition, I began to repeat, "Lord Jesus Christ, only Son of God, please help Miranda and me, sinners," and repeated it softly over and over to myself in front of the flickering candle I'd lit. When Miranda said to me, "There's Father Tran," I snapped out of the reverie and realized that I was no longer sad. My wife would be blessed and we would be fine.

■

Instead of walking at the park across from the church, we drove to our favorite area of the river parkway and wandered downstream for a change, toward the city's center. The paved trail was filling up with the youthful after-work crowd, so Miranda and I as usual veered onto the horse trail in the heavy brush close to the water. Everything became much quieter, a fair trade-off for the dusty footing.

Small birds skittered from bush to bush all around us, and somehow the water smelled fresher than usual. Maybe everything smelled better. "When I talked to Nancy—"

"What does she really want?"

I stopped and took her hand. "I think...I think she wants to be back with me because our old life represents stability to her."

"It represents instability to me," Miranda said. "How would you feel if my ex-husband was bugging me to take him back?"

"He'd only bug you once if I knew about it."

"We've enough stress in our lives without her," she added.

"You're right, but she's not in our lives as far as I'm concerned." We hugged and I kissed Miranda's ear, then her lips. As we embraced I heard a hollow, wooden sound like a musical *clunk*. "What's that?" I asked.

We both looked around and my wife said, "Is someone playing an instrument—maybe up by the bike trail?" We had on occasion encountered guitarists, and at least one harmonica player, up there.

Clunk! It reverberated like something I'd heard from Incan musicians years before.

"It sounds like it's up—"

Clunk!

"Look," said Miranda, and she pointed at a large, dark bird weaving through foliage toward us until finally it settled on a branch only twenty feet or so above our heads—a raven.

Surely it could see us, but it showed no concern. I was shocked by the size of its ebony beak — a formidable apparatus indeed. Then it hopped to a higher branch and dipped slightly. Its throat bulged and its wings lifted like a person shrugging shoulders, and we heard *clunk!* It repeated the musical performance, while we stood motionless below. A moment later, it *clunked* once more, then again, and my wife wrapped both her arms around one of mine.

From far off, we heard another faint *clunk!* The bird above us dipped and *clunked* again, then flew away, the swish of its wings distinct. We stood for a while longer, hearing the faint *clunks*, then I said, "We're going to be okay, aren't we?"

"Of course we are."

■

"Marty, I need to see you," Nancy told me, her voice cracking. "Please come by while I'm at Lea's."

I wished I hadn't answered the phone, but I said, "I'll be over," feeling trapped by my own emotions.

"Don't forget."

"I won't."

Miranda wasn't due home for nearly two hours, so I decided to drive over right away and get the visit with my ex-wife over. Once Miranda returned home, her medical problems would dominate my thoughts.

My daughter answered the door. She was holding the baby. "Daddy, I didn't know you were coming over."

"I thought I'd visit the boys and say hello to Grandma."

My daughter smiled, handed me the baby, then said, "Mom's in here," and led me to the small den. "Look what the cat dragged in," she announced as I followed her into the room.

Tyler was on the floor playing with Legos, and he looked up and said, "Hi, Grampa Marty."

"Hi, Squirt."

"Wanna play?"

"In a few minutes," I replied.

Nancy, still beautiful, stood up. "I love seeing all you boys together," she said with a smile, then crossed the room, put one of her hands behind my head, and caressed it in the familiar way as she kissed my cheek. To my surprise, she held my head a moment longer, then kissed my lips.

It wasn't a long kiss but a warm one. Sexual excitement shot through me, then I recoiled and gazed into her eyes. My ex-wife gazed back at me with something like yearning as our daughter said, "Hey, you two. I can't leave you alone for a second."

I plopped with Dougie squirming on my lap into the rocking chair across from the couch where Nancy sat.

"I didn't expect to see you so soon, but I'm glad you came over," she said.

"You said it was important that we see one another."

"Legos are fun," said Tyler.

"You look great, Marty, especially for someone who's had so much go wrong with him lately. It's just hard to believe. You were always so healthy and strong—"

"You look fine, too."

Lea tapped my arm and said, "Let me take the baby, Daddy. He needs changing. Tyler, come on with me. It's time for your snack."

"Wanna snack, Grampa Marty?"

"Later, Squirt."

He looked sad, so I added, "Afterwards we can wrestle."

"I'm gonna win you," he said as I passed Dougie to Lea. Then Tyler followed them toward the kitchen.

There was no point in mincing words. "Are you okay, Nancy?" I asked. "Your voice sounded strange over the phone."

"I'm lonely, Marty. I know I made a mistake after Doug's death, but I was distraught."

"We both were," I said.

She took a deep breath and looked away from me. "I know." After another sigh, she said very rapidly, "I could never unlove you, Marty. I tried, but I couldn't. I left you because I unloved myself."

I didn't want to think about the implications of what she was saying, so I concentrated on that strange word, "unlove."

"Oh, Marty," she said, "I'm sorry I wasn't here to help you through this, but I had to deal with Doug's death in my own way. Now I've lost you both."

"You haven't lost me, Nan, but we're not married anymore," I said, thinking that in this life you take what you get and make the most of it. "At least we had those early years," I added. "Some people don't even have that."

"Is that *all* we're going to have?" she gasped and began blinking back tears.

The answer was no, since we now shared a grandchild, but I really didn't want to pursue the topic. As I was about to reply, Lea entered the room and cried, "Mom, what's *wrong?*"

■

The phone rang right after supper and I waited for the answering machine to respond, then heard, "Mr. Martinez, this is Dave Cole, Melissa's husband. I wanted you to know that Ned, my father-in-law, died last night."

I picked up the receiver and said, "Dave, this is Marty. I'm really sorry to hear that."

"It's better than what he was going through," the younger man said. "He really suffered at the end."

"The hospice workers . . . ?"

"They did their best, but it was in his spine."

"Oh. . ." I had to pause for a moment, then I continued, "Will there be a service?"

"No, he didn't want one. Melissa and I will try to start a journalism scholarship in his name out at State, though."

"I'll call his old buddies from the paper," I volunteered. "I know they'll want to contribute." I *had* to do something to memorialize the old pal I'd let down.

35

We decided that Miranda would immediately begin radiation on a small lesion in her brain, and that she would also begin chemotherapy to deal with the lung tumor as well as any systemic disease. To me it seemed as though one day she had been well, the next she was gravely ill. I had trouble believing it.

Her first treatment was scheduled for early on Monday morning, so we drove to the hospital making light talk to fill the silence. The infusion center was on the third floor; we rode the elevator up and Miranda waved at the receptionist, then walked directly into what she called "the war room." It was painted in bright colors, and cheery prints decorated its three walls—the fourth side was a vast window. On each of the walls, a large television screen was mounted. Near the middle of the room was a nurses' station, and fresh flowers adorned the desk. A small brown woman doing paperwork looked up, then smiled at Miranda, who waved and said, "Hello, Guadalupe."

"Hi, Dr. Mossi. Dr. Washington's on her way," the nurse said.

"No hurry."

Obviously someone wanted this room to look as appealing as possible. Along those three walls were lounge chairs, comfortable-looking units with leg rests. Next to each was a metallic stand and some kind of electronic panel, which I assumed would monitor the infusions. There were also headphones at each chair.

Four women and one man sat in the loungers, all wearing headphones and gazing at the television screens while chemicals dripped into their veins. Two of the women looked at us, then smiled in recognition and waved at Miranda.

"Patients of mine," she whispered to me. No sound was emitted by the TVs, so I assumed the headphones were providing it, something even Sherlock Holmes could have figured out.

Dr. Washington walked hurriedly into the room accompanied by a plump, gray-haired white woman. "Miranda," she called, "sorry I'm a bit late, but I got hung up in a meeting. Hello, Marty."

I nodded and smiled.

The oncologist turned toward my wife, saying, "This is Pris Simmons. She'll be your infusion nurse. Pris just joined us from UCSF."

We all shook hands. "I've heard all about you, Dr. Mossi," the nurse said.

"Only believe the good stuff," Miranda replied.

"As we discussed," Dr. Washington then said, her tone suddenly business-like, "we'll get you started on Navelbine today, then do a scan late next week to make sure it's working. As it accumulates in your system, it might make you a little sick. Keep me posted on how you're feeling. We can usually stay ahead of most side effects if we know about them early enough.

"You're going in to start the radiation process with Paul Nimitz tomorrow, aren't you?" the oncologist added.

Miranda nodded. "I've got a three o'clock. He'll start the telemetry."

"Good. The sooner the better," Dr. Washington said, then like a headwaiter she extended a hand and said, "Choose a seat and Pris and I'll get you started."

I returned to the waiting area. A few minutes later, Dr. Washington stopped by on her way out, saying, "Miranda's doing just fine."

Upset that my wife was even at such a place, I asked, "Does being an oncologist ever get discouraging, Dr. Washington?'

She paused and seemed to examine me, then said, "Sure, at times it does, but mostly it's satisfying. Patients I see really need help; I'm usually their last chance and we're able to save more all the time."

■

To my surprise, Chava stopped at our house the next afternoon on his way to a regional fire captains' meeting, and he began ragging me about my series on the predatory priests, which the Merced newspaper had belatedly begun reprinting. I was in no mood for it, but Chava was always Chava. "Man," he said, "you were everyone's favorite altar boy. Remember how Gonsalves used to say they wouldn't fire you if they caught you boogering the bishop? Now I wonder if you *did.*" He grinned.

I shook my head.

"That one guy you wrote about — what's his name? Damien? — he must be a real scumbag," my brother said. "Man, if a priest had touched us, Papa would've hung his balls on the front fence." My brother burst into guffaws then, saying, "You were gone when old Father Kiernan finally retired and Father Nelson replaced him. I was in high school then. Did you ever meet Nelson?"

"No."

"He was a young guy, and word on the street was that he was a *puto.* He hung out with Mr. Silva — remember, we called him the queer director instead of the choir director." Chava's eyes were twinkling, and he could barely control his laughter as he continued: "Anyway, by then I was on the wrestling team with Jimmy DeCosta and Mike Patton — you wrestled with their brothers. The three of us figured out a secret way to make fun of the new priest. Stand up and I'll show you."

Normally, I would never stand up to let Chava demonstrate anything on me, but I'd been feeling so empty that it was just easier to do what he asked than to argue, so I stood.

"Okay," he said, "we'll do this in slow motion, so don't resist. Imagine you're a kid who's new to the wrestling team: I want to show you the three most important holds." He slid one of his arms around my left one and braced his against my neck and shoulder, saying, "First, the half nelson. Next, the full nelson," and he slid behind me, trapping both my arms and bracing his hands against my neck and shoulders. "Now," he announced, "the Father Nelson," and he humped my rear a couple of times, then released me and jumped back as I swung a heel upward toward his crotch.

"Well," he added as I shook my head at him, "that really wowed 'em on the wrestling team. And by the way, *vato,* you almost nutted me."

"One more bump and you'd've been singing soprano."

"You're still mean for an old fart." He paused, then asked, "You okay, Marty?"

"Yeah."

Chava reached over and placed a large hand on one of my shoulders, then asked, "What's wrong, *vato?* I can tell something's eating you."

"Ah, it's just my heart," I lied. "Being sick pisses me off." That last part wasn't a lie.

"How about your cancer? It under control?"

"Yeah, the hormone blockers I've been on have beaten it back."

Chava's hand was still on my shoulder and he squeezed when he said, "Stay on top of that shit, *vato.* I don't want to lose my last brother."

"I don't want to lose you, either."

■

Sick or not, Miranda had gone to the hospital for her rounds, so I was alone in the house. After Chava left, I made myself a small lunch, then wandered into my den to see if I could work up an article for the paper, but I checked for e-mail first. There was the usual spam — get-rich-quick scams, videos of teenage girls on the farm, variations of pyramid schemes — but near the bottom was a note from Mort O'Brien.

Marty:

Did you hear about the priest who won the lottery? The officials asked him if he had to turn it down, and he said he didn't turn anything down except fat boys, and he turned them face down.

Long time no see, buddy. The guys in the group keep asking about you. We've all been reading your series on the priests and several of us are thinking of taking holy orders so we can rev up our sex lives.

Everybody'd like to see you. We've got a guest speaker next week. I hope you can make it.

Mort

P.S. *Bill, the guy who joined the same night you did, is going on chemotherapy, since hormones have failed. The poor guy hasn't had much luck.*

Sighing, I sat back. The support group had seen me through those first lonely, trying days after the cancer had been diagnosed. Now that I had Miranda in my life, and suddenly two grandsons, and my writing career too, I just couldn't seem to find energy or time for it. That realization brought an acknowledgment: I couldn't find extra energy because I didn't have any, even though I'd begun taking my depression medicine again.

I knew I should at least visit the prostate cancer group every month or so, as Miranda did her breast cancer support group. She also still attended the scripture class with some regularity, which was amazing to me, given her health and her schedule.

■

Late that afternoon, I was waiting for my wife to arrive home from work when the phone rang. "Marty," Miranda said, and the tone of her voice told me something was wrong. "I'm afraid I've got terrible news." I immediately thought of her cancer, then she continued: "Johnny died a few minutes ago. His heart gave out, but the ALS did the real damage."

"Oh God."

"He didn't suffer at the end," she added, "and the debilitation had really begun to frustrate him."

I could say nothing. I'd visited him regularly, so had observed his steady decline. One part of me was grateful that my old pal had not had to endure total paralysis, but I was really going to miss him. His death would diminish my world substantially; only my family connected me so intimately with my youth.

"Are you okay?" Miranda asked. It was the second time today I'd stimulated that question.

"I'm okay," I puffed. "We'll talk when you get home, babe. Are you going in for your infusion first?"

"Yes. As soon as I'm done I'll be home," she said. "And Marty, I love you as much as Johnny did."

"I'm a lucky guy," I said.

Only a minute or so later, Johnny's son Gabe telephoned to tell me his father had died. "It was his heart, they said," Gabe told me, sounding dazed. "It, like, just wore out, they said."

I didn't tell him I already knew, and in a second he was weeping. When he'd settled down a bit, I said, "Some of your dad's friends have put money away for his funeral and any hospital bills, so don't worry about that stuff."

"He, like, wanted to be buried in Merced. Is that okay?"

"That's fine, Gabe. Anything he wanted he can have. Do you want me to call the funeral director in Merced? He's an old family acquaintance."

"Yeah, I don't, like, know anybody down there. My dad he just wanted a Mass, no Rosary or stuff. Could you, like, do the whatmacallit, the sermon or whatever at my dad's Mass?"

"The eulogy?"

"Yeah, the eulogy."

"I'd be honored," I said, and I gulped hard. Johnny was really dead.

"Thank you, Mr. Martinez. My dad always said you were, like, his best friend."

"A lot of people loved your dad, Gabe. He was a special guy."

I immediately called Babe LaFranchi and put the wheels in motion for a grand send-off, then sat at the kitchen table, feeling gutted because I hadn't been there to hold Johnny's hand and help ease his journey into death. I'd been home feeding my face while he was dying.

■

"Father Tran was making his rounds at the hospital," Miranda told me that evening. "I called him and he gave Johnny last rites."

"You should've called me, too."

"No. You're a sick man, Marty, whether you admit that to yourself or not," she replied. "Your heart didn't need that stress. I decided as a physician not to call you. If I was wrong, forgive me, but I can see how close to the deep end you are over my health. You didn't need more stress, and Johnny wouldn't have known you were there. Besides, you *were* there in your heart . . . and in his, I'll bet."

She reached over and grasped my right hand, saying, "You're going to laugh at this, but I'll bet when you get to Heaven, Johnny'll be there saying something like, 'Hey, Champ, where ya been?'" Her voice descended to a growl like my late pal's.

"I think I didn't tell you when it happened," I said, "but Johnny said not long ago, 'Your lady's a champ, too, Champ.'" She smiled and her eyes glistened when I added, "He was right, Champ." I felt myself edging toward tears. "He was a great pal."

Miranda embraced me, saying, "Johnny would be crying for you if the situation was reversed," she said. "You two're the toughest men I've ever known, that's why you're brave enough to cry."

But that wasn't true of me. I wasn't tough, and now so damned much was going wrong; my emotional shield was sagging. Well, there was one thing I *could* do.

I walked into my den and dialed the newspaper's phone number. "Bud," I said when the editor answered, "Johnny O died today. I want to write a feature on him."

"The fighter? Sure. Boy, he was a tough sucker."

"He was a good man and he was my friend."

"That's right," the editor said. "You guys were both from Merced, weren't you?"

"Same neighborhood. I've known him since we were kids," I told him.

"Write as many takes as you want. We can feature it on the sports page, and run a break-out on page one of the local section."

There was a pause, and I thought he was about to hang up. Then he asked, "Oh yeah, didn't you write something a while back about that ex-'Niner, Reggie James?"

"Yeah, why?"

"Well, he died, too. It just came over the wire."

That stunned me. He'd looked so healthy when I'd seen him. "He *died?*"

"Yeah, at UC Hospital in San Francisco, of—this must be a misprint—it says he died of breast cancer."

"That's no misprint," I replied.

"No kidding . . ." His voice trailed off, then he said, "And, Marty, if you reconsider about writing more on the priests, let me know."

"I won't — reconsider, that is."

Bud's tone changed then, and he said, "We've been friends for over thirty years. Something's wrong. Is your cancer back?"

Bud could keep a secret, so I told him the truth. "This is strictly off the record, but my *wife*'s cancer is back."

"Oh God," he said. "I'd hate that more than having it myself. If I ever lost Tish, man, I'd be cooked. Let me know what I can do."

"If there is anything, believe me, I'll let you know."

"And take care of yourself, Marty. Take care of yourself."

■

I was moping around the house, considering what to write about Johnny, when the phone rang. Miranda answered it, saying, "Marty, it's Lea."

"Hello," I said into the phone.

"Hi, Daddy. Listen, can you and Miranda watch Tyler for a little while? Randy and I want to catch the new George Clooney movie at Cinema 12. We'll take Dougie, but Tyler gets way too antsy. We'll only be a couple of hours."

I was feeling so low that my impulse was to say no, but I cupped my hand over the mouthpiece and called to my wife, "Do you want to watch Tyler this evening?"

"Sure," she replied without hesitation.

A quarter of an hour later there was a knock on the front door, and when I opened it Tyler flew in like a charge of buckshot. "Hi, Grampa Marty. I got a new Transformer — "

I grinned at Randy, who'd delivered his son to the door. "Lea's waiting in the car with the baby," he explained. I said, "Tyler's only been here thirty seconds and I'm already tired."

Randy chuckled. "Marty, thanks for babysitting. It's okay if he watches cartoons on TV. You don't have to entertain him, but there're books in this bag" — he handed it to me — "plus crayons and a coloring book, and his new Transformer."

"That oughta do it," I said. "We've still got that box of Legos out from the last time he was here. They've been a good investment, so thanks for recommending them. We'll see you when you get back."

"Right."

Miranda appeared and Tyler said, "You got a hat."

She was wearing a slick "head-rag," as she called it. "I've been thinking of adding fruit to it and changing my name to Carmen Miranda Martinez," my goofy wife had earlier told me.

She scooped up the boy and gave him a hug. "You want to try it on?" she asked.

"No way," said Tyler.

"Okay, Squirt," I said to Tyler, "what'll it be? Legos? Transformers? Or do you just want me to pinch your bottom?"

He giggled, the asked, "Can I have a mint?"

The kid knew my habits, but as I dug a Life Saver out of my pocket a crazy thought occurred to me: Could I be accused of abuse for pinching a little boy's butt . . . or for wrestling with him . . . or for hugging him?

After Randy and Lea had taken Tyler home that evening, I mentioned that idea to Miranda, and she said, "The answer is yes, if the wrong person heard you were doing those things and assumed the worst, you probably could be in trouble. Crazy world, isn't it?"

"I had an Aunt Antonia," I told her, "my mother's sister, who never spanked us or slapped us, but she always pinched us if we were bad. She left bruises."

"Well, she'd be in big trouble today," Miranda said.

"It worked for her. We were always well behaved when she was babysitting."

"It still sounds cruel."

"My older brother was always defying Mama," I told her, "jumping in the irrigation canal that ran near our house. Tia Antonia caught him one day and pinched a chunk out of him. Well, a week or so later, after a summer storm, a kid named Beto Acosta dared Manuel to jump in with him. Manuel never turned down a dare, but he didn't want Tia to pinch him again. Beto jumped in by himself and drowned. True story."

"Sad story," my wife said.

36

I wasn't able to schedule Our Lady of Mercy for a funeral on the day Gabe wanted. The priest there had referred me to Merced's new church, St. Patrick's. I was reluctant since we'd all attended Our Lady of Mercy when we were kids, but I really didn't have any choice. I'd talked over the phone to a Father Echeverria at St. Patrick's, and he was cordial, even agreeing to a few embellishments of the traditional ceremony.

Ironically, I didn't even see the church until Miranda and I, accompanied by Chava and Cindy, drove into its parking lot for Johnny's service. "Man," I said, "where did all these houses come from? This was all fields." The area was full of new homes, many of them large and all, it seemed, with SUVs parked in front. These certainly weren't poor folks.

"Hey, it was fields just a couple of years ago. Now there's gonna be the new university campus out this way," my brother said, "so this is where development is happening."

I noticed folks working in their yards and turned toward Chava. "This is a mixed neighborhood, isn't it? When we were kids, the town was pretty damned segregated: poor whites here, rich whites there; blacks here, Mexicans there, a few Asians over there . . ."

"Yeah, but today if you've got the bucks you've got the digs," my brother said.

My wife asked, "Isn't that better?"

"I guess," grunted Chava, but I could tell he wasn't sure.

We entered the sparkling new church — larger than Our Lady of Mercy and much lighter inside — and sought out the priest. We were nearly two hours early, and as luck had it he was directing the arrangement of flowers around the altar, so we didn't have to search for him at the rectory.

Father Echevarria turned out to be a large, bearded young man with a bald spot that could have been a tonsure. "Nice to meet you face-to-face, Mr. Martinez," he said. "We've had a ton of calls about Mr. Orozco's funeral Mass. He must have been pretty popular."

"Yeah," I replied, "he was a famous boxer, but mostly he was a genuinely good person. Everyone loved him."

The priest was a generation too young to have heard of Johnny, but he smiled and said, "Let's hope people will say the same about us one day."

I'd wondered how many locals would remember my old pal, but the church was jammed, with many fight people from Southern California and the Bay Area crowded among the locals, and even guys like Sol LaBarra and Kid Tommy Murphy from New York; they'd both fought Johnny at the old St. Nick's Arena forty or so years before. There wasn't a casket — Johnny had been cremated — but honorary pallbearers sat in the front row, and among them were my wife and me.

I'd never seen a female pallbearer before, and I'll bet few in the church ever had either, but Johnny was his own man and he had dictated funeral instructions to Gabe, naming both Miranda and me. We sat holding hands in the front row with an assemblage of old Merced chums, ex-fighters and even Babe LaFranchi dressed in a silk suit the size of a three-man tent. In the pocket of my jacket was the short speech I'd written, a condensed version of the long eulogy the *Sacramento Tribune* had carried.

When it came time for my talk, I felt myself on the edge of tears. By the time I'd finally finished speaking, my eyes were spilling and my throat was soft.

Several times I'd had to stop and take deep breaths to regain control of myself, but I couldn't seem to shake the deep sorrow that gripped me, especially when I closed with "As a Christian, I know I'll see Johnny again, so I won't say good-bye. I'll say, Hasta luego, amigo. Hasta luego. Till we meet again." As I walked back to my pew, tears streaming down my face, my brother stood, stepped into the aisle, and hugged me. "You did great, Marty," he said. "Just great."

"That was wonderful," Miranda whispered when I sat down, and her hands grasped one of mine. But I felt hollow. My friend was gone forever, and all I could offer was words.

Later, just as the priest finished intoning the final passages of the Mass, he gave a high sign to Ruben Quintana, who sat on the bench with the altar servers. Ruben stood and three times clanged a boxing-ring bell mounted on a wooden frame. The audience jumped as the sound reverberated through the building.

As the final clang echoed and startled mourners exchanged glances, a stooped, white-haired man rose from the far end of the pallbearers' row and shuffled to the pulpit. Miranda raised her eyebrows and looked at me. "That's Dapper Danny Delaney, the famous ring announcer," I told her. "He flew out from Florida."

One of the deacons handed Dapper Dan a microphone. The old man turned to face the crowd, then nodded at Ruben, who pulled the bell's cord three more times. "Clang! Clang! Clang!"

"Ladies an' gen'lemen," called the announcer, his voice still strong, his tone still melodic. "Let us say good-bye to the uncrowned welterweight champeen of the world . . . The Merced Mauler! The Mexican Menace! El hombre mas peligroso del mundo!"—Dapper Dan paused dramatically after each new designation—"A credit to boxing! A man among men! A loyal friend to all! *Johnny 'El Tejon' Orooooozco!*"

Much of the crowd leaped to its feet and burst into loud applause as the announcer dragged out the name. One voice shouted, "*Adelante,* Johnny, *adelante!*"

I found myself smiling and clapping as though my pal had just won the title.

Then Dapper Danny turned toward Ruben and again nodded. Slowly and more softly, the bell tolled ten times, and I saw many men with scarred eyes and flattened noses wiping tears from their cheeks.

As soon as the service ended, Gabe found me and hugged me, clinging for a long time while I felt his body surge with sobs. "If you ever need anything, son," I told him, "just call me." He thanked me, then slouched away to a clutch of younger people.

■

In the parish hall later, I was surprised to find that someone had set up a life-size cutout of Johnny in fighting garb — the remnant of some long-ago boxing promotion. It stood with fists at the ready, and next to it several photo boards showing everything from Johnny as a baby to his last fight, with Julio Martin thirty-plus years later. I was particularly struck by his First Communion portrait: a sweet, angelic kid with big, dark eyes and curly hair. But he had been an angel with a warrior's heart and a powerful punch, and those things had determined the course of his life.

Now he was gone, and I felt again a shudder of deep sorrow. For an instant I thought I would once more burst into tears, and Miranda said, "Marty?"

"Our generation's window on life is closing," I choked.

Miranda squeezed my arm and asked, "'El Tejon'? What's that mean?"

"The badger."

She thought about it, then said, "Yes, that's the Johnny who fought the disease. He was a badger."

"That was the Johnny no one enjoyed fighting in the ring or in the street, either."

Miranda squeezed my arm again. "He was quite a guy," she said.

At lunch we washed down enchiladas and tamales with jug wine. Two of Johnny's ex-wives — Marie and Lorraine — sought me out and thanked me for my words. Several old pals did the same thing, and later Miranda and I listened to story after story of Johnny's exploits. My younger brother recalled, "Back in grade school us chile chokers used to bring burritos for lunch every day, so by Thursday we'd be tired of 'em, and we'd send Johnny and my big brothers to convince some of the rich Anglo guys to trade their sandwiches with us. No one ever refused. What was it, do you think, Marty? Logic? Reason?" He laughed.

"Yeah," I said, "I used to explain to them that it was better to eat a burrito and not have Johnny and Manuel kick the shit out of them. They caught on right away."

Then an old boxing trainer named Charlie "Smoke" Leoni recalled, "Those guys was smart, because that Johnny he was tough. When we was in Rome in '64, they never give Johnny a chance to warm up before the fight, and that Eyetalian, Ricci, he roughed the kid up, dropped him twice in the first. The kid comes back to the corner and I asks is he okay. He looks up at me from the stool and he says, 'Yeah, but that Wop's in deep shit.' I says, 'Hey, I'm a Wop!' He says, 'Yeah, but you're a lucky one. Johnny's not after you.' He stopped Ricci in three, busted him up good."

Babe LaFranchi spoke up then: "Remember when the referee was gonna stop the fight against Moore because Johnny had that big cut on his nose?" He wheezed, sounding like a bellows. "Well, Johnny he said to the ref, 'Just one more round,' and the ref he looked over at me sittin' in the front row and I nodded. Damned if Johnny didn't nail Moore with three left hooks in a row, put him on queer street, and the ref stopped the bout. You couldn't ever count Johnny out. Am I right or am I right?"

"When my little girl dyin' with the leukemia," a slim man with a scarred face the texture and hue of a walnut said quietly, "Johnny he come by every day. He bring us food, he cry with us, he pray with us . . . he say 'Cookie, they ain't nothin' you and Joellen need Johnny won't do for you. You just give yo' energy to yo' baby.' I tells you right here, they don't make mens no better'n Johnny O."

I realized then that the speaker had to be Raymond "Cookie" Daniels, who had been the lightweight champion of the world forty or so years ago. I would never have recognized him.

Chava lightened things up, asking, "Did Johnny ever tell you guys about the time he, Raul, and Marty burned a big *S* on our football field the night before we played Stockton High?" He began chuckling as he continued: "The next day the other football players were claiming they'd almost caught the Stockton guys, said they chased them all the way up Highway 99 past Ceres, but lost 'em by Modesto. Raul and Johnny and Marty, they just listened and nodded and said, 'No shit?'"

That reminded me of something: "You guys remember Eddie Rivers? He was one of the ones who claimed they almost caught the Stockton guys?"

"A benchwarmer," said Junius Peppers, who had been a football stud in high school.

"Did you know his mother was Mexican? He was half."

"No shit," said Junius. "He sure didn't let that get around. I heard him talk some bad shit about beaners, man."

"A *pinche pendejo,*" my brother said, and everyone laughed.

As we were leaving, I asked Al Robles, "Where's big Ben today? He and Johnny were tight buddies."

"Gonsalves?" he replied. "Didn't you hear? He had a stroke and he can't walk or talk very good yet. He's at that nursing home across from the hospital. Me and Junius go by to visit every Tuesday and Thursday night, give his wife a little break."

■

Miranda and I decided to stay at a motel that night. We could have slept at the house of my brother or one of my sisters or any number of pals, for that matter, but my plumbing problems still embarrassed me. As we drove to the Best Western, we tuned in to a Beatles retrospective on FM, Miranda humming along softly to "Yesterday."

Once we entered the motel room, though, I turned on the clock radio to find the same station, but heard instead the raucous voice of Little Richard: "Long tall Sally she is built for speed . . ."

"Whooo!" I whooped, imitating Little Richard. "Now we're getting to *real* music."

"Really? You like this better than the Beatles?"

"This and Jerry Lee Lewis, Dorsey Burnett, Chuck Berry, Elvis Presley, Carl Perkins, Wanda Jackson, Fats Domino . . ."

"*Really?*" Miranda seemed genuinely shocked. "To me, the Beatles created a whole new direction in music. Their songs seemed . . ." She searched for a word. "*Profound.*"

"Out here in the Valley rhythm 'n' blues and rockabilly cut through all the pop music and gave us a sound we could actually identify with," I said. "I can still remember the first time I heard Little Richard — he's my all-time favorite. He knocked my socks off."

"Well, I heard the Beatles when I was in college, but I kept my socks on."

"In those days that was probably *all* you kept on."

She punched my shoulder as she laughed again. "You're nasty. My mother warned me about boys like you: fast music, fast cars, drive-in movies."

The voice of Nat "King" Cole — hardly sounding like the same species, let alone the same era — followed Little Richard's. Nat was singing "Unforgettable," so I slipped behind Miranda and enveloped her in my arms. "I take back what I said about your socks," I whispered, then kissed her ear.

"Do you swear you love the Beatles?" she demanded.

"I swear," I lied.

"You silver-tongued devil." She turned and kissed me for a long while.

We were reading in bed later when Miranda put down her book and said, "I've been thinking about what you said about music. You were serious, weren't you, about preferring Little Richard to the Beatles?"

"I'm afraid so."

"Well, I don't think that's a big deal in itself, but I wonder if it's linked to the way you hometown guys always talk about fights and things when you're together?"

"What brings this up?"

"I was listening today, and I saw the way your eyes lit up when you talked about those . . . what? . . . those brawls. Was Merced really that tough?"

"I think the whole Valley could be rough during those years. There was a lot of social churning then."

"But violence doesn't settle anything," she said, her tone more reasoned than passionate. "It just begets more violence."

"Well, if some guy's coming after you and you can knock him on his ass, that's something settled," I said. "But I think you're generally right. Johnny became a professional fighter in the first place because boxing and the military were the hope for poor guys. Other people had more options."

She paused, then said, "Johnny was a soldier, too, like you? I don't think war settles much either."

"Tell a European Jew that, honey. Tell them that stopping Hitler wasn't important."

"Of course," she acknowledged. "I was thinking of Vietnam." Miranda sat silent for a moment, then she asked, "Today, as a Catholic Christian, would you fight or turn the other cheek if someone hit you?"

"Well, that'd depend on how hard I was hit. If somebody really belted me, he might knock the Catholic Christian right out of me—I mean, knock any conscious restraint out. Then I would fight in a primal way just to survive. And I think almost everyone else would, too."

This wasn't stuff I wanted to be discussing on the day we'd buried a special pal, but when I changed the subject I didn't lighten it much. "You know what I've been thinking about all day?" I asked.

"Sex?"

"That's a good guess, but no," I replied. "I don't understand why I'm alive when so many people I love are gone. It just doesn't compute."

"Life doesn't compute, dear. We just live it."

37

The clan assembled for breakfast the next morning at Chava and Cindy's house. After surveying the crowd, Miranda winked at me and said, "I thought Mexicans were supposed to be brown." This was an old joke between us.

Chava overheard her and said, "Martinezes forgot the rules."

"We're brown enough, Champ," I added.

My brother asked, "What's with the 'Champ' stuff?"

"Johnny named her that."

"Johnny did?" He turned toward Miranda and said, "Come on, Champ, let's eat."

Breakfast featured my mother's menudo recipe with all the trimmings, cooked by Chava's distinctly non-Mexican wife; homemade tortillas and salsa brought by my sisters; and a twelve-pack of a Central Valley beer called Dos Okies, carried in by Marcus, one of my brothers-in-law. "Hey," he said, "there's *dos* of us here, me and Cindy. She's a white one and I'm a slightly darker one."

After we'd eaten ourselves nearly into a stupor, and told story after story in the process, I excused myself and used the nearby bathroom. As I stood washing my hands, I heard children's voices outside, so I peeked out a small window and saw some kids choosing sides for touch football. All of them were mixtures of something—whites, Asians, Latinos, blacks—and all of them family or neighbors. The new California. I also saw faintly reflected in the window my own face: gray hair, wrinkled skin, tired eyes. The old and the young caught for a few moments on that pane. And I thought of Johnny and Manny, of Raul and Junius . . . of all of the kids I'd grown up with and played with here, many of them now dead. Enjoy it, was all I could think to say to those youngsters on the lawn. Enjoy it.

After a moment, I washed my face and returned to the dining room, where Chava said, "You know, we really need to start having a reunion like this—maybe even a whole weekend—every year. We should've started doing that before Manuel died, but like he used to say, today's always a better day to start than tomorrow."

"Amen," said Alicia. "Marcus's family does that over in Oakland. It's a kick."

Her husband, whom most people would likely identify as African American, smiled. "We go to an Oklahoma reunion down in Lamont and a Louisiana reunion in Oakland, and they're both somethin' else. At the Oklahoma reunion, folks from the same town get together—everyone from mine is part Choctaw, seems like—but the Louisiana one used to separate whites and blacks. Nowadays, man, if you're a Delacroix or Fallandy or Dupree, you just go to these big, long tables signed with your name, and you sit there and eat and listen to music and dance with pearl whites and coal blacks and everything in between—everybody kin."

"It's really fun," my sister agreed.

I thought of those kids rollicking on the lawn next door, and I said, "There used to be some pretty strong racial barriers in this town. Things seem better now."

"It is better, Homes," agreed Chava.

Homes. Homeboy. He hadn't called me that in years.

"But not perfect," Alicia said. "Marcus and I can still raise eyebrows. At a potluck at the high school last fall some *gringa* who'd just moved into the new section from San Jose said, 'I don't mean to be rude, but what nationality are you?' I said, 'American.'

"She smiled and said, 'But what are you *really?*' I thought, My father and my uncles fought in World War II. My brother was killed in Vietnam! I was *really* steamed."

"You could've fried an egg on that pretty neck." Marcus said. "I wouldn't've wanted to spar with her then."

"I nearly slapped her face!" snapped my sister.

"Calm down, baby," urged her husband, who hugged her and planted a kiss on her cheek. "She really told that gal off."

My older sister, Esperanza, had disappeared after eating. "What's up with *la jefa?*" Chava asked, and her husband, Bob Mardikian, whom we called "the foreigner" because he was from down the road in Fresno, said, "She's got a surprise." For the taciturn Bob that was an oration.

My brother once observed, "Anybody married to Sis couldn't get a word in edgewise. I hope she's a great piece of ass."

Esperanza finally reappeared a few minutes later, carrying a cardboard box. She placed it on the dining room table and announced, "We were cleaning out the storage locker, and I found this box of Mama's keepsakes. I'd forgotten we'd stored them after she died."

My stomach immediately churned, and coppery saliva puddled at the back of my tongue.

"Anyway, look at this," my sister said. She pulled a tiny sailor suit from the box and held it up. Then she reached in and brought out a little cap and one small bunny slipper. "Do you remember these, Marty?" she asked.

"No," I croaked. I really didn't, but I knew whose they had to be.

"They're yours, baby, they're yours."

My mother had once dressed me in these clothes, and had loved me enough to save them, but I had abandoned her.

"Marty," Esperanza said, "are you okay?"

I blinked hard and swallowed, then managed to say, "Yeah." Miranda patted my thigh.

I saw Chava give Esperanza a high sign, and she raised her eyebrows, then put the clothes back in the box and said, "We can look at this stuff another time."

My wife and I excused ourselves a few minutes later. "I've got chemo this afternoon, and I'm starting radiation right away, too," she explained casually, as though talking about a tennis lesson. "Busy day," she added.

"How's that going?" Alicia asked.

"Well, I'm really just starting, so it's not bad," Miranda responded. "This particular drug doesn't tend to cause much of a problem with nausea, although before I'm done it'll have me looking like . . . who's that chrome-domed villain in the Austin Powers movies? . . . Dr. Evil? Fortunately, Marty's always been attracted to bald-headed women."

That comment broke the tension. "That right, Homes? You like baldies?" asked my brother.

"I'll like this one," I said, and I squeezed Miranda's hand.

"Oh yeah, speaking of baldies," said Chava, "do you remember Raul Acosta?"

"The guy we called Segundo?"

"Yeah, Nacho's little brother."

"What's up with him?"

"I saw Nacho the other day and he said Segundo has prostate cancer bad. Had to have his *huevos* cut off."

"Oh God."

■

As we drove back to Sacramento, my wife sat close to me, one hand on my thigh. "Does your mother's death still haunt you?"

"No, but my performance that night does."

"You told me you'd confessed that sin."

"I have."

"You've been absolved, right?"

I knew where she was going with this. "Yes."

"Then it's over. God's forgiven you. You know good and well that your mother has. What're you hanging on to?"

"*I* haven't forgiven me."

"Will you stop wallowing in self-pity?" she demanded, the first time in our relationship that she'd sounded that agitated with me, and I almost flared at her — she couldn't understand how I felt. I swallowed my anger and said nothing.

After several miles of road fled beneath us, Miranda said, "I know what you're doing is purgatorial, I understand that, but don't cultivate it or you'll be right back in depression. If you're still holding on to that, you need to see Dr. Molinaro."

"Miranda," I said, "have you ever thought that this world is all there is, and that how we feel about what we've done is the real Heaven or Hell?"

She sighed, then answered, "Sure, but that would mean that sociopaths who hurt people and don't care about it would suffer no consequences. I can't believe in an existence that crass."

I hadn't thought of it that way.

"Churches may only be guessing about what comes next," she continued, "but I honestly believe it's tied to morality and love and forgiveness. That belief keeps me going. All I ask is that you keep yourself open to that possibility, too." She snuggled back against me. "Besides, I just don't want you to be sad."

"Okay," I said. But the sadness didn't depart.

■

I accompanied my wife to her first radiation treatment at the same place where I'd been radiated . . . unsuccessfully. Vonda and Dr. Nimitz, and even the receptionist, knew my wife by her first name. The tone of the visit was as I'd expected, almost like a small party. I remembered from my own stops here that everybody seemed to put on their best faces for as long as they could.

Miranda seemed genuinely relaxed about what was going on, though. She had earlier come in for the telemetry measurements, so a frame customized to fit her head was ready. I couldn't go into the treatment room with her, of course, so I didn't see her wearing it. Instead, I remained anxiously in the waiting room trying to concentrate on old magazines.

I wondered about the people I'd met while I was being radiated here, about how many of them were still alive. Had their good spirits allowed any of them to survive this long? It seemed to me that biology was all that mattered, studies to the contrary notwithstanding; one mutant cell, then more and more finally snuffing out their own environment. I found that terribly threatening. Praying might not cure anything, but it certainly took my mind off all that plagued me, so I silently mouthed an Our Father, then a Hail Mary, and was about to begin a Glory Be when Miranda emerged from the treatment area.

"One down, twenty or so to go," she said, smiling.

I smiled back but felt lousy. I knew I needed to call the psychiatrist, but kept putting it off. I moped around the house later, still burdened by Johnny's death, by the sailor suit, and mostly by Miranda's obdurate cancer. When she later returned from her office, she walked in through the kitchen door and announced, "Let's drive up to Castella this weekend. I want to see my property. I probably won't feel much like it a week from now." Although she had thrown up after eating last night, her voice retained the old playfulness.

"Are you sure you feel up to it?" I asked.

"There's a toilet up there to barf into, isn't there? And no one in Castella will know I wasn't always bald." Her hair had come out in clumps and she was wearing her "head-rag," actually a rather expensive and attractive cross between a cap and a scarf. She usually only put on her gray wig when she left the house, and she looked pretty slick in it, I thought. "I'm fine," she continued, "and we both need to get away. We can leave Friday afternoon after my infusion and come home Monday morning in time for the next one. Okay?"

"Okay," I replied, not certain she should be traveling.

She poured herself a glass of ice water, then asked, "When do you see your cardiologist again?"

"Tuesday afternoon."

"And the oncologist?"

"Yikes!" I said. Since I only went in every three months, I'd forgotten another appointment was due. I walked into the kitchen and looked at the calendar. When I returned to the family room, I said, "Thanks for reminding me. I go in tomorrow morning, so I need to go down and do blood work this afternoon."

"Do you want me to go to either appointment with you?"

"No need," I answered. For serious consultations, we always went together, but these were "well-baby" visits . . . I hoped.

She smiled and said, "Do you feel like a nap?"

"I could fire up my pump."

"Forget the pump. Let's just cuddle."

"I feel a tingling in my Depend."

"I suspect that reports of a tingle in your Depend are greatly exaggerated," she correctly surmised.

My wife never ceased to amaze me. While I still sagged toward depression, she never revealed that tendency, let alone fear. She always seemed to make the best of situations, and she carried me along with her.

■

After watering the lawn late that afternoon, I reentered the house just as the phone rang. I let the machine answer and heard Bud Hartley's voice. I picked up the handset and said, "Hey, Bud."

"Hi, Marty. Sorry to bother you this late, but I really need to talk to you." His voice sounded strange. "Look, I know I said I wouldn't involve you anymore in the story about Catholic priests, but I just had a call from one of my sources at the *Express,* and he told me Monica Salinas is going to break a story about a gay priest at St. Apollinaris. Those two over there are your friends, aren't they?"

"They're my friends."

"Well, Monica has learned that one is gay — the young one — and she's going to expose him."

"Expose him for what?" I asked.

Bud didn't answer at first, then he responded, "For being gay, I guess."

"Being homosexual isn't a crime or a sin as far as I know, even for a priest." I wasn't shocked to learn that a priest was gay, even Father Tran. In fact, I wouldn't be much shocked to learn that anyone was, because it no longer seemed very important to me. "I read recently that as many as 50 percent of younger priests may be gay. So what's the big deal?" I asked him.

"What about his work with altar boys?" the editor asked.

"What about the other one's work with altar girls?"

Bud cleared his throat. "Look, I happen to agree with you, but *you,* not I, need to write the *Tribune*'s response to whatever the *Express* asserts, and I don't know for sure what slant Salinas will give this. We'll need an op-ed piece if it turns out she's just casting about for a story. What I just heard you say would be a good start for the response.

"Here's the skinny," he continued. "Some priest named Andrews told Monica that the whole child-abuse problem is that gays have infiltrated the priesthood and that they're being harbored by liberals. He says this only happens in America, where true Catholicism is no longer practiced . . . You want to hear more?"

"Naw." I shook my head. "I'll pick up an *Express* and read the piece, but I know Andrews, and I can tell you he's a nutcase. I guess Monica really wanted an angle if she took him seriously."

"Can you help us on this one?"

"On this one, I can." Writing it wouldn't be exactly returning to the pedophile-priests story — something I'd vowed to myself not to do; it would be helping a friend. My energy was low, worrying about Miranda and dealing with my own illness drained me, as did those memories that I couldn't seem to shake.

Although I'd said nothing to anyone about it, I was also concerned that my once prodigious memory seemed damaged; I now had to reach for information that was once right there. Nevertheless, I knew I could do a job if Salinas was unfair to Father Tran. "After I read what Monica writes," I told Bud, "I'll decide how to approach this."

"Keep me posted," the editor said, then hung up.

I sat at the kitchen table and swirled my cold decaf and even did a few deep-breathing exercises to settle myself, then I called, "Miranda! Are you awake, honey?"

No response.

"Babe!"

She appeared in the doorway from the bedroom. "I was listening to *Porgy and Bess.*"

"Bud just called and said the *Express* is carrying a story claiming a priest at St. Apollinaris is gay."

"Yes."

"Father Tran," I said.

"I know."

"You know? Why didn't you tell me?"

She smiled, but her tone was serious when she replied, "How was it your business? Father Tran is my patient and my friend, and he has the right to expect confidentiality from me. If he'd wanted you to know he'd have told you. Besides, he's celibate, so what difference does it make?"

"How do you know he's celibate?"

"The same way I know you're faithful: because he's someone I believe." She seemed to measure me for a moment, then added, "Was it important to your friendship with him that you know his sexual orientation?"

"No, I guess not."

"I didn't think so."

"It's just that my own son . . ."

"That may be why Father Tran is so fond of you."

■

Monica's whole story turned out to be a revelation that Father Tran was gay, then a discussion of gay priests nationally, plus considerable credence given to Father Andrews and his opinion of all this. She also quoted a couple of unhappy parishioners and asserted that "at least 40 percent of American priests are homosexuals." Since she cited no source for that figure, I assumed it was a guess.

I turned on my computer to begin writing, but as usual checked my e-mail first: Two ads about penis enlargement and a chance to share a fortune in funds from Ghana, but no personal messages.

I began this way: *"Just last fall our rival newspaper editorially endorsed tolerance and understanding of personal sexual preferences. Last Sunday, in a front-page story, the same newspaper attacked a respected parish priest for being homosexual.*

"Which stance represents the paper's actual position—tolerance or bigotry? It can't have it both ways.

"Celibacy is celibacy whether a priest is gay or straight. Not even the writer suggests that Father Nguyen Tran has broken his vow . . ."

38

Mort's introduction of the guest speaker at the prostate cancer support group went on far too long. He made the guy sound like a combination of Mother Teresa and Albert Schweitzer, but he looked like an aging hippie to me: gray beard and ponytail, with the mandatory smock, sandals, and beads. "Dr. Wendell Phelps is a leader in the holistic psychology movement," Mort concluded, "so we're extremely fortunate he's taken time from his busy schedule to address us. Dr. Phelps."

We applauded, and the slender man put his hands together in a prayerlike position and bowed slightly, a pale-faced Gandhi.

"Since I was diagnosed three years ago myself," he said, "I'm a prostate cancer brother. As a result, I'm delighted to share my experiences with you, my prostate brothers. One of the first things I heard after word got out about my condition was that prostate cancer isn't really serious; you can live forever with it, I was told. Then, brothers, I read that it's the second-worst killer of men."

"Oh *brother,*" I soto-voiced to Al Royster, who chuckled.

Phelps paused to allow his words to sink in, although everyone in this group was well aware of the disease's deadliness. The psychologist then lightened the discussion when he observed, "By the way, I see that I'm the only one here still wearing love beads, though I'll bet some of you rolled around in the Summer of Love just like I did. I wonder if you know how many ex-hippies it takes to control this disease?" He paused, then said, "Four. One to buy the green tea and three to roll it into joints."

That drew overly hearty laughter, probably because it broke whatever tension his clothing and hairstyle might have caused among our largely conservative membership.

Once the laughter subsided, the guest speaker continued, "Like many of you, I'm certain, I really do make green tea one foundation stone of my response to cancer. Tofu, soy milk, and soy cheese are another. My diet is strictly vegan. Like most of you, I hope, I have resisted attacks on my body sponsored by the American Medical Association. No surgery. No radiation. No chemotherapy or hormones. All my treatment is natural—acupuncture, bodywork, meditation.

"Lately I have been taking a mixture called Sun Soup—I'll tell you more about it later—and I ingest maitake and shiitake mushrooms rather than the wondrous 'shrooms of my youth," he said. "I also make brown rice and flax seeds foundations of my regimen. I take one PC-SPES capsule a day, as directed by my healer and spiritual counselor. My alternative course for dealing with this experience stresses deep spirituality."

He paused then, and seemed to search the room before continuing: "Notice that I said *experience,* not struggle or battle or fight. We have been deceived," he said softly and opened his arms in a Christ-like gesture. "We have been deceived, brothers, by the medical establishment."

I exchanged a glance with Al Royster, sitting across the table from me. He rolled his eyes.

"What we need," the psychologist continued, his voice almost somnolent, "is to learn how to live *with* our cancer. Don't resist it. The prophet tells us that if we resist the charging dog, it will bite. If we merely accept it, the dog will submit.

"Don't try to destroy your disease, brothers," he chanted. "Go with it. *Go* with it. We must accept cancer as our companion, perhaps our friend. Then and only then can we transcend . . ."

"Excuse me, Dr. Phelps," called Dr. Royster. The psychologist smiled beatifically as he replied, "Yes, brother?"

"With all due respect, *brother,*" the physician said, "you're full of shit."

■

"It's been thirteen months, and your PSA's stayed at zero," Dr. DelVecchio reported. "I think it's time we took you off the hormones for a while."

"Really? That's great!"

The oncologist sat in a chair and I sat on an examination table. He was making notes on my chart as we spoke. "How've the side effects been? Still having hot flashes?"

"Yeah, but they haven't been bad—more like sweats than what I've heard other guys describe."

"Any breast swelling or tenderness?"

"A little."

The oncologist looked up, then said, "How's the heart doing? Are you exercising? Push-ups? Sit-ups? Walking?"

"Yeah, all of those."

"Good." He smiled. "And you're really okay with going off the hormones for a while? I've had patients who panicked when they realized that nothing was being done about their cancers."

"I can't wait."

"I'd like you to stop by the lab on your way out and have them do a testosterone-level test. This first time off, I'd like you to do that monthly, along with a PSA so we can graph how fast those things come back. After the next round, whenever that is, we'll do a bone-density test, too."

"Okay. I'm really grateful that you've had me on this therapy, but I've begun to feel weak and listless, so I'm hoping that my time off will pep me up."

"It should." He stood and extended his right hand. "Unless something goes haywire, I'll see you in three months."

"See you then."

He turned and opened the door, then stopped. "Oh yes, one other thing," he said. "Please give Miranda my best wishes. We docs are really a small community, and she's one of the very best. I'm pulling for her. I know she's a Catholic, but tell her my wife and I are sending some Jewish prayers her way."

"You're Jewish?" I asked, impolitic as that was.

"I converted after I married Deborah." He added, "People ask me that all the time."

■

That Friday night we joined Rollie and Audrey for dinner at their house in Dunsmuir. He was in rare form. "How come if Jesus was a Jew he had that Mexican name?" he demanded.

As laughter subsided, I countered with, "I always thought he had an Okie name, J.C."

"You danged rascal," my ex-brother-in-law yipped.

As the evening wore on, the wine jug emptying, the laughter and yips growing louder, Rollie said to my wife, "You sure got some bargain-basement deal whenever you got this ol' boy, Champ"—he'd quickly seized her new nickname. "Why, I heard from his brother that folks used to lock their daughters up whenever he came around . . . and their livestock, too."

He was still guffawing when I said, "Well, Rollie was noted down there in Bakersfield where he's from as a veterinarian who serviced lonely heifers."

Audrey stood then and said, "Okay, boys. That's enough. I'm cutting off the wine supply." Then she turned to Miranda and said, "When the conversation reaches this point—and it always does—it's time to put them to bed. Do you guys want to stay here with us or drive back to the cabin?"

Champ asked, "May I leave Marty here?"

"No way," Audrey responded.

"Hell," her husband said, "let him stay. We might could have him weed the garden. Chili beans're good for that."

"You know what Okies're good for?"

"No," said Audrey, "and I don't want you to tell us."

My designated driver wheeled the five miles back to the cabin, swooping us up onto the highway, then off again at the Castle Crags exit in the Sacramento River's canyon. "It's really dark up here," she said. "There's not even much moonlight."

Beside the road, fir trees showed as black on black, and the river was a deep murmur. On the side street, we crossed the bridge over Castle Creek, crossed the railroad track, then drove the final couple of hundred yards to our cabin on an uncrowded street, with the river tumbling behind our backyard. Several of our neighbors were year-rounders, retired mostly, but also a logger, a fishing guide, and a single lady who taught school in Dunsmuir. Cordial folks all. With the exception of one shack surrounded by old cars and nondescript dogs and owned by a grizzled gent who talked to no one but who posted anti-government signs all over his fence, the houses were well kept.

Champ parked the car on the dirt driveway and sighed. "It really is beautiful up here, Marty, and it smells so clean."

"The river does that," I said.

In bed a few minutes after entering the cabin, I was still feeling good, so I gently nudged her and said, "Care to do a little horizontal dancing, Champ? My wick may be broken, but the fire's still there."

She kissed my cheek and said, "Talk to me in the morning. But tell me something—why do you guys always end up joking about sex?"

"Because we're insecure about it."

"You talk as though sex is important all by itself, not as part of a relationship."

I reached over and stroked her nose, her lips, her chin with one finger. "I think guys have to learn what's really important about it. There was a lot of pressure to be sexually active—or talk as though you were—when I was in high school."

"You didn't go to a Catholic high school, did you?"

"No, my folks couldn't afford that even if there'd been one in town. I went to Merced High, but my mother made us attend catechism classes with the black crows—nuns."

Miranda laughed, then said, "Well, at St. Anne's, where I went to school, they spent a considerable amount of time warning us not to lose our virginity, not to French-kiss, and not to ever, ever, ever touch anything that emerged from a zipper. Most of all, we weren't supposed to go on a date to a drive-in movie. I took that stuff seriously, and so did most of the girls."

"Hey, I used to hear that Catholic school girls were hot."

"Did you ever date a girl who went to a Catholic high school?"

It was my turn to laugh. "Naw. That's why I could imagine anything I wanted."

Miranda's voice changed then, and she said, "It seems quaint to say it now, but I was a virgin when I married Arthur. I don't think I was so much virtuous as scared. I think he was too, by the way—a virgin, I mean, but you'd have to shove bamboo slivers under his nails to force him to admit it."

"His lack of early experiences could explain his womanizing," I said. "Guys put a lot of pressure on their peers to be sexually active, and some never get over it."

"He got active, though," Miranda said, "sleeping with any willing young woman he could find." She paused, then added, "As a result, I learned that you can enjoy sex with someone who's promiscuous, but you can't value it. Before long you can't value him either.

"I've never regretted waiting until marriage before having sex. And now let me really shock you: You and he are the only men I've ever slept with."

I didn't know what to say to that. "I guess I can't be worse than second-best, then," I finally responded. "I'd love you no matter what, Champ. I just plain love you."

"I know. That's why I told you."

■

The next morning, we walked hand in hand on the old road below the highway and parallel to the Sacramento River until we reached a bridge. I pointed across the stream and told Miranda, "That's where Nancy and I used to bring the kids to play in the shallows. When it got hot, I'd go in there myself and sit in the water, then the kids'd spend all their time splashing me." I grinned at the memory.

"My kids didn't get much outdoor activity. My husband was a city boy from San Francisco," she explained, "and he never felt safe in the woods. But he was good about taking them to places like the zoo or the museum." She smiled then, saying, "We once went up to Yosemite Valley and stayed in a cabin. Poor Arthur was awake the whole night worrying that bears might join us."

"He may have been right."

We continued strolling and dropped onto a dirt track near the water. "There's a better trail on the other bank," I told her, "but I like this old fisherman's path. The one over there's 'improved,' so it's like a freeway."

I'd walked this side scores of times when fishing, and I knew Miranda would appreciate the forest's complexity and the river's rapids and runs from here, and that we might see birds or animals not visible from the heavily traveled trail across the river.

Soon road noises were obscured, and all we heard was the stream's resonant voice, plus the calls and skitterings of birds. "That big rock out there used to hide a huge trout," I told her, pointing to a boulder the size of a car, submerged but visible at midstream. "In low water you could sometimes see the fish's tail fanning if you had on Polaroid glasses. Rollie and Doug and I spent hours casting flies here, but no luck. Finally, Rollie said, 'That's not a real fish. It's a mirage.'

"Then in 1991 there was that big poison spill when a railroad tank car full of chemicals fell into the river upstream at Cantara Loop, and that grandfather trout was killed. I was sent up here to cover the story of the spill, and as it turned out, one of my Castella neighbors just happened to have been in this area when the chemical plume reached here. He said there were dead and dying fish everywhere, and the big guy just sort of popped to the surface, still alive but dying. Anyway, Bob — the neighbor — waded out and recovered that fish and took it into Dunsmuir. It weighed almost twenty pounds, which is huge for a non-sea-run trout. The folks at the market displayed it in a freezer for a couple of months, and I understand that one of the local guides eventually paid to have it mounted."

Miranda said, "Oh, so this is the stretch that was poisoned. I remember reading about that. It looks fine now."

"It's not, though — or not entirely, anyway," I told her. "The riparian community, plants and trees both, plus underwater vegetation, was badly damaged. When the first fish migrated downstream from the upper reaches, they didn't find much to eat because the insect cycles were disrupted. But it does look pretty well recovered now. That's taken over a decade."

A memory made me smile. "When I was up here interviewing folks about the spill I ran into an old-timer, and he said, 'Well, the good side is that we'll be rid of the trash fish,' and a young environmentalist who overheard him said, 'Are you nucking futs? That stuff is killing *everything!*' I think it was the 'nucking futs' that broke the tension, because there sure wasn't much upside to the story then."

We moved on, almost immediately disturbing some sort of small critter — I couldn't tell what in the dense undergrowth, but I knew it was a mammal because I saw a blur of gray, grizzled fur. Farther upstream, we reached a curve in the channel where a long, swooshing run had cut a pool into the far bank. It was another favorite fishing hole. "Oh, look!" the Champ pointed as a kingfisher seemed to bounce off the water, a minnow struggling in its beak.

"This used to be my son's favorite hole," I told her. "He'd cast wet flies or nymphs here, and I swear he always caught trout, too. He was a catch-and-release man."

We sat then on a fallen log, watching and listened to the water rush by. "You really miss him, don't you?" she said.

"I really do."

"After a long pause, Miranda said, "I'm glad we came up here together, Marty. It's a special place."

"Yeah," I said, "it is." I put my arm around her and squeezed, hoping that the two of us would be up here many more times together.

■

We were in the car, about halfway back to Sacramento, when she broke the news: "I didn't want to tell you this while we were enjoying our weekend, but the chemo I've been on, Navelbine, doesn't seem to be working anymore. The tumor mass isn't shrinking; it may be growing. My numbers haven't gone down."

My belly knotted and I exhaled loudly. "Shit!" I said.

"There's good news, too," she added. "The radiation's shrinking that tumor in my brain."

"That's fine, but what's next with the chemo? What therapy, I mean." I'd been in the cancer world long enough myself to know that series of treatments were often available, and sometimes one worked when others didn't. I also knew they usually bought time but cured nothing.

"We'll try Navelbine just a bit longer, and Jeaneve has some weapons we haven't tried."

The amazing thing to me about all this — my health problems as well as hers — was how matter-of-fact they'd become; there was no movie background music, no crescendos or diminuendos, just two people alive and responding as best they could to tough problems. Although I knew it was dumb, I couldn't help remarking, "After all you've been through, for this not to work just isn't fair."

"Come on, Marty," she sighed. "Don't be silly. Cancer's not fair. It doesn't grasp that concept."

"I know, sweetheart," I replied, feeling even dumber for having said that in the first place. "I know, and it really pisses me off."

"Marty," she said, sounding exasperated, "I hate it, too, but this is the way it's *supposed* to be, older people dying, younger ones procreating, new ones being born. It's just that when someone you love dies, part of you does too, no matter how old. We all march to the abyss together, and it's always been this way. Now it's our turn."

"But you're only sixty-five," I stammered.

"Which makes me pretty old in terms of life expectancy the world over."

"I'm not worried about the world over . . ."

The Champ put her hand on my thigh. "You have to let this go," she said. "We've both known we were on borrowed time since we met. Don't make this more difficult than it already is."

That stopped me. I guess I *was* making it more difficult.

■

The nap we took immediately upon arriving home turned into a bit of light necking before sleep, even though the chemo had caused sores to develop in Miranda's mouth. But snuggling for us was life holding out against death, and it calmed me.

The Champ was still adrift in her nap and I was lying next to her, unasleep, once more growing disturbed as I read the newspapers that had arrived while we were gone.

I heard the front door open, then the voice of Dougie and Tyler chirping at their mother. A moment later, she called, "Daddy? Miranda?"

Tyler called, "Papa! Gramma!"

I rolled out of bed wearing only shorts and a Depend, then shrugged into a robe and slippers. "I'm here," I called down the hall as I left the bedroom.

"Oh, hi." My daughter smiled as I entered the dinette. She sat at the table holding her squirming son. Tyler said, "Can I watch TV?" Then he headed for the den before anyone could answer.

"That boy!" Lea said. After surveying me for a moment, she asked, "Were you in bed, Daddy? Are you sick?" Her voice was concerned.

"Yes I was in bed, and no I'm not sick."

"Then why . . . ?"

"Miranda and I were in bed."

"But . . ." My daughter grinned suddenly. "You weren't *you know what,* were you?"

I smiled, not feeling obligated to outline for her what we were or weren't doing.

"Daddy, you're almost seventy years old." Her playful tone turned serious. "You have a bad heart. You have cancer. Does your doctor know that you're doing *that?* Can that be good for you?"

"It's wonderful for me, as a matter of fact," I smiled, "and my doctor knows exactly what I choose to tell him. Why didn't you knock, by the way?"

"Tyler did," Lea said, and I immediately understood that his light rapping wouldn't have carried into the bedroom.

"Well," I said, "maybe *you* ought to in the future, if only for the sake of the children. You never know what you'll catch us doing or where we'll be doing it."

"You're kidding, right?"

I grinned and didn't answer her question.

39

"Hello, this is James and Cynthia. We're not available to take your call, but please leave a message and we'll call you back as soon as we can." I assumed that they monitored their phone just as I did, so after the beep I said, "James, this is Marty Martinez. I'm calling to let you know—"

"Hello, Marty," Miranda's oldest son said. "What's up?"

"I'm calling to let you know that Miranda's cancer is back. Has she already told you?"

"Crap!" he said. "No, she hasn't. She's not one to complain."

"She's doing radiation and chemotherapy right now, with mixed results so far. I'm sure she'd be bucked up if you or your brothers called or visited."

"How mixed are the results?"

I explained what I knew, concluding, "It could be worse, but it could damn sure be better, too."

After a loud sigh, James replied, "Cynthia and I were hoping to come out for Thanksgiving, meet Nick and Kathy there too, and join you guys, but maybe I can work something out sooner."

"You'll call your brothers?"

"Sure," he said. "Nick'll be in touch with Mom right away . . . I know him. But Robbie's still got a bone stuck in his craw. He hates you and doesn't respect her right now."

"What's his problem, anyway?"

"He's the baby of the family and he's accepted Dad's version of everything. He also said he'd had a run-in with you."

"He didn't *have* a run-in with me, he *caused* a run-in with me." I told him the story of that afternoon.

"You sure got his attention," James said. "He's scared of you now. I think that's the main reason why he hates you."

"He can do anything he wants about me, but he owes his mother respect."

"That's what Nick and I've been telling him, but he says no, not while she's with a Mexican. He's pissed and scared and looking for excuses."

"Well, she's not with a Mexican," I pointed out, "and he'll be sorry if he doesn't visit her no matter who she's with. He'll regret this behavior when he finally realizes what he's done."

■

Miranda was soon on a new chemo, Xeloda. There was no infusion this time, just three pills twice a day, and she suffered few side effects. She did seem to be losing weight, but her body actually looked pretty sleek. This new stuff not only was easier than the infusion with Navelbine had been but also seemed to be working better.

At the weekly consultation with Dr. Washington, we learned that the tumor in Miranda's lung appeared to have stopped growing and was perhaps shrinking. The one in her brain had definitely shriveled, so the therapy was working after all. "I hope this is worth the side effects," the oncologist said.

"It is, because I haven't had many at all," Miranda replied.

"Good. We never know for certain how people's bodies will respond to these chemicals," Jeaneve said. "The big thing is that the tumors are responding."

"Amen," I said.

Miranda and I felt like whooping on the drive home, and I was thinking that I had to call her sons and give them the good news, but first I proposed an idea to her: "How about a taco salad at Casa Garcia?"

"Will you throw in a little walk along the river afterward?"

In the glow of good news, I'd entirely forgotten Miranda's lingering problem with nausea, and her taco salad went nearly untouched while I wolfed mine down. I carried hers in a box to the car after lunch, and we motored to a parking area near the pedestrian bridge at Sacramento State.

We almost didn't get there, though, because I lost concentration and turned the wrong way onto a one-way street.

"Marty!" my wife screeched just as I realized what I'd done. Traffic was thin — one older man in a sedan who honked at me and two gals in a convertible who laughed — so I managed to U-turn back the correct way.

Miranda was laughing as she said, "That was a thrill! You drive like an old man."

"How else *could* I drive?" I asked, a little shaken. Then I grinned. "Just what I needed, more evidence that I'm losing it."

"Mostly but not entirely." The Champ squeezed my thigh and laughed again. "There's still a little left."

A brisk breeze was blowing up the river's channel as we crossed the levee to the footpath. "I've said it a thousand times, but I love it out here," Miranda said. "What are you grinning about?"

"Well, I'm standing here wearing a damp diaper; I haven't had a natural erection in years; my body is drooping and my face is sagging; I'm driving the wrong way on one-way streets. And I'm a happy guy."

"You're also a goofy one," the Champ said, and we hugged.

"You know," I said, "that bit about life being more intense when you might lose it is true. I used to think that was just a platitude."

"It's a platitude that's true," she said. She gazed at me then and said, "I've been so wrapped up in my own problems that I haven't asked you how you feel now that you're off hormones. You've certainly been acting livelier."

We were walking hand in hand on the horse path along the river, hearing joggers and skaters passing above on the paved trail. We occasionally stopped just to watch the water slide by. "I don't really feel very different," I told her. "I never did have the serious problems with the therapy that some guys do, and now that I've been off it for a while, I feel as good or as bad as always — with a little more pep, though."

"Well, we've talked about this before. If you start that treatment early enough — and I'm sure you did — it can be effective for a relatively long time."

"Now if my heart will just stay healthy, I'll be fine," I added.

She smiled at me and said, "To quote you, 'Always some damned thing.' Let's head back for the car, dear. I'm starting to poop out."

I drove home the long way, via north Sacramento and the pleasantly overgrown old homes there. On one large lawn three stooped brown men were working, probably pulling weeds. "You know," I said, "sometimes when I see people working like that I feel like I'm spying on my own grandparents."

"In this valley," she replied, "probably a lot of people could say the same thing."

■

For reasons I didn't and don't understand, I again began having problems controlling my bowels. It was a strange and decidedly unpleasant return of an old dilemma, and it immediately affected my life, since I became afraid to go out or to make appointments to go out. Most days, I minced around the house until the big event, after which I was usually okay.

I told Miranda one evening, "You're having chemo and I'm having pooh problems. We're a pair."

She replied, "I'll bet it's stress. You have a weakness there from the radiation, and when you're under stress those weak points give out. You've been drinking unleaded coffee in the morning, haven't you?"

"Yeah."

"Well, try leaded," she advised. "It's a bowel stimulant. With luck it'll get you into the bathroom right away, then you can go on about your day."

The next day I drank a cup of French roast, then waited for it to take effect.

Miranda wandered into the kitchen shortly thereafter, poured herself a glass of water, and asked, "Any luck?"

"No luck, still stuck," I chanted, remembering a line from a children's book we'd been reading to Tyler and Dougie, and she burst into laughter. "It's so nice to start your day with a discussion of BMs, isn't it?" I added.

"It doesn't add much to the conversation," she agreed.

■

Later that morning I as I emerged from the bathroom—Miranda's caffeine cure had worked—I heard Bud Hartley's voice on the answering machine. I picked up the receiver while he was leaving a message. "Oh, hi, Marty," he said. "I thought you'd like to know we had that magazine photo of the pederast priest you sent computer-enhanced. It's him, all right, but guess who else is there in the background? Marvin Bearheart."

"Bearheart? No kidding?" I shifted the telephone receiver, then asked, "Are you sure?"

"As sure as a photo can let me be. Remember how he used to stand with his head tilted back like he was challenging everyone? That was the giveaway."

"Why would a state senator let a photo like that be taken, let alone published? I don't get it."

"I don't get it either, but people do it . . . over and over again, it seems."

Marvin Bearheart had been found shot dead in Mexico a few years back. Rumors had circulated about a highly placed circle of gay and bisexual men in state government and big business who supposedly held private parties with boys. I'd covered the murder for the *Express,* but neither I nor any other reporter ever dug up any concrete evidence of those activities, although the way people clammed up when I asked questions left me certain that a story of some kind was there to be told. Before I could investigate further, my son had died and I'd dropped out of life.

"Curiouser and curiouser," I said to Bud.

"Listen, Marty, you wouldn't consider dropping work on your tree rustlers or tree huggers or whatever it is, and look into Marvin's murder again, would you? Take as long as you like. This just looks like too much of a coincidence."

The Bearhart murder felt like unfinished business to me, but I was in no rush to assume more responsibilities right now, with Miranda so ill, so I said, "Let me think about it, Bud."

"Okay, but the story's yours for the taking. I'll hold the assignment for you."

"I'll let you know soon."

■

"Listen, Marty," Father Tran said, "I want to thank you for what you wrote. It means a great deal to me."

We were standing in the garden beside St. Apollinaris Church after a week-day Mass. "It meant a great deal to me, too, Father. You've been a wonderful friend, and I wanted to nail those birds at the *Express* for their hypocrisy."

"I don't know what it meant to the bishop," the priest went on. "I'm being relieved of my pastoral duties and reassigned to the diocesan office, where he can keep an eye on me — make sure I don't run out to a gay bar or something, I guess."

"You're kidding!"

"No, it's a done deal. I'll be there by next week. Father Andrews will replace me."

"Now I *really* hope you're kidding."

The young priest smiled, "That's exactly what the monsignor said when he heard, and he rolled his eyes as only he can. He's not a fan of Andrews."

"Who is?" I could only shake my head.

The young priest continued, "Well, this won't necessarily be a bad move for me, because the bishop does have a job for me. He's thinking of developing an outreach program to the gay community and another one for Asian immigrants, and I'll help with both — but I prefer parish work."

"We much prefer to have you here," I said, knowing he was trying to give the best spin he could to the situation.

Father Tran paused and seemed to blink hard, then he said,

"Marty, I told you a long time ago that I haven't dishonored my vow, and I really haven't. I wasn't always celibate, but I have been since I entered the priesthood. If I ever can't be, I'll resign. I'll never let my parishioners and friends down. Never."

"I know you won't," I said. "Have you heard the rumor that the Pope is going to ban the ordination of homosexuals?"

The cleric sighed deeply before he responded, "Yes. As a practicing priest I wouldn't be much affected, but the seminaries are apt to become mighty empty mighty soon."

"I don't think the Vatican gets it," I shook my head. "Every study I've ever read, including those commissioned by the Church, shows that the majority of abusers are heterosexuals."

"Me, too, but it would be self-serving and probably counterproductive for me to get involved in that argument. I agree with you, though. Celibacy is celibacy."

That a good man was being placed in the position Father Tran was in really ticked me off. I was, I guess, grinning grimly as they say in the detective novels, like a dead dog, as I hissed, "Well, I can flex my typewriter and I will if that really turns out to be the new policy. I'll challenge the hierarchy to ban the ordination of heterosexuals, since they cause most of the problems."

Although I was serious, that comment seemed to break the tension and the priest laughed. "You really are a troublemaker. Miranda's right!"

The mention of her name stopped me. "Before you leave, can you say another Mass for Miranda?" I asked.

One of his hands touched my forearm. "Is she worse? The ladies in the scripture class keep asking about her."

"She's in a tough battle. This last chemo' seems to have worked, but you never know for how long . . . ," I had to swallow hard then because I was suddenly just barely able to control my voice. "I'm afraid I'll lose her."

"Marty," he said, grasping my arm now, "you won't. You'll never lose her because you love her. She may die, but you won't lose her, and she won't lose you. Love is stronger than death. It really is."

40

When I arrived home, I called to Miranda, who'd slept in, as she often did since she'd begun the therapy. After a moment, she appeared in the kitchen doorway wearing her robe and her fancy head-rag. "Hello," she said.

"I forgot to tell you, but I've got some bad news."

"What?"

"Father Tran's being transferred to the diocesan office and your old pal Andrews is coming back to St. Apollinaris."

"*Great,*" she groaned.

"Well, I have a feeling that Andrews won't last very long with the monsignor. He may suffer his own personal apocalypse if he starts any trouble in this parish."

Entering the dining room where I stood, she said, "I've got some bad news, too," and my alarm bells immediately went off.

"What's up?" I asked.

"Jeaneve called while you were out. The last tests and images weren't good," Miranda reported. "Sometimes it seems like this stuff has an intelligence, even a wiliness. It's apparently figured out how to deal with the Xeloda, because my numbers are up and tumors appear to be growing again."

"Shit!" This was becoming a long-running play, and every act seemed to end the same way.

My own PSA remained near zero, and I had hoped that the Champ's numbers would also stabilize. Wishful thinking, as it turned out.

"So where do we go from here?" I asked.

"Back to see Jeaneve. She's looking into clinical trials for me, and she's still got one or two weapons we can use."

One or two weapons against this cancer didn't seem like a very formidable arsenal, and I said so.

Miranda agreed. "No, it's not. But if I'd been diagnosed with this disease in Somalia or Bangladesh or someplace like that, there'd have been no weapons at all."

"I just wish you didn't have it."

"I do *not* need to hear that!" she snapped. "Do you think I don't know how grave my situation is? 'I wish you didn't have it' isn't one of my options, Marty. I *do* have it, and I have to deal with it. You've been a fighter all your life. Would you say 'I wish I wasn't fighting' halfway through a battle and turn your back, or would you just keep fighting as long and as hard as you could?"

Her passion shocked me, and I stammered, "I'm sorry, honey. I just wasn't thinking . . ."

Miranda said no more, but instead sort of collapsed in my arms, and we held one another. The Champ was looking her opponent straight in the eye, remaining engaged and staying far stronger than I, reading everything she could, surfing the Web, talking to other physicians and survivors, but never giving in to pity or hindsight. I finally grasped that the battle itself, not victory, had become her focus.

"I love you so much," I said, as I embraced her. "I was with Nancy for over three decades, but I don't know her nearly as well as I know you. And she didn't know me either because those were the years when we just floated through life . . . no challenges. Then when something went wrong we fell apart.

"But you and I started under stress and it's welded us. I know I let you down sometimes, but I'm weak. Chew me out, but forgive me."

She said, "Consider yourself chewn and forgiven."

"We've had a lot of good days," I added, "but we haven't had many easy ones."

"We'll have more good ones, too," she replied.

■

I picked up James and his family at the airport while Miranda was at the infusion center, then we all assembled at home. In no time Grandma was playing

Barbies with James's daughter, who carried on an animated conversation about Ken's new camouflage clothing: "He looks real cool, huh, Grandma?"

"He looks cool to me, honey," Grandma replied, and I noticed Cynthia, Annette's mother, beaming.

James and I, meanwhile, sat at the dining room table drinking coffee and watching the gals. "Mom's sure lost a lot of weight, hasn't she?" he said.

The weight loss had been gradual, so I'd barely noticed it. "Now that you mention it, she has, yes," I replied. My wife suddenly appeared gaunt to me.

"It's ironic that she probably looks better by Barbie standards now because of that," he said.

"She always looked fine to me."

"Me, too, but you know what I mean."

"Yeah," I agreed, "I know."

He chuckled then, saying, "Cynthia was one of those mothers who said no dolls for her daughter, so Annette had every kind of educational toy money could buy. But when she'd visit other little girls, she would immediately head for the dolls. Finally, Cyn gave up and bought her one. That opened the floodgates."

"It's great all of you could fly out," I told him. "I didn't expect that. I haven't seen your mother so animated since before she started the chemo."

"Speaking of which," James said, "I'm grateful you called me, and I'm sorry we don't live closer so Mom and Annette could really get to know one another. My wife's folks live near us, so they see us all the time. Cynthia's dad is retired and Annette's their only grandchild, so they moved from Chicago just to be close."

I nodded. "Yeah, my daughter and her family live just across town, so I see them regularly. Miranda's really good with them, but it's not the same thing. She's cut her hours way back, but I doubt she would ever retire completely; medicine's too important to her."

"I know. From all I hear, she's a wonderful doctor," he said. "After all she's done for breast cancer patients, it's ironic that she'd be in this condition." He paused, then smiled sadly, "I'm just reaching the age when I can see who she really is, and if you don't mind me saying so, I'm wondering how my dad could have been such a jerk."

"His loss, my gain," I said.

"Amen." James was tall, one of those attractive people who combine luminous blue eyes with olive skin and dark hair. Except for those eyes, he strongly resembled his mother.

"Do you know what her prognosis is?" he asked.

"Not exactly, but from what she's told me, I'd say not good."

"Nick and Loni and their kids will be out in a couple of weeks," he told me.

"He and I have decided to alternate visits, and to try to come out once a month each. We know Mom's not going to be around forever."

"She'll really appreciate that."

He grinned then and added, "Hey, it's only money, and we can use the air-mileage points."

From the picture window in our living room, he and I viewed light traffic and a few pedestrians bouncing along the sidewalk. We stood there momentarily, then I said, "You guys will never regret one moment you give to your mother, but your little brother is digging himself a hole."

"He's so damned spoiled that he thinks he should always get his way. I'm just as glad he isn't here, because if he acted like he did the last time I talked to him, there'd be trouble between us. And he'd better hope that Nick doesn't see him."

"Have you talked to your father lately?" I asked.

The younger man chuckled, then replied, "Oh yeah. He's got new hair plugs, his skin's been scraped, his chin lifted — in fact he's had everything lifted that would come up, even" — he began laughing — "even his pecker. My little brother told me Dad had a penile implant. Poor Dad, he's like the mirror opposite of Mom. She's naturally attractive, accepts aging and even illness, while he's terrified of all that stuff."

"Most of us are," I told him.

"Well, if you are, you and Mom sure handle it better. Have you ever met him?" he asked.

"Your dad? No."

James smiled. "I thought not. He talks like he knows all about you."

"He can say all he wants to about me, as long as he leaves your mother alone."

"He will. He's afraid of both of you, I think. An insecure guy . . ." James paused, then added, "But without a gray hair."

■

Dr. DelVecchio didn't mince words at my next oncology visit: "I'm really surprised that your PSA is climbing this fast. It's unusual . . . and not a good sign at all."

That familiar knot immediately swelled my stomach. "How high?"

"It's 0.9," he replied. "Candidly, I'd expected it to still be at zero. It seems to have shot up pretty fast. We'll do another test in a month so we can determine the exact doubling time — that'll be revealing — then get you back on hormones if it's still climbing."

"Crap! Why would it be up so soon?"

"If I could answer that definitely, I could probably solve a whole series of mysteries about this disease. Basically, this is a very complex problem, with everything from heredity to prostatic phosphorus in the blood being possible causes."

"So what's this do to my prognosis?" I asked.

"Well, I won't know exactly where we are until we do another PSA and probably do some imaging, too. You're not in any imminent danger, but I know that having to take the hormones doesn't add much to your quality of life."

"No."

"On the other hand, if it keeps you alive . . ." He shrugged. "We've talked about this before, but let me repeat: there *will* be a breakthrough treatment for this cancer. We just have to keep you alive until that happens."

At that moment, I was far more interested in a breakthrough to treat my wife's disease.

As he turned to leave the treatment room where we'd been talking, Dr. DelVecchio paused and said, "Please give Miranda my best wishes."

■

Along with Dr. DelVecchio's good wishes, I mentioned the Marvin Bearheart photo to Miranda, as well as Bud's request that I look into the old murder. She seemed only mildly interested, but when I said, "I don't think I'll work on it. I just don't have the energy anymore," she replied, "It would be better if you did. You're too wrapped up in what's happening to me. If you don't get your mind on something else, you're going to relapse."

"But—" I immediately thought about what my oncologist had just told me, which I hadn't yet mentioned to Miranda.

"You said you're not going to have to leave town for this story and you wouldn't have a deadline, either. Do it, Marty. You're good at it, and maybe you'll develop something important when you dig into it.

"Our lives aren't a movie where everything stops because some dramatic scene's playing out," she added. "This is real and life goes on constantly. I'm still consulting because patients are still getting sick. Don't quit just because I'm ill."

Just because I'm ill, as though she had a cold: She was the one person I knew who could say that and mean it. Miranda had begun another chemotherapeutic regimen, gemcitabine/carboplatin, and it had immediately sickened her. She had trouble holding food down, and felt so generally lousy that she began remaining in bed much of the day. She didn't complain, but she did say, "I hope the cancer's having as much trouble with this stuff as I am."

"What can I do?"

"Just hold me . . . and stop looking so sad. You should see yourself. You look like the mask of tragedy."

That evening as I helped her out of the recliner in the family room I couldn't help noticing how much lighter she had become. She returned from the bathroom and plopped next to me on the couch, leaning against me.

"A glass of wine?" I asked.

"No thanks."

"Mind if I do?"

She smiled. "I insist. It'll make you romantic."

In the kitchen I opened the bottle of a $3.99 special that I'd picked up at the store, then poured myself a glass.

I returned to the living room, sat down on the couch next to the Champ, and took a sip.

"Well?"

I replied in a grave voice, "It's an audacious little vintage, with a butter base and hints of nutmeg and apricot, and an aftertaste like . . ." I paused and smacked my lips. "Like a turd."

For a second Miranda said nothing, then she exploded with laughter, a sound I'd heard too little of late. "A *turd,*" she choked, then laughed again, her eyes filling with tears.

"This is the worst shit I ever bought."

Her cheeks wet, her voice still deep in laughter, the Champ said, "You make a fine wine critic. A turd!"

"Not if I have to drink this kind of stuff!" I grinned, infected by her guffaws.

For the next few minutes we made small talk, but every so often she'd again burst into laughter. "A turd! You should have seen your face when you took that sip!"

"I'm saving the rest of it for my brother."

That set her off again.

I returned to the kitchen, emptied the offending wine into the sink, then poured myself a small glass of cream sherry and went back to the family room. We cuddled on the couch and, with the remote, I surfed channels on the television until we heard a rich tenor voice with a dark-haired kid younger than any of our own children wielding it. "This okay?" I asked.

"Sure, it's fine," she said, "but who is that?"

"I don't know. He can sure sing."

As the young man performed, Miranda leaned back against me, and I rested my chin on her bald head. Then I kissed it and she kissed one of my palms. I kissed her ear then, and whispered, "I love you."

She responded with a contented "Mmmm."

We fell silent as the music surrounded us, and I reached over and turned off the lamp so that only the television's glow illuminated the room.

A pledge break interrupted the music and the singer was identified, then two pleasant people asked for donations . . . and asked . . . and asked. Since we'd already sent our dues in for the year, I hit the MUTE button and we sat silently, my cheek against her scalp. Then Miranda asked softly, "What're you thinking, Marty?"

At first I was speechless because I wasn't thinking at all, just lost in the wonderful songs and her proximity, and if truth be told, in a certain romantic nostalgia. After a moment, though, I said, "I was thinking how terrific it would've been to have necked with Yul Brynner."

Miranda's bald head turned around and she grinned. "You!" she said.

"Let's get away for a day or two if we can, okay?" I suggested.

"Sure. A day one way or another isn't apt to make much difference."

After that, there was really nothing left to say, so we cuddled.

41

While Miranda was at the infusion center the next day, I drove to the nearby Rathskeller, a bar where most local journalists slam-dunked drinks. Slip Kennealy, a colleague who'd retired a decade earlier, still held court there, and it was easy to pick him out since he still wore a slouch hat on the back of his head, a wrinkled dress shirt, and a tie but no jacket, his costume for nearly fifty years as a crime writer for the *Express.* Although he was a native of Los Angeles, he also still affected an Irish brogue: "Martin, me lad, how are ya? What're ya drinkin', me boy?"

"A draft," I replied.

"Draft it is. Dieter!" he called to the bartender, "A brewski for me friend and hit me again."

"Coming up, Slip," Dieter responded, and immediately delivered a tall beer for me and a squat glass of Irish whiskey for Kennealy, who had broken into journalism back in its hard-drinking days and who still emptied a glass with the best. Ned Schmidt had once said, "Old Slippery must have a liver like a saddle by now." That was twenty years ago.

"So what brings ya back to this dive?" the older man asked.

"I've been looking into Bearheart's murder again," I said. "I remember the rumor that he was queer. Was he?"

"Does a bear shit where?" Slip grinned. "Yeah, Beerfart was queer as a four-dollar bill. Funny thing is that he was one hell of a good guy. Everybody liked him. He'd buy a round of drinks without blinking. He was tough, too. Never backed off." Slip paused and seemed to gaze over my shoulder, then said, "Ya know, when it gets to sex, there's no knowing what a guy'll do. Remember that sheriff down in San Joaquin County they discovered dead wearing women's underwear? And that clown in Rocklin with the broom up his ass?"

"How about the Black Orchid?" I asked. "Any truth to that story?"

"The Black Orchid." He smiled. "I haven't thought of that bunch for a long time . . . dead now, most of 'em anyway. But yeah, it wasn't common knowledge, but that was a bunch of high rollers who liked boys. Old Chief Conlon was supposedly a member, and Bob Haron, the county supervisor, a couple of state senators and assemblymen — I forget their names right now — Baxter, who was head of protocol for all those years, Katz, who ran that big department store, and Goldman, the attorney. Old Beerfart, the law-and-order king of the senate, was supposedly a master link in the daisy chain, but he was untouchable. We didn't report stuff like that then."

"You know who killed him?" I asked.

"Beerfart? There *was* a rumor that he and some Mexican guy had a dispute about a kid."

"This is all pretty damned strange."

"So," asked Slip, "are ya gonna break the story?"

That was easy to answer. "Not unless I find some solid, corroborated evidence. I won't accuse a dead man who can't defend himself. But I'll keep digging."

"Try Buster Conlon. He might verify what I've heard."

"Conlon? The cop? Jocko's brother?"

"Yeah, he's a retired copper now, living over in Davis. Give him a try. He's in the phone book."

"Thanks, Slip. I'll call him."

"Nothin' to it, me boy. Nothin' to it."

■

The next morning Miranda and I drove south out of Sacramento down Highway 99, our first outing in a while. We buzzed toward Merced, where we'd agreed to meet Chava and Cindy. They were going to take us to lunch at what he claimed was the best Mexican restaurant in town, then maybe on a drive up toward Mariposa.

The car's radio picked up a station playing Merle Haggard, and once the song ended, I told the Champ, "My mom and dad used to sing together in the car when our family traveled."

"They sang aloud together?" Miranda asked. "I thought that was something that only happened in movies . . . you know, Mickey Rooney and Judy Garland harmonizing."

I laughed, then said, "Well, when you don't have a car radio . . . and we didn't . . . you make do. Besides, they were from a different time. A lot of people sang, and danced, too, then. They'd also take all of us kids to dances on weekends."

"That was a different world from the one I was raised in."

The radio announcer launched into a commercial for "Testosterboost," a compound developed by Dr. So-and-so, who guaranteed it would turn an earthworm into a tenpenny nail and thus "renew your marriage."

"I wonder if Dr. So-and-so ever thinks about the men with occult prostate cancer who might naively use that stuff and fuel their tumors?" said Miranda.

"I doubt they're thinking much about tumors," I said. "Guys have always followed their peckers into trouble." I thought of Bearheart.

Once we arrived in Merced, my brother drove us to the site of an ancient, run-down-appearing drive-in restaurant on the road to Yosemite: Taqueria Hernandez. There were no other cars in the parking lot, but two older women stood at an outdoor window. "This is it?" I asked. "We drove from Sacramento for this? You think the headwaiter can find us a table?"

"Wait'll you taste the food, smart-ass."

Inside, we ordered at a counter—*tostadas de pollo* and lemonades for Miranda and me—then sat at one of the small tables to await the food. The front door opened and two kids, not much more than in their mid-teens, I judged, walked in with a toddler wearing a miniature soccer uniform. The guy wore jeans and a T-shirt inscribed NO TEMAS NADA, while the gal was attired in a tank top and short overalls unhitched and drooping so her plump brown belly was exposed. When she turned, something else was revealed below a lower-back tattoo resembling an electrified Chihuahua, and Chava whispered to me, "I think that's the quarter slot there under the dog."

I nearly choked on my lemonade, spilling it on my shirt. "Shit!" I said.

"No big deal," said Miranda, patting my knee. "You've got spares in the car."

After I grabbed a shirt and undershirt, Chava accompanied me to the men's room, informing me he had to pee. While he stood at the urinal, I removed my wet garments, and my brother said, "Marty, what happened to your chest? You used to have the most hair of all of us. You're bald now."

I started to answer, but he interrupted, "And, man, your pecs? You've got *chichis, ese.* Boobs! Where're your muscles?" His voice had lost its usual smart-assed edge; he sounded shocked.

"Mexican hairless," I said, trying to lighten things up. "The hormones do that. I can be dead with muscles or slowly be feminized by my therapy. There's no middle ground."

"Oh, man," he said, and he hugged me for what seemed like a long time.

"Don't try to cop a feel," I warned.

Later, as we were finishing an unusually quiet meal for Martinezes, my brother announced, "Oh yeah, I brought you the Irish sporting page," handing me the folded newspaper he'd carried in, "and you'll notice a Carlos Conner, only thirty. Well, that's Trini Garza and Bob Conner's son — remember them in Manuel's class? The kid ODed."

"Man. . ." I shook my head. He tossed the newspaper onto the table. I snapped it open and turned to the obituaries to see if any old friends or classmates were listed. None were, thank God.

As we were chewing on the last ice in our drinks, I said, "Did you notice the first names in these obits?" I handed him the sheet back across the table. "Check 'em out," I said. Many, especially those of folks originally from the Southwest, were rare indeed in the contemporary world: Waunona Veramae Owens, Buddy Don Gittens, Clarence Elmer Reese, Opal Minnie Wright.

"Now look at the grandchildren's first names," I urged. Breanna, Justin, Jordan, McKenzie, Lennon, Kaitlyn, Carson, Allison, Kennedy, Madison. It struck me that something important was revealed in that contrast, something I could write about.

"There aren't many Okie or chile choker names anymore, are there?" my brother observed. "Everybody uses those Yuppie names . . ."

"To help the kids fit in, I think," Cindy interjected.

"Most of the popular ones today I never heard when we were kids," Chava continued. "But the Bloods haven't given in. There are a lot of Nikeshas and Lateshas and Willies in Merced, but I've never known or heard of a black kid down there named Lennon or McKenzie." He grinned and added, "Besides, you're only allowed to use those names if you own an SUV, like us."

He turned toward the Champ then, and said, "I almost forgot. Miranda, there's a woman here in Merced, a Mrs. Allen, the aunt of one of the firefighters, who's got . . . lymphoma, I think it is . . ." His voice trailed off momentarily. "Anyway, she was told a couple of years ago that she just had months to live, and she began taking something called colestrum, derived from cow's milk from what she says, and she's fine now. No sign of the cancer."

He stopped there, not urging Miranda to try colestrum, but leaving the anecdote for her to consider.

"That's wonderful," she replied.

My brother turned to me then, saying, "And Marty, Chicano students at MHS are agitating for a *la raza* graduation."

"A what?"

Cindy interjected, "I think it's about demanding easier graduation requirements. You wait: separate graduation, separate diploma, separate curriculum. Just what racists love."

"Exactly what we need." Miranda shook her head. "A society flying apart instead of unifying."

"Who's demanding that?" I asked.

"I don't know exactly, but you can bet Dr. Montoya's kids aren't," my sister-in-law replied. "Or ours. They want to go to Stanford."

As we walked to the car, my wife whispered, "Marty, let's find a motel near here, then drive home tomorrow. I'm really tired."

I'd been too involved to realize that she increasingly appeared exhausted. I replied simply, "Of course. I'll smooth it over with Chava and Cindy."

"We can't stay," I told them. "Miranda's got to be home tonight. Medical stuff..."

"Oh, damn," he said. "I wanted to swing by Alicia and Marcus's, then up to Mariposa." Apparently as an afterthought, he asked, "When're you gonna join this century and buy a cell phone, *vato?*" He turned to my wife then and said, "He always was a tightwad—wouldn't share his gum or anything." That made me laugh because she didn't realize he meant sharing gum I was already chewing.

"Miranda's got a cell phone," I told him, "but it's for professional calls. If I want to talk to you I just dial 1-800-P-E-N-D-E-J-O on the old-fashioned one."

"Dial *this, cabrón!*" He pumped his arms, the timeless screw-yourself gesture. Then, to my astonishment, he hugged me.

■

After we arrived home late the next morning, I checked my e-mail for messages, but only spam awaited me: "Important news for your colon!" I logged off, then telephoned Buster Conlon. He answered on the second ring, sounding a little boozy but friendly enough after I introduced myself. Once I explained that I was looking into the Bearheart murder, though, he suddenly sounded less friendly: "My advice is that you just leave it alone," he said. "There's nothing to be learned, nothing that won't hurt somebody. Bearheart made his choices and he died. That's that."

"But if his choices *have* hurt someone—a child forced into prostitution, for instance..."

"You're dealing with real trouble here, Martinez. Bearheart was connected. Let it go before you stir something up."

"Mr. Conlon," I said, "this is going to come out. Bearheart's photo appeared in a pederasty magazine. Can't you at least suggest someone else I can talk to?"

I heard him sigh and half expected him to hang up on me. "You reporters have to stick your noses into everything, don't you?" he finally said. "Call Kyle Holmes if you want to chase this farther, but watch out."

I knew who Kyle Holmes was, so I asked, "Why the threat?"

He sounded genuinely angry when he responded, "I don't have to threaten the likes of you, Martinez. I can whack you anytime I want. I'm just trying to warn you, but you don't seem to want to hear it. You don't know what you're getting into."

Well, I did know that Holmes had been Bearheart's administrative assistant for a number of years. I'd talked to him more than once, and found him a little too squeaky clean and self-serving for my taste. He'd moved to a private lobbying practice after Bearheart's death and kept a low profile ever since, though his office made a bundle representing clients in Sacramento.

His secretary answered the phone and said, "Whom should I say is calling?"

"Tell him Martin Martinez from the *Tribune.*"

"And to what does this pertain?"

I felt like saying, "It pertains to buggery, my dear." Instead I replied, "I'd like to talk to him about a story involving the late Senator Bearheart."

"Just one moment. I'll see if Mr. Holmes is in."

He was in, which must have come as a great surprise to her. "Yes?" he said.

"This is Marty Martinez. I'm looking into the murder of Senator Bearheart pursuant to a story I may write for the *Tribune.* I wonder if you'd be willing to answer a few questions?"

"I might."

"Does the 'Black Orchid Society' mean anything to you?"

I heard his breath catch, then after a moment he snapped, "Certainly not."

"Were you aware that the senator's photograph appeared in a pederasts' magazine?"

"I was not. What kind of a photograph was it?"

Aha, I thought, he's worried that it's explicit. "A shot of a group of men identified as 'boy-lovers.' Can you suggest why he might have allowed his photo to be used in that context."

For a moment he did not reply, then he said, "A magazine might identify a photograph any way it chooses. That doesn't make the identification accurate."

"Why would the senator be pictured in a pederasts' magazine at all?"

Again there was a pause, then Holmes said, "The senator was part of a group involved in setting up an orphanage for homeless boys in Guadalajara. Perhaps in that capacity he was somehow photographed . . . with constituents or associates."

"What was his interest in boys?"

"He funded charities that helped homeless street children."

"Why not girls, too?"

"This is growing tiresome, Mr. Martinez. That was just a choice he made because, I suppose, he had once been a poor boy."

"Did he have sex with the boys?"

"I don't know what he did," Holmes snapped, "but I can tell you he never coerced anyone. I knew him well enough to tell you that! What is this crusade you're on, anyway? Can't people decide for themselves what they want to do? Do they need people like you to control their lives?"

"How about the argument that sex like that can never really be consensual because the youngster can never be on equal footing with an adult?" I asked.

"Oh, spare me the false moralism! *Spare* me!" His voice dripped condescension.

"I'm not interested in sparing you, asshole!" I snapped, but he'd already hung up.

I sat there for several minutes, a little startled at my own sudden rage, knowing that Miranda's situation had me on an emotional brink. The Champ was facing cancer with grace and courage, while this chump wanted moral acceptance for buggery. He'd better hope his fate never depended on me sparing him.

42

Nick and Loni, with their son and daughter, visited for three days of nearly nonstop action. Miranda came to bed each night and slept as though drugged—and, of course, she *was* drugged—but the next morning she arose for her infusion, then returned home ready to play with Jason and Courtney. He was four, she was six, and it was fun for me to watch them interact with Grandma and one another.

At one point, for instance, Courtney talked Jason into wearing clothes backward—front in back—and he began walking backward all over the house, bumping into walls and furniture. They got along remarkably well, it seemed to me, but when he grabbed a coloring book from his sister, she slapped him and he began throwing wild punches. Loni separated them and sent them to different chairs to cool off, rolling her eyes as she said, "Aren't they fun?"

Miranda said, "You should've seen Nick and James at that age. It was like Saturday-night wrestling."

"We didn't fight that much," Nick argued. "Mostly we just tested each other. It was all in good fun."

"Then you can repay me for the repair of James's tooth and remind me where you got that scar on your chin," his mother said, smiling. "You two were pretty evenly matched."

Before long Courtney was chasing Jason around the long loop of dining room-kitchen-family room-living room-dining room again, both of them giggling and squealing. When their mother admonished them to stop, Miranda said gently, "It's all right with us if they run. Marty and I don't hear that kind of laughter often enough."

Nick asked his mother, "Has Robbie been by?"

Miranda answered, "No."

"That little shit. I'm going to straighten him out."

"He's not little anymore, Nicky," his mother said.

"He will be when I get through with him," Nick responded. He wasn't a huge guy, but he'd played football at Arizona State and he looked pretty fit and formidable to me.

Robbie never did appear, and after Nick and his family departed, Miranda stayed in bed for much of the next two days.

■

The new chemo regimen really beat her up, but the Champ rarely complained. She knew that she was running out of options, so she was grateful for having any therapy at all. Still, the nausea, the night sweats, the aches, and the general lethargy seemed almost worse than her disease . . . almost.

Most evenings, I would as usual nod off early under the covers, but I'd vaguely feel her churning next to me, in and out of bed. The irritated bladder that had resulted from my radiation had me up peeing several times most nights, and when I arose I'd often see her owl-eyed, sitting in the den reading, but when I'd ask if she was okay, she invariably smiled and said, "I'll be back in bed soon." In the light from the reading lamp, her skin appeared almost orange and her abdomen seemed swollen, but I tried not to notice. Many nights, she didn't seem to rest until dawn neared.

One morning as I lay next to her and listened to her snoring softly, I reached over and ran my hand lightly over the smooth skin of one of her exposed arms until I reached its crook, where heat concentrated. I left my hand there and gradually I began to sense her pulse, wondering how long that brave heart would continue beating and what I'd do — what I *could* do — when I lost her. Lea and Dougie would be there for me if I called, as would my brother and sisters and even Nancy, but nothing could ever be the same. My world would be so empty without Miranda.

■

I returned to the prostate cancer support group feeling a bit like a stranger, since it'd been so long since I'd last attended. Mort, though, treated me like a prodigal son, welcoming me effusively: "Hey, Marty! Great to see you."

As we shook hands, I glanced around the table and noted only a few familiar faces, then took a seat, since it was time for the meeting to begin. Mort's opening remarks that night were the kind of goofy thing I was used to hearing from him: "Do men over sixty prefer boxers or Jockeys?" He paused while we shook our heads, then said, "Depends!"

Amidst the chuckling, I didn't know about *prefer,* but I knew I wasn't the only guy sitting there in a diaper.

After announcements, he asked, "Are there any new members tonight?" When no one spoke up, he asked, "Any reports?"

"Have any of you guys tried this new stuff that's supposed to be better than Viagra?" asked a young Asian man I didn't recognize.

No one answered, but many heads were shaken. Finally an old-timer named Ed grinned and said, "Hell, I shellacked my pecker years ago. Been hard ever since."

"I think you also shellacked your brain," Mort added, and everyone laughed.

Mort then announced, "Some of you fellas don't know Marty Martinez, but he's been a member for several years. He's the same guy whose stories you read in the *Tribune* — used to be in the *Express* — and he's a cancer survivor like the rest of us. Marty" — he turned toward me — "why don't you bring everyone up to date on your history with prostate cancer and tell us what's going on."

I did that as succinctly as possible, then I got to the point: "Let me tell you why I most wanted to come tonight. My wife is losing her fight with breast cancer. I wonder how many others of you here are dealing with or have dealt with this. I feel so damned helpless."

Three hands went up, and a young man across the table said, "I lost my wife three years ago. She was thirty-seven and we have four kids. Let me tell you, that was much worse than learning I had cancer. I wasn't prepared to lose her, and I'm still not."

One of the older men followed. "My ex-wife had a radical mastectomy four years ago. She's been on tamoxifen ever since and, so far at least, she's okay."

Al Royster spoke then: "My wife has ovarian cancer, Marty, and it won't be cured. Our situation is different than yours because we're older and both slipping, although Dorothy still looks just fine. I hate what's happening, but she and I've had one hell of a run — fifty-three years, six kids, fourteen grandkids, lots of pals and good memories. That's what I cling to. As a doc, I saw a lot of people who never had a shot at what I've had in life.

"I'll go to my death in the hope that Dorothy and I will be together again. You know, I don't think anyone has a clue about death . . . or post-death, I mean . . . so I'm just hoping there's something there."

Thinking of my own belief, I asked, "Are you a churchgoer?"

"I'm a temple-goer, actually," the physician replied. "We're Jewish, and I find it a great comfort."

"Do you take it literally?"

"I take it figuratively and, as I said, it's a great comfort. I don't know much about theology, but I know the spirit is real. I saw it in others when I was in practice, and I sense it in me. I think it's the only part of me I'm capable of healing, so that's what I'm working on."

■

On my way home from the meeting, I stopped at St. Apollinaris to kneel and pray. I hadn't been back much, except for Sunday services, since Father Tran left, but the old comfort was there as I said an Our Father, a Hail Mary, and a Glory Be, then an Act of Contrition. Those formal prayers finished, I simply sat in the dark building, and breathed deeply, feeling myself calm. Then I asked God to help Miranda, to see her through whatever she must face, and to help me deal with it, too.

Finally, I rose and walked outside onto the lighted parking lot. As I strolled toward my car, I heard the familiar voice of Monsignor Kelley saying, "You must've committed some great whoppers of sins to come here at night, Marty."

I smiled, then responded, "It's the only time I can come by when you're not taking up a collection."

The cleric laughed and slapped my back. "How're things going at home?" he asked.

"Miranda's not getting better."

"And you?"

"I'm okay," I replied.

"You don't look okay, my friend. You look wretched, to tell you the truth."

"I feel wretched, Monsignor."

"About Miranda's health?" he asked.

"Yes, and about elements of my own life that won't seem to heal. I have this eerie notion that punishment for my earlier sins is being inflicted on those I love." That was something I'd not intended to reveal.

Monsignor Kelley looked startled for a moment, then he asked, "Have you a bit of time, Marty?"

"Sure."

He motioned toward a bench among the roses outside the rectory, saying, "Let's sit down and chat about this."

As soon as we were seated, the priest said, "If you can, tell me what deep down inside most troubles you."

Deep down inside . . . I thought for only a moment, then said, "On the night my mother died, I abandoned her." I told him the story and how on some irrational level I felt it was linked to my son's death, to my failed marriage, to Miranda's cancer — to all the pain I'd delivered in my life.

When I finished, the monsignor sat quietly for several moments, then said, "My parents had six girls and one boy — me. My mother prayed I'd become a priest, but you know what I became? A bit of a ruffian, a bit of a rounder, a bit of a drunk. That led me to take up prizefighting, traveling with a carnival from town to town all over Ireland, taking on all comers. I was handy with my mitts, and having a high old time with the drink and the women, and I basically forgot my family.

"Then one day a message came for me. My mother'd had a stroke and died. I rushed home and no one blamed me, not my da' and not my sisters, but I knew how unhappy I'd made my mother, the woman who'd given me life.

"That's when I went back to school, then to seminary. That's why I'm here. But I don't think my sins are still floating around causing troubles. I think a God who's not really comprehendible to humans is immeasurably understanding and has long since forgiven me, but expects me to have learned from my mistakes. That's what I try to do."

He paused and seemed to measure me, then continued: "That's why He sent you here to talk with me, I think." He halted again, then added, "If you open your heart, you'll be given opportunities, too. And be careful, because sometimes guilt becomes an excuse for not dealing with life."

I guess I've been a newspaperman too long, because as good as I felt after that conversation, on the drive home I found myself wondering if the priest's story was true. It was too much like a *Reader's Digest* moment, yet I couldn't believe Monsignor Kelley would fabricate such a tale just for me.

Miranda was resting when I walked in the house, so I went straight to the Rolodex and found Robbie's telephone number. I dialed it and, after several rings when I expected an answering machine to reply, he said, "'Lo?"

"Hello, Robbie, this is Marty Martinez. I've called to tell you that your mother is pretty sick. It would really be good if you visited her."

After a long pause, he grunted, "My brothers told me."

"Will you come by, then?"

"Not while she's with you."

"I won't be present," I said.

"I mean not while she's still living with you."

I kept my voice calm. "She's my wife."

"That's her problem." In the background I heard a female voice call, "Robbie, come *on*!"

"Gotta go," he said to me.

"Listen, Robbie . . ." The line went dead.

43

Again the roller coaster swooped upward: Miranda's newest chemo was working. She was somewhat nauseated and tired, but her numbers were improving, so cancer cells were being killed. The most recent imaging revealed a shrinkage of the tumor in her lung. When Jeaneve called with the good news, and Miranda told me, I was standing in the kitchen still disheveled in pajamas, and I said, "I've become a decrepit old fart, but I'm a *happy* decrepit old fart. Would you like to dance?"

"You're also a goof," the Champ replied, then added, "and yes, let's dance."

I embraced her and, to the sounds of the oldies-but-goodies station we listened to each morning, we became the Fred Astaire and Ginger Rogers of the geriatric set. When the tune ended, I mentioned that, and my love laughed. "Fred in his tux and slicked-back hair you're not . . . but I'll take you."

"I'll sure take you," I choked, and I had to pause to control my voice. "How much longer will you stay on this treatment?" I asked.

"Well, no one can stay on it forever, but as long as it's effective I'll likely do three weeks on and three off."

I hated those words, "as long as it's effective," but I'd become a pragmatist about such things because I feared that nothing else would work.

"When you're feeling stronger," I suggested, "let's take a ride, maybe drive down to Merced to visit the family or go up to the cabin."

"You're on . . . Champ." She smiled.

■

My rather passive search for more details on the Bearheart story led me to Wendy Gottlieb, an old colleague at the *Tribune.* I'd helped her break in when she'd come to the paper right out of college, and now she was editorial page editor. In the past she'd covered the state legislature, and when I told her about the photo of Bearheart in the pederasty magazine, she literally whistled. "Wow," she said, "he was always so careful to keep his private life hidden, I can't understand why he'd let something like that become public."

"Maybe he didn't, since he's just in the background. Maybe it was just a lucky break — lucky for us, not him."

"I'm still amazed. Can you fax me a copy?"

"Sure," I said. "Listen, what was that kid's name who was his driver and general flunkie? Bud hasn't gotten around to sending me the file."

"Yeah, his driver. I've got it here," she said, and I assumed she was spinning her Rolodex. "P-e-l-l-e-t-i-e-r, Bob Pelletier. I've got a phone number, too, but it might be out of date: 916-673-6329."

"Thanks."

After we rang off I made a note to send a copy of the Reilly-Bearheart photo to Wendy, then dialed the number she'd given me. I got an answering machine and left my name and number, but before I could hang up, a voice came on and said, "I'm here."

"Me, too," I replied. "This is Marty Martinez from the *Tribune*. We met a long time ago when you were working for Senator Bearheart and I was with the *Express*."

"I remember."

I told him about the magazine photograph, of the stories I'd already heard, even of my talk with Bearheart's erstwhile administrative assistant, Holmes. When I finished, he was silent for several moments, then he said, "Why don't you leave this alone? The senator's dead."

"Because I want to be certain the boys in a Mexican orphanage aren't still being used as sex toys."

He was silent for several moments, then said, "They'd starve otherwise."

I was having none of it. "That's a convenient morality."

To my surprise the young man responded, "Yeah, I guess it is. Is this off the record?"

"It can be."

"Well, off the record, Kyle, he used to bring boys north for parties. He's that way, too."

"That way?" I wanted to be certain of what he'd just said.

"He likes boys, but this is off the record, right?"

■

The conversation with Pelletier, and what exactly I'd do with it, buzzed in my head that night. After Miranda turned in, I retreated to my office to once more assemble the Bearheart material I'd gathered. When the telephone rang, I let the machine answer it and heard: "Martin? This is Eduardo Rivera. I have a story for you."

I guess I'll never learn — I picked up the receiver and said, "What's the story, Eddie?"

"How are you, *ese?*"

"I'm okay. What's up?"

"I've just learned from a private source that the superintendent of schools intends to cut the budget for bilingual education in elementary schools. That's cultural genocide! Latinos Unidos is going to launch a campaign to halt it, and we're having a strategy meeting at Cafe la Azteca. We hope you'll join us."

This cordiality after our last heated conversation didn't surprise me because I knew it was my newspaper connection he really wanted. "So what exactly does the superintendent intend to do?" I asked.

"She wants to limit grade-school instruction to English. She wants to rob Mexican children of their language and their heritage!"

To the extent that I'd ever thought much about him, I'd always considered Eddie a pain in the ass. Now I could enhance that to *ignorant* pain in the ass; he seemed to know nothing about language acquisition. I replied, "Twenty years ago my wife and I visited Chichén Itzá. We had a Mayan guide there, and he told us that kids in Yucatán spoke Mayan until they reached school, then Spanish was mandatory. They still spoke Mayan at home, but at school they had to learn the public language of Mexico."

"What's your point?"

"What's the public language of the United States?"

After a pause, he hissed, "It doesn't have one! I keep forgetting that you've sold out, don't I?" and hung up.

"Yeah," I said to the silent phone, "one of us has."

I went to bed and tried to read but quickly dozed. Miranda, though, was up when the late call came and she answered the phone in the den. Only half asleep, I could vaguely hear her voice but couldn't discern what she was saying. After what seemed a long time, she called, "Marty, are you awake? It's Nancy."

Nancy? What in the world could she want? I walked into the den, noting that my wife's face looked distressed. She knew I didn't want to talk to Nancy if I could avoid it, so she mouthed silently, "It's important."

"Hello," I said, more than a little wary.

"Marty," Nancy choked, "Audrey asked me to call you. There's been a tragedy. Rollie passed away this evening . . . his heart."

My gut seized as if I'd caught a punch. I couldn't respond, so after a long interval, Nancy said, "Marty? Marty?"

"How's Audrey?" I finally asked.

"She's lying down. Both the girls will be here tomorrow morning, and Tommy will be home in the afternoon."

"What can Miranda and I do to help Audrey and the kids?"

"Services haven't been arranged yet, but probably his lodge will handle them. But can you give a eulogy? You were always his favorite." She seemed to cluck before she added, "The irony is that he was worried sick about *your* health. Now he's gone."

"He's gone," I said. After several moments I added, "Of course I'll talk at his service." I was giving eulogies too damned frequently anymore.

After I hung up, I sat staring at nothing. It didn't seem possible that Rollie could be dead. On the wall on one side of my desk was a photo of him, Doug, and me taken at Lake Shasta a lifetime ago. I gazed at it: my son so young that he still had baby teeth with little gaps between them; Rollie with a full head of hair and a cigarette between his lips; me wearing a hat festooned with artificial flies, my arm around Doug's shoulders; all of us holding fishing rods. I remembered the day well. We'd almost lost the outboard motor in the middle of the lake because I'd forgotten to check the mounting. Doug hadn't even known how close we'd been to having to paddle back to the landing. It was another of those wonderful moments you recognize too late.

"Everyone's dying," I said.

■

Over the years, I'd encountered only a handful of Rollie's friends and neighbors, so I didn't know most people seated around Miranda and me at the memorial service. His lodge brothers, wearing fancy sashes and bibs, read aloud in what was to me an emotionless ceremony.

The best moment came when the lodge's chaplain nodded and a small guy I'd noticed earlier because he wore a cowboy costume stood and, carrying a guitar, walked toward the lectern. "Ladies and gentlemen, Shorty Bryan," announced the cleric.

I recognized the name as that of a local entertainer to whom Rollie had occasionally referred, but whom I'd never met. The Stetsoned man who slumped to the microphone looked none too healthy himself, as he adjusted his guitar strap, then said, "Thanks, Parson. Me and Rollie had some real good times together, fishin' mostly, and I know he wouldn't want any sad stuff today, so I'm just gonna sing a couple of his favorites." He strummed the strings, then burst into song: *"Hey, good-lookin', what you got cookin' . . . ?"* Around me I noticed a few people grinning and even bouncing a bit, and the singer suddenly appeared far more robust than he had a moment before.

When Shorty finished, I could tell that a lot of people wondered if applause would be appropriate, but he solved the problem by immediately launching another song: "*Too old, he's gettin' too old, he's too old to cut the mustard anymore!* . . ." After that song, Shorty returned without fanfare to his seat. His performance had been the only thing so far that truly reminded me of the Rollie I'd known.

When the time came for me to speak, I emphasized how much fun Rollie had always been, told a couple of stories about him and Jimmy Dean that evoked considerable laughter, then noted that the sound of laughter was exactly what Rollie'd like to hear at his memorial. But when I began to talk about what a special pal he'd been and how much I'd miss him, I began to weep — I seemed to have no control over that anymore.

As I walked from the lectern, Audrey stood and embraced me, whispering, "Thanks so much, Marty." Her daughters and son did the same thing, and so did Nancy and Miranda. A few minutes later, the chaplain offered a final prayer, then a military honor guard composed of high school cadets presented a flag to Audrey and the formal service concluded.

Afterward, everyone wandered from the ceremonial hall to a large dining room with a bar at one end. Miranda whispered, "I need to drive back to the cabin and take a nap, dear. I'm exhausted. You stay."

"I'll go with you," I said.

"No," she insisted gently, "your family needs you here. I'd love to stay, but I'm just pooped. Call if you need a ride home."

"Honey, I . . ."

She smiled. "I really do think it's important for Audrey and the kids that you stay."

She was correct, of course, but the idea of her driving back to the empty cabin to rest while I socialized seemed wrong to me. Nevertheless, I acquiesced, walked her to the car, kissed her, then rejoined the party in progress.

Lea and Randy immediately found me, and she embraced me, saying, "Uncle Rollie was such a hoot. In fact, you two together were like a comedy team. I'm so sorry for Aunt Audrey."

"Me, too," I replied, "but that's just the real world for you. Rollie came from a hardscrabble background, so I think he'd just acknowledge that this is natural. We gain a Dougie, but we lose a Rollie."

"I know it's natural, but that's a lot easier to accept when it's abstract. When a real person like Uncle Rollie dies, there's a gap left in the world."

I immediately thought of her dead brother and my ill wife before I said, "The gap is natural, too. But only the best of us leave much of one, I suspect."

Lea nodded, saying, "Uncle Rollie was sure one of the best. What's going to happen to his dog?"

"Jimmy Dean? Oh, he and Audrey will pal up. The goofy dog will remind her of Rollie and, of course, she'll remind the dog of the same thing. Where are your kids?" I asked.

"Audrey found us a babysitter," Randy replied. "This would be way too much for them. We're going to leave in just a few minutes and pick them up. I want to drive back early because I should be at work tomorrow."

"Oh, Daddy," my daughter added, "I forgot to tell you that Dougie said 'papa' when he saw a photo of you Thursday, and kissed it."

"You're going to be astonished at how soon he grows up," I said. "I never understood 'seize the day' when I was young, but I sure do now. It's almost too late in the day for me to seize any of it, but you two — "

"Daddy, don't talk that way. There're always days to be seized as long as you're alive. In fact, that's what it means to *be* alive."

She was a bright girl.

At the luncheon — that bar much patronized by Rollie's lodge brothers (and sisters, too, for that matter) — boozing rather than dining seemed to be the first order of business, although it was midday. I grabbed a beer and joined my ex-brother-in-law, Toshio, and his spouse, Janine, at a small table off to one side; like me, they knew few of the locals. Then Nancy, who'd been sitting with her sister, approached. "Why don't you guys come sit with Audrey and the girls?" she asked.

"She seems pretty busy with her friends," Toshio replied. "We'll see her back at the house."

"I hope you'll be able to visit her occasionally from now on," Nancy said. "It's going to get lonely for her. Believe me, I know."

I started to ask how she could be lonely at the commune, but decided to remain silent.

To my surprise, she volunteered, "I've decided to leave Madre Maria. I want to be closer to family. I'll keep Audrey company for a while."

"Where's Miranda?" Toshio asked.

"She tired out, so she went back to the cabin to rest."

"How's she doing? She looks awfully thin," Janine said.

I shook my head. "Not well. She's on a new chemotherapy, and it's tough."

"She looked so drawn at the service," said Nancy.

"Yes." This wasn't my favorite topic.

"Marty," Nancy said softly, one hand on my arm, "if there's anything I can do for either of you, just ask."

"Thanks, Nancy."

She embraced me then, hugged tight before releasing me. "Are you coming over to the house after lunch?"

"I have to check in on Miranda, but probably."

Later that afternoon, back at the cabin, I realized that Miranda was just too weary to drive with me to Audrey's, so I telephoned and explained that we wouldn't be coming over. Audrey understood.

■

On the return trip to Sacramento, the Champ leaned against me and softly hummed along with popular songs from the '40s and '50s playing on the car's radio.

"You know this end of life isn't going the way I thought it would," I said.

Miranda lifted her head and gazed at me for a moment, then asked, "How did you think it would go?"

I could only reply, "Death is so matter-of-fact. Sickness is so matter-of-fact. To me, it was always mystical."

"You're sick, but you go on writing your stories, and I keep seeing some of my patients, but finally our lives will run out. We're really not very important in the great scheme of things."

"So I've noticed," I said. "I saw too many movies when I was a kid: I keep waiting for music to crest or lights to flash."

"We're important to one another . . . maybe to God . . . and that's really what matters," she suggested. A few miles farther, she added, "Let's have a party at our place soon."

I glanced at her — thinner than I'd ever seen her but smiling at the thought of a gathering. She was a pistol, a champ who wanted to enjoy her celebration before she was dead, and I was the lucky, lucky man who'd found her. I didn't want her to *be* sick, but she was and I had to help her deal with it on her own terms. "Let's," I replied.

44

The week after Rollie's funeral Miranda still seemed exhausted. I'm sure she had a good idea about what was going on in her body, but she said nothing to me, doing her best to remain upbeat. Dr. Washington thought more tests were in order, the results of which were terrible. I found myself wondering aloud, "How can this have turned around so fast? Surely that one trip to Dunsmuir didn't cause a relapse."

"No, of course not," Miranda said. "Don't blame yourself for something that goes on at the cellular or subcellular level. Earlier results were probably anomalous. Sometimes something, maybe your diet, masks the cancer. Sometimes the cancer quits growing for a while on its own. We just don't know why, but I'm glad I had that respite. Now we'll have to try another counterattack." She smiled then in that indomitable way of hers and said, "We've been dancing on the edge of the abyss, Marty, and it's been wonderful."

"Let's keep dancing . . . in fact, are you busy right now?"

"Do I look busy?" She smiled.

"Well, I seem to remember where we keep the baby oil, and I'd like to rub some on you."

"I'd love that," she said.

"But first let me help you undress," I offered.

She slipped into sleep as I massaged her back.

■

That evening, I again telephoned Miranda's sons. Nick and James both promised they'd be back for a visit soon, together if they could coordinate it. Robbie said only, "Okay," and hung up.

When the Champ and I drove to the infusion center the next morning I tried to be cheery, but we knew this might be Miranda's last chance. The nurses did their best to lighten the tone, too, but their efforts seemed strained. When my wife finished, the infusion nurse, Pris, said brightly, "See you tomorrow, Dr. Mossi," but, looking at Miranda, I wasn't certain there'd be many more treatments. As soon as we arrived home she lay down for a nap.

I sat at my desk and basically twiddled my thumbs, unable to concentrate on any of the projects I had in process. I didn't even want to call anyone connected with the Bearheart story. Finally, I reached for the telephone and dialed my daughter's number. She answered right away. "Yes?"

"I called to talk to Dougie."

"To Dougie?" She hesitated. "Are you okay?"

"Sure."

"Just a minute, then." After a brief pause, she urged, "Say hi to Grandpa," then that little voice chirped, "Papa!"

"Hi, Stinker, how you doin'?"

"Papa! Papa! Papa!" said Dougie.

"What's Tyler doing?"

"Ty-Ty," said the little voice, then Lea came on and said, "He just kissed the phone, then took off for his box."

"His box?"

Randy bought Tyler a bike and Dougie claimed the box. He puts his head in it and says, "Hide! Hide! Hide!"

"I'd like to hide," I said.

"*You'd* like to? What's wrong? Not your heart?" Her voice swooped.

"Miranda's back on chemo."

"I thought she was better," said my daughter.

I sighed, "Honey, she's not going to get better."

For several moments my daughter didn't reply. Finally she said, "Are you sure?"

"I'm sure."

Again her end of the line went silent, then she said, "I've got to go see what Dougie's into, but, Daddy, I really didn't realize it was so bad," and she began to weep, saying, "Maybe I haven't wanted to. Miranda's been so good for you."

■

My visit with my own oncologist was brief and to the point. "Well," said Dr. DelVecchio, "your PSA is rising much too fast. We need to drop it with hormonal ablation again. We can do a Lupron shot today and I'll give you a prescription for Casodex."

"Starting today?" I asked.

"Right," the oncologist replied. "There's no point in delaying."

"I know," I said, but psychologically I wasn't ready to admit that my cancer, like Miranda's, was obdurate.

He must have read my face, because the young doctor said, "These treatments will prolong your life, perhaps until better treatments are developed."

That seemed to be everyone's hope—hang on until a cure was found—so I said simply, "I understand," and waited until a nurse came into the treatment room to inject me.

■

Since it was on my way, I stopped by the office of the *Tribune* and caught Bud Hartley at his desk. "Hey, what brings the phantom writer in?" he asked, grinning as we shook hands. "We don't get many visits from old-timers."

"I stopped by to say howdy . . . on my way back from an appointment with my oncologist."

"How's that going?"

"Okay."

"And your wife? How's she doing?"

"Not well," I admitted.

Bud exhaled loudly, then he said, "Well, I'm really sorry to hear that."

"Yeah," I agreed. "Listen, I just want you to know that I followed up a bit on that Bearheart story, and there's not much question that he was involved with bringing boys north from Mexico for sex, but no one is willing to speak on the record."

He sipped at the cold coffee that always seemed to be available on his desk, then asked, "You got enough to write about it?"

"No. Unless I have on-the-record testimony or other hard evidence, I wouldn't feel right about publishing accusations. Someone needs to go to Mexico and read the files, do some interviewing. I don't have the energy."

Bud leaned far back in his chair, popped a stick of Doublemint into his mouth, then said, "You're old school. The *Express* would've done a front-page story based on rumors."

I nodded and said, "It probably will eventually."

■

James and Nick arrived together that next weekend without their families. To my astonishment, though, they weren't alone. They brought an obviously reluctant Robbie, who avoided me but did hug his mother. James and Nick had alerted Miranda that they'd be coming by, and she somehow managed to look pretty and behave vitally, although she was much thinner. Her sons appeared shocked when they saw her.

Most of that evening was spent on small talk, family gossip, with Robbie largely silent unless prompted by one of his older brothers. I stayed out of the way, provided coffee and soft drinks, plus a tray of snacks. After hearing about James's and Nick's families, Miranda turned to Robbie and said, "What're your prospects, Robbie? Have you found the girl yet?"

"He's found too many," interjected James, then laughed.

"No one special," the youngest son finally said. "I date some girls."

"Have you gone back to school?" asked Miranda.

The lanky young man shrugged and seemed to gaze over her shoulder, then replied, "I'm gonna take a couple courses at the J.C. next fall."

"Tell her about your new job, dude," urged Nick.

"I'm working at a computer store, setting up systems."

"That's wonderful," his mother said. "Do you enjoy it?"

"It's okay."

Nick grinned. "He doesn't enjoy any work. Right, dude? He was to the manor born."

Robbie made a face, but James replied, "Who does?" and everyone except Robbie laughed. He seemed like a strangely humorless young man to me.

"Hey, Marty," said Nick, "Mom sent me copy of that exposé you wrote about the pedophile priest. Nice job."

"She sent me a copy, too," said James. "I'll bet you rattled some cages with that one."

"I won't be invited to tea with the bishop anytime soon."

Robbie spoke up then. "Dad knows him."

"Knows who, dude?"

"The bishop."

"What'd Dad think about the exposé?" Nick asked.

Robbie shrugged. "I dunno. Shocked, I guess."

"A lot of us were," said his mother, "and sad."

Later, as the three young men were leaving, James and Nick said they'd be back tomorrow for another visit before flying home. Robbie said good-bye.

Miranda watched him leave, saying, "Poor Robbie. He was such a bright, funny little guy, and now he's so morose."

"Some people cultivate that," I remarked. I could have added, "Including me."

"But not him, I don't think. I hate to say it, but I think my ex-husband has played him like a harp, probably as a way to get back at me. It's so unfair to Rob."

Before I could frame a response, Miranda rose and said, "I'm going to have to lie down for a bit. Oh, and about that party I suggested the other day . . ."

"Yes?"

"We'll have to skip it. I've decided to call hospice. It's time for them to come in."

Standing in the doorway wearing her bright turban, she looked lovely, so I had trouble connecting what she was saying with what I was seeing.

"Hospice?" I'd known for a long time that I'd be hearing this announcement, but it nevertheless stunned me. In order for hospice to begin services a patient had to be terminally ill with a prognosis of no more than six months. Miranda'd all but stopped eating solid food and was surviving with cans of Ensure.

My love read the distress on my face and said, "We're going to need them before long, so I want to make contact."

"But I thought the new chemo was working," I said.

"It is, but trust me, it's time to call hospice."

After going back on hormonal ablation to treat my own cancer, I'd once again been silently feeling sorry for myself. But now the Champ was telling me without dramatics that she had reached the beginning of the end. I was once again nearly overwhelmed by reality and had to excuse myself, walk into the other room, gaze out the window, and breathe deeply. After a while, I walked into the bedroom where she was resting and said, "Okay."

Miranda had lived with me long enough to know how I operated, that I always needed a bit of time to adjust to new situations. She'd once said to me, "You'd be a terrible businessman. By the time you made a decision the opportunity would be lost. But I guess it's that thoughtfulness that makes you such a good writer." I'd chuckled then . . . but not now.

"When the hospice workers come, Marty, I want you to know that I'm going to remind them that I want the lightest dosage of painkiller that will work. I want my wits about me for as long as possible. I can always countermand that request if I need to," she added, "and so can you, because you have my power of attorney for health care."

Medicine was Miranda's business, so I said nothing, although I was unhappy. "Don't look so glum," my wife said. "I know hospice symbolizes the end, but these people aren't bringing death. They're really bringing a little more life, because they'll be able to medicate me in ways that will allow me to be comfortable and active as long as possible. The cancer, not hospice, is bringing death."

"I know."

"And take your antidepressants."

■

Three women arrived the next afternoon. I don't know what I'd expected, but they were attractive, middle-aged gals who could have been arriving for a book-club meeting. "Mr. Martinez," said the lady in the lead, extending her right hand, "I'm Starchild Morgan—guess whose parents were hippies." She grinned. "This is Diana Monteverde and Lois Rothstein. We're with hospice."

"We've been expecting you," I said as cordially as possible. "Please come in. Miranda's in the den . . . this way."

The ladies all greeted the Champ with great warmth. "Dr. Mossi, we worked together with Mrs. Toliver," said Lois as she shook my wife's hand.

"Of course, Lois," Miranda replied. "Good to see you again. And you, Starchild—still the bingo queen?"

"When my husband lets me out," said the tall woman. "Have you met Diana? She's just up from the Modesto unit."

"Welcome." My wife smiled as she shook hands with the other hospice worker.

"I've heard so much about you, Dr. Mossi," said Diana.

The conversation that followed was less technical than I'd expected, since my wife was familiar with how hospice operated, and the three ladies were familiar with Miranda's background.

As they stood to depart, Lois said to me, "Are you the Martin Martinez who writes for the *Trib?*"

"Yes."

"Well, thanks for exposing that pervert priest. Keep up the good work."

As they walked toward the door, Starchild called over her shoulder, "And don't forget to call us as soon as you think we're needed, Dr. Mossi. We'll be right over."

After they left, the Champ said, "Nice gals. Not one of them has to do this, but here they are." After a moment, she said, "Why not invite Lea and Randy and the kids tonight? We need a change of pace."

She didn't say there might not be many more evenings when she'd feel up to a gathering, but I got that unspoken message.

■

My wife rested until the gang arrived. The two little boys entered at a run. "Know what?" Tyler immediately said. "There's a mean girl in my class and she's Anastasia!"

"What'd she do?" I asked.

"She . . . she . . . she chased me."

Dougie was on Miranda's lap. Then off. Then on again.

The Champ remained in her chair sipping Ensure while everyone else ate ordered-in Chinese food on TV trays, then she played again with the children. She read each a book as they sat on her lap. From across the room, I observed that bittersweet scene. Miranda accepted Randy and Lea's kids just as she did her own sons' youngsters.

When would that sparkling consciousness evaporate into atoms, leaving no trace on the universe? I stood and walked to the picture window and gazed out, breathing hard and telling myself that there was no profit in thinking that way.

"Marty?" Miranda's voice was faint. "Are you okay? When you stand over there, it usually means you're upset."

"Just thinking," I replied.

She was wearing down, so I quietly advised Randy and Lea that it was time to leave. Each of the little boys gave her a kiss before departing, and Tyler insisted, "No, wait! No, wait!"

"What?" asked Randy.

"I got butterfly kisses for Gramma Miranda!" He once more scrambled onto her lap, then moved his face near hers. The Champ's eyes closed as the little boy's eyelashes brushed one of her cheeks. Her last butterfly kiss? I thought, then jarred myself out of that mood. Some people never get even one.

"Ty-Ty!" Dougie squealed, and they were gone.

"That was a wonderful visit," said Miranda.

"It sure was."

Just as we were turning in, the phone rang and I soon heard the voice of my sister Alicia leaving a message. I hurried into the den and picked up the receiver. "Hey," I said.

"Marty? Tia Beda died."

"Aunt Beda?" She was my mother's older sister, and the last of her generation. "What happened?"

"She was ninety-three, Marty. She just got old and tired and died, or at least that's what Margarita, her oldest, told me. Tia was living with her down in Oceanside."

"When's the funeral?"

"It's all over," my sister replied. "Margarita said she didn't want family to feel obligated to drive down from all over the state, so they just had a simple requiem Mass and had her mother cremated. She's in a niche down there."

Despite her age, I was genuinely shocked to learn of my aunt's passing. I'd always hoped we could take my mom's photo albums to Aunt Beda so she could identify all the unfamiliar faces in the snapshots. "She's the last of the old folks in our family," I replied.

"Not really," my sister countered. "There're still plenty of old folks, and we're them.

"And, yeah, did you tell Chava something you didn't tell the rest of us? He's really been worried about you. He got all teary the other night, and I haven't seen that happen since . . . well, since Manuel died."

45

When Miranda fell ill at the infusion center, I knew that she and Dr. Washington would have to take a close look at her blood work to decide if she had maxed out on this chemotherapy. If she had . . . well, I didn't want to think about that.

"There's really no other proven chemo I can take for this now, Marty," my wife later explained. We were seated in chairs in the bedroom, and in that light her complexion appeared mottled; she held a handkerchief near her mouth and paused to gulp, as though trying to avoid upchucking. "Jeaneve and I are looking into an immunotherapy protocol at UCSF," she continued, "but I may not be eligible. If I'm not, it'll be time to tell the hospice volunteers to come over."

I embraced her, feeling bones under her shrunken flesh, then said, "Look, we can afford to go anywhere and try anything. How about those apricot pits in Mexico, or the coffee therapy down there or something?"

She leaned back, then said, "Unfortunately, dear, if it's not being tested at a major medical center, it's hooey. I'd love to believe in something like that, but those options you mention are traps for desperate people."

"The medical profession doesn't know everything about this," I argued. "Surely the —"

"It knows far more than anyone else." she said, cutting me off. "Trust me, if there was anything to those treatments I'd try them without hesitation. But there isn't. I have all the fears and hopes any other patient has . . ." Suddenly she was weeping.

I wrapped my arms around her, and after a few moments she gasped, "I want to live as much as anyone does, Marty. This illness really angers me! I want to enjoy our old age. I want to see my grandchildren grow up."

I'd taken her strength for granted, but now I realized how close to the edge she was, and that my whining had caused her unnecessary upset. I stepped back, my hands on her shoulders, and looked directly into her eyes as I said, "I'm sorry, honey. Really sorry. It's just that I'm desperate."

"I am too, but sometimes I don't think you realize it."

■

On the afternoon after Starchild and Diana initiated their ministrations, Miranda began coughing and sneezing uncontrollably. We never figured out if her medications caused it or a seasonal allergy or what, but she also began to vomit, and Starchild immediately elevated her head and said, "Get me a towel, please. We don't want her to aspirate this stuff."

When I returned, the coughing and sneezing were tapering off; tears streamed from Miranda's eyes and she puffed like a spent runner. She whispered something to the hospice worker, who then said, "Will you excuse us, Mr. Martinez?"

I started to leave, then turned and said, "What's wrong?"

Starchild rose and walked to me, then whispered, "She's had an accident. All that coughing caused her to lose control of her bowels. I'll take care of it."

For a moment, I let the news sink in, then said to the nurse, "I'll clean her."

"Mr. Martinez, I don't think . . ."

"If the situation were reversed and I was the one who'd had the accident, who do you think would clean me?"

Starchild had more to say, I could tell, but she stood silently for several seconds, then nodded and responded, "I'll bring you warm water, soap, and some towels."

She departed and I walked to my love's bed and said, "I'll help you clean up, honey."

Miranda looked away, then said, "I saw this happen to a few of my patients, and I thought I understood how they felt, but I had no idea how humiliating . . ."

"You know virtually the same thing has happened to me, and your support helped me get through it. And we both know you'd clean me if I was the one in bed right now."

"Yes . . ."

"So relax. Just tell me if I do anything uncomfortable."

Later, when Starchild and I carried the wet, soiled towels to the laundry room, the hospice nurse said, "I have to tell you that I've never seen a husband do that before. Usually even the most devoted ones aren't interested in that kind of job."

I gave her what was to me the simplest of explanations: "I love her, Starchild. Anything I can do for her now is to make our bond unbreakable."

"She's a lucky lady, Mr. Martinez."

touching

■

Miranda rested little that night, or so Lois, who was on duty, told me. I dozed in the lounger that we'd moved into the bedroom, not sleeping with the Champ because I didn't want to disturb whatever rest she managed. In the morning Lois helped Miranda bathe while I showered, then I returned to the bedroom and read parts of the newspaper to her until she dozed.

Monsignor Kelley, who brought Miranda Holy Communion twice weekly, arrived that morning with his great grin, his hearty handshake, and some news, "I hope you aren't too upset, Marty, but I've dumped your mate Father Andrews. I told the bishop that I'd had enough."

"I'm heartbroken," I replied, trying to smile.

"I thought you would be. Are you still investigating the pedophile priests story?"

"No, I burned out."

"I can understand that, but don't let that bunch convince you the world's morally ambiguous."

"I didn't and I won't."

"But you look glum."

"Sometimes I wonder if there can be any higher plan behind the suffering Miranda's going through."

The priest nodded, then said, "I sometimes think our lives are fragments and fragments of fragments—this little relationship, that little experience—and what we call God gives us the power to unify them."

"God's a verb, not a noun?" I asked.

"Too metaphysical for me." He smiled. "However you explain it, the abyss awaits. For Christians, though, the possibility of something more can make suffering sacramental." He placed a large hand on my shoulder and continued, "Right now, you two're alive and together. You've been called to this ministry," he said. "Not everyone gets to show their love this powerfully. Relish the moment, my friend, relish the moment."

In truth, I didn't relish anything about it. "It's tough not to be sad," I said.

"I didn't say not to be sad, boyo. I said relish the moment, sad or not. I suspect that you and Miranda are sharing something that not many people ever experience," he added. "A wonderful gift."

I hadn't thought about how our lives looked to others because I'd been so involved in living mine, but I guess it was unusual for people our age to be so obviously swept up with passion for one another. To me, Miranda was a kind of miracle in my life.

"Are you praying for strength?" he asked. "'Come to me all you that labor and are burdened and I will refresh you.' You *will* be refreshed, but not on your terms—on God's. Stay with it, Marty, and stay with the idea that nothing on this earth—good or bad—lasts forever. That won't lighten your sadness, but it'll put it in perspective.

"Now let me visit that spouse of yours."

We walked toward the bedroom, and the priest stopped me just before we entered and said, "One more thing: If what we believe is true, then Miranda will be waiting for you in Heaven, and so will all those others you love. That may be simplistic, but what have you got to lose by believing it?"

"Nothing," I said.

"Ah, Miranda," the monsignor called as he entered the bedroom, "we've missed you at Mass, dear."

■

For me this process was much too fast. Before I could adjust to one diminution, another occurred, so I wandered around feeling breathless and depressed. What the monsignor had said seemed to be correct, but in the face of loss it wasn't very comforting. Later that week, my wife experienced trouble walking, so the hospice volunteers brought a wheelchair. During her good hours, we began to take Miranda outside, usually into the backyard under the arbor or up and down the block.

One afternoon out on the deck as we leafed through the thin photo album we'd assembled of our lives together, the Champ said, "This is what we've had, Marty, and it's been wonderful, so leaving it is dreadful."

I could not reply.

"People have always died," she said, as though talking to herself. "Even Jesus."

"And people have always prayed for cures," I added.

"I don't. I *do* ask to be spiritually healed and for the strength to deal with whatever's coming, though."

I couldn't comment on that either. After several moments, I offered something Lea had suggested: "May I wash your hair?"

"Wash my hair? What hair?" In fact, a little had begun to grow back, so she smiled at me, saying, "I've never imagined you as a hairdresser."

"I'll even wear tight pants and unbutton my shirt to the navel, call myself Mr. Marty."

It was wonderful to hear her laugh again as she said, "You're on, Mr. Marty."

I pushed Miranda's wheelchair into the master bath and positioned her next to the large sink that had a spigot on a hose, draped a towel over her shoulders, then eased her head back so I could bathe it with warm water that would drain into the sink. Her eyes closed and she all but purred. Although I used a dab of shampoo, what I performed was more like a scalp massage, but I did it slowly, allowing the warm water to relax her.

And relax me: Just touching her, rubbing her, feeling the tension leave her neck and see her face in repose, was a new kind of intimacy for me; I should have done this before, long before. Once I finished — Miranda appeared to be asleep — I gently toweled her head, leaned over to kiss her ear and neck, then left my cheek against hers for a long, long time.

■

More than anything else to pry my mind away from Miranda's situation, I telephoned Joaquin Sandoval-Mendez, a Tijuana cop I'd met a few years back while I was writing a piece on illegal immigration. I had his home number, and he answered on the second ring, *"Bueno?"*

"Hola, Joaquin," I said. "Es Marty Martinez. Como está?"

"Hey, Marty, good to hear from you. Que hay es nuevo?"

"Tengo una problema — "

He interrupted me to say, "You've got a big problema speaking Spanish. Let's keep it in English so I can understand you."

"Okay. Didn't you used to work in Guadalajara?"

"Sure. Why?"

"Do you remember the Marvin Bearheart murder?"

"Of course. His name was unusual, even for an American."

"Rumor has it that he was involved with boys at that orphanage he helped sponsor — sexually involved, I mean."

"Yes," Joaquin replied. "I've heard that too."

"Have Mexican authorities pursued it?"

"No need. He's dead."

"I mean pursued the problem."

The Mexican policeman chuckled, then said pleasantly, "You Americans constantly make the mistake of trying to judge the world in terms of good and bad instead of better or worse. You've all had it too easy up there, I think. As for your Senator Bearheart, unofficially of course, I can tell you he got what he asked for."

"Meaning what?"

"Some information surfaced not long ago, and we confirmed it. He was killed by a father."

No surprise, since Mexican parents, even if they'd had to leave their children at an orphanage, would stop at nothing to protect them. "Some kid's father killed him?" I asked.

"Not that kind. A *sacerdote,* not a *papi.*"

"A *priest?*" I gasped, momentarily discombobulated.

"Yes, a Catholic priest."

"Who?" I asked.

"Remember, this is strictly unofficial, but a priest from your East Coast had come to Mexico to look at the orphanage because he and his group thought they might help sponsor it. They ran into the senator and some others from up your way and the priest figured out what was going on."

"So he killed him?"

"He warned all of them. Everyone but Bearheart got the message."

I shook my head. "He was a hard-nosed bastard."

"Not for long. Some men in the priest's organization were enforcers, I guess, because they killed him, then left our country."

"Why don't you come after them?"

"For what? Doing us a favor? I'm glad someone killed him; I wish I had. He's dead now and I've got living criminals to deal with."

I'd always considered Sandoval-Mendez to be a good cop, but his brand of pragmatism shocked me. "Well, can you tell me the name of this priest or his group?" I asked.

There was a pause. "I don't remember his name. I could look it up... but his group was called Mother Maria."

"The what?"

"In Spanish, the Madre Maria," he said.

"The *what?*" I gasped. After hanging up, I sat on a stool next to the phone and gazed out the kitchen window.

46

Sleep had become my refuge. Most nights I seemed to drift dreamlessly until I heard the muted sounds of the hospice volunteers in the morning, then remembered who I was and what was happening. That night, however, Joaquin Sandoval-Mendez's story churned through my mind. Nancy's membership in the group deepened everything. I had to discuss this with someone, so I telephoned my brother, who responded, "I can't see why Nan needs to know."

"But she seems to hold some allegiance to Madre Maria."

"You'll have to judge that. I think your detective friend is right. It's over."

His attitude surprised me. "But a murder was committed."

"Or an execution," he said. "Sounds to me like he was a bastard who needed killing."

"And if Nancy finds out later?"

"Come on, Marty," Chava chided. "How's she going to know that you knew if you don't tell her? I'm sure as hell not going to. When we hang up I'm going to forget we had this conversation. Leave Nancy out of it."

"But..."

"You've got more important things to think about, *vato.* Don't search for reasons to worry."

After we hung up I again gazed out the kitchen window. I guess I didn't know my little brother, either.

■

Many people telephoned to check on the Champ's condition, and at first I tried to respond to all of them, but I soon tired of the calls. Most asked, in hushed tones, "How is *she?*"—as though mentioning Miranda's name might somehow worsen her condition or perhaps transmit it to them.

Finally, I all but stopped answering the phone and put a new message on our answering machine: "This is Marty. Thanks for calling. Leave your name and number and we'll try to get back to you." I didn't try to get back to very many at all, but did pick up the receiver if I recognized a special voice . . . Kathy Mettler, say, or one of Miranda's sons.

Get-well cards were another thing: We were swamped, and at first my wife tried to read and respond to each. Eventually, though, I became a kind of filter for her, although she knew so many people that I'm sure I missed some important messages. One day what appeared to be a homemade card written in Spanish appeared, and Miranda read it with a smile, then said, "Marty, you translate this for me. My Spanish isn't great and the handwriting isn't very good, but I know who these ladies are."

I smiled and said, "Me translate? The blind leading the blind, but I'll try." Once I began reading, all humor vanished from me: "Esteemed Dr. Mossi: You are in our thoughts and prayers. We know that God will soon call you home and reward you. You will be seated at His right hand. We are beginning a novena to Our Lady of Guadalupe for your intention.

"You have been a saint to us. We do not know what we will do without you, but Our Lord will provide." It was signed with varying degrees of legibility by seven women.

"They're the poorest of the poor," she told me. "Even buying that stamp had to be hard for them, but they're praying for me." She looked up then and said, "Marty, I've been so blessed to have been able to help people like these and not be the one needing help."

"And Dr. Mintz agreed to replace you at the clinic?"

"Yes, Charlene Mintz. She's fresh from residency and full of energy and idealism."

"Big shoes to fill," I said.

"Size nine," Miranda replied.

■

"Are you taking the meds for your mood?" Miranda asked.

"Why?"

"Have you looked in a mirror lately? The mask of tragedy looks happier. Do us both a favor and go see Dr. Molinaro."

I had no snappy comeback. "Okay," I said.

A week later I was in Len Molinaro's office. His black hair had grayed a bit, but otherwise the psychiatrist appeared little changed. "How've you been, Mr. Martinez?"

"My physical health isn't great, but I've been happily married now for over three years . . ."

"To Dr. Mossi, correct?"

"Yes."

We made small talk for a while, me telling him about how I'd been able to rejoin my family. "I've got a new grandson . . ."

"But?"

It took me a few seconds to reply: "My wife is dying. Her cancer is back."

He sat quietly before replying, "I'm truly sorry."

I cleared my throat, then added, "I'm beginning to feel like crying all the time."

"Well, I'll give you a prescription. We need to get something started again." After another pause, he asked, "What else is troubling you?"

"Sometimes it seems like the people who constitute the world I care about are all going or gone, like the world's emptying."

"Mmmm-hmmm." The psychiatrist nodded. "It's awful to lose those you love. My dad passed away recently and I'm still hurting. There's no way to sugarcoat those feelings. But also consider the people who've entered or reentered your life in the past five years or so. Your daughter, of course, and the others you told me about: Tyler, Dougie, those priests . . ."

"Father Tran and Monsignor Kelley."

"And, of course, Miranda. And that's just the list I know about. There must be others."

I nodded. "People've always coped with this, I understand that," I said, "but when it happens to you . . ." I had to pause and swallow hard. "I know different people are filling up our lives, too, but that doesn't make losing loved ones easier."

"It's not supposed to be easy," he responded gently. "It's the price we pay for love, an inverse relationship: the greater the love, the worse the pain. But also the more wonderful the relationship. Be grateful, Mr. Martinez. Be grateful . . ."

■

I was gently massaging her feet, rubbing them with baby oil, when Miranda spoke faintly, as though the words were too painful to utter aloud, "You know, people used to lose children at childbirth . . . in infancy, but we lose some who live, don't we?"

"Robbie'll come to his senses," I said, thinking too about my own son and that as sad as his death was, my experience was better than what Miranda faced with her youngest. And I inevitably thought for a moment of what my mother had faced.

"I hope so," she said. "I miss him. He was my baby." She paused and gazed out the window for several seconds, then said, "Marty, can we take a walk?"

"You want to go out back?"

"Along the river, I mean."

That shocked me, so I stammered, "Do you think you should?" She had an IV connected to her left hand and a catheter draining urine.

She smiled again and said, "What've I got to lose? Besides, I'm a doctor."

"Okay," I said, toweling her feet. "Let me tell Lois."

"I wouldn't recommend doing that, Mr. Martinez," the hospice nurse responded confidentially. "It might be too much for her. Why not just take her for a stroll around the yard or maybe around the block?"

"Because she wants to walk at the river, and we both know it won't make any difference in her life expectancy."

"All right," the nurse said and quickly turned away. Then she added, "If you'd rather another volunteer came in, you can call the office."

Just what we needed, a temperamental nurse. I touched her shoulder, saying as she turned to face me, "Lois, I'm sorry. I know you're doing everything you can for Miranda and I don't mean to be pulling rank or causing trouble, but you know my wife's a realist. She'd rather have an hour at the river than a day stuck in here, so I'm going to take her. I'd like your help."

The woman blinked, and her eyes grew moist as she stood silent before me. "We all love Dr. Mossi, too," she finally said, "and I don't want her to suffer for one moment, but I'm afraid it's too late in the . . . the process . . . for a walk."

"Help us find that out one way or another," I urged quietly. "*Please.* I'll assume responsibility."

One of Lois's hands grasped my forearm then, and she sighed, "I just want to help your wife."

"Miranda understands what's happening, but she . . ." I responded, then all of a sudden tears began to flood my face.

"I'll get her ready," Lois said.

■

On the drive over, the Champ seemed to perk up and take in everything. "The trees are so pretty this season," she observed and I agreed, my mind churning with thoughts that couldn't be helpful: Is this the last time we'll walk together? Will she ever see the river again? How can I live without her?

After parking near the pedestrian bridge at the university, I removed the folded wheelchair from the trunk, then helped Miranda into it. She wore a catheter bag strapped to one leg, and I was careful not to knock it loose when

I tucked a blanket in. Then I hung a small pack with emergency supplies on the back of the seat, busying myself so that my sense of farewell wouldn't overwhelm me.

As I straightened up and my face wasn't hidden from her, I burlesqued, "Where to, Champ?"

"You'd make a terrible poker player," my wife smiled, "but you're a wonderful husband. I'm glad you don't hide your emotions, Marty. Keep them out there, and everyone, mostly you, will be better off." Her voice was weak, but not foggy or slurred.

"Yes, Doctor." I blinked. "How about a kiss?"

"I thought you'd never ask."

After a soft kiss, I began pushing the wheelchair. Where the meadow opened up, birds seemed to be in concert, so I stopped pushing the chair along the bike path and put my hand on Miranda's neck. We heard the faint honking of geese in the distance. My wife turned and smiled at me.

"Would you please request that there be no flowers at my requiem Mass, but memorial donations for La Clinica de las Mujeres?"

"Anything you want, honey."

"And don't let that dreadful tenor sing. He hasn't hit a note on key in all the years I've been listening to him."

"Okay."

"No long-winded eulogy."

"Okay."

The path seemed strangely devoid of runners and walkers — only an elderly couple strolling and a young woman jogging with a black Lab on tether had passed us — but suddenly a string of high school kids began running by, lean boys and girls in various workout costumes. "A cross-country team, I'll bet," I said.

The runners were strung out and each that passed us seemed to be moving measurably slower than the one before. Once it seemed all were gone, I said, "That was a real gaggle of kids."

"It sure was," Miranda agreed just as a chubby girl puffed up behind us, apparently shuffling after the earlier group. As she passed, she glanced our way and managed a smile. I gave her a thumbs-up. "That's a lady with some guts," I said.

We paused at one of the many memorial benches along the trail and I sat. "Marty," Miranda smiled, and I expected she'd say something about the runner, but she fooled me. "Do you remember the look on Mrs. Donati's face that day when we said we liked holding people's hands in Mass? It was like someone had prominently farted." Miranda began chuckling.

"That was almost the first time we ever talked to one another," I said. "Wasn't it that day we discussed the face of Jesus appearing on a tortilla or something?"

"It was. And you'd just come from the psychiatrist?"

"Not just, but recently . . . like being born again. I met you and things *really* looked up. I was twitterpated," I said.

"I hope you still are."

"You have no idea . . ."

"Oh yes I do." The Champ took my left hand in both of hers, kissed my wedding band, then rested her cheek against it, saying, "It's been *so* much fun."

■

Father Tran snuck over from his office as often as he could for visits, usually during his lunch break. "The good news," he told us, "is that I really do have a job there. The bad news is that there's no such thing as an 'Asian community.' There're Korean and Viet and Cambodian communities, and so on, but they really haven't much in common . . . except for being Christians."

"That's something," I said.

"Yes," he smiled. "The Gay Outreach is far more satisfying because there's a defined community and a genuine need."

Miranda asked, "And the bishop's supportive?"

"He really is. There's more to him than I anticipated."

I hope so, I thought but did not say.

As he left, the young priest took my hand and said, "Marty, you can call me anytime, day or night. I'll be there for you and Miranda."

"I know." We stood for a moment, still gripping hands, and I added, "Thanks . . . from both of us."

Jeaneve Washington also dropped by frequently, visited with Miranda and me, and even with Starchild, who was an old friend. "It's nice you're making house calls again," my wife said on one of her last good days, and Dr. Washington, who had picked up my nickname for Miranda replied, "You won't think it's nice, Champ, when you get my bill," and both had laughed.

■

Miranda's final decline lasted less than a month, with fewer and fewer minutes out of bed or outside the house for her. She consumed progressively less Ensure. Both Father Tran and Monsignor Kelley remained regular visitors, and their presence always cheered her, and me too, for that matter. James and Nick flew out four times during that period, and when they left the fourth time,

James said, "Be sure to call us if it looks like we're losing her. We'll fly back right away . . . and we'll bring that twerp Robbie, too."

They were already losing her, but I didn't point that out. It was difficult enough to admit it to myself—the once robust body now wispy, the sensual voice a whisper. She awakened one afternoon following a long pull of drugged sleep, looked at me and said, as though dreaming, "Sometimes, when the pain goes away, I'm me again."

Later that day, following a visit, I walked with Dr. Washington to her car. "I think you'd better call Miranda's sons, Marty," she said as we strolled. "It's about over."

I knew that was true, of course, but hearing the oncologist who'd been fighting to keep the Champ alive say it jolted me. I tried to control my face, but couldn't restrain tears. "I know," I choked.

To my astonishment, the physician embraced me and held me for a long time. "We all hate this, Marty," she said. "We just *hate* it. Miranda's so special."

"Yes," I said.

47

I felt her die . . . my wife, my love, my life. After all her struggles, breath slipped from Miranda's exhausted body with the faintest of sighs, and I perceived a sudden settling in her and in my own consciousness, too, like fluid flowing into fluid. I sat holding her hand as it cooled; when I finally let go, it remained half closed, thumb forward, three fingers bent, little finger curved inward.

Her wedding band caught my eye, so I leaned forward, kissed it, and rested my forehead against it until Monsignor Kelley put his arm around my shoulders and said simply, "She's with God, Marty." I slid the ring from Miranda's emaciated finger and dropped into my breast pocket, thinking only that she wasn't with me.

Later the monsignor's voice lowered as he said, "What was it you called her, the Champ? Well, she was certainly all of that."

Father Tran arrived soon after Miranda's body had been picked up and transported to the mortuary. He seemed momentarily nonplussed when I asked, "What's the point of suffering, Father? Why did someone like Miranda have to go through all that?" My face was out of control, lips quivering, tears spilling.

"Marty . . . I . . . I don't have any quick or easy answer for that. I saw some horrible things in Vietnam when I was a child . . ."

"How can I not be pissed off at God? Why shouldn't I be?"

He grasped one of my arms then and said, his voice suddenly firm, "Didn't Jesus suffer? A rabbi once said something like, 'Not to know suffering means not to be human.' That's our role in this life and we should be grateful for the times we don't."

I shook my head. I didn't trust myself to speak.

"God's ways are far beyond me," he admitted, "but if I don't believe in them my life, and yours, and Miranda's, will be meaningless. I believe there's some purpose, probably unknowable, behind all this, and that's what makes it worthwhile at all. You know, we educate and educate our conscious minds, but I suspect we really live somewhere deeper." He paused, then embraced me and said, "Marty, let's pray together."

Miranda's remains were cremated and interred in one of the adjoining niches we'd purchased at the Catholic cemetery. If the paths of glory, like the paths of mendacity and villainy, do lead but to the grave, so do the paths of compassion, of concern, of virtue. She was really dead. I would never hold her again.

■

Four days later, St. Apollinaris Church overflowed for her requiem Mass. After the family had been seated and the rest of the church crowded with mourners, a procession of clergy entered to solemn organ music and walked to the altar, priests from every Sacramento parish. To my great surprise, bringing up the rear, resplendent in purple vestments, was James Ignatius Moriarty, bishop of the Sacramento diocese. He sat in a chair facing the altar while Monsignor Kelley celebrated Mass.

I quickly forgot him, but the deep comfort I hoped for from the service didn't permeate me; I felt like an actor at a dress rehearsal, observing myself being observed. The final words of Father Tran's brief eulogy, however, did pierce my shell: "Along with mourning for our dear lost friend, we should also give thanks for having known her. Just think of all the unfortunate souls who never did." I began to sob, my daughter cradling me like a child, while a strange notion swept me: Someone who had known her, her first husband, had to be present. Well, I wasn't awfully sorry for him . . . unchristian as that was.

Sitting in the front row with James and Nick and their families, as well as with Lea and hers, I was thinking, There's no way to undo this. There's no way to undo anything. And there's no way to know exactly what happened between us as she died, only that it did happen.

Robbie, who'd been summoned home from Cancún after his mother's death, fidgeted on one side of me. I don't know what his brothers had said to him, but despite a robust tan and newly bleached hair, he appeared sick. When it came time for the Our Father, and we all joined hands with the people beside us, he hesitated to take mine, but finally did, his touch nearly incorporeal. When we exchanged the handshake of peace, he averted his eyes.

Since Johnny O's service had proved to me that the unconventional was now allowed at Catholic requiems, I'd asked the monsignor if we could play Nat "King" Cole's version of "Unforgettable" over the sound system to close the celebration. He'd eyed me for a moment, then replied, "Of course. I loved that song when I was a lad, and I can't think of anyone who deserves it more." By the time "Unforgettable" was finished in the actual Mass, though, I once again could not control my tears, and neither could many of those in attendance.

After the service the bishop brought up the rear again as clergy filed out the front doors. We family members followed and formed a receiving line just outside. The bishop immediately approached me, extended his hand, and said as he grasped mine, "Mr. Martinez, please accept my condolences. I'm sorry to meet you under such sad circumstances. Your wife was an extraordinary woman and Catholic. Would that we could all put our faith into action as she has. The repose of her soul will be in my prayers, and so will the hope that your grief will pass. Your wife is with God." He reached up then and with his right thumb inscribed the sign of the cross on my forehead.

"Thank you so much, Your Excellency," I said, and he moved on to the rest of the family. That unexpected gesture of blessing brought some of the solace I sought.

■

I wanted the luncheon reception in the parish hall to be the party Miranda had requested, and the building was crowded with people sharing memories of her. Despite good music, rich food, and abundant drink, the gathering never took off. There was no sing-along, no dancing, and little joy. I sat at one of the round tables with my daughter, son-in-law, and their boys, while James and Nick and their families each occupied a nearby table. My siblings filled other tables near the center of activity, along with Nancy with her brother, Toshio, and his wife.

One after another, old friends — Miranda's, mine, ours — commiserated with me, offered condolences, invited me to lunch. Bud Hartley said, "That was a terrific piece you wrote about your wife, Marty . . . a great piece. I'm sorry I didn't get to know her." I thanked him.

Lester Jackson placed a large hand on my shoulder and said, "Dr. Mossi was a wonderful lady, Marty, just wonderful. You a lucky man. God bless you." Then he hugged me. Lester was followed by the ladies from the scripture class, who had apparently attended as a group, then some women I didn't know from

Miranda's breast cancer support group, plus Mort and several other guys from mine.

Buzzy stopped by my table, as did Slip and Will and even Monica Salinas, and a gang of my old chums from Merced who'd barely known my wife but were nevertheless there to support me, as I knew they'd be. And more and more. Whatever else was true, I was not abandoned.

After I'd eaten a bit, three small, dark ladies, Indians it appeared, approached me with lowered eyes. They told me in a dialect of Spanish I barely understood that they'd been treated at La Clinica de las Mujeres and said that they'd pray for my wife, whom they called *"una santa."* The tiniest, darkest one added, *"Una santa verdadera!"*

I could only agree and thank them.

Nancy, who'd been sitting at an adjoining table approached me then. "I've never, ever seen an outpouring like this," she said. "Miranda really *was* an extraordinary person. Until today I don't think I understood all she did." She sat down next to me then, and I thought about the story of Bearheart and the Madre Maria Society; she would never hear it from me.

"I was a lucky guy," I said. "I'm not sure I appreciated how special she was either." All I recognized for certain was the grievous wound her absence had left in me.

Nancy's voice lowered then, and she took one of my hands, then said, "I have to say one other thing. You've changed. You were never very demonstrative . . . that used to bother me and the kids, but I just accepted it as the way you were, but I didn't like it. I've seen you with Miranda since she's been so ill, and your affection for her, for our grandchild, and how openly you wept today . . ." My ex-wife blinked away tears, but I could say nothing.

Robbie wandered past, so I excused myself, then motioned for him to join us, but he ignored me. His brothers didn't invite him to their tables, I'd noticed. In the crush of old friends offering condolences, I soon lost track of him. Chava wandered over carrying a beer in one hand and the remains of a burrito in the other. He plopped into a chair left empty by my son-in-law, who'd been hailed by a pal, and said, "I don't know how you hold yourself together, Marty."

"Everything's hollow right now."

"I hear that," he said. After a moment of silence he asked a bold question, as he was wont to do. "Listen, what was up with the bishop being here? I thought you guys were living in sin."

"Her first marriage had been annulled and, besides, we hadn't been able to have relations for a while. She went to Confession and received the last rites from the monsignor." Then I added, "I think the bishop genuinely respects her work—"

"How could he *not?*" my brother interrupted.

I continued, "And maybe wanted to mend fences, too."

As I spoke, Changito was living up to his nickname, climbing all over me. "Dougie, don't crawl all over Grandpa," Lea said, just as Tyler insisted, "I wanna go potty with Grampa Marty."

"Grandpa Marty's busy," my daughter responded.

"It's okay, hon," I said. "I'll take him."

"Meeee!" called the *changito* as Tyler and I rose. "I go too!"

"I'll take them both," I said, and I picked up the smaller guy, held hands with the larger, and marched to and from the men's restroom, thinking that Miranda would never be able to take her grandchildren to the potty or anywhere else.

When the three of us returned to our table, Chava said, "You're a good-looking grandpa . . . or at least the kids look good."

He was trying to lighten the mood, I knew, so I smiled. Nancy and Lea exchanged nods. Beyond them I noticed Robbie slinking out a side door, so I rose and followed. I caught him in the parking lot as he trudged away from the hall, his head so low that his neck seemed to have disappeared into his shoulders. "Robbie," I called, "wait a minute, please."

He stopped and turned. "*What?*" he snapped.

"I know your brothers have ostracized you, but your mother never did and never would. She always prayed for you and always loved you. There's nothing you could do she wouldn't forgive."

The young man swayed in front of me, and I wondered if he'd actually heard me, but then he said, "If you hadn't married my mom I'd have *been* with her. It's *your* damned fault!" He began weeping then, great gulping sobs, and I reached for his shoulders to comfort him, but he spun away and fled to his car. A moment later it roared out of the parking lot.

I stood there gazing up the road my wife's son had just taken, watching other anonymous vehicles pass where he had driven. Then I heard Nancy's voice. "Marty? Are you okay?"

I turned and saw her standing on the porch of the hall, the sun illuminating her, slim as a college girl. "Are you okay?" she called again, a desperate edge creeping into her voice.

On the far end of the parking lot, a vast oak mantled. Beyond it, nearer the river, spread a field where Miranda and I had once walked. As on that distant day, tall yellow stalks swayed like dancers in gusts that also tugged and parted thick green turf beneath. Beyond that field stood the riverine forest.

After a moment, I made my way through those weeds in search of the trail to the river, but couldn't seem to find it. Then from far away I heard the atonal, compelling *bleeks* and *squacks* of geese, their voices like vintage car horns. That stopped me, so I stood searching the sky until, far to the northeast, I saw a fluid chevron — Canadian honkers. Then a second undulating wedge appeared behind the first, all engaged in conversation. As the geese winged closer, they altered positions, and their voices beckoned.

I watched until the flight passed above me, then to the south, their few final notes lingering like memories of the brief interlude Miranda and I had enjoyed, of the small and precious time any of us ever have together, of how quickly we and it and they are forgotten . . . as though we'd never lived.

But we did. We did . . .

Six weeks later, a memorial bench with a bronze plaque was erected along the River Parkway. On the plaque I'd had inscribed:

For Miranda who loved this place.
From Marty who loved her.

I began to visit it daily, running my fingers over the raised letters so often I learned them like Braille. Then, a week or so ago, I arrived to find our bench occupied by a young couple smooching. That jolted me momentarily, but I quickly realized that was the proper use for it, and I smiled as I strolled away.

terrific ending
Sat. 6/21/2008